STUDIES

OF THE

EIGHTEENTH CENTURY IN ITALY

BY

VERNON LEE

A New Edition

London
T FISHER UNWIN
26 PATERNOSTER SQUARE
MDCCCLXXXVII

CONTENTS.

STUDIES OF THE EIGHTEENTH CENTUKY IN ITALY.

INTRODUCTION.

This book is at first sight heterogeneous and anomalous : heterogeneous, because it treats two subjects which are rarely treated by one individual, and never treated under one binding, literature and.music; anomalous, because it is far from dealing Avith all that goes to make up the Italian Eighteenth Century, while it deals with not a few men and things belonging to the sixteenth and seventeenth centuries. Why not deal exclusively and completely with either music or literature ? Why not study the satirist Parini by the side of the playwright Goldoni, rather than study the .gumposer Jommelli, who seems to have no connection with him ? Why examine the comedies of the time of Salvator Rosa and pass over the tragedies of Alfieri ? Why linger over forgotten composers and singers while scientific and philosophic writers, whose works are still read and discussed, remain unmentioned ?

The book is seemingly most incoherent in subject, and most incomplete and digressive in treatment. But the apparent incoherence of subject is in reality unity of treatment; and the apparent incompleteness and irrelevance of treatment is in reality completeness and restriction of the subject. The book deals both with literature and with music, because the point of view of the writer is neither exclusively literary nor exclusively musical, but generally assthetic; because the object of the writer has been to study not the special nature and history of any art in its isolation, but to study the constitution and evolution of the variautL^axts-compared with one another; and the arts whose constitution and evolution can be studied in a work on the Italian Eighteenth Century happen to be the dranui and mjasic, just as the arts which might be studied in a work on tlic Athenian fifth century n.c. would be the drama and sculpture. The Avliter of this book is neither a literary historian nor a musical critic, but an aisthetici an ;_ and both literature and music belong to the a^sthetician's domain. Thus far concerning the incoherence of subject: now with respect to the incompleteness and irrelevance of the treatment The book

B

Introduction.

does not treat of all that is contained in the Italian Eighteenth Century because much of this does not belong inherently to Italy, but is merely a portion of the universal character of the century itself, a character far more spontaneous and strongly marked in other countries; and it treats of many things belonging to the sixteenth and seventeenth centuries, because all that was really national in the Italy of a hundred years ago, the great musical and dramatic efflorescence, has its roots deep hidden in Italian character and civilization, and germinates slowly throughout the sixteenth and seventeenth centuries.

The notion of there having been a spontaneous efflorescence of national art in Italy during the eighteenth century may amuse some persons and will doubtless astonish many; but efflorescence of national art there was, nevertheless—an efflorescence of national art which has remained hitherto unperceived because the Italian Eighteenth Century has, as a rule, been not only not studied, but not even seriously considered as a reality, except by a few specialists who could see nothing but antiquarian details; for, with regard to the Italian Eighteenth Century, we are at present much in the same condition as our ancestors of the days of Montesqnieu and of Robertson were with regard to the Middle Ages in general. They knew that the middle ages had existed, they knew that certain wars had been carried on and certain laws enacted during that period, but that the middle ages had had any civilization of their own, much less any art, never entered their minds: the word suggested a blank, and no one cares to investigate into a blank. So also is it with the Italian Eighteenth Century. There is a general notion in other countries that the eighteenth century did exist in Italy, though the fact has never been brought home to any one. There is also a vague knowledge of the fact that a certain number of writers—some, like Goldoni and Alfieri, still read—others, like Metastasixi, remembered as names, belonged to the Italy at that period; but what was their connection with that time, or what was the civilization which suiTonnded them, is a question which seems to occm- to no Englishman, Frenchman, or German, as indeed it occurs to veiy few Italians. The very few Italians who do trouble themselves on the subject are either laborious bookworms, who find broken and minute fragments of the eighteenth century as they do of every other century, but are unable to unite them so as to constitute any definite shape; or else they are philosophical historians, who are interested in the eighteenth century only inasmuch as it contains germs of the nineteenth; who study Parinij _Beccaria^ Verri^ and Filangieri because they view them as ^'ecursors^of Ihi) social, political,vjind literary movement of our own day, but who turn aside with contempt fron) Metastasio and Carlo Gozzi because they see in

Introduction

them no political foreruuners_ofthe j)resent, and arc incapable of recognising in them the artistic product of the past. To foreigners, therefore, the Italian Ei<,diteenth Century is covered wth an historical mist, to be rent and dispelled only by shock of the cannon of Montenotte and Lodi. Any amount of artistic life may be safely hidden beneath that mist from the English, French, and Germans who think it their duty to be well versed in the art and literature of the Italian Middle Ages and Renaissance; who are intimately acquainted with the exact pictorial character of Liberale da Verona and Ugolino di Prete Ilario, and with the literary value of Ricordano Malaspini and Giannozzo Manetti, but who do not know that Metastasio wrote opera t(>xts or that Marcello composed psalm music; who know very exactly whether Agnolo and Taddeo Gaddi were or were not father and son, but who are not sure whether Pergolcsi and Paisiello may not have been the same person. The philosophical Italian historians, on the other hand, take notice only of philanthropic poets and of economic writers ; all that is art entirely escapes their notice.

Now it so happens that, inasmuch as it was a forerunner of our own civilization, the Italian Eighteenth Century was poor, weak, and uninteresting, because in all this it was a mere insignificant copy of the English and French Eighteenth Century. The political and philosophic tendencies of the days of Montescpiieu, of Voltaire, of Hume, and of Smith, did indeed exist in Italy, both because they were naturally produced there as elsewhere by the preceding civilization, and also because they were largely imported from other countries; but they were so comparatively feeble that Italian civilization would never have spontaneously made the stride which it did, would never have got to its modern point, had it not been borne along by the whirlwind of the French revolutionary invasion.

^arini, Alfieri, Bcccaria, Filangicri, interesting and valuable though they are in themselves, are wholly uninteresting and valueless considered as the products of a spontaneous Italian civilization. They are essentially cosmopolitan and eclectic. To naderstand them we must not seek in the remoter layers of Italian life; we must look round at the general character of the eighteenth century. Without j?opc, without Kousseau, without Montesquieu and Diderot, they are unintelligible; by their side they gain in intelligibility but they lose in importance. Italy in the last century got her philosophy and philosophic poetry, like her dress and her ^ furniture, from Paris and London; but Italy in the last century got her jjraiaa. and her comedy neither from Paris nor from London, but from her own intellectual soil, where they had been germinating for centuries; and

""Italy, in the eighteenth century, gave her own spontaneous national-music to the whole of Europe.

B 2

-k

v#;

\..^

Introduction.

In this national drama and national music Ups for us the interest^of the Italy of a hundred years ago. Not only is this artistic efflorescence the only really national and spontaneous thing which Italy then pos-^ sessed, she being in all else inferior to other nations, but that Italian_ artistic efflorescence was the only thoroughly national and spontaneous artistic movement which took place anywhere in the eighteenth century. The other nations had spontaneous philosophical life, but Italy alone had artistic life. The .plastic arts were dead everywhere, and had not yet been galvanised by criticism into a spectral semblance of life. Poetry, in France and in England, under Pope and Voltaire, was mere phi-losophy decked out in Dresden china pastoral furbelows ; in Germany ^ it was, when it re-appeared late in the eighteenth century, only partly spontaneous, and, in the main, 4ihiJosopdiy again of a different sort, and either draped in classic garments, manufactured on Winckelmann's patterns, or trapped out with pseudo-mediasval jingles. The sole vita.l___ thing throughout the eighteenth century appeared to be philosophy^ France, England, and Germany were sterile of all else; Italy alone possessed living and growing artistic, organisms; Italy alone had art which was neither decrepit nor eclectic, art which had been germinating unnoticed for centuries; comedy whose seeds had been sown in the old^^ Latin and Oscan days, before Plautus and Terence were born ; music_^ which had been slowly developing throughout the middle ages, and which now blossomed out in mature perfection, spontaneous, Italian, absolutely national, and which, even transplanted into the favourable soil of Germany and cultivated by the greatest Germans, ceased not to be Italian. During this eighteenth century, while all eyes were fixed upon /other countries,, Italy^ insignificant and backward, developed to maturity the art germs which had remained dormant during her brilliant Middle Ages and brilliant Eenaissance;..she possessed,then what she had not possessed in the time of Dante, nor of Lorenzo di Medici, nor of Ariosto, a drama as national as the English drama of the days of Shakespeare and the Spanish drama of the days of Lope de Vega. For her, in this obscure period, was reserved the last great art, of which antiquity had not dreamed, which the Middle Ages had not divined, which the Kenaissance had but faintly perceived—Music.

Does it matter if the eig;hteenth century, strutting complacently in its philosophic dignity and eclectic grandeur, did not perceive the art istic movement which was going on in Italj.? if, in its satisfaction with the plays of Voltaire and of Schiller, it mistook the national Italian stage for the planks of a fair-booth ? Does not all pseudo-classic and eclectic art, like its archetype

Voltaire, mistake all real art, be it the art of ^Eschylus, of

Shakespeare, or of Calderon, for mountebanks' ranting? The Italian national stage did exist none the less. Does it matter if the nineteenth century, critical and misled by critical theory, fixing its eyes on the people who are the critical and theorising people above all others, fails to perceive the Italian national efflorescence of music in the eighteenth century, and considers as spontaneous German products the works of Handel, and Gluck, and Mozart, although every inch of Germany was colonised by Italian musicians, and although there is not a form of melody in the works of the^ great Germans of the eighteenth century which has not its necessary predecessor and its absolute equivalent in the works of their Italian masters and fellow pupils? Are not critical theorists always blinded and misled by critical theorisings ? The greatness and supremacy of the Italian music of the eighteenth century did exist nevertheless.

And it is this national Italian drama, unnoticed by the puristic eighteenth century; it is this national Italian music, still overlooked by the critical nineteenth century; it is__this spontaneous art, which constitutes the real importance of Italy in the time of Pope, of Voltaire, and of Lessing. The Italy of a century ago is interesting because, in a time of me re philosophic speculation, it alone created artistic form, not eclectic, but national and spontaneous; because to it belongs perhaps the last

great artistic efflorescence, which was , jiot, like that which produced Shelley and Keats,^ a reaction; jior like that which produced Goethe and Schiller, a revival; but was like the efflorescence of art to wliicli we owe Phidias, Raphael, Dante, oTShakespeare, the culmination of a long and unbroken series of artistic phenomena.

^ It is therefore from the festhetical. pcjiiut of view that the Italian Eighteenth Century appears to us interesting and worthy of study; it is the art of the day, musical and dramatic, which absorbs our attention. But, in studying the art, we have incidentally been led to study the times. Following the sound of the music of Pergolesi and Cimarosa^ trying to catch closer glimpses of the Bettinas and Lindoros of Goldoni^ of the Truffaldinos and Brighellas of Carlo Gozzi, we have strayed into the every-day world of Italy in the eighteenth century, the world of fine ladies-in stomachers and hoops, of dapper cavalieri serventi, of crabbed jpedants, of hungry Arcadian rhymesters, of Gallo-maniacs and Anglo-maniacs—a world of some good, some evil, some folly, and mucli inanity; rambling through which, in search of some composer or singer, of some playwright or mask actor, we have occasionally seen at a distance noble intellectual figufes like Parmi and Alfieri, and have stopped to look at them, although they were not the objects of our pursuit; or we have glanced at one or two faint forgotten celebrities like RoUi and Frugoni;

or we liaA'e wandered into some assembly of drolly solemn pedants, dreaming of pastoral life and dinner-giving patrons; or again into the drawing-room of some beautiful Sappho, some Faustina Maratti or Silvia Verza, seated, sentimental and coquettish, in a circle of enamoured poetasters. Often also we have idly followed the crowd of periwigged and stomachered citizens through the squares and streets of old Italian cities, or have watched them, chatting and card-playing, in their country houses. Strolling about and prying in odd nooks and corners in hopes of meeting a buffoon of Goldoni, or of hearing a snatch of song of Jommelli, we have come across quaint little old-fashioned figures, droll little old-world groups fit for Hogarth or for Watteau, and have stopped and tried to sketch their grotesque outline. Thus has originated the first essay of our volume, that on the Academy of the Arcadi, which may serve to give a general notion of the times that witnessed the arti stic efflo-rescence jvhich is our principal subiect. Our true work lies with the composers, and singers, and playwrights, and actors; with MetastasiOj^and Goldoni, and Gozzi; but these cannot be well understood unless we previously reconstruct the societj- in which they lived, and unless we reassemble aroimd them those men who, though seemingly indifferent or insignificant, yet indirectly influenced their lives, their art, and their fame. We deal with that part of the Italian Eighteenth Century which is sterling and imperishable; with art_ which, though now forgotten, still remains and will once more be remembered; and our book is in so far serenely cheerful; but ever and anon, by the side of the imperishable, arises the thought of that which has perished; and we may once or twice forget for a moment the plays of Metastasio and Goldoni, and the music of Marcello and Pergolesi, forget our persuasion that they remain and will remain, as the impression comes home to us how deep an abyss separates us from the men and women for whom the plays were written and the music composed, and how many faint and nameless ghosts crowd round the few enduring things bequeathed to us by the past.

THE ARCADIAN ACADEMY.

THE ARCADIAN ACADE]\IY.

I.

Frosi the year 1680 to the year 1790, Italian literature is mainly represented by Filicaia, Vico, Metastasio, Goldoni, Parini, Gasparo Gozzi, Vincenzo]\Ionti, and Vittorio Alfieri. But these men merely ^represent, they do not constitute, the intellectual life of the nation; for that we must look in the innumerable academies, \ietworks of molecular life spreading all over Italy, and^connecting all the classes of society which possessed, or were supposed to possess, any knowledge of literature. These academies were countless and multiform; they sprang up and died out on all sides, growing out of pompous receptions in the palaces of cardinals or of princesses, and out of disorderly carouses at literary jcoifee-houses; they fairly exhausted the stock of intelligible appellations; their names were allusions, riddles, jokes, or gibberish, such as the Transformed (Trasformati) of Milan, among whom were Parini, the three Verris, and Beccaria; the Frozen Ones (Gelidi) of Bologna; the Crazed Ones (Intronati) of Siena; the Erithrean Shepherds of Naples; the Phleginatics, Frigids, Fervids, and Drunkards. They were all local— very limited in numbers and fame—all except one, whoso name resounded with equal glory from Trent to Messina, from Savona to Treviso, whic h comprised among its members all the great_writers, philosophers, or artists, all the noble lords, all the rich bankers, all the astute lawyers, all the well-known doctors, all the sainted priests, all the beautiful ladies, that lived or travelled in Italy; and this academy was the Academy of the Arcadians.^ By means of colonies established in all the Italian towns, iT^aught, like a huge spi der-web, everyone distinguished in any way whatever. The establishment could profit by every sort of advantage of which its members might be possessed: the use of literary talents was obvious in a literary institution; artists could paint pictures and make plans for the Academy; musicians could afford agreeable interludes in its meetings; princes, senators, and ministers could grant diplomas and honours; bankers might give or lend money; and last, but far fi-om least, ladies would form a pleasing leaven, a charming cement to all the remainder. With views so liberal, and principles so grasping, what

wonder was there if the institution flourished, if it spread in all quarters, and if there appeared on the title-pages of half the books published in Italy during the last century the pastoral pipe, and laurel and pine cr own, y emblematic of the Arcadian Academy?

In the course of our studies of the eighteenth century we were so continually coming upon |he Academy of the Arcadians, every person and every thing seemed so connected with it, jt.so pervaded the whole of the Italy of those days, that we began to feel curiosity concerning this once renowned institution, and to wonder what had become of it in our own ~~ day. Had it been swallowed up in the convulsions which changed the face of Italy, or were its broken fragments still crumbling away in silence ? Although we were in Eome, the head-quarters of the Academy, it was long before we could obtain any answer to this question. Most persons had never heard the name of the Arcadians, while those who had, associated it with vague impressions of absurdity and imbecility. However, little by little we obtained a few scraps of information on the subject, mostly erroneous and contradictory, and invariably accompanied by not a few expressions of contempt; and just as we were giving up all further inc^uiry in despair we received an authorisation to visit the hallowed spot, once the meeting-place of the Arcadians, and now the only remnant of their possessions.

The Bosco Parrasio is situate on the road winding up the Janiculum towards the Villa Pamphili, but so utterly forgotten are all things Arcadian that for a long time we wandered close to its gate, through the dirty street leading to Ponte Sisto, up the battered Via Crucis of S. Pietro Montorio, and down the slippery mule-path of the mills, asking vainly after the villa of the Arcadians. No one had ever heard of such a place as the Bosco Parrasio, nor of such beings as the Arcadians; the beggars who hung about the gate of the monastery hard by, the sacristan of the Sette Dolori, the dyers hanging out their skeins of scarlet and blue wool, the peasants loading their mules with sacks of flour, all answered in the same astonished negat've. At the top of two slippery mounds, between the Vigna Corsini and the mills, was a little garden, at whose gate stood a portly priest: we determined on accosting him. True, there was no reason why he should have heard of a place unknown in the whole neighbourhood, but he was our last hope. So we repeated to him the old, hopeless question: "Did he happen to know where was the Bosco Parrasio, the villa belonging to the Arcadian Academy?" The priest, as jolly, slovenly, and demonstrative a one as could be found, turned with alacrity towards us—" The Bosco Parrasio? This is it." So, when we least expected it, we were actually standing at the gate of the Italian Parnassus, and, what surprised us still more, in the company of one of the dignitaries of Ai-cadia.

Tlie Arcadian Academy.

We returned from this first visit with the most dismal impressions of the Bosco Parrasio—of muddy paths, dripping bushes, flower-beds filled with decaying ilex-leaves, lichen-covered benches, crumbling plaster, and mouldering portraits—grim spectres looking down on the final ruin of Arcadia. Nor had the live inhabitants of the place conducecT to raise our spirits. The villa was inhabited by some peasants, whose furniture and provisions filled the state-rooms. The Arcadian who did the honours of the place did not know one portrait from the other; could not recollect his own, or anyone else's, pastoral name; and took an interest in nothing, save some beans spread out to dry, which he examined, criticised, and calculated the market value of, in company with the gardener's wife. Such was the first effect Arcadia produced on our imagination; but gradually, as the remembrance of meanness and decay became fainter, the disagreeable impression wore away, and left instead a whimsical interest in the forgotten. Academy; the Bosco Parrasio impressed us no longer as a damp, decaying casino in the suburbs, but as a weird habitation of Jiterary goblins. The result of this new phase of humour was that we revisited the villa of the Arcadians, and found it strangely different from what it had at first seemed. It was now June, the time when Rome receives her crowning beauty before being made hideous by dust and decay, when the Campagna is one living, waving, chirping, humming mass of green; when grass and flowers spring up in every interstice of the old pavement, in every crevice of the crumbling walls. The little triangular strip of ground on the Janiculura was a tangle of flowers: belated jonquils and daffodils drooped in the shade of the velvet-leaved medlar-trees; jessamines, lupins, and wild geraniums were entwined among the box and yew hedges; garlands of tiny pink and yellow roses were slung from ilex to ilex, drooping over the marble slab carved with the Arcadian pipe:

Fistula cui semper decrescit arundinis ordo, Nam calamus cera jungitur usque minor.

Behind a clump of tapering laurels and pines was hidden a grotto, covered with long ferns and maiden-hair, trickling with the icy water of the Acqua Paola. In front of the little yellow villa splashed a fountain, and the miniature amphitheatre was overrun with ivy, morning glories, and tomatoes. The house, once the sunmior resort of Arcadian sonnetteexs^ was now abandoned to a family (»f market gardeners, who hung their hats and jackets on the marble heads of improvvisatori and crowned poetesses; and threw their beans, maize, and garden tools into corners of the desolate reception rooms, from whose mildewed walls looked down a Im-f nf cele-bvities—brocaded doges, powdered princesses, and scarlet-robed cardinals, simpering drearily in their desolation. Sad, haggard jwetesses, in sea-green and sky-blue draperies, with lank, powdered locks, and meagre

arms, holding lyres; fat, ill-sliaven priests in white bands and mop ^vigs; sonnetteering-ladies, sweet and vapid in dove-coloured stomachers and embroidered sleeves; jolly extemporary poets, flaunting in many-coloured waistcoats and gorgeous shawls; and among this crowd of rococo figures, looking down on the homely furniture, holy water vessels, hallowed box sprigs, and smutty prints of saints and soldiers, here and there stood out some strongly-marked individuality:—Alfigri in semi-military dress, with the collar of his own Order of Homer, glaring fiercely round him, his red hair waving as if in the draught of a furnace; the dapper Algarotti, pMru losopher for ladies, versifier for kings, and hanger-on of celebrities, his long beaked face peeping out from a huge wig and pelisse; JohnJV^ of Portugal, dark, apelike, his head covered with a mass of black horsehair, his body encased in shining armour; the Abate Metastasio, reclining on his sofa, fat, easy, elegant, languid with selfish, self-complacent sentimentality. It was strange to turn from this assembly of literary ghosts, their gala dresses and gala looks fading away in oblivion, to the bright, noble nature surrounding the mouldering casino. Close beneath stretched the Vigna Corsini, overrun with tall grass, poppies, and vines; further off, the pines of Villa Lante, St. Peter's with its background of the bald round Monte Mario, and far in the distance, Soracte, rising out of the hazy blue plain. In front, stretched at the foot of the Janiculum, lay Rome, bounded on one side by the ilexes of the Pincian and the Quirinal, and on the other by the Tiber winding past the green Testaccio Mound. Perhaps it was just in this contrast between the grand view and the blooming garden, and the time-stained portraits of long-forgotten men and women, whose frail talents had withered and fallen to dust with time, that lay the charm of the Bosco Parrasio. We returned often and often to spend the burning afternoons in the shady garden, or in the cool, dismantled rooms, going home at sunset, carrying away bunches of flowers, tiny roses, polyanthuses gorgeous as an Oriental brocade, sapphire-coloured irises, exquisitely delicate in texture and perfume, tied up with long sprays of maidenhair fresh from the trickling grotto; sketches, too, of some brocaded Lycidas or powdered Chloe, and above all, vague impressions, quaint and sentimental, of the long-deceased and long-forgotten world of the last^ century.

During the intervals of our visits we procured, not without great difficulty, old books relating to the Arcadian Academy. We sought for them in dingy dens near the Piazza Navona, and on stone benches behind the Pantheon; among rows of musty, faded, worm-eaten, volumes, and among heaps of soiled prints, engravings, and etchings. Thus, one by one, we discovered many of the heavily-bound, childishly-printed books with the invariable Lnjmmatur, and "Approbation of the Superiors," and the no less invariable pages of dedicatory nonsense, in huge characters, mth

windmills and cupids as initial letters; the books which contained all that remains of Arcadian glory, and whence we extracted the materials for the following history of the once famons Academy of the Arcadians, round which centred the general intellectual life of the Italian eighteenth century, of which we would fain give some notion before proceeding to study its special artistic products.

II.

The grand literature and art which burst into full efflorescence at the beginning of the sixteenth century had their origin in the strong, active, cheerful life of the previous age; the sixteenth century, the time of foreign invasion, of Spanish and ^apal pi-eponderance, of despair, brutality, and fanaticism, in its turn produced and bequeathed to the succeeding century its artistic and literary fruit—the crazy, meretricious architecture and sculpture of the Jesuit churches; the theatrical and ecstatic Bolognese painting; and the wild conceits and languid affectation of the literaiy scliool of Marini. These were the products of a time of unhealthy excitement; they grew to maturity in one of national lethargy, and the poor exhausted seventeenth century was reviled not only for its own indolence and incapacity, but for the extravagance which it had inherited from its predecessor. The mystic sibyls and tragic martyrdoms of Guido and Domenichino became simpering sentimental ladies and romping opera murders in the hands of Donato Creti, of Giro Ferri, and of Luca Giordano; the briUiant paradoxes of Marini and the elegant effeminacy of Guarini turned into systematic nonsense and studied vapidness among their successors: the sun cooled itself in the waters of rivers which were on fire; the celestial sieve, resplendent with shining holes, was swept by the bristly back of the Apennines; love was an infernal heaven and a celestial hell, it Avas burning ice and freezing fire, and was inspired by ladies made up entirely of coral, gold thread, lilies, roses, and ivory, on whose lips sat Cupids shooting arrows which were snakes. In short, if in England the rage for ^nceits injured not a few excellent poets, in Italy it made the fortune of scor es of p oetasters; for the indolent, ostentatious nobles, who presided over the innumerable academies, required mad paradoxes and vapid hyperboles in their birthday odes and dedicatory sonnets as much as they required fluttering smirking goddesses for their gardens, and curling masonry and waving stucco work for their chapels. Yet it was during this despicable _^eriod of exhausted repose that took place the partial renovation which pi-oduced the modern Italian world; it was among these languid, \'7d)ompous, artificial people of the seventeenth century that modern society began to be formed, and it is in dealing with them that we first find that we have to do, no longer with our remote ancestors,

\

12 Tlie Arcadian Academy.

living in castellated houses, travelling on horseback, fighting in the streets, and carousing at banquets; but with the grandfathers of our grandfathers, steady, formal, hypocritical people, paying visits in coaches, going to operas, giving dinner parties, and litigating and slandering rather than assassinating and poisoning. As the century advanced and the stormy times of invasion and reformation were left further and further behiml, Italy, indolent, pedantic, and ostentatious, saAv the slow consolidatioii__of^ regular, formal governments; despotic, but not illegal, letting peppledo what they chose except think and act for themselves j^^while the spiritual authorities, with their well-organised Jesuit schools and officially-managed . Inquisition, relaxed their sway, or rather let their zeal die out into self-complacent meddlesomeness. Heresy had long been crushed, indifference was rapidly spreading, and free thought was almost becoming a possibility; in short, the ponderous inert mass of Italian society Avas imperceptibly slipping onwards.

At this time Rome was, with the exception of Venice, Genoa, and Lucca, the only truly independent Italian State, and the only true republic remaining. The Papal 8ee had become a most perfect oligarchy; the sacred college was mainly recruited among the nobility, and the pope was the doge or gonfaloniere for life of an ecclesiastical senate. Religious zeal there was no longer: the race of Caraffas and Perettis had died out; poor monks remained poor monks, and inquisitors remained inquisitors; the Protestant and Catholic States Avere treated with the same bland civility; all ideas of giving laws to Europe had been laid aside as folly. The popes were elected sovereigns, whose only thought was to secure to their relatives wealth and a chance of succession; the cardinals were rich senators aspiring to sovereign power, and consoling their disappointment with pomp and ostentation. Still, this languid system of nepotism was not without its advantages: each pope brought with him his family and friends from Bologna, Lombardy, or Venetia; Roman life was kept up by a continual influx of foreigners, and Roman society obtained a more liberal and active character than it could otherwise have had. The papal families vied with each other in tasteless magnificence: the Borghese enlarged the great villa outside Porta del Popolo; the Odescalchi of Como built the vast yellow palace opposite the SS. Apostoli; the Altieri erected the hiTge clumsy structure near the Gesu; the Pistojese Rospigliosi established themselves on the Quirinal, the Florentine Corsini on the Janiculum; everywhere, in short, the strangers colonised Rome. To them are due those enormous palaces with spacious courts and low-stepped stairs, bedizened with plaster dragons and flowerets and curls of masonry without, and with gilt Cupids, and brick and chalk-coloured frescoes, within; and the many villas with straight walls of clipped ilex and box, and innumerable ill-restored, worthless statues in fantastic temples.

^ r*

They employed the fiigkl INIaratta and the stiff Sacchi to cover their ceilings with earthy-tinted Gods and Nymphs, and the clnmsy Dnrpicsnoy and the theatrical Legros to ornament their chapels with gigantic saints in Hying marble robes. Thanks to them and their hangers-on, Rome was in the middle of the seventeenth century a handsome modern-looking town, for most of the houses with shell, pinebranch, and other stucco ornaments which abound in what are now the dirtiest quarters, were then resplendent with whitewash. The prince nephews were likewise patrons of music, which was then struggling to free itself from the inexorable composers of madrigals and canons ; theatres were built, and cardinals had wonderful private concerts, at which sang all the charming sirens of the day, Milton's Baroni and Evelyn's Laurettos and Pasqualinos. But above all the Roman aristocracy favoured literature and men of letters; not a wedding could take place, not a cardinal could be promoted, without volumes of poems being published on the occasion, and the innumerable lay ecclesiastics who hung on to the princes of the church were all poets, members and perhaps founders of academies. In short, thanks to foreign colonisation and nepotism, there was in Rome a vast literary bustle without aim or result.

But, as the centuiy of incapacity and indolence drew towards its close, Italian intelk'ct began once more to stir; music, destined to attain to perfection in the succeeding age, rapidly superseded the plastic arts; and a new style of poetry, free from conceit and extravagance, soon showed itself. It would certainly be difficult to find in any Italian verses of the end of the seventeenth century the feeling and grace of the songs contained in Salvator Rosa's music-book, but nevertheless a great literary revival did take place. While Redi let his droll humour riot in his burlesque Triumph of Bacchus, and Menzini Avrote his sharp, harsh Satires, Filicaia and Guidi struck a note whicli had been mute for more than two centuries; instead of addressing the descendants of the " un-conquered Hippolytus" and the "magnanimous Alfonso" of Ariosto and Tasso, they addressed Italy, France, and Germany; they spoke to a nation in the name of a nation, and their poetry has the nobility as well as the bombast of newly-obtained and as yet misunderstood independence. At the same time the conceits and fustian of the poets of the preceding generation began to lose favour, and the simplicity and elegance of the early Italian classics began once more to be admired. In Rome especially a society of literary purists formed itself, which included some of the most gifted poets and some of the most eminent pedants of the day; for literature had sunk so low that mediocrity could easily associate with talent, nay, that talent and mediocrity might be found strangely united in a single individual. They found a staunch patroness in Queen Christina of Sweden, who, in return for the amount of bombastic flattery usual in

that day, received them as friends and presided over their meetings in her gardens. They even introduced her majesty's bad verses into their own poems, a better proof than the most servile flattery that these writers of the seventeenth century were without station, fortune, or a literary public. They turned their attention especially to extirpating what remained of the metaphysical poetry of the previous age, and to rehabilitating Petrarch and his followers, Bembo, Molza, and Costanzo; and their influence became daily greater and more acknowledged. However, they did not succeed in bettering their own fortunes, for, on the death of the munificent Christina, they lost their fixed meeting-place, and had to send their servile muse to Don Livio Odescalchi to ask for an invitation to Frascati, and to Cardinal Corsini to beg admission into his gardens— a favour readily granted, for the Komau nobles were idle, conceited, and loved to play the Maecenas. However, one fortunate spring morning of the year 1692, Fate decreed that they should find no better place of meeting than the large pasture tracts behind the castle of Sant' Angelo, usually known as the Prati di Castello. The party niimbered fourteen, and included some of the most illustrious men of letters then flourishing: Alessandro Guidi, the humpbacked favourite of Queen Christina, regarded by himself and his contemporaries as a second Pindar, and who boasted that his poetical stables contained a hundred winged coursers, ready to carry up his misshapen little person in the track of the horses of the sun; Giambattista Felice Zappi, a young Imolese lawyer, of noble birth and elegant person, of whose graceful though rather insipid poems we shall speak more than once; Silvio Stampiglia, historiographer and writer of tragi-comical opera texts to the Emperor Leopold; the Calabrian jurist and critic Giovanni Vincenzo Gravina; the Abate Crescimbeni, one of the stupidest and most self-important of Eoman pedants; and nine others, mostly satellites of the two last-mentioned writers. The Prati di Castello form a quiet, rural peninsula, separated by a bend of the sluggish yellow river from the vast grey town, with its innumerable cupolas and belfries shining in the sunlight; the ground is covered with grass and mint; crushed and browsed by the shaggy Roman horses and long-horned, white oxen; here and there a hedge of flowering thorn or a clump of slender elms, and to the back, the round mass of the castle of S. Angelo and the long extent of the Vatican terrace gardens. The quiet pastoral scene impressed even our fourteen literati, for after they had read and improvised verses, and applauded each other as indiscriminately as was their wont, one of them exclaimed: "It seems to-day as if Arcadia were reviving for us! " His speech was hailed as an inspiration, and it was immediately determined that, since Arcadia had been thus happily resuscitated, it should be kept alive by their care. The first and most obvious necessity was to exchange their real names for such as

would suit tlioir new capacity of Arcadian shepherds, and fourteen pastoral names and surnames wore foi-thwith written on as many slips of paper, which were extracted, in the order that fate ordained, out of the hat of one of the company. This being done, the fourteen shejdierds in black coats, white bands, and horsehair wigs, pastoral physicians, lawyers, priests, and professors, set about framing the constitution of the newly-created state. It was republican, but paternal; the elected head of the state was called cnstode (custos), and to him were given two subordinate, or YicG-ciistodi: such was the rudimentary form of government.

Scarcely was the existence of Arcadia known than everyone in Rome longeil to bo admitted into it, the learned literati and the stupitl nobles being equally charmed Avith the notion. Meanwhile the Academy elected its president, or, more properly speaking, the sheep looked out for a head shepherd. The choice unanimously fell upon one of the least brilliant of the members; yet the choice was a happy one, as events proved in after years. Guidi was old, conceited, and too little interested in the institution; Zappi, on the other hand, was too young and simple-minded; Silvio Stampiglia was a writer of plays, and had no connections in the ecclesiastical city; Leonio was insignificant, and the other unnamed ones still more so; the choice therefore remained between Gravina and Crescimbeni. Gravina was a man of about thirty: tall, thin, with a fine worn, thoughtful face, thin lips, a long weak chin, dreamy eyes and a massive forehead, whence his scant hair fell in light ringlets; he had a considerable fortune for a Roman writer in those days, and held the chair of Jurisprudence at the Sapienza. As a jurist his talent was undoubted, his great works on Roman law being read to this day, and having served, with those of Vico, to produce a new school of Judicial Philosophy, headed by Montesquieu; he Avas besides a great classical scholar, his critical writings were ingenious, his style elegant ami noble; and his society was eagerly sought by all the most intelligent men in Rome. Gian Mario dei Crescimbeni was a priest of about forty, born at Macerata in the March; he was small and ungainly in figure, dark complcxioned, with a nose of such liuge proportions as to gain him the familiar appellation of Nasica; his crabbed aspect was that of the pedant which he was. He had Avritten on literature, in a stiff, hard, low style, mere awkward compilations, and the only original idea he Avas ever known to have struck out was that the Dirina Commedia was a comic poem and the Morgante Magqiore a serious one. Yet, in spite of all the recommendations of person, talents, learning and position on the one hand; and of all the disadvantages of ugliness, stupidity, pedantry, and poverty on the other, the general choice fell not upon the dignitiod and ingenious Gravina but upon the awlcAvard and pedantic Crescimbeni; nor was the choice a wrong one. For Crescimbeni had a high conception of the honour and responsibility attached to the position

of Gustode Generate d"Arcadia; he was a good-natured man, who couUI flatter the great and soothe the humble, and whose only thought Avould be to further the interests of the Academy which had honoured him with its choice. Martello, writing some years later, describes him as discreet, fair and modest, able to distinguish a good writer from a bad one, yet condescending even towards a raven decked out in swan's feathers.* Gravina, on the contrary, was neither entirely liked nor entirely respected in Rome; his being a Neapolitan, though certainly no recommendation to the Romans, is not sufficient to account for the rather hostile feeling which he inspired. " He is proud and eccentric according to the general belief" [che strano e altero e nel concetto altrui], writes Martello; he was cold, conceited, and had an insatiable appetite for praise; to be tolerated by him it was necessary to concur in all his notions, which were often extravagant and pedantic, as, for instance, he affected to consider Trissino's Italia

Liberata equal to the Iliad and immeasurably superior to Tasso's Jerusalem. " You must concur in all his notions," continues Martello, "for the weakness of this great man is to imagine himself possessed of all human wisdom. Praise him, and he will love you as a son." Unfortunately the Roman literati of established position found such conditions intolerable, although profuse enough of praise towards wealthy patrons; so Gravina remained as Opico Erimanteo., a mere member of the Academy, distinguished only by his own talents; while Crescimbeni, under the name of Alfesiheo Cario, took possession of the supreme rank of Custode Generale d'Arcadia.

However, as the Academy grew in numbers, Gravina came into greater notice, for the institution needed a code of laws, and this work naturally fell to the great jurist and scholar; the result was considered worthy of Cicero, both for wisdom and latinity. Meanwhile Crescimbeni, who could not shine by his pen, set to work quietly and patiently at gaining members and patrons for the Academy, with which his heart was bound up. Among the Roman nobles who aspired to the position of Maecenas, the most conspicuous was Don Livio Odescalchi, of Como, nej)hew of the proud pope who had dared to thwart Louis XIV. He was the successor to Queen Christina's position in Roman society; in his elegant palace between the SS. Apostoli and the Corso he gave concerts at which (as the irate Bourdelot complains) all the ecclesiastical musicians of Rome sang profane music, and literary receptions at which verses were read and improvised by conspicuous writers; nay, he even invited whole

* Vi notai Crescimbeni e il suo Leonio, Ch'ambo discreti, equanimi e modesti,
San chi sieda e chi no nel coro Aonio. Ma giii non sono al van desio molesti D'un corvo che di cigno abbia le piume.
Pier Jacopo Martello, Sat. .^3.

ncademios to his sploiulid villa in tlio hills. Don LiA'io, Avho Avas always willint; to buy literary fame at the price of such invitations, immediately understood how important it Avas to connect liis name with that of the rising academy, and Crescimbcni took care to foster this belief. Don Livio appears to have been the only noble who invited the whole Academy to his country seat, Prince Corsini and Cardinal Farnese deigning to receive the hungry shabby literati in their vineyards and gardens, but not in their palaces.

There i5eems at the end of the seventeenth century to have lingered among the Italian upper-classes a remnant of Spanish gravity and pomposity, which disappeared in the eighteenth century, when the true Italian character came once more into notice, mingled perhaps with a little French levity. It is impossible to conceive how an institution like the Arcadian Academy could have assumed the importance which it did, except in the midst of that stately and solemn civilisation, marked by straight-walked gardens, heavy, gilt coaches, black clothes, and huge curly periwigs; or in any other place than Rome, among its upstart princes and idle prelates, whose only thought was ostentation of some sort. Sixty years later, in the days of Goldoni and Gaspare Gozzi, such an academy would have been regarded as a mere whimsical congregation of crotchety pedants and blue-stockings, whose only use was to make people acquainted with each other, and whose sittings were an avowed amusement, enlivened by music, small-talk, and cards; but between the years 1690 and 1710 things were viewed in a very difierent light: the Arcadian Academy, besides reviving the simplicity and innocence of the golden age, was to reform literature throughout Italy ; it was to make or unmake the reputation of writers ; it was to eradicate vice and ignorance ; it was to restore to Rome the glorious days of Augustus and of Leo X. ; it was to erect monuments to kings and emperors, and to supply Homers for any chance Achilles who might turn up. All this was sincerely believed by Crescimbeni, Don Livio Odescalchi, and probably nearly all the Roman Arcadians, nor do they ever seem to have suspected any ludicrous discrepancy between what they were and what they were intended to be; these poetasters, priests, and lawyers, living for the most part off" dedications, and their munificent patrons, the illiterate nobles, met in the prim box alleys and ilex groves of the Roman villas, and fretted to read their own compositions, and yawned over those of theu' companions, in the full persuasion that they were engaged in most important work, and that the whole world watched them with anxious interest. Everything had to be literary and solemn, and even Arcadian amusements took a ponderous and pompous shape, as is proved by Crescimbeni's account of that celebrated and delightful game called the Giuoco del Sibillone, invented by the illustrious shepherd Domenico Trosi. •' In this game of the Sibillone (i.e. great male sybil),

c

otherwise called game of the oracle" (writes the Custode Geiieralc d'Arcadia), " one of the company is chosen to personate the oracle, and answers in a single word whatever question may be put to him by the spectators, which word is afterwards explained and shown to be suitable to the question by two others, who play the part of interpreters. For the sake of enjoying this most noble and curious game, after some time there came not only friends, but other persons, and we ourselves have seen more than once gentlemen and ladies of the highest rank, and even Cardinals ; and in truth this was an amusement worthy of any great personage, because, as the interpreters were mostly men learned in every science, their interpretations were usually full of rare information, especially philosophical . . . nay, sometimes the interpreter would fulfil his duty with wondrous perfection, speaking extempore in elegant Italian verses, sometimes even in rhyme."

As the Academy increased in numbers and importance, Croscimbcni took to publishing octavo volumes with large margins, endless dedications, and the syrinx surrounded by pine and laurel branches, the chosen emblem of Arcadia, in which he chronicled the meetings of the Arcadians and the Olympic Games, performances in which the clumsiness and sloth of litei'ary racers and wrestlers were displayed in honour of some illustrious stranger. The cost of printing these works must have greatly surpassed any small profits made from their dedications, and, as many of them were published anonymously, we can ascribe their production only to the sincere faith which Crescimbeni placed in his vocation, and his awe-stricken belief in the institution which had placed him at its head. Later appeared volumes containing lives of distinguished menibers, and others filled with biographies of the deceased ones. In these productions Crescimbeni was assisted by various other Academicians, whose style is rather less insufferable than his own, but who write about Arcadian matters with as much solemnity as their chief From these works it appears that Arcadian colonies were beginning to be founded all over Italy, and that scarcely a single distinguished man of letters of any part of the country had been missed by Crescimbeni's pastoral fishing apparatus. These books also give an insight into the literary circles of Rome, inasmuch as they wore connected with the academy. The principal one had for its centre the beautiful and accomplished Faustina, daughter of the famous painter Carlo Maratta, and wife of the then scarcely less celebrated poet Felice Za\'7d)pi. Zap]ii was considerably older than his wife, but handsome, elegant, and highly talented, and there aj^pears to have existed between

them an affection which never diminished, and of which Faustina's
beautiful sonnet to an old love of her husband's is a proof such as one
rarely meets among the vapid Arcadian love poems. She was likewise
skilled as a painter, and the Arcadian Academy still possesses a little
portrait in which she has reprospntod herself in the fnll maturity of her beauty, dressed in
flowered yellow brocade, her black hair raised in a high structure, and one long curl falling on
her finely-modelled neck. The face, with its straight, delicate features, and opaque, ivory
complexion, has a sort of sedate, intellectual coquetry, like that of Pope's lady—" an equal
mixture of good humour and sensible soft melancholy "—which makes one understand the
courteous and admiring afVcction which Faustina Maratti Zappi inspired in the most euiiucnt
men of Italy, a feeling quite unlike the flat gallantry of those times, and which Manfredi has well
expressed in a pretty sonnet:

Pur con questi occhi al fin visto ho I'altero Miracol di bellezza e cVonestate, Cui sol per
adombrar, mille fiate Oltr' Amo ed Apennin spinto ho il pensiero.

E pur con queste orecchie udito ho il vero Fregio c il vivo stupor di nostra ctate : Or gli
uni e I'altre omai paghi e beate Chiudansi pur, ch'altro da lor nou chero.

No tu i gran templi e i simulacri tuoi Vantarmi intatti aucor dal tempo cdace, Neir ampie
spoglie della terra doma;

Cho gloria antica o nuova altra non puoi Mostrar pari a costei, sia con tua pace, Bella,
invitta, superba, augusta Roma.

Rolli and Frugoni and all the principal Italian poets addressed Faustina Maratti under her
Arcadian name of Aglauro Cidonia ; but their verses were mostly inferior to their subject, and
Felice Zappi himself, although his vein was generally rather insipid and finikin, was, on the
whole, the sweetest and most elegant of the j>oets who sang the charms of the beautiful painter
and poetess. Faustina is the heroine of a romantic incident, strange enough in the jog-trot literary
Italy of those days. A young noblemen, violently enamoured of her and enraged at her
contemptuous treatment, determined to destroy her beauty in d(>fault of her reinitation, and
threw in her face some dreadful liquid, probably vitriol, of Avhicb, however, only a single drop
touchetl her, leaving on her temple a black patch, the size of a sticking-plaster motiche, an
indelible record of this semi-miracle, which she, of course, recorded in a sonnet. It is curious
with what simplicity Count Corniani, writing sixty years later, asks mth indignant surprise how
such an atrocious attempt could go unpunished ; but its author was perhaps the nephew of a
Pope, and in the eighteenth century it is a great proof of the liberty enjoyed by Italians that the
crime should not have been punished on the victim rather than on the criminal. An old friend and
constant visitor at the Zappi's was Pier Jacopo Martello, who resided for some time in Rome as
fcjecretary to the Ambassador of the Bolognese Senate to the Holy See. Martello was, like most
of his

c2

contemporaries, a learned man—he had Avritten Latin verses and treatises ; but he had
been in Paris and acquired a taste for French literature, which, joined to his secular Bolognese
education, gave him a light and genteel air compared with the solemn Eoman clod-hoppers. A
volume of his works contains a finely-wrought little engraving of his portrait, suspended Avitli a
pastoral pipe on an oak tree: Avith his carefully crimped hair and fur pelisse he has much the
look of a dandy; and his thin lips, heavy eyelids, and scraggy profile, give the general impression
of conceit, inoff"ensive, intellectual, and benign. Martello Avas perhaps the first Italian who
made his fellow-countrymen acquainted with French literature, and who, while the subtle and icy

Gravina was constructing plays on what he conceived to be the Greek model, Avrote tragedies in the correct and polished French style, and in a species of Alexandrin, invented by himself, and of such uncouthness of sound as to do him little credit. Occasionally the cheerful little Bolognese society at Faustina Zappi's house was increased by the benign and elegant mathematician Francesco Zanotti and his rough, merry brother, the painter and poet Giampietro. Then there was the intimate of old Carlo Maratta, the famous violinist and composer Arcangelo Corelli, whose works are still remembered and admired, while Martello, the Zanottis, Zappi, and even the beautiful Faustina herself have long been forgotten.

But while colonies were being founded in all directions, and the illustrious names—not only of princes, and senators, and cardinals, but of the last Gonzagas and Estensi—were being exchanged for pastoral appellations, danger threatened the Academy from within, and a spark was set alight which well-nigh blew Arcadia back again into chaos. The haughty and eccentric Gravina had not seen without a pang the growth of an institution which had declined having him at its head, nor the glory which had thence accrued to his rival Crescimbeni. This ill-favoured, awkward pedant had become the acknowledged head of the whole hierarchy of Italian literature, petted by cardinals and princes and flattered by poets and ladies; and meanwhile he, Gian Vincenzo Gravina, the greatest scholar and jurist in Rome, the author of luminous treatises and elegant poems, the handsome, dignified, eloquent Gravina, was left to muse and study in his rustily-furnished rooms in Via Giulia, and to hold forth thrice a Aveek before the students of the Hapienza. Gravina's jealous irritation was increased beyond all control by the ill success of his tragedies, which, as Martello informs us, no one Avould read; and the illwill pent up for twenty years suddenly vented itself on the unlucky Crescimbeni. The j)retext for the quarrel is confused and obscure. Gravina accused Crescimbeni of passing off the famous Arcadian Code as his own work; Crescimbeni declared that Gravina had merely translated what he himself had suggested; which was in the right and which in the wrong none

Can now tell, and no one perhaps understood at the time; bnt this much is certain, that a schism ensued, Crescimbeni retaining the main body of the Arcadians while Gravina marched off at the liead of the minority. And now a\'7d)peared the influence of Gravina's undoubted talents; one Arcadian after another abondoned Crescimbeni and rallied round his rival. Between the two parties poor Don Livio Odescalchi was i)erfoctly lost; he felt bound to protect from heresy the Academy that was rendering him immortal; but he could in no way discover which was the orthodox branch, and which the schismatic, wavering between the authority of Crescimbeni, long and intimately connected with the institution, and the influence of Gravina, the most brilliant scholar of Rome." At length, and in despair, Don Livio lot himself be won over by Gravina, but reluctantly, and casting a half remorseful glance back at Crescimbeni. Although he installed the Anti-Arcadia in one of his villas outside Porta del Popolo, and even accepted the nominal title of Custode Generale, he yet tried to keep on good terms with Crescimbeni, who takes care to inform us of this fact (^Vite degli Arcadi Morti), at the same time hinting darkly and solemnly that the unhappy Prince was the victim of a conspiracy, of whose existence he became aware very soon, but too late, alas ! to be saved. In the midst of those awful events, which the scofEng Baretti ridiculed with more coarseness than wit fifty years later, one of the original founders of the disturbed Academy, Domenico Petrosellini, had the levity to sing the war between Gravina and Crescimbeni in a heroic-comic poem, which had great success at the time, but is now extrenily difficult to procure. But the schism, begun about 1711, was not of long duration. Gravina's coldness, intolerant and intolerable conceit, and real want of interest in Arcadian matters, little by little sent back the penitent schismatics to the orthodox institution, and after some time the heresiarch found himself shunned no less by his own former disciples than by those of his opponent. 80 Gian Vincenzo Gravina hid his humiliation in his house near Palazzo Farnose, and soothed his disappointment by doing his best to make his young pupil Metastasio an eminent lawyer, instead of letting him waste his powers on being a poet.

The Arcadian Academy appears already to have possessed some sort of fixed abode, called Serbatoio, a word that might be translated into reservoir or conservatoiy, and about which Baretti made the following etymological remarks : " Serbatoio, a Greek word derived from the Chaldean, is in Eome equivalent to poetical Secretaries office, while in Florence it has the meaning of a closet in ivhich are kept meat, vegetables, poidtry, and other eatables." However, the Serbatoio appears to have been a very humble apartment, judging by a letter of Giampietro Zanotti, in which he says : " I have been to the Serbatoio, a very little thing, oruaniontod with very little things." Indeed, the only large thing that

it contained was Crescimbcni's nose : " I assure yon " (writes Zanotti to his wife) "that it impressed me miich more than the obelislc of the Piazza

del Popolo Oh, what a nose! A statue ought to be made

of it and placed in the Capitol. What is the cupola of St. Peter's or the Colosseum compared to that nose? A wretched trifle. Let us pray Heaven to preserve that nose yet a while, and let us give thanks for our living now-a-days and seeing so grand a sight." The Bolognese painter could not recover from the impression made by Crescimbcni's nose, and again spoke of it in a letter of the 19th December, 1719: "Saturday last the lightning fell with tremendous crash on the Capitol, and, strange to say, broke a bench on which three lawyers were seated, without hurting them. Think if it Avere to fall on to the Serbatoio d'Arcadia and hit the nose of the Custode ! "

When Giampietro Zanotti wrote this rhapsody on Crescimbcni's nose GraAdna had already been removed from the scene of his shortlived glory and long humiliation. Unable to brook the final victory of his rival he had apparently accepted the invitation of the King of Sardinia to fill the place of professor of civil law at Turin, when, in 1718, he suddenly died, leaving the bulk of his fortune to his favom-ite pupil Pietro Bonaventura Trapassi, the son of an ex-soldier and small druggist, who was later to fill the world with his fame under the name of Pietro Metastasio. Soon after Gravina's death, his friends, Vincenzo Leonio and Pier Jacopo Martello, informed Crescimbeni that the deceased had chai'ged them to make known to the Custode Generale d'Arcadia that he deeply regretted having provoked the schism in that institution, but that he had done so from no want of respect towards it. This extraordinary posthumous self-humiliation of one of the vainest of men may possibly have touched even the rusty heart of his rival ; at all events, the merits of Gravina were appreciated more universally than before, and by a general decree of the Arcadian Acedemy the name of Gian Vincenzo Gravina, erased during his lifetime from its registers as that of a malignant schismatic, was inscribed once more in them a short time after his death.

Two events, more brilliant than even this one, were reserved for the last years of Crescimbcni's reign.

In 1725 there arrived in Rome the most illustrious Signer Benedetto Marcello, patrician of Venice and Provveditore of Pola, celebrated for his patronage of poetry and music. Crescimbeni and his pedants, who were utterly incapable of appreciating the musical genius of Marcello, and who, in their happy state of self-delusion, doubtless considered musicians as miserable buffoons, not worthy of a look from an empty-headed man of letters, were yet capable of appreciating the great Venetian composer's high rank. So Marcello Avas forthAvith admitted to the inestimable honour of belonging to the Arcadian Academy, and, when his psalms were performed

in Cardinal Ottoboni's palace, Crescimbeui and his colleagues embellished this solemnity by reciting their own verses in the interludes of the music —a splendid instance of self-sufificient folly patronising genius. Marcello, however, was of very little importance compared with the heroic prince who graced these performances with his presence ; and, if sonnets were made for the patrician who deigned to cultivate music, Olympic Games were decreed in honour of the king who stooped to pay attention to poetry. The king in question was Don John V. of Portugal, one of the most licentious, superstitious, and spendthrift princes of the day, and whose portrait at the Bosco Parrasio, representing him in full armour and a black horse-hair wig, from under which peers his swarthy, apelike countenance, reveals one of the most brutish natures conceivable. Cres-cimbeni, however, was too much dazzled by the glory which surrounded John V. to perceive any of his Majesty's uncouth peculiarities, and the king, in return for the Olympic Games above mentioned, made a present to the Arcadian Academy of a triangular strip ofgi'ound on the Janiculum, Avhich, being laid out with flowers and shrubs, was designated by the name of Parrhasian Grove, and became the summer resort of the shepherds in black broadcloth and full-bottomed wigs.

Meanwhile the Academy was gradually changing, as one after another of the old members dropped away and new ones started up instead. Alessandro Guidi had not long survived Queen Christina and the seventeenth century; Silvio Stampiglia had for years been replaced in the imperial service by the Candiot dramatist and reviewer Zeno; Carlo Maratta, last of great painters, and Corelli, first of great violinists, had followed each other to the grave; the intelligent and accomplished Martello had also gone, leaving, however, a growing crop of French imitations and Alexaudriu verses behind; even Prince Livio Odescalchi, would-be Maecenas, had died, ha\'7d)py, doubtless, in expectation of immortal fame. This gradual change in the members of the Academy indicated a much more important one in the whole republic of letters, nay, in the whole of Italian society. The men educated in the seventeeth century were rapidly dying out, while those already educated in the eighteenth were beginning to take their place. The solemn period of stagnation, nejjotism, and Spanish rule was over, and the time of French influence, levity, tolerance, and national reconstitution, had come. There remained, it is true, not only then, but throughout the whole eighteenth century, much that was childish, pedantic, and servile : there were vast numbers of dunces who passed oft' for learned men, and vast numbers of fools who got credit as poets; worse still, there were truly learned men wasting their time on the most futile disputes, and real poets throwing away their talents on the most insignificant subjects; there was, still worst of all, the basest adulation of princes, and prelates, and fine ladies; this was the miserable inheritance of the previous age,

but by its side was what tlio previous age had not possessed—learning put to worthy use, talent developed in the right way, and protection granted generously and intelligently. But of these new characteristics we shall speak later, when we come to treat of the time when they were more highly doveloped than at the mere beginning of the century. We must, however, mention some of the new Arcadians, who went to the Bosco Parrasio before its laurels and ilexes had grown out of the state of bushes. Paolo Antonio Rolli is one of the most conspicuous of these more or less forgotten celebrities. He was born near Rome, in the valley of the Tiber, about 1686; and, after having vainly attempted to make his fortune at home by his talents for both written and extemporary poetry, went to London, wrote libretti for Handel and his rival Porpora, translated Paradise Lost, was put into the Dunciad for his pains, and pronounced to be a vermicelli-maker or pastry-cook, the only profession besides that of musician for which the Britons of those days gave the Italians credit. In Italy, on the contrary, Rolli got more consideration than money; his elegies were translated into Latin, and he himself, being a native of Todi in Umbria, was dignified with the title of the modern Propertius. Although Rolli was far from being a first-rate poet, this epithet was founded upon more than the mere accident of his Umbrian origin and elegiac tendencies, for, living when he did, he had a strange, unaccountable antique air about him, such as became common only much later. He was trifling and superficial, yet, among the colourless, insipid imitators of Petrarca, he stood out as does a second-rate copy of some mythological picture by Titian among a lot of hazy, woe-begone Guidos and ^asso-ferratos. While his contemporaries composed in loose, limp rhymes, he was the first to make Italian hendecasyllabics; while they were satisfied with the barest, slightest outlines of conventional scenery, he went into minute descriptions of the split sides of figs, of the crackling of burning juniper berries, of the scent of Monte Porzio wine, and the weight of ripe melons; while they indited canzoni upon the beatification of saints, he wi-ote a hymn to Venus, a patchwork of imitations from half the writers of antiquity, but not without a pantheistic, pagan tone, such as was rare before Goethe; * indeed, his antique tendencies were carried to such a length that

    * O bella Venere, figlia del Giorno, Destami affetti puri nell' animo, E un guardo volgimi dal tuo soggiorno. Te non accolsero da' flutti infidi, Nata dall' atro sangue Saturnio, Di Cipro fertile gl' infami lidi: A te non fumano Tare in Citera, Nc ti circonda con Ic Bassaridi De' fauni e satiri I'impura schiera.

    he thonglit it prndout to liead his works by a dodaration that, " by tlio Divine Grace, I was born in the faith and in tlie bosom of the Imly Catliolic Roman Chm-ch, which I have everywhere and at all times imli-licly professed." Rolli never departed further from the models of his times than in the series of little poems adtbessed to his E,<^eria: she is certainly not the Cynthia of Propertius, still less the Delia of Tibullus, yet she is more closely related to them than to the colourless semi-nymphs, somi-nuns, of Rolli's contemporaries; he makes no attempt to substitute tli(^ conventional pseudo-classic details for modern ones, and it is perhaps the very minuteness and distinctness Avith which he describes Egeria at her miiTor, dressed in brocade trimmed with gold fringe, flowers and lace on her powdered hair, waiting- for her heavy gilt coach, Avliich brings him nearer to antiquity than his classical brethren. Rolli, though ofteii graceful and lively, and sometimes almost pathetic, was after all only a second-rate poet, but a piece by him has become a sort of relic from being connected with a great poet,—the canzonet " Solitario Bosco Ombroso" having been a favourite with Frau Rath, who taught it to the little Goethe even before he knew a word of Italian.

    A more brilliant and universally admired poet than Rolli was the Abate Carlo Innocenzo Frugoni, but his subsequent literary fate was worse than that of Rolli, for, while the latter has been permitted to remain in inglorious peace, Frugoni's name has been used as a bye-word by thousands of Italians who have never read a line by him. TlvAi frngoncria means high-sounding nonsense, meaningless fustian, is well known by every student of

    Le sagge favole sull' onde chiare Poserti in vaga conca cerulea, A fior del tremulo tranquillo mare; Pereht' il tuo vivido spirto sovriuio Penetra c scorre negli umor fluidi Che p.adre rcndono I'ampio Oceano, II qiuil con runiide ramose hraccia Lo porta e infonde nel grembo all' aride Cose clie mutano colore e faccia;

    Tu quando i tiepidi venti amorosi II dure ghiaccio sui monti sciolgono, E i tiumi a Tetide vaniio orgogliosi; Tratta dai rapidi tuoi bianchi augclli Scendi nel suolo che per te germina Erbette tenere c fior novcUi. Tu rcndi a gli alberi o frutto e fronda; Per tc gli ai'ati canipi verdeggiano, E cresce prodiga la messe bionda; Per te di panipini veston le viti, E il caro peso dei folti grappoli Per te sostengono gli olmi mariti.

Italian literature, but who and what Frugoni was, few have cared to investigate. He was, when we really get to see him, a lamentable instance of fine talent, not wasted, but ruined out and out by a disorderly character, a ramshackle career, and a stupid public. Of noble Genoese family, Frugoni had been forced into a monastery at sixteen; many years were wasted in getting out of it, with the help of the good-natured Pope; many more in vainly attempting to recover the fortune which, on his embracing a monastic life, had been seized by his relatives; and the remainder of Frugoni's days passed in trying to obtain a fixed mode of life, an attempt frustrated by political events, by his antecedents and by his own reckless, disorderly habits, which would have been punished by any but the easy-o-oing hierarchy of the eighteenth century. In the midst of all this, Frugoni's brilliant, prolific, unsteady talents suffered as much as his worldly career, for their possessor seems to have been totally destitute of patience, of desire of improvement, and of judgment: he poured forth sonnet upon sonnet, ode upon ode, stanza upon stanza, without any thought of attempting a large work, or perfecting a small one. Perfectly satisfied with his facile vein and the easily excited applause of his hearers, and firmly persuaded that he would be immortal, Frugoni's talents were, as we have said, not merely wasted, but irretrievably ruined, for in his works the good is not embedded in the bad, but sense is inextricably interwoven with nonsense, and a grand thought or beautiful image is (we can find no other expresion) so mixed and amalgamated with trashiness as to be absolutely irrecoverable. Yet his poems were very popular, nor was their popularity entirely undeserved, for they have a flow of versification, a magnificence of sound, and a splendour of colouring and imagery which dazzle the mind before it has time to reflect on the meaning. Frugoni's epithets always raise up confused visions of beauty and wonder, and the mere sound of his verse impresses you, but on trying to analyse one of his pieces you find that he evidently had no idea of what he was writing, and that he did nothing but heap together brilliant pieces of trash and gorgeous fragments of real value, which only serve to make the absurdity of the remainder more lamentable. However, Frugoni's time was not one of inanity, although it may have been one of bad taste, and Frugoni himself was not an inane poet; on the contrary, his grandiloquent and highly-coloured nonsense was probably enjoyed just in proportion as it differed from the pale, correct, languid truisms of the poets of the preceding generation. Frugoni was a man of real and brilliant talents, and talents like his, however much wasted and ruined they may be, cannot fail to excite what they do in some measm-e deserve, momentary admiration and everlasting abuse. A third poet was beginning to be spoken of at Arcadian meetings, although probably much less than either Rolli or Frugoni, and this was the Abate Pietro Metastasio. He had been early brought into notice by the fact of his being the adopted son of Gravina, of ominous memory; and after his benefjictor's deatli he often appeared at the Bosco Parrasio, first witli a tiresome frigid elegy to the memory of the deceased, and then with other trifles of which the great Crescimbeni deigned to approve. People expected him to be another, though less dangerous, Gravina, and praised him for his erudition; but unfortunately, having consumed his protector's legacy, he got into idle ways at Naples, neglected the study of the law, and abandoned the company of the wise and learned Arcadians for that of composers and singers and similar riffraff". What would poor Gravina have done if he could have foreseen such an end for his adopted son ? said the Arcadians at the Bosco Parrasio, and shook their heads at the prodigal. One day, however, in the year 1724, news came from Naples that a play called Dido, set to music by 8arro and written by Gravina's pupil, had had the most extraordinary success, and soon after the worthies at the Bosco Parrasio heard to their amazement that Mctastasio was the greatest di-amatist Italy had ever produced, and the greatest poet she had given the world since Tasso.

But there was another poet who, while infinitely less esteemed than any of his contemporaries, was yet infinitely more flattered; and who, while everyone knew that he would, nay must, be forgotten by the very next generation, yet received what Rolli, Frugoni, or Metastasio would vainly have sought for—an honour which, while the greatest Italy could give, she yet ventured to offer only to an inferior sort of beings. The cro^vn of the Capitol had got to seem such a theatrical honour that it could be given only to a kind of theatrical performer, and such was the Cavalier Bernardino Perfetti, the greatest of the Italian improvvisatori. If we have been speaking in a paradoxical style it has been from the very nature of our subject, for never did there exist a stranger paradox than one of these extemporary poets, possessed of a splendid endowment which every other sort of poet would have despised, displaying his talent in an exercise which was an avowed waste of it, and, while producing nothing but commonplace nonsense, giving a greater impression of genius and inspiration than the best of his worthier contemporaries. It is therefore easier to condemn and ridicule such poets and poetry than to judge them with fairness, or even to get a distinct notion of the case under judgment. However, before speaking of Perfetti himself, we must make a few remarks on the class to which he belonged. Italy appears at all times to have produced extemporary poets ; and we meet them, male and female, almost as often during the Eenaissancc as during the eighteenth century. Lorenzo de' Medici is said to have improvised his spirited " Falcon Hunt " at a convivial meeting, and both he and his son Leo X. had regular improvvisatori among their satellites; but it seems probable that the gradual institution of a number of academies, of which the eighteenth century was

particularly prolific, and the gradual spreading of literary interests among the more frivolous parts of society—another characteristic feature of the eighteenth century—favoured the profession of extemporary poets, and caused it to become a perfectly independent one. For besides the poets who, like Eolli and Frugoni, extemporised verses at a party or at table, without thinking any more about them, and whose fame rested entirely upon their written compositions, there was a class of men and of women who would improvise, not a couplet here or there, but whole poems of thirty or forty stanzas on any given subject and before assemblies convened for the express purpose of hearing them; people who did not write and perhaps could not Avrite, for the exercise of their profession rendered them incapable of anything but the most slovenly work, besides accustoming them to compose only under a kind of stimulus which they had not when calmly writing at a table. To be a successful improi-visatore real poetical faculties were undoubtedly required: great vivacity of mind and brilliancy of imagination, besides extraordinary powers of expression and versification, but besides this there were qualities which an ordinary poet rai-ely possesses—a nervous excitability and a warmth of, we should almost say, sensational feeling, which generally developed at the expense of the body and the mind. Most improvvisatori showed signs of utter exhaustion, such as Avas rapidly destroying the young Metastasio when the Princess Belmonte Pignatelli induced Gravina to forbid his improvising any longer. How much depended upon the practice of improvising, the habit of getting into this extraordinary state of physical and intellectual excitement, is shown by the fact that Lorenzo d'Aponte, the librettist of Mozart, gradually developed the faculty in himself and in his brother; while Metastasio, Avho had possessed it when a mere child, afterwards declared that he could neither extemporise a single line nor understand how he had ever been able to do so. That the product of these anomalous talents must have been a very anomalous one is evident; and that the improvvisatori talked a vast amount of trash, nay that there was in their performance no real originality or literary merit, is undeniable; that, as Metastasio, who in after-life could not endure the thing, tells us, the poems thus produced were full of " Angelicas with the helmet of Orlando and Rinaldos wearing the nightcap of Armida;" that, as we learn from Forsyth, the scraps of improvised poetry written down by persons of the audience proved the vilest rubbish—all this is very true, and yet it is even more true that the performance of a good improrvisatore was a wonderful performance: the rapid out-\'7d)Ouring of sonorous verse, the succession of image on image, flashing past the mind in vague splendour, the air of inspiration, and the sensuous eloquence which is more potent than that of the reasoning faculties—all this made the exhibition of a Perfetti or a Gorilla something fascinating; but a mere exhibition it was, like that of fireworks

or some strange theatre scene, and it was absurd to seek in it a poem or any sort of real work of art.* Among the many accounts whicli remain of the performance of the greatest imptwrisatore of the last century we choose the following one, written by the lively and int(>lligcnt President de Brosses to his French friends from Rome in the year 173U : " You have heard of the class of poets who think nothing of composing an extemporary poem on any subject one may propose to them. The subject we gave to Perfetti was the Aurora Borealis. He meditated, looking downwards, for at least half a quarter of an hour, to the sound of a harpsichord preluding sotto voce. Then he rose, and began to declaim in rhymed octaves, softly, and stanza by stanza, the harpsichord continuing to play chords while he was declaiming, and preluding during the intervals between the stanzas. At first they succeeded each other slowly enough, but little by little the poet became more animated, and in proportion to his doing so the harpsichord also played louder and louder, till at length this extraordinary man declaimed like a poet full of enthusiasm. The accompanier on the harpsichord and himself went on together with surprising rapidity. When it was over, Perfetti seemed fatigued; he told us that he does not like to have to improvise often, as it exhausts his mind and body. His poem pleased me very much; in his rapid declamation it seemed to me sonorous, full of ideas and

imagery You may be sure, however, that it consisted in

reality of much more sound than sense: it is impossible that the general construction should not be most often maimed and tortured, and that the fiUing-up be not mere grandiloquent rubbish." Bernardino Perfetti, thus described by the President de Brosses, was of noble Sienese family, a knight of the order of St. Stephen and professor of jurisprudence in his native city, nor does he seem ever to have exercised his talents for improvising except for pleasure and glory. In 1725 the Grand-Duchess Dowager of Tuscany, Violante Beatrice of Bavaria, sent for him to Rome, where she was a guest of Benedict XIII. on occasion of the Jubilee. During this visit Perfetti excited such admiration by his improvisations at the Clementine College, at the palace of the Grand-Duchess, and at that of the French ambassadoi', Cardinal Polignac, that the Pope, no doubt influenced by Crescimbeni and his adherents, decided that the hnprorvisatore should receive the crown of the Capitol, and gave the necessary instructions to the senators and chief magistrates. Perfetti had, however, to undergo three consecutive

* The !mj)r(irr!niif(irl were probably aware of their shortcomings, and aware of their right to be excused, as I gatlier from the following answer made by an extemporary poet of the first years of this century to a Cardinal who cried out," Too many syllables : " " Chi ferra, inchioda, e chi cammina, inciampa ; S'improvvisa, Emincnza, e non si stampa."

ordeals in the palace of the Grand-Duchess, and in the presence of all Arcadia, twelve of whose members were chosen as judges. These twelve, divided into batches of four, proposed a theme to him on each evening; he improvised on them all with the greatest success; and the last evening, when everyone thought that he was utterly exhausted, he suddenly rose and epitomised all the previous arguments in the light verse called sdrncciolo, and, according to Crescimbeni, " Strung together the themes with wondrous felicity, and in such a way that, without altering the order of their succession, he formed out of the most different subjects a perfectly constructed oration." The delegates of course decided that Perfetti was well worthy of the crown worn by Petrarch. This was a very serious opinion, and the character of Benedict XIII., of Crescimbeni, and, above all, of the solemn, stately time, excludes all thought of the ceremony being a mystification like that played off by the facetious Leo X. on poor Baraballo. The day after these trials Perfetti dressed himself after dinner, that is to say, after tAvo in the afternoon, in a robe of black damask, and betook himself to the palace of the Sapienza, where he Avas received by a magistrate, who carried him to the Capitol in one of the great gold-embossed and painted coaches of the senators. In the hall of the Horatii and Curiatii, bedizened Avith Arpino's clumsy frescoes and decked out for the occasion Avith draperies and plants, Perfetti was met by the unique representative of the Roman Senate, in his gold and purple robes, with his adjuncts, the Conservatori, the chief magistrates, innumerable pages, mace-bearers, and nobles, by the Grand-Duchess Dowager of Tuscany, the Princess Ruspoli, sister of the Pope, and her daughter the Duchess Gravina, and by Arcadia rei)resented by Crescimbeni and the most illustrious members. In the midst of a croAvd of cardinals, prelates, long-Avigged princes, and enamelled-cheeked ladies, Perfetti advanced to the foot of the senatorial throne, and the Senator Marchese Mario Fran-gipani, taking the laurel Avreath from a page, who held it on a silver embossed salver, placed it on the poet's head, making the folloAving Ciceronian speech: " Eximium hoc laudis poeticae decus, quod tuo capiti inqjono, sub felicissimis auspiciis S.S.D.N. Papae Benedict! XIII. sit publici non minus erga argumentum quam obsequentissinii animi significatio erga amplissimam illam et plane regiam benevolentiam, qua, decoraris." Perfetti Avas not loss glib in improvising Latin prose than Italian verse, and ansAA'ered: " Poetica laurus immeritae imposita fronti, excelsam S.S. Patris ac Principis Papae Benedicti Xlll.munificentiamque, effusainque senatus populusquc Romani erga me voluntatem testatur, quarum utraque aut honore dignos invenit ant facit." Then the crowned poet Avas seated on a chair of state prepared for him, and seven Arcadians, headed by Crescimbeni, repeated laudatory poems, to the accompaniment of a tremendous noise of trumpets and drums, and the firing of a hundred

mortars. Afterwards the notary of tlie 8cnate drew up an Act by Avhicli the citizenship and nobility of Rome were conferred on the Cavalier Perfctti and all his descendants. There is or was a picture of Porfetti at the Bosco Parrasio, not in the black damask robe and laurel wreath, but in a strange combination of many-coloured garments, green, red, and yellow, with an open collar and loose blue necktie, and an orange-coloured scarf rolled round his close-shaven head; a mass of colour harmonising Avell with the very swarthy complexion, brilliant eyes, and full, laughing lips of the poet. This picture, gaudy and yet harmonious, rich and outlandish, serves to help out our conception of the strange, theatrical, poetical medley of talents which made up the successor of Petrarch.

III.

Crescimbcni's glorious reign ended soon after the donation of the Bosco Parrasio and the coronation of Perfctti; and the Arcadians of Rome and of the colonies lamented in innumerable sonnets and elegies the veteran founder and champion of the Academy. The raised seat beneath the laurels of the Bosco Parrasio, loft vacant by the death of Crescimbeni, was filled by his friend and colleague the Abate Lorenzini. He had been edixcated as a servant in the house of the poet Guidi, and had early acquired a literary position, though less by his works, which cannot now be found, than by his familiarity with writers, having contrived to keep on good terms both with Crescimbeni and with Gravina. He was a large, rawboned man, with a face at once sarcastic and good-humoured, and strange, humorous, astonished-looking eyebrows. He had probably more talent than Crescimbeni; at all events a much juster appreciation of men and things, and a tendency to regard Arcadian affairs as not so very much more important than other human concerns. The accession of the second Custode Generale marks a ucav phase in the history of the Academy : during his government Arcadia extended its frontiers to the utmost, and became supreme throughout the peninsula; but, like Rome and Venice, it did so at the expense of its original spirit and constitution. The Academy became lost in its legions of members, and as people of every sort, and in every part of Italy, became Arcadians, to bo an Arcadian soon meant merely to be a member of the society of one's native town, and a holder of one's own principles, just as one would have been had Arcadia never existed. In short, Arcadia ceased to be an academy and became the whole literary and social life of the country.

V And now let us sto\'7d) and glance round the Italy of the eighteenth century, a century displaying in all countries so strange a mixture of

strength and of weakness, of vigorous modes of thought which had not the force of habit, and of Lizy modes of life which were enforced by custom; of philanthropical aspirations and tyrannical institutions; of goodness masked by frivolity and scepticism, and villany hidden beneath solemnity and moralising; of corruption and renovation, mingling and fermenting in unlovely fashion. In Italy this movement was less strongly felt than in other countries, and especially less than in France, and not merely because the race was less prone to exaggeration and excess. In Italy tliere was, of course, a great deal to sweep away—vicious modes of thought and life due to long inertion and protracted rule of Spaniards, Jesuits, and little local tyrants; but, on the other hand, there still remained much of the influence of the Renaissance. The Italians were

' not tlie great-grandsons of semi-barbarians, like the Germans and ourselves, but of free, enlightened, and polished burghers; they had the remembrance of commercial commonwealths, and not, like the French, of a hideous feudal system; there was no inequality of classes, no great misery and great power opposed to each other for centuries; and when the stream of progress of the eighteenth century reached Italy it joined insensibly with the remains of civilisation left in the country by antiquity and the Renaissance, and of which no amount of political and social disorganisation could ever deprive it. The eighteenth century in Italy was, therefore, not a violent reaction against feudalism as in France, nor against Puritanism as in England, nor against foreign domination as in Germany; it was a mere gradual waking up from lethargy and a shaking off of its bad effects. There was no war against nobles, or priests, or foreigners, and thence it is that Italy in that time seems scarcely to move in comparison with other countries, and its very movement, when examined, appears rather droll than revolting in the contrasts it brings to light.

Let us pass by the four great towns most visited by the travellers of the eighteenth century: Venice, crumbling gaily away, a place where Beckford could dream Oriental dreams of luxuriousness and hidden terrors, and compare the motley population, not less than the cupolas and minarets, to the strange world of Vathek which he carried in his mind ; Naples, feudal and antique, at once so backward in social

\ institutions and so happy in natural endowments, which could make Goethe feel even more of a Greek than he naturally was—Naples, which from amongst intellectual and physical filth gave Italy in the eighteenth century her philosophy and her art, her Vico and her Pergo-lesi, her Filangieri and her Cimarosa ; Florence, with her Frenchified rulers and intensely Italian people, painted in all her frivolity by the frivolous Mann ; and Rome, of whose uneducated princes and half-barbarous lower classes the President de Brosses speaks like an earlier

c

and less eccentric Stendhal. Let us leave tlie great centres, each representing some extreme, of artificially produced vice, of artificially kept up barbarism, of artificial credulity, and artificial pedantry; and let us look at one of the innumerable smaller cities which attest the vigour of the Italian spirit of earlier days, a vigour which foreign interference or foreign pressure has succeeded neither in entirely extinguishing nor in entirely warping. In these c^uiet mediaeval towns,—where crumbling monuments ovei'shadow grass-grown streets, and only a few heavy gilt coaches rumble across the time-worn pavement; where the popular vitality is concentrated in the market-place, the barbers' shops, and the coffeehouses,—intellectual life sputters and crackles cheerily. The noble counts and marquises, descended from republican merchants, feudal princes, or mercenary generals, mix freely with the upper middle classes, their equals ill race, in education, in manners, and very nearly in fortune, and who feel neither jealous nor idolatrous of their superiors in rank. The dull, serene life of these inglorious grandees and placid burghers is wiled away in the cultivation of science and erudition, literature and art; nobles and commoners meet on equal footing; they study together in the same colleges, where the master may be a patrician general like Marsigli, or a plebeian professor like Zanotti; they help eacb other in editing inscriptions, publishing chronicles, and compiling guide-books and histories; they make each other presents of their materials, or lampoon each other most frightfully. The women are not left out of the literai-y bustle; of course there are some who have been brought up by pious nuns who could not or would not teach them reading or writing,* as there are young men after Parini's model who remain in bed till twelve, and read only wicked French novels, brought up in unconsciousness of classical studies by dingy priest tutors, who run errands and carry lapdogs for their pupils' mothers. All this there is of course, for, unless we placed the ignorant apathy by the side of the restless inquisitiveness, we should give a false picture of the eighteenth century, whose characteristic peculiarity was that it united the evil things that remain with the good things that are coming. All this there is—ignorance, sloth, and corruption ; but there are also good qualities. There are the innumerable ladies who, as soon as they have exchanged the convent for their / husband's house, become refined, literary, nay learned: poetesses, composers, and presiders over intellectual society, the friends, patronesses, and counsellors of the greatest writers in Italy, yet without aspiring to the position of the Dottoressa Bassi, who lectured on Newton's Optics before she was twenty.- There arc also the innumerable young men, elegant dancers, and fencers, and sturdy players at racket, who in their youth

* This was the case with the grandmother of a Tuscan friend of ours, from whom we have the anecdote.

D

are spoken of by well-known writers as of excellent morals and great literary acquirements, and who, later in life, when dancing and fencing and racket have been abandoned, collect libraries, write verses and satires on surrounding frivolity, take interest in agriculture, imitate the Georgics in poems on the cultivation of rice or silk, and in a few places keep up some amount of industry and commerce.* The domestic life is strange enough ; the marriages are mostly made up by the families, though, according to Baretti, not usually against the desire of the young people. The husband and wife are not permitted to be on bad terms, yet there is the inevitable cavaliere servente, chosen by the husband or the wife's family, obsequious, useful, tiresome, meddlesome, treated with contemptuous consideration; often much in the way of both husband and wife, as Goldoni shows him in the play, where Don Koberto and Donna Eularia run away from town and bury themselves in a village where society will not force cavalieri serventi on to them ; that he disturbs family peace or endangers family ties few even of the satirists, no, not even Parini, will admit; he is a respectable institution. Another institution is that of putting all the daughters for whom no eligible husbands can be found into rich convents, where they can enjoy comparative freedom; and of making the younger sons enter the Church or some military order, unless they can turn magistrate or something similar. The upper middle classes do without cavalieri serventi, convents, and military orders ; and make their sons lawyers, doctors, professors, or priests, commerce, except in the sea-ports, being reduced to shopkeeping. The social life is a queer mixture of gaiety and dullness, unless we go into the madly spendthrift society of the dissolute Venetians or Frenchified Lombards and Florentines ; the same people meet day after day; everyone is intimately acquainted with his neighbours. The literati— and every educated person belongs more or less to them—sit in the bookseller's shop, and discuss new works and enter into a literary conversation with any stranger who comes in, as the amiable people at Padua did with Goethe when he was in search of Palladio's works. They meet also in the garden or palace of one of the company; and the lofty rooms, hung with faded tapestry and portraits of worthies in black doublets and

* In the little oligarchy of Lucca the principal families kept up their industrial and commercial connections until past the middle of the eighteenth century, some of the nobles possessing silk-manufactories and banking-houses even in Flanders. These same Lucchesc nobles, who managed one of the finest theatres in Italy off the savings in their incredibly small State budget, were great publishers, and re-edited t\\e\\'\w\c FjW 11 el(>]>(■ (lie when prohiliited in France. It has often been remarked that the Italian nobles of the last century were comparatively better educated than their descendants, because the progress of Liberalism, while it raised the intellectual standard of the inferior chisses, frightened the nobles into stolid opposition to all improvement, and ccmscquently into an illiterate and bigoted stagnation.

scarlet caps, or sliining ^Yith new gilt stucco and high-backed white and gold chairs, are crowded with senators in full-bottomed wigs, pour literary priests in rusty little cloaks, smart young men with their hair tied in queues and their pockets crammed full of sonnets, and beautiful ladies with rouged cheeks and long-sleeved brocade dresses ; they read and recite verses, talk of the new books from Paris, and of the new opera from Naples; play at cards and sing. Often, in the long winter evenings, they learn some French tragedy, translated or imitated by one of the party, and act it with all possible solemnity ; nay the noble ladies and gentlemen even dance ballets, as was particularly the fashion at Verona, where Ippolito Pindemonti, Knight of St. John of Jerusalem, gained such applause in performing the part of Pygmalion that he determined to turn ballet-dancer and unite his fortunes to those of the famous Le Picq; a plan which, luckily for poetry, he was prevented from executing. In some towns, Bologna for instance, the young men have little tournaments; in the winter, if it snow very hard, they drive sledges, and, incredible though it may sound, the young ladies of the highest birth go out on riding parties, dressed in almost masculine fashion, no one taking offence thereat, and the poets telling them that in this garb they look like Paris and Endymion.* In the aixtumii the nobles retire for the vintage to their villas, from whose belvederes they can see the old, silent, many-towered town, and their friends hm-rying to and fro on the dusty road. The villas are never without literary guests ; some of them, like the splendid Villa Albergati, near Bologna, contain large theatres; and even in comparatively poor country houses there arc enthusiasts, like Count Giaconio Gozzi, who make their children act when scarcely more than babies. A place of villegyiatara, some shady nook, or breezy hillside near a town, is a collection of five or six large villas, whose owners live in each other's houses, meet twice and thrice a day, play at cards, go out shooting together, read to each other, and saunter about the primly laid-out grounds, or among the upturned fields strewn with decaying leaves. The lawyers, and priests, and poor literati, who have been unable to leave the stifling city, are not forgotten, and presents of grapes, figs, mushrooms, and game are sent to them by beautiful blue-stockings, and are duly acknowledged in verse and paid for with sonnets on lapdogs and elegies on canary birds. Then there are little musical farces performed in the open air, in suburbs or villages, and to them rush all the listless villa inhabitants, and laugh at the drollness of the music or the inexhaustible witticisms of the masks. Once or twice a year the great theatre is put into order, the senators, prelates, or delegated managers enter into treaty with some groat performer, male or female, and the whole town is in a tumult of excitement.

* Sec FrufTOui's ei;;lit enorraous volumes. T> 2

/ A new opera is composed and brought out in the presence of all the population and of innumerable visitors from neighboitring places; amidst a sliower of sonnets and flowers, occasionally intei'spersed with oranges and medlars thrown at the head of an offending composer, as he sits directing the performance at his harpsichord. Faction runs high for rival singers : people at the coffee-houses fight with sedan-chair sticks to defend the reputation of their favourite, and in the theatre almost die of rapture : the powdered Achilles or Eegulus becomes the tyrant of the place, bullies the nobles and prelates, and condescends to permit the ladies to wear five portraits of him at a time. This annual musical enthusiasm, while showing the life that remains in the people, serves at the same time to dispel for the moment what is trivial and local in Italian civilisation.

Such a state of society was admirably suited to produce a vast amount of worthless poetry. For, while literature had got to be considered as a sort of social amusement, it had by no means gained the honourable independence of the other arts and sciences, and a man of letters, although doubtless considering himself as the perfection of the human type, lived either in a more limited or in a less stable fashion than a surgeon, a painter, an architect, or even a singer: Benedetto Marcello's virtuoso remarking to a great poet that the position of literati was far less honourable than his own, as singers had always plenty of money while men of letters were usually starving. Nor was this entirely erroneous ; the man of letters, who was neither a noble nor a well-endowed priest, nor a well-paid lawyer or professor, and who, according to Baretti, had no chance of reasonable remuneration for his literary productions, the profits of which belonged entirely to the publisher ;—the man of letters who was nothing but a man of letters was necessarily more or less of an adventurer, living off flattery and humiliation. His life was sj^ent in continual efforts to obtain some fixed employment, which, if he was nothing more than a poet, was naturally more or less a sinecui-e, and in the gift of some great personage; most often the employment was promised and not given, or, if given, taken away from caprice, and the poet had to continue his vagabond life, hunting for dedication fees, translations, odd jobs, and occasional dinners. The happiest thing for such a poet was to live in the midst of literary nobles, who would give him lodging and food for a minimum of flattery, instead of making him loiter about ministerial antechambers. Literature was a trade, but scarcely an independent or honourable one, for what was sold were not books but dedications of books. Romance literature, that rich field for poor mediocrities, did not exist in Italy, the few novels that were read then being translations from Marivaux, Le Sage, or Richardson. Theatrical literature could hardly be said to exist either; there was no tragic stage whatever, for there were only singers and mask conierlians; the few tragedies written for the closet by men like IMalTi-i and Martello, and the translations from the French, amply suffing for private performance. There was only the old mask comedy, which consisted mainly of mere adaptations of old Italian and Spanish plays, all the best scenes of which were left unwritten and

/ were filled np by the wonderful extemporary performance of the Brig-hellas, Trufifaldinos, and Tartaglias who had taken possession of comedy ever since the fall of Italian national literature and the reign of dialects in the seventh century; nor was it till Goldoni that Italian written comedy reappeared. There remained, it is true, the opera stage, which was as splendid as its rivals were miserable, but in a time when the same play could be set to different music twice or thrice by the same composer, . Metastasio's many operas were quite sufficient, being, as they were, a mine (of beautiful dramatic and lyric poetry. There remained, therefore, nothing but the smaller forms of lyric poetry—the ode, the elegy, and above all the sonnet; and luckily, as people could not live off such trifles, especially when the market was overstocked with them, the number of poets who were not something else besides was—as indeed is still the case in Italy—very small.

Here we have, then, a national literature in which the tragic and the comic stage are respectively monopolised by two men, Metastasio and Goldoni; from which the epic is excluded by the very nature of the civilisation, which could afford neither natural nor imaginary historical colouring; in which the minor lyric forms, the ode, the canzone, the elegy, and the sonnet, are not spontaneous, but maintained by mere scholarly habit, and in which these latter forms are yet the commonest, because within the reach of almost everyone. And what are the subjects of this lyric poetry, whose forms, well-nigh petrified, belong to very different states of civilisation ? All political subjects are excluded because there is no poli-

*r tical interest in a country cut up into little despotic governments, mostly of foreign extraction; and in this line there remain only general lamentation over the decline of Italian arms and influence since the days of ancient Rome—lamentations which, if sometimes genuinely felt, are yet too vague and aimless either to alarm the police or to interest the reader. Then there are religious lyrics; but in the eighteenth century religious ardour is not sufficiently strong to be poetical, and when a man writes canzoni to the Virgin and sonnets on Judas in the style of those of Betti-nelli, and Lambcrti, and Varano, we cannot help thinking him either narrow-minded or hypocritical. After jtolitical and religious subjects come personal ones, but the individual was not much more poetical than the patriot or the believer ; neither married life nor conventional cava-liere-serventism was prolific of inspiration, and, as to unhappy and ill-fated affections, never surely were fewer to be found than among the

s/

Italian poets of the last century. Not that these good people were without such sorrows, but the time had passed when men did not shrink from weeping in public over their dead loves, while consoling themselves with living ones, like Dante, Petrarch, and Lorenzo de' Medici; and the time had not yet come when romanticism taught them to alleviate their woes by retailing them to the public, and to tear open their bleeding wounds fer the amusement of their readers. There were doubtless Werthers and Consalvos, but they preferred to keep their misfortunes hidden, and to write poems on the cultivation of silkworms, or on the absurdities of pedants, rather than declare themselves ready to commit suicide for their Charlottes, and to be kissed when corpses by their Elviras. Lyric poetry —we mean the poetry which is lyric in spirit as well as in metre— requires the constant appearance of the poet himself, the constant laying bare of the poet's personal feelings ; and, whether from obiuseness of feeling, reserve, or any other cause, the Italian poets of the last century could not and would not make themselves their own subject—so much so that Rolli takes care to impress on his reader that his love poems are all

addressed to ladies as purely imaginary as his feelings towards them

yet lyrics were written in plenty, very correct and elegant in language, and very cool and vague in sentiment. There are the elegiac patriotic pieces, in which, after a splendid description of ancient Rome, and the loudest lamentations over the fallen state of Italy, we are informed that the man, the hero, the demigod has come from whom the country expects deliverance from her woes, and this hero and demigod may be a viceroy of Naples, a Venetian proccuratore, a Tuscan senator, or, as Manfredi thinks, Don Annibale Albani, " who with universal applause has just taken his doctor's degree at Urbino." There are the long, intensely subtle, and metaphysical canzoni to ladies taking the veil, who, either forced into the convent by their families or entering it from worldly disappointment and 67171111, are supposed to be so many St. Catherines and St, Theresas; there are the sonnets for the same occasions, full of Cupids, Dianas, and flourishes, as profane as the fat cherubs and languishing saints overhead among the stucco and gilding, and printed off by the dozen to be handed round to the guests with cakes and ices, while the powdered hair of the novice is being shorn to the accompaniment of church music with fiddles, flutes, and roulades. There is the still more numerous and nauseous class of bridal poems, mostly written by priests, in which Venus, the Graces, Cupid, and every manner of personified feeling are introduced to bring about the union of two persons who, in all probability, care nothing for each other, and are merely following the will of their parents or the suggestions of their worldly wisdom; when the marriage is an aristocratic one, Italy is brought in as a spectator, and prophesies that a new Alcides will be born, and that the proud Turk will soon tremble at the

name of the heroic infant. Sometimes—and this is often the case when the jioet is a superior one, and cares nothing for the marriage—the bride and bridegroom are left behind after a few lines, and some classic fable is brought forward in their stead; but even then the best we get are poetical paraphrases of Albani, with loves climbing into trees, coquettish nymphs, and languishing heroes. After this we meet poems on all sorts of trifles—lapdogs, canaries, horses, gifts of fruit and wine, new hats, and what not; some of which, written under the influence of beautiful poetic ladies by elegant frivolous poets like Frugoni, are certainly very pretty; and finally, to exhaust the stock of lyrics, we come to the sonnets destined to be showered down on to successful performers, and which, although often written by celebrated poets, are so trivial, vague, and verbose, that we can only hope that they were used as curling papers by the singers, a few of whose extemporary flourishes and embellishments contained infinitely more genius, more art, and more poetry, than all the verses of all their admirers. But, despite this miserable poverty of subject and sterility of fancy, the amount of lyrics written in Italy during the last century passes all belief: for every one who could hold a pen—men, women, priests, nuns, lawyers, doctors, barbers—every one wrote poetry. The works of each poet are excessively voluminous— five, six, seven, eight, ten, fifteen huge volumes being quite iisual, and the greater portion of their contents, as well as that of the innumerable collections printed at weddings, deaths, veil-takings, christenings, and the still more innumerable academical collections, consist of this uninteresting, vapid, verbose, intolerable rubbish. In the presence of all these myriads of sonnets, odes, elegies, and canzoni per nozze, per monacazione, per gentil dama, per musico, and ^;er elevazione alia sarp^a porpora, we feel crushed and speechless, and regain the use of our faculties only to cry out at the indefatigable imbecility of the Italian eighteenth century.

There is no exaggeration in this, and yet there is no exaggeration either in saying that of all the centuries during which Italian literature has flourished the eighteenth century is one of the most honourable. We have seen as yet only what the men of that time could not but fail in, and in which they persisted so obstinately that they left behind them the appalling mass of rubbish we have described ; but there were other branches of literature in which the Italians of the last century as necessarily succeeded, and in which they reached a far higher point than any of their predecessors. The poetry which required individual activity of life and feeling, in which all depended upon strength of passion and abundance of movement, upon the poet's own individuality—this kind of poetry had ceased to exist; but in its stead appeared that other poetry which depends upon contemplation and examination of types, whose excellence is due to the knowledge of the minute shades and transitions

of feeling, upon the power of the poet to divest himself of his own character and to enter entirely into that of others : the epic, the lyric, had become impossible, but tragedy, comedy, and satire had taken their place. The reader must not, however, imagine that, because the literary forms requiring the development of the poet's own individuality had disappeared, this was a period when, as in the time of Anne and of George I. the real poetic artistic element had been replaced by thought, wit, and elegance of expression; on the contrary, in tragedy, comedy, and satire there appeared the greatest wealth of the really tragic and humorous elements, to the utter exclusion both of oratorical pomp and brilliancy of wit: the tragedy was real tragedy, the comedy real comedy, and more so than either had been in the hands of the too eloquent Eacine or the over witty Moliere. It may also appear contradictory to our previous remark on the absence of a regular stage in Italy to affirm that the dramatic form was the one then brought to perfection, yet this seeming paradox can easily be explained. There was no tragic stage in Italy in Metas-tasio's time, and it is to that very fact that Metastasio's excellence is due ; for, had he attempted real tragedy, he would have produced at best only a feeble repetition of the French oratorical plays. Instead of this \ being the case, Metastasio was called upon to write dramas for music, for music which was then in its heroic youth, simple, grand, pathetic, and, above all, beautiful; and which, in its vigorous movement towards perfection, could drag along with it the style of poetry arising from its requirements. The opera was then still in its simplest condition; melody did not attempt to follow dramatic action in concerted pieces, but was restricted to short speeches and soliloquies, bursts of feeling or flights of fancy, in which the poet gave the musician only a general framework, while all the body of the play—the scenes of narration, dialogue, altercation, and movement—were left to the musically noted speech called recitative. The recitative required even more than did the melody that the verbal expression should be as simple, concise, and natural as that of the regular tragedy was the reverse; and, above all, it required that the action of the play should be rapid and strongly marked. The noted declamation could not be united with a rhetorical style of poetry, for the modulations of the recitative were suggested by the inflexions of the speaking voice, and the long carefully-constructed periods of tragic oratory necessarily reduced these inflexions both in variety and force. The requirements, therefore, of the music produced a new style of drama, simpler, stronger, more pathetic, less eloquent, and less formal than tragedy, while the tendency of the music itself, its beauty, pathos, grandeur, and yet richness, did much to influence the poet's conceptions. When we compare Metastasio's poetry with the -^ music to which it was set avc feel, that, if the individual pieces were

suggested by the words of the poet, those words were themselves suggested by the general style of composition then prevailing. Metastasio's principal characters, so distinct and yet so noble, so clearly and delicately drawn, ardent or tender, pathetic or solemn, so full of life and feeling, and yet never either realistic or sensational—Achilles, Regulus,^ Timanthes, Aristea, Megacles, Dirce—are conceived in the same mannerC as the music which Pergolesi, Leo,

Jomelli, and Hasse made them sing;^ we meet again, what we meet so rarely, emotion used as an artistic means. A similar paradox has to be explained with respect to Goldoni, who found no regular comic stage in Italy, and owed his peculiar excellence to this fact, just as Metastasio did his to the non-existence of a regular tragic stage. By a singular process of decentralisation, Italian literature, ever since the breaking-up of the commonwealths and the rule of foreigners in the sixteenth century, had become less and less national and more and more provincial; till, in the seventeenth century, all vitality seemed to have been absorbed by the dialects, and the feebler the writings in the universal language of the country the more original and racy became the poems and plays in Venetian, Milanese, Neapolitan, and Sicilian.* Now to each of these dialects belonged a figure, a type or caricature of the particular provincial character formed by the people of the province. When the Neapolitans gave the reins to their boisterous humour it was in the character of Pulcinella or of the Fuego ; when the Venetians wished to represent themselves they brought forward the drolly cautious Pantaloon; when the Milanese wished to criticise the Spanish airs of their nobles they made the simple, sensible, clownish Meneghino their spokesman ; when the Bolognese felt inclined to laugh at the professors of their university they brought forward their blustering-pedantic Dottore; in short, every province—nay, in some cases every town—had its popular representative, unchanging in dress, manner, and speech, as every such type must be. As this typical buffoon, or mask, as he was called, for his unchanging costume easily gave rise to the appellation, was brought on to the stage, so very soon there began to appear actors who never played any part except that of the humorous patron of their native town, and as soon as several of these actors—say a Venetian Pantaloon, a Bolognese Dottore, a Brighclla from Bergamo, and a Trutfaldino from Brescia—met on the same movable stage, the comedy of masks, or, as it was called, the eommedia delV arte^\ was created. Goldoni found this eommedia delV arte in absolute possession of

    * The most original Italian poem of the seventeenth century, Kedi's dithyramb, is far less national than Tuscan, even in language.

    f Arte here probably has the older meaning of trade, for it literally was a man's trade to play Arlccchino or Brighclla all his life.

    the theatre, and, as many of his admirers and perliaps he himself believed, he dethroned it. But he did so only in appearance, and when Voltaire congratulated him upon having " freed Italy from the Goths " he was much mistaken in thinking that Goldoni had done so in order to install a semblance of French comedy in their place. In reality Goldoni's reforms were merely that he put a limit to the improvisation of the actors, and that he divested the masks of their characteristic costume, and even sometimes of their characteristic dialect; for Goldoni's action merely represented that of his time, which tended once more to swallow up the provincial in the national. Goldoni's comedy was to be for all Italy, and no longer for a single province ; it was to show the life of the whole country, and therefore what was unintelligible to the whole nation and what was illustrative of only local life had to be eliminated to a certain extent; but Pantaloon remained Pantaloon, although stripped of his red hose and black long-tailed hood, and put into the dress of a Leghorn merchant or a country proprietor; and Harlequin remained Harlequin despite the loss of his parti-coloured clothes and the adoption of modern dress; the Italian comedy remained the same in spirit and system, although it ceased to be called commedia delV arte. Goldoni did not attempt to meddle with the arrangements by which the same types were constantly reproduced by the same actor; he did not introduce new characters, but merely new combinations of characters ; he did not make the stage a vehicle for satire ; in short, consciously or unconsciously, he merely developed the Italian comedy without imitating the French one.

There were radical differences of origin and conception between the French and Italian comedies, and to these are due the absolute difference that exists between Moliere and Goldoni, a want of perception of which has so often led to the grossest misjudgment of the latter by persons who expected to find him like the former. French comedy was mainly a court and drawing-room production, like all the other literary forms of the age of Louis XIV.; it had no roots among the people, and was constructed to suit the wittiest, most cans tic, and most elegant class of the wittiest and most caustic of nations—to suit the contemporaries of Boileau and La Rochefoucauld, of Mme. de Sevigne and La Bruyere, people all the power of whose mind consisted in delicate appreciation of character and neat expression of paradoxes, brought to the highest point of perfection. The Italian comedy, on the other hand, had arisen among the people, and, what is more, among the provincial middle and lower classes, who disdained the national speech, utterly ignored smartness of expression, and asked only to be amused with humorous pictures of themselves; simple, jovial, honest folk, with charity at the bottom of all their humour. Moliere, in compliance with the wants of his audience, accepted a few trumpery, mostly unnatural and uninteresting plots and situations, and

gave all liis attention to the creation of original powerful types : Har-pagon, the Malade Liiaginaire, Tartvife., the Femiiies Savantes, and, above all, the Misanthrope and his companions, Celimene and Philinte and Oronte and Arsinoe, the heartless coquet, the easy-going, benevolent man of the world, the dandified fool and the court prude ; each a bitter satire, couched in the tersest and most brilliant language, which in itself forms almost a series of epigrams. Goldoni, who had no courtly wits among his audience, accepted the old popular types given by each province; types neither very sharply marked nor very satirical, for the Italian people is neither personal nor unkind in its buffoonery; and lavished all the richness of his fancy in contriving new plots, new scenes, new situations, new combinations of the old characters, in which a trifle—a fan dropped, a dress expected, a pi'omise not to be jealous, a promise to be silent—produces in the simplest and most spontaneous way an infinite concatenation of droll situations, of droll exclamations, of droll movements. Moliere's characters, when not absolute and almost repulsive caricatures, make us smile the subdued smile of perception of wit rather than of drollery ; Goldoni's characters, even when so faintly marked as to be no types at all, make us laugh the free happy laugh of unconcerned amusement. Moliere's men and women, even the stupidest, are continually saying clever things which do not move us; Goldoni's people, even the cleverest, never say anything either epigrammatic or unamusing. Moliere may be as much engaged in the closet as at the theatre, and even there requires only subtle intonations and clever looks ; Goldoni, however delightful when read, even out loud, cannot be fully appreciated except on the stage, where alone we understand that inexhaustible energy and movement, that amazing overflow of life and animal spirits, which made the performance of the Barruffe Chiozzotte a kind of revelation to Goethe.

The third branch of literature in which the Italians of the last century were destined to succeed was satire, but satire also altered and made into a separate category by national influence. The satire of Parini is not much more like the satire of Boileau or of Pope than the tragedy of Metastasio is like that of Eacine, or the comedy of Goldoni like that of Moliere. Parini's great poem, the epic, as one might call it, of satire, seems at first sight to be conceived in gre ater bitterness than any other work of the same kind, since it is the satire of a whole class by a man belonging to a totally different one; yet in reality there is no animosity of any sort in the Giorno, because its writer is not actuated by any personal dislike. Parini was doubtless a utilitarian, a philanthropist, more or less of a moral lawgiver, but he was not a moraliser nor a stoic ; he had no abstract ideal of virtue, but he had a strong aversion to what is bad or merely mean, and throughout his poem we

feel that what he wishes to brand is not so much the corrupt as the idle, the vapid, the useless ; what he constantly brings before us is not the wickedness of his hero's life, for it is not wicked, nor its absurdity, for it is not ridiculous, but its want of everything manly and ennobling. What Parini hates is the incompleteness, the emptiness of this dandy's existence ; the trifles turned into important concerns, the possession of useless objects, the feeble attempts at pleasure; we understand how different a life, how full of strong healthy action and enjoyment, of State service, of literary employment, of domestic affection, of rural pleasures, the poet conceived ; a life, alas, not granted to the poor sickly priest, obliged to gain his livelihood like any other schoolmaster in the close hot town.* At the same time Parini has great artistic feeling ; while satirising, he does not distort; on the contrary, it is extraordinary what gi'ace he lends to everything he touches. The luxurious life of his giovin signore becomes one of almost oriental splendour ; the hundred trifles strewn about on his toilet table become so many little masterpieces; the smart stiff dress of the last century becomes under Parini's fingers the daintiest, most graceful of garbs, nay, the very movements and gestures become beautiful and noble, and the young fop seems to forget his dancing-master under the poet's orders. Add to this beautiful tendency a wonderful swiftness of movement, and simple elegance of verse and diction, a delicacy of colouring, and, above all, a subtle subdued ridicule, never taking the sharp crnde shape of an epigram, and we shall yet have but an incomplete picture of the great Milanese satirist.

An inferior style of satire, and an inferior poet when compared to Parini, nevertheless deserve to be mentioned among those which did most honour to the eighteenth century. Count Gasparo Gozzi, better known by his agreeable and amusing letters, wrote a few of those blunted

* Perhaps Parini might have heen an Italian Cowper, with all the grandeur of form of which Italian rural scenery could give, had he lived in the country. The famous odes on the purity of the air, and on rustic life, contain nothing equal to the following lines in the Givrno, so superior was Parini when using blank verse :

Poi sul dorso portando i sacri arnesi,
Che prima ritrovar Cerere e Pale,
Va, col hue lento innanzi, al campo, e scuote
Per lo aMgusto sentier da' curvi rami
Il rugiadoso umor, che quasi gemma
I nascenti del sol raggi rifrange.
Then with his load of sacred implements,
Ceres' and Pales' earliest gifts to men,
He seeks his field, his tardy ox ahead ;
And in the narrow pathway brushes off
From the curved boughs the dewdrops, which like gems
Refract the rays of the just rising sun.

generalising satires called by the Italians sermoni, which in their line are excellent. Gozzi has none of Parini's tendency to beautify, none of his high intellectual aspirations ; he is a simple, honest, sensible man, averse to all the corruption and affectation of his times ; and his poems, very l)lain and elegant in metre and diction, contain clever descriptions of Venetian life: of the crowd pouring into the square of St, Mark's on summer evenings ; of the young dandies buying hair-pins for their ladies; of the barges going up the Brenta to the places of ville(ifjialura; little pictures with no attempt at caricature and of a pleasing sobriety of colour; to which may be added the sketches, full of life and grace, contained in some of his single lines, as those of the racket-player, the mask actor, and similar then familiar figures of Italian life.

"We ought perhaps to have mentioned the brother of Gasparo Gozzi by the side of his rival Goldoni, but, although he had the audacity to enter into competition with Italy's greatest comic writer, Carlo Gozzi can be appreciated only when seen alone and when the vast superiority of Goldoni is kept out of sight. Carlo Gozzi thought that Goldoni wanted to destroy the national theatre for the sake of imitating the French one; and, indignant at this supposed insult, he determined to show the public that the most absurd nonsense, with the help of the old masks, was more amusing than the best French comedy. His first attempt succeeded so well that he continued to write in the style he had taken up for a mere momentary purpose. His plays have long since been forgotten, as a sort of posthumous retribution for his injustice towards a greater man than himself; yet these strange wild things, stories from the Arabian Nights and from Basile's Neapolitan collection, such as are still told in the Venetian States, made into tragi-comedies, with transformations, deeds of heroism, and buffooneries, are not without their peculiar charm : the wizards and enchanted princesses, the blue monsters^ the serpent ladies, the kings transformed into stags, the Venetian Pantaloons and Lombard Brighellas talking dialect in their Chinese and Persian dresses, the mixture of heroism and jargon, of childishness and tragedy, all conduces to make Carlo Gozzi's plays the quaintest, queerest, and in some respects almost the most amusing products of his time ; it was chaos, but a chaos contrived and arranged by a very fertile and original mind.

We have, while glancing at the literature of Italy in the last century, hurried through a space of upwards of thirty years since the death of the great Crescimboni, and we have also got a long way from the Serbatoio d' Arcadia and its poetical inmates, for which misdemeanours we hope, by pleading our good intentions, to be forgiven by the shades of the Arcadians, and also perhaps by the i-eader. Meanwhile the best and speediest mode of showing our contrition, and of making amends, is to return to the history of the Academy, and with that view to get

back to the city which was the head-quarters of Arcadia after having been the capital of the world.

The eighteenth century had got its pope. Prospero Lambertini, Archbishop of Bologna, mounted the throne of Julius II. and Sixtus V. in the year 1740, under the name of Benedict XIV. to the great surprise of everyone concerned, and of himself most of all. The first thing that the new Pope did was, in no very decorous language, to reprove the master of the ceremonies for instructing him to keep his cap on in the presence of the cardinals ; the second, to inform his nephews at Bologna that they were on no account to come to Kome unless he sent for them, which he took care never to do ; in short, Benedict astonished everyone by showing that he was going to be a very different pope from his weak, bigoted, ostentatious, formal predecessors. He had been a lawyer, and continued a writer and a wit, a lover of science and literature, without any pretensions to eminence ; he lived simply and spoke bluntly; he made friends with the heretics without making enemies of the Jesuits ; he bad the Roman streets cleaned, and left the travertine of the Roman churches to get spongelike from neglect ; he reformed many abuses, and hoped to reform many more; he even designed to suppress a number of the holidays which fostered the idleness of the lower classes, and to diminish the religious orders which burdened the country. He accepted with alacrity the dedication of Voltaire's 3'Iahomet at the very time Cardinal de Tencin dared not open his doors to its author. In short, Benedict XIV., a priest without bigotry, a sovereign without ostentation, revered by Catholics, respected by Protestants, as Walpole's famous epigram runs, was the typical pope of the middle of the eighteenth century, before free thought had grown into over-bold action, and attempt at radical reform had produced violent reaction ; while the Austrians in Lombardy and Tuscany were tolerant and reforming, and the Bourbons in Naples and Parma were anti-feudal and anti-Jesuitical: in short, while the people were still so loyal and obedient that the governments could amuse themselves with being a little radical and revolutionary.

A curious feature of Rome throughout the century was that everyone who was not a noble or a soldier was a priest in dress and title ; married men, lawyers, doctors, writers, even strangers, wearing the short black dress and little cloak, and being addressed by the title of Abate. The priests had an amount of liberty bordering on licence, from the cardinals, who had their boxes at the theatre, and gave gay parties to the low ahati, who crowded the pit and loitered in the coffee-houses. If we may believe Winckelmann, who was rather inclined to exaggeration, people might express themselves very freely on religious subjects, and cardinals laughed at the Inquisition.* There was much licence, but perhaps less hypocritical

* It was not so in Tuscany. Tommaso Crudeli, a physician and talented poet, was

vice, than among the priestliood of earlier and of later days ; and altogether the Pope himself was by far the most devout and rigid, though perhaps the most frcespoken and least priggish, of the hierarchy. While Benedict was most parsimonious in everything save works of public utility, his cardinals vied with each other in profane splendour. Foremost among them were the two brothers Albani, Annibale and Alessandro, rivals in their attempts to obtain the tiara, in their collections of antiques, and in their many quasi-bankruptcies; next to them was Cardinal Pietro Otto-boui, who was in a permanent state of bankruptcy ; an old, shabby, jolly disgrace to the Church, who, despite his beggary, had a splendid collection of antiques, and gave magnificent private concerts or sacred operas, at which all the great performers sang, out of liking for the disreputable old fellow. Of the family of the last Pope but one there was the beautiful young princess d' Arce Orsini, composer, poetess, and general patroness of literati, a great improvement on the other Roman ladies if we may believe the President de Brosses. Another great Eoman figure was the King of England, James III. who had taken to devotion in his old days, and lived dismally in his palace near the SS. Apostoli. And there remains yet another figure in the Rome of those days, which, although then scarcely noticed, was a more important one than all the cardinals and pretenders. A German priest, a hanger-on first of Cardinal Archinto, then of Cardinal Alessandro Albani, a sort of pedant after the German fashion, a kind of hiimble companion, eating what the charity of his employer gave him, and wedging his way into the company of his protector's grand friends ; a cynical, pleasure-loving, information-seeking man, hanging on to the rich and intelligent painter Raphael Mengs, and who yet gave himself strange airs towards Roman artists and antiquaries. There he was, continually poring over books, though no lover of literature ; continually examining works of art, though no artist, clambering on to the pedestals of statues and into the holes of excavations. "What was he about ? What was he trying to do ? The Romans got the answer, although they probably did not fully understand it, when there appeared the first volumes of A History of Art among the Ancients, and when it became known that, in the midst of the cockle-shell and mirror art of the eighteenth century, Winckelmann had discovered the long-lost art of antiquity.

We returned to Rome with the full intention of resuming our task of chronicling Arcadian affairs, but on examination we find that during the

accused, apparently merely because lie had been seen with " suspicious foreigners," of the terrible crime of having derided the Church; and, although in very bad health, was shut up first in the Inquisition prisons, then for some years in the citadel of Florence, desi)ite the sympathy of the Minister Kichccourt, and the constant jirotcc-tion of the famous singer Broschi Farinello, then the omnipotent favourite of the King of Spain.

V A:':\"\\\ f lid prosperous reign of Lorenzini there is nothing, to chronicle, ..xoi 'It It be the Olympic games and the admission of new members, ■.vliioh would, we fear, be found rather tedious by our readers. But ;t the beginning of the reign of Lorenzini's successor, Morei, Arcadia began to be threatened, if not in her existence, at least in her glory. We have already remarked that little by little the limits of the institution had been overstepped, so that in the middle of the eighteenth century it had become boundless and shapeless, a mass of incoherent social and literary life. Now practical philosophers, of whom there were great numbers to be found when the practical j^oint was one of no consequence—practical philosophers began to ask themselves and each other what this huge shapeless institution could signify, and of what earthly use Arcadia could be. Of course, as is usual in such cases, they never took into consideration that Arcadia, inasmuch as it was the largest of the many literary associations of the country, united by a common bond people of all parts of Italy, and broke down those local distinctions, kept up by prejudice and jealousy, which were so great an obstacle to national feeling ; that, moreover, it levelled ranks and fortunes, and gave not only introductions into Milanese houses to Neapolitans, but, what was much more important, secured an entrance into good society to low-born talent; that, for instance, Goldoni, a Venetian, could, as an Arcadian, gain admittance into Pisan circles merely by going to the Serhatoio d' Arcadia of Pisa ; and that a poor peasant educated by charity, like Parini, could become acquainted in the Milanese colony with the Counts Verri, with Beccaria, and with women like the Countess Castiglione ; that by this moans all the old stupid exclusive-ness of the aristocracy was got rid of; that men of letters became refined by mixing in good society, and good society became ennobled by containing men of letters ; that it gave a higher tone to social existence, and a greater sociability to literary life, and that a great step in national progress was thus made. All this the practical philosophers of course entirely overlooked ; they did not cai'e for the effects of the real nature of the institution, but set about investigating those of its imaginary one. They asked, 1st, Whether pastoral life was consistent with civilisation ? 2ndly, Whether, if it were, the members of the Arcadian Academy were more simple, peaceable, and virtuous than other people ? 3rdly, Whether literature had been reformed by the Arcadian Academy ? The answers to these questions were obvious: pastoral life was incompatible with civilisation (Baretti proved it by pointing to the nomad Tartars); the Arcadians were not in the least shepherds, indeed most of them had never possessed a sheep or any animal save a lapdog; and, finally, literature was by no means reformed. If, then, Arcadia had not cured the evil, it was evident that it must have fostered it, and that all

the artificiality of modern society, all the French idioms ■which -were creeping into the langnage, all the bad sonnets that were being written, all was due to the enervating, stultifying influence of Arcadia.* A few of these critics admitted that at the beginning things had been different, and that the institution had entirely degenerated since the days of the wise and far-sighted Crescirabeni, who would doubtless have been shocked at the sight of the prevailing folly. To this charming practical unprac-ticalness, this folly in the garb of wisdom, of which the last century shows so many glorious examples, must be added the fact that the turning-point in the eighteenth century, the moment when romanticism began to exist, quite tiny, by the side of utilitarianism, had come, and that Rousseau had already suggested that there were real rustic life and real shepherds, by no means resembling the Arcadian ones. A minority began to cry out that truth and action were needed, and that Arcadia was a humbug. Already Bettinelli had suggested that for the benefit of literature Arcadia should be shut up for a hundred years, at the end of Avhich it was scarcely likely to be re-opened; but Bettinelli had done so in a work, the Virgilian Letters, in which existing literary opinions were smartly lashed, and Dante was ridiculed, so that the whole of Italy rose in indignation against it. Bettinelli had, however, begun the work; a more formidable attack was coming from a strange, whimsical, original being, whom we must stop to look at, for, although but little noticed by his contemporaries, he did much to prepare the way for future generations. This enemy of Arcadia was Giuseppe Baretti, a wonderful, wild, coarse, tender, angry creature, a kind of maniac in the eyes of his contemporaries, who could understand the originality neither of his talent nor of his character; and who, not satisfied with attacking Goldoni, Frugoni, Algarotti, the Verris, and nearly all the most eminent Italians, did not shrink from making an onslaught on Voltaire in French and on Smollett in English. He had travelled much, read much, known many distinguished men, done everything, in short, that might be expected to tame down a man and a critic, but which had, on the contrary, merely increased his eccentric ferocity. He was decidedly clever; " he has but few hooks," said Johnson, " but. Sir, he grapples very forcibly with them;" and his very superiority, inasmuch as it consisted in extraordinary independence, in titter contempt for the world's opinion, and intense loathing of everything weak and false, led him into numberless acts of injustice and ill breeding. He could not endure Frugoni on account of his obscurity and emptiness ; he could not endure Goldoni

* We are sorry to say that modern Italian writers still talk in this strain, quite as ehildish, thouf^h in the opposite sense, as Crescimbeni and Don Livio Odescakdii, when they imagined Areadia to he an infallible remedy for all evils. See Kanalli's Sforhi (h'Ur Belle Art'i.

on account of liis designs against the old national comedy ; he could not endure Algarotti on account of his scientific frivolity and his truckling to Voltaire ; he could not endure Voltaire because he protected Goldoni and Algarotti; he could not endure the Verris and Beccaria because they admired the French and set up a rival journal to hie own. Of living Italian literati he admired only Metastasio, because Metastasio had no apparent connection with eithei- Frugoni, or Algarotti, or Voltaire, or Goldoni, or the Verris ; and he personally esteemed only the two Gozzis, Gasparo and Carlo, because they were eternally at war with Frugoni, Algarotti, Goldoni, Voltaire, and the Verris. Above all, Baretti abominated Arcadia, all its founders, members, and abettors, because Arcadia bad fostered all his enemies, and because it seemed to him—wild, strong-minded, practical, ill-mannered philosopher that he was—the most imbecile, effeminate, pedantic, frivolous, and utterly useless institution on earth. Now Avhen Baretti once despised or disliked anyone or anything that person or that thing was doomed in his eyes ; it had no merit, no excuse, it was to be abused, calumniated, scoffed at, annihilated.

In 17 G3 Baretti started a species of literary review, more or less on the model of The Spectator, to which he gave the ominous name of La Frusta Letteraria, the " Literary Whip." Like Steele and Addison he contrived an awkward frame for this work, pretending to be an old soldier, Aristarco Scannabue (Aristarchus Massacre-the-dunces), who had lost an arm in Persia, was served by an idiotic slave named Macouf (who afforded comparisons with Goldoni, Chiari, Frugoni, and the two Verris), and whose intimate, his Sir Roger de Coverley, was a pipe-smoking, quiet, sensible, Bolognese priest, Don Petronio Zamber-lucco. This seems dull enough, but it must be admitted that the Frusta Letteraria was not only infinitely less pedantic than most other reviews of that day, but that, in the midst of coarse ill-humoured injustice and wild buffooneries, it contains much sound sense, good feeling, and independent thought, and some really humorous notions. Unluckily for Arcadia, the new Custode Generale Morei, who appears to have inherited much of Crescimbeni's reverence for the institution and want of intelligence—unluckily Morei thought fit to publish just at that time a General History of Arcadia. Here was Baretti's opportunity. He had already, in his English work on Italy, showered abuse on Arcadia; but now was the moment to let loose all his long pent-up contempt, disgust, and hatred. Down he pounced on to Morel's book. He concentrated all his modes of attack upon it: he reasoned, he laughed, he shouted, he ranted ; he went through the usual argument as to the nature and effects of pastoral life ; he decried Crescimbeni, Gravina, and the other founders as pedantic idiots ; he battered Zappi about as an effeminate coxcomb;

he trampled upon the early Arcadians; he hooted at the story of the foundation ; he went into convulsions of angry caricature over the narration of the schism ; he cried and shrieked at the present institution, and sank down exhausted, but triumphant, with the assertion that every intelligent creature knew that Arcadia was the stupidest, most pedantic, most mercenary, vilest institution in Italy. Barctti's onslaught had but little effect on his countrymen. They did not believe in Arcadia any more than himself ; but they were all Arcadians, and thought it rather pleasant than otherw'ise to be called Mirtillo, Labindo, Polianzo, instead of Francesco, Giacomo, or Antonio, and once a fortnight to read their literary productions to so many Chloes, Lesbias, and Aglauros.

Arcadia was no longer of sufficient interest to be quarrelled about; that had been possible only in those far-off solemn days of Crescimbeni and Gravina, before people read the Encyclopedie and Voltaire's novels. Yet Baretti's example was not entirely lost, for Baretti was a forerunner of a new generation, which was soon to become the reigning one. What distinguished Baretti from men of the class of Frugoni, Gozzi, and all the other representatives of the then established literature, was that he had travelled, and had brought home broader ideas on literary and social points than those of his countrymen. The generality of Italians of the mjddle of last century had never been out of their country, and knew of no foreign ideas save those of the French, which, together with their fosliions, their language, and their dancing-masters, had become as supreme as they could in a country which differed from France in spirit, m tradition, and in tendency. But for this reason French^ideas could not thoroughly permeate the Italians; they listened, admired, but "accepted^only a very small proportion of what was offered them; they did not abuse Voltaire, Rousseau, and the Encyclopedie with the fanatical rag^^ the English and of -the Germans; they found in them much sense, much elegance, much usefulness, but also much profanity, much in'decency, atnll miich violence. They regarded the French as Parini did Voltaire, as "too much praised and too much blamed ;" jogging quietly along on the road of progress, they could not keep pace with the French in their wild rush onwards towards chaotic change. Add to this the difference in national character, the impossibility of an Italian being satisfied witii wit, paradox, and elegance ; the difference in traditions, and consequent impossibility of an Italian, with Dante, Ariosto, Tasso in the past, and Metastasio, Goldoni, and Gozzi in the present, being satisfied with the philosophical, colourless, emotionless, pseudo-classic literature of France; sum all this together, and it will be evident that as long as there was only French influence in Italy there was comparatively very little foreign influence at all. But, little by little, as the middle of the eighteenth century was left behind, another influence—that of England—

K 2

began to be felt in Italy, first indirectly throngli the French, and then directly from the English themselves. The Italians had, early in the century, got acquainted with a few English writers—Milton, Pope, and especially Addison—whom not only Baretti but Gasparo Gozzi largely imitated. Richardson's novels had also reached Italy, and even suggested plots to Goldoni; but on the whole there was but little intellectual communication between the two countries until after the year 1750. Till then the English had been too insular, too coarse, too overbearing, to see in the Italians anything more than opera singers and vermicelli makers, and for the Italians to consider the English otherwise than as stupid pedantic miloj'di, a fit prey for innkeepers and ciceroni. Besides this, England could influence Italy and Germany, and strongly influence even France, only when she had shaken off that French element which permeated her literature from the time of Charles II. to that of George III. The force of England lay in her intellectual originality, in her being at the head of what was afterwards called the romantic school, as opposed to the pseudo-classic French one. Dryden, Pope, Addison, pleased the Italians and the Germans, as they pleased the French ; but they could not strongly move any of them, for they were not sufficiently unlike the long-established Racine, Boileau, and La Bruyere. But when Shakespeare reappeared in the hands of Gar-rick, when Sterne and Gray threw aside all the traditions of the age of Anne, then England made a sudden and deep impression on foreign literature. This return to nature, to passion, to imagination, on the part of English literature, shook the French literature world, loosening the foundations of the merely elegant and clever school, which was to be finally destroyed by Madame de Stael and Chateaiibriand ; it threw the newborn German literature into full romanticism, and it made the Italians feel that at last there were people who could sympathise with them, who could see in Dante something beyond a monster, and in the comic masks something more than barbarians; making them acquainted at the same time with a people who could be free without licence or profanity, and philanthropical and utilitarian without rhetorical grandiloquence; whom they could follow on the path of progress more safely and easily than they could their over-excited French neighbours. Then it was that Italians began to go to England for their education and amusement, as even Parini's giovin signore is supposed to have done, though without becoming acquainted with anything else than the racecourse. The Italians could get acquainted with English life and thought only by going to England, for the English travellers, although, according to Goethe, they carried their tea-kettle up ^tna, came to Italy for the sake of art and autiquit\'7d', but not at all to propagandise their political and literary notions. In this point Baretti was the forerunner of the men of the

generation of Pinclemonti and Alfieri. He knew England and English institutions twenty years before the rest of his countrymen, and his independent utilitarian spirit, his hostility towards the French, towards grandiloquence and 'persijlage, did much to form the school which culminated in the MisogaUo, the first assertion of Italian political feeling since the time of Machiavelli.

So, gradually, as the nation moved onwards in the wake of its neighbours, as foreign, and especially English, or at least Anglo-French, influence became stronger, people grew either more indifferent or more hostile towards Arcadia. At Milan its members themselves began to despise it. The Verris and Beccaria had set up a journal called the Caffe, in which, together with literary topics, they discussed whether the aristocracy would not do well to resume commerce. The journal succeeded. Young men of the nobility studied agriculture and legislation, Pietro Verri and Beccaria nobly carrying out their own recommendations, the former in his works on political economy, the latter in his famous treatise against the then existing criminal laws. Joseph II., then master of the Milanese, did all he could to further this philosophical movement, being himself, after a fashion, philosophical. In Naples the minister Tanucci, while letting the young king grow up in the most woeful ignorance, set about refoi-ming the State in the arbitrary manner then in vogue, while Filangieri spread liberal and philanthropical doctrines in the court of Ferdinand and Caroline—doctrines which were to be paid for terribly in the year '99. In Parma the French minister Du Tillot set up as a wiser and more philosophical sort of Sully, building factories, suppressing convents, and sending for Condillac to be tutor to the heir apparent, who, however, did not profit much by his teachers, since he spent his life serving at mass and ringing church bells. In Tuscany Peter Leopold changed the rather barbarous laws dating from the early grand dukes, and expelled a few dozen monks; finally, in Pome itself, after the death of Lambertini's bigoted successor Rezzonico, Clement XIV., better known as Ganganelli, signed the bull suppressing the Jesuits, although probably aware that he was, in so doing, signing his own death warrant.*

While in the rest of the world philosophy reigned in more or less boisterous fashion, Italy accepted quietly, prudently, rather timorously. Even poetry was influenced by this philosophical tendency. Not only were

* See Mutinelli's violent diatribe, " Gli ultimi oO .aniii della rcpubblica di Venezia," written in 1854, in an Austrian and Papal spirit. About the year 1780 there were masonic lodges at Venice, Padua, and Vicenza. unforbidden by the government, and among whose members were many nobles. In 17G8 the Venetians secuhu-ized several monasteries, forbade ecclesiastical purchase and the begging of the mendicant orders, and ordered that all monks should be tried by civil courts for temporal offences, forbade novices under twenty-one years, and professions under twenty-live.

utilitarian odes written in imitation of tlie one by Parini on the salubrity of the air, or, more strictly speaking, on the bad Milanese drainage, but poets, although probably not grown careless of dinners and pensions, began to hold np their heads and talk of human dignity—a quality of which they had never before suspected the existence. Here, again, ^^arini, as the poet of civilisation, to use the modern phrase, was the general model. He had said, what he doubtless sincerely believed, that " he was not born to knock at the hard doors of the great; that the kingdom of the dead should receive him a poor, but a free man—

"^ me non nato a percuotere Le dure illustri porte, Nudo acorra, ma libero, n regno della morte—"

and men, quite destitute of his proud, honest spirit, repeated the sentiment in other words, while continuing their modest little raps at illustrious doors. Virtue began to be talked of no longer as a necessary accompaniment of high birth, but as something infinitely to be preferred to it; poverty was declared to be a sort of advantage ; war was decried as an abomination ; ladies were conjured not to give out their babies to nurse ; late hours, fashionable dresses, and rouge were execrated; in short, there was a general enthusiasm for nature and virtue, an enthusiasm which seems to have had but little effect on things artificial and vicious. These doctrines, of course, brought the fact that the Arcadian Academy was not a very rustic or natural institution into great relief. It began to be thought that all this verse-scribbling was not really poetical; and the excessive enthusiasm for Ossian, who had just been translated by Cesa-rotti, induced very unlucky comparisons between the Celtic bards and the Roman ahati, between the rocks of Morven and the Serbatow d'Arcadia. People began to suspect that Poetry positively refused to inhabit the halls of an academy, and that she asked for crumbling ruins, virgin forests, and misty mountain-tops. In default of these places, where people of fashion might find it inconvenient to visit her, the Muse was invited to little quiet circles in palaces or villas, where, under the patronage of some beautiful lady, and out of reach of hungry little priests, poetical enthusiasts might meet without fear of artificial or prosaic intei-ests being thrust upon them. The colonies of Arcadia began to be neglected for the drawing-rooms of woinen like the Countess Castiglione at Milan, the Countess Grismondi at Brescia, the Marchesa Silvia Verza at Verona, the Countess Roberti at Bassano, and, above all, of the lovely Isabella Teotochi Albrizzi at Venice, where the most eminent poets, Parini, Pindemonti, Pompei, Cesarotti, were constantly to be met, together with an occasional classical sculptor or emotional singer like Canova or Pacchierotti. Very delightful those little literary circles must have been, where the

most talented men lavished their intellectual gifts to please be, ntiful and refined women ; little circles meeting in some cosy drawing 'oom in the quiet dark town, or on the terraces and in the cypress and Sj ca-move alleys of the villas along the Brenta and between the Monti Berici ; so delightful that their remembrance made those who long survived them, and even ourselves, who have merely heard of them, feel quite elegiac at the sight of the now desolate country-houses where they met, and of the faded pictures of the ladies who presided over them. The poetry which was produced in such societies was, of course, far less conventional, verbose, and worthless than that of the large academical assemblies; less was written, and that better, than in the days of Frugoni, but great excellence was scarcely attained to. The poems of Pompei, Mazza, Masche-roni, and even of Ippolito Pindemonti, who far surpassed his contemporaries,* give us the impression that, agreeable and elegant though they are, their authors were more interesting than they. There was a general mild, elegiac tone prevalent, which, though not without a certain charm, was rather languid and insipid ; nor was there produced, towards the end of the last century, any work to be compared with those of Metastasio, Goldoni, Parini, or even of the Gozzis. The spread of philosophical and humanitarian ideas had no perceptibly good influence on literature, for, although a tendency to take interest in individual sentiment had arisen, it was neither sufficiently strong nor sufficiently spontaneous to produce true lyric poetry; and the gradual adoption of foreign and the revival of antique modes of thinking and feeling merely weakened the national literature. Metastasio could not have written his operas, nor Goldoni his comedies, had either been fresh from reading Ossian, and Homer, and Gray, and Rousseau, and Gessner; so true is it that intellectual cultivation by no means implies intellectual productiveness. Imitation was in vogue, as it must always be when anything striking first becomes known to a whole people; and by the side of the newly-acquired knowledge of foreign literature came the newly-revived interest in antique art, the enthusiasm for both mingling strangely towards the end of the last century, but without a better effect than that of making people tolerate tiresome classicism by the side of tiresome romanticism. In Italy the classical tendency was on the whole the stronger of the two, although largely tinged with northern romanticism ; Italians began to go to Rome with the express purpose of seeing ruins and statues, which had hitherto interested only professed archaeologists, and more especially for the purpose of musing over them. Winckelmann's Italian works, and those of his followers Fea and Visconti, excited interest in antique art, while the gradually-spreading liberal

     * His poem Antonio Foncarinl would be a masterpiece were its subject a more moral one. Tet even in nobility of feeling how superior is it not to a poem on a somewhat similar subject by a living author, Pratt's famous Edmcnegarda?

     doctrines revived interest in Roman history, which for two centuries had been a kind of dead letter; in short, romanticism, which, being in rcahtj'^ only the revival of literary and artistic appreciation due to critical study, included even classicism—romanticism made Rome once more a capital, of which we personally are very glad, since it enables us to return once more to Arcadia, and to show it in a more flourishing state than it had been since the middle of the century.

     This revival of Arcadia was marked in the year 1775 by an event which brought back for a moment the glory of the Academy, and at the same time cast great ridicule on it. The reputation, if not the talents, of Perfetti had fallen to the share of a woman who became famous under the Arcadian name of Gorilla Olimpica. Maria Maddalena Morelli was born at Pistoja about the middle of the last century, and her early years are involved in such obscurity that, betwixt the enthusiastic lyrism of her admirers and the vile scurrility of her lampooners, it is impossible to tell whether she was a pattern of virtue or the very reverse. She married a Spanish gentleman named Fernandez, whom, together with her children, her enemies accused her. among other wickednesses, of having shamefully abandoned. However, her iniquities could either not be proved or were hushed up in consideration of her amazing talents, for we meet her everywhere received, honoured, and courted in the most signal way, despite an ominous hum of contempt on the part of the less polite or more scrupulous literati. She received several invitations from Joseph II., from the Republic of Venice, and from the Bolognese Senate, Clement XIV., an austere man for his time, gave her, in the most flattering manner, a permission to read books prohibited by the Inquisition; and all the most distinguished of the foreign visitors—Orloflf, the Corsican chief Paoli, and the Duke of Dorset—lavished honours on her. Her receptions were much frequented by the most brilliant company, for, besides her poetic talents, she was pretty despite a squint, amiable, and accomplished. She was also a musician, for when Dr. Burney went to her house at Florence* he heard her play the violin; and she was particularly gracious to Mozart as a boy, for whom she even condescended to write a sonnet. In 1775 she was invited to Rome by her fellow Arcadians, and excited such enthusiasm, that the Senator spontaneously sent her the diploma of citizenship; and the Abate Gioacchino Pizzi, Custode Generale d'Arcadia, crowned her at a private meeting of the Academy. To this first ebullition of admiration is also due a beautiful bust of Gorilla, presented by an English

* This house, with General Miollis's mouuniental, but not very intelligible, inscription, " Qui visse Gorilla in secolo XVIII°." is at the corner of Via della Forca, a street running towards S. Lorenzo, and Via Cerretani. It has au additional interest for us on account of Mozart, who was so often her guest.

sculptor, Christopher Hewctson, to the Arcadians, in whose possession it still remains. Jndging from it and from a smutty portrait of licr dressed in brown brocade decorated with flowers, Gorilla Olimpica must have been at that time a stout woman of thirty-five, handsome, lively, intellectual, withal rather heavy and coarse iu feature; she had besides a squinting eye, which was supposed to make the immediate conquest of anyone upon whom she chose to fix it while in the enthusiasm of improvising; and, if contemporary scandal may be credited, Gorilla had made frequent use of this faculty. At any rate she turned the heads of many people in Rome, filling them with madness of some sort or other—love, ambition, or avarice—to serve her purposes. The young Prince Gonzaga Gasti-glione (the Prince Gastelforte of this rather realistic original of Gorinne), a certain Monsignor Mazzei, and, above all, the Gustode Generale d'Arcadia, Pizzi, moved heaven and earth, begged, and promised, and threatened, until the Pope consented to give Gorilla the crown whicli had been worn by Perfetti. But times were changed since the solemn reign of Grescimbeni. A Gustode Generale d'Arcadia was no longer omnipotent over men's minds, a pope was no longer infallible in all his decisions, an improovisatore was no longer an inspired poet; things could no longer be looked at in the grave and dispassioned style of the year 1725 ; the coronation was regarded as a farce or a profanation, the Arcadians as conceited pedants, Gorilla herself as an impudent adventuress, and, above all, the feelings of the Romans were conceived to be outraged by this arbitrary and undeserved bestowal of what was thought once to have been a national reward. Gorilla's dubious antecedents, her theatrical profession, the exaggeration and intrigue of her partisans, did much to awaken public contempt and indignation : the ready buffoonery of the Roman people burst out in more or less scurrilous fashion ; it was solemnly announced by Pasquino—that undaunted stone advocate of an oppressed but not disheartened people—that

Ordina e vuole Monsignor Mazzei Che sia la Gorilla cinta dell' alloro, E che non le si tiriu buccie no pomidoro Sotto multa di bajocchi sei.

Other epigrams averred that this coronation, like that of Daraballo, was meant as a jest and ought to be taken as such:

Venez-y, riez-en ; et puis vous pourrez dire Que tout cela n'a ete fait que pour rire.

Pizza and Gorilla's other partisans seem to have taken fright at these pasquinades, and, fearing perhaps that, despite the alleged fine of six baiocchi on whomsoever should throw orange rinds and tomatoes at the poetess, they might run the risk of some unpleasant scene if they

performed the coronation in the daytime, they determined that the ceremony sliould take phice at midnight. This precaution did not, however, entirely suffice, for, as CoriUa was advancing to receive the crown of the Capitol, a young priest pushed his way through the crowd of bystanders and handed her a paper; the poetess, finding the missive to be in Latin, handed it to Prince Gonzaga, who, under the impression that it contained complimentary verses, read them out aloud, discovering, only too late, that they were most infamously insulting to her. The ceremony of coronation was hurried over, amid the acclamations of Gorilla's enthusiasts ; but the very next day a storm of invective burst out. Lampoons against Gorilla, her partisans, and even against the conniving Pope, were pasted on all street corners and handed round in every house;

the Abate Pizzi was accused of having plotted to introduce Gorilla at an Arcadian meeting with a crown on, which was to be passed off for that of the Capitol; of having been induced to do so by the bribes of Prince Gonzaga, and by his own desire to play in regard to Gorilla the part played by Grescimbeni in regard to Perfetti; the whole coronation was decried as illegal, and punishment required for its perpetrators. Poor Pizzi, in despair, wrote a solemn letter of explanation to the Pope, who would appear to have ratified the whole proceeding. But rumour could not so easily be put down, or satire so quickly silenced: a long, and rather clever, but extremely irreverent, poem was published, in which, in the strain of the Dies IrcB, Gorilla lamented her- unfortunate fate, cursed all who had invented Gapitoline crowns, and especially devoted to celestial vengeance the xmlucky Abate Pizzi:

Pizzi iniquo, maledetto, Tua mercc gia m'affretto Al ferale cataletto. All crudele! ah scellerato ! M'ha ridotta in questo stato D'avarizia il tuo peccato. Tu sol fosti che inventasti Nobilta. corona e fasti, Tu che mi sacrificasti. I miei vizii, i miei difetti, Di canzoni e di sonetti Oggi sono i soli soggetti.

Gorilla had excited much admiration, and met much adulation ; Madame de Stael, who saw everything through the beautifying and ennobling medium of her own character, heard of her in after years, totally misconceived her talent, her position, her triumph, saw in her a radiant sibyl, a sort of personified genius of Italy, and wrote Corinne. Thus poor, misused, pasquinaded Gorilla Olimpica unconsciously gave rise to a masterpiece; but those Romans who still remembered the scene at the

Capitol in the year 1775 must have suppressed a smile in reading the magnificent description of Corinne's coronation.

The reigns of Clement XIII. and of Clement XIV. had been dull enough for Rome and Arcadia; both popes were austere men, one engrossed in bigotry, the other in reforms, caring respectively only for beatifications and consistories, and for politics and Church government. The reign of Pius VI. was a very different one. Giovan Angelo Craschi, the handsomest, vainest, and most artistic pope who had reigned since more than a centiuy, seemed inclined to abandon the principles of his immediate predecessors, and to return to the notions and habits of a Paul V. or an Urban VIII. Nepotism, a thing long out of use, reappeared in full force, together with the most lavish expenditure and the most childish ostentation. The Pope's nephew, Braschi Onesti, was made a duke, a grandee of Spain, a prince of the Holy Empire, and was given a large fortune, large estates, including the famous villa of Hadrian, and a large amount of political influence : a striking contrast to the Lambertinis, whom their uncle Benedict XIV. had invited to stay at home and leave him alone. Pius VI. had something of the feeling of Louis XIV., and a vague idea of playing the part of Pericles ; he did a few things handsomely and a great many in the most shabby style of ostentation ; he bought a number of very valuable ancient statues, which would otherwise have been scattered about in foreign collections, and built to receive them the noble rotonda and staircase of the Museo Pio-Clementino, the most beautiful of all galleries; he caused considerable excavations to be made, and em])loyed Canova and other first-rate artists to restore antiques; at the same time he built that monster of heavy pastry-cook architecture, the chapter-house of St. Peter's, and a number of trimipery buildings of a similar style; and to whatever he did, good or bad, he appended his name, hoping to gain immortality by means of the tablets with the heraldic wind blowing down lilies, and the inscription, "Munificentia Pii Sexti," which he sprinkled all over the streets, museums, and monuments of Rome. In his reign, and partly owing to his personal influence, Rome became for the first time a great cosmopolitan centre; not merely a place like Venice, Bologna, and Milan, in which young men on their grand tour remained for a short time, but the permanent residence of numbers of foreigners who came to study art or to wile away a lazy existence. Soon there was a regular set of French artists, another of Germans, and a small colony of English of rank and fortune; nay, Rome became so cosmopolitan towards the end of the eighteenth century that when Beckford was there in 1780, the Senator—that is to say, the supreme magistrate— was a Swede. These foreigners did not necessarily mix with Roman society, except with the artistic and literary part of it; and whereas, in the year 1740, Charles de Brosses found himself in the midst of a strange

people, Dr, Burney informs us that as early as 1770 he met more Englisli than Italians in Rome, and eighteen years later Goethe seems scarcely to have known a single Italian; for, in proportion as the foreigners colonised, the natives became more national and exclusive. This new condition of things naturally affected literary life; there was no longer in Rome either a Don Livio Odescalchi in search of literary retainers nor a Crescimbeni in search of rich noble protectors; the nobles had ceased to play the Maecenas, the literati had ceased to be their humble attendants; literature was gradually being turned out of noble Roman circles and seeking refuge in the cosmopolitan society which collected in Rome for the sake of art, of music, of archaeology, and of that general intellectual improvement which Goethe was the first to analyse and define; the intellectual part of different nations was beginning to consider Rome as its home. There were, of course, lots of Roman fine ladies and gentlemen on the lists of the Bosco Parrasio; but the really intelligent pixblic, the one which could still take pleasure in meeting for literary pm-poses, was a mongrel one: there was the Duke of Dorset, a great giver of private concerts; there was Councillor Reiflfenstein, a great collector of antiques; there was Zoega, the Danish archaeologist; Piranesi, the engraver; Fea, the translator of Winckelmann, and his more famous rival Visconti; there were Canova and Angelica Kauffmann, and Tischbein and Gavin Hamilton;, there was a crowd of artists, and literati, and musicians, Italians and foreigners, with whom they associated; there Avere aspiring young men trying to create a national stage: the Abate Monti, a poor secretary of the pope's nephew Braschi Onesti, whose Aristodemus was vehemently applauded, and Count Alfieri, a rich, half-mad Piedmontese, always driving a lot of horses and getting into dreadful quarrels, whose Orestes created a still more violent sensation, and gave the younger generation a certain impatient contempt for Pope Pius and his rule, and a desire to return to antiquity, and freedom, and paganism. While Roman society was thus losing its national character, Rome itself was unchanged: with its old-fashioned, half-classic practices, its riotous Carnival, its races of riderless horses, its people living and sleeping in the streets, its processions and popular festivals, and old Christian and heathenish customs; so that, in this wonderful mixture of newly discovered antiquity, of modern artistic life, of picturesque old-fashioned custom, of polished modern society, Goethe could feel all his wishes fulfilled, save that of never cjuitting so delightful a mode of existence. The imbecile and uncultivated natives had retired, the imbecile and uncultivated foi'eigners had not yet come; there was art and music, and antiquity and nature, apparently for the sole enjoyment of the intelligent and cultivated minority, to whom new and vast horizons of philosophy, of liberty, of art, of literature, were gradually disclosing; and altogether things seemed to be going on in a

strangely agreeable way, as indeed they did immediately before the great storm which was to shake, and bhast, and uproot all. This was the state of Kome when, in 1788, Coimcillor Wolfgang von Goethe, minister of the Duke of Wieniar, author of Werther, the most popular book that had ever appeared, was admitted into Arcadia as Megalio Mclpomenco, and had allotted to him by the Abate Pizzi the " fields of the Tragic Muse " —rather an unnecessary piece of property for a man who was finishing Tasso and Iphigenia, and had the first scenes of Faust in his portfolio.

This delightful state of Roman life was not destined to last long. Scarcely had Goethe recrossed the Alps when there came news from France which diverted the thoughts of intelligent men from literature, art, and archfBology. Liberal doctrines had long been working their way in Italy, though in a subdued and inoffensive way, but it was not till the year 1789 that the Italians became aware that those doctrines might be practically applied; as it is possible that even in France people did not know what changes might be effected until the first great effort had shown them their own force. But, when once the movement had begun, it was irresistible; men found themselves suddenly hurled from out of the sphere of mere wild speculation into that of violent action. The Italians seem to have received a shock of surpi-ise; what the French had so long hinted at and then ranted about was absolutely taking place. The reforms, which had seemed mere dreams, were being enforced, philanthropy was being put into practice, freedom was being established; those far-gone times of Brutus and the Gracchi, which had seemed mere poetical ideals, were really returning; humanity was being changed, renovated, transfigured. •Such was the feeling of many ardent young men in Italy, and many more moderate and wiser men sjTnpathised to a certain degree with them, but felt less sanguine than they did; nor does there appear to have been any attempt at imitating the French in their revolution. Very soon, however, the horrible excesses of the republicans, their theatrical bombast, their want of patriotism, their insolent defiance of all law, human and divine, disgusted even the most ardent philanthropists of Italy. The Governments looked on in stupid fright or stupid apathy; some thought to stay the revolutionary wave by imprisoning a few Frenchmen and uproarious youths; others trusted in their concessions to the people. Tuscany remained placid and happy. Venice, despite the warning voice of Francesco Pesaro, determined to jog on comfortably, and let the banner of St. Mark and the twenty-five old cripples of Peschiera scare away all invaders.* Pius VI. immediately ordered a creature of his, named 8pe-dalieri, to ^vrite a book to prove that man had a right to equality and

* The following gives an amusing picture of the times, which we transcribe from Professor Krnesto Masi's very learned and at the same time amusing book on the

liberty, and that the Sovereign Pontiff' was tlie likeliest person to obtain it for him. The King of Sardinia called out his people to defend their independence and their rulers, and opposed his elaborately-trained army to the French. x\ustria moved, England moved, France moved; the independent Italian States found themselves between the belligerents, caressed and bullied now by the one, now by the other, vainly attempting to maintain neutrality, and to suppress the seeds of insubordination. In Kome the French minister and his secretary drove through the Corso wearing tricolour cockades-—the mob fell upon them and cut them to pieces; Monti wrote a poem in honour of the murdered Basseville, but that did not atone. The French soldiers, without bread, Avithout clothes, without shoes, were told at the foot of the Alps to avenge their countrymen massacred at Eome; they poured into Italy, a hideous barbarous mass, bm'uing, sacldng, and pillaging, while they declared that they were bringing liberty to the Italians. Napoleon reorganised them, disciplined them, soothed the population, and prevented all but official plunder. The Austrians then came and sacked and ravaged in their turn. The French planted trees of liberty, stole pictm-es, statues, manuscripts, money, all they could lay their hands upon. The Italians rejoiced because they had been made free, and wept because they had been made beggars. Some false enthusiasts cringed to the conquerors and obtained posts under them; some timorous conservatives went over to the Austrians; some generous-minded visionaries plotted to exterminate the foreigners of all sorts and set up an Italian kingdom; some wanted a democracy, others an oligarchy; some approved of the French system of levelling and wholesale changing; others wished to preserve some of the old traditions; a few truly noble men put aside their prejudices and united, priests and freethinlvers, republicans and aristocrats, determined to serve their country under whatever rule it fell, trying to save it from the ruin which seemed impending; among these we meet, for the last time, a man of Avhom we have already spoken at considerable length, the Abate Giuseppe Parini.

Meanwhile the frivolous part of society chatted and danced, and went to operas and masquerades, and adored now the Emperor of Germany, now the French general, but especially that greatest, most heroic of men, the

amateur playwright Albergati, a book which unfortunately fell into our hands only after the pubUcation of this essay in Fraser"s Magazine: —

" In the year 1792 the Bolognese Senate discussed various plans, and finally assigned to the most excellent Signor Gonfaloniere (head of the Senate) 120 Bolognese livres, wherewith to provide for the safety of the State. This worthy gentleman resolved in his mind how best to employ the money, and finally distributed it, in sums of .30 livres, to the various Capuchin monasteries and to the convent of the Barefoot Nuns, that they might implore Heavenly assistance on account of the French invasion of Savoy" (p. 442).

siii.n'or Marcliesi, Avhoiu Alficri called upon to buckle on his helmet, and march out against the French, as the only remaining Italian who liad dared to resist the " Corsican Gallic" invader, although only in the matter of a song. And in this confusion of contrary opinions, and of absence of opinions, in this chaos of strife and of utter helplessness, of vain-glorious rascality and unnoticed heroism, there remained one man who, taking no part, looked on in contempt, and left the world the most extraordinary monument of his feeling. Alfieri had only two feelings, strangely fused into one—hatred and contempt. He hated and despised the savage republicans, the formal Austrians, the grandiloquent French spoilers, the barbarous German invaders, the inane republics and grand dulses, the retrogrades and the radicals, those who acted and those who were passive, the servility and the tyranny; and this hatred and contempt he expressed in the collection of epigrams which he entitled Misogallo, with the harsh bitter terseness which was his literary weakness and his political strength. The whole order of things in Italy was subverted; all was plundered, regulated, arranged for the better by the French; the Austrians and Pied-montese made terrible reprisals. Venice was handed over to the Austrians; Naples was abandoned to Caroline and Cardinal Euffo; colleges Avere instituted, statues carried off, trees of liberty planted, fireworks let off, while prisons and fortresses were crowded, while whole families, once wealthy and powerful, crossed the Alps on foot as beggars, and the best blood in the southern provinces was shed in torrents.* Carlo Botta, a patriot and a thinker, who had suffered in his youth for the French cause, has left a heartrending account of the feelings of men like himself at the close of the eighteenth centmy, looking upon their country ravaged, pillaged, enslaved; dishonoured by those who had pretended to bring liberty, and crushed by those who had pretended to defend independence; all illusions were dispelled, all hopes gone, and there is something like a stiiled sob in the words in which the historian tells how the \'7d)opulace rejoiced when the Republic of St. Mark was dissolved, and predicts that soon the time will come when Venice will be a mere heap of ruins, washed over and half hidden by the compassionate lagoons. So, indeed, it seemed when Botta wrote; nor could he foresee that what appeared final destruction was, in reality, but the beginning of renovation; and that the freedom and independence of Italy, lost amidst devastation and oppression when the feudal monarchies of the North reached their highest power at the begni-ning of the sixteenth century, would be recovered, thanlcs to that second

* Perhaps no better picture could be given of Italy in the last years of the ciiilitt'cntli century than that contained in the Covfrxs'inyil dl vn Ottua(irnario, by the hitc Ippulito Nievo. This very rennirkable, tiiongh occasionally tedious, novel reads like a real autobiography; and it is wonderful how a young writer of our own day could so realize the condition of Italy ninety years ago.

The Arcadian Academy.
foreign invasion due to the fall of feudalism at the end of the eighteentli century.

What became of Arcadia in that great storm? Did her members continue writing and reading sonnets, while Pius VI. was being dragged lo Avignon, while Pavia was being sacked, while Venice was being sold, while Cirillo, and Eleonora Pimentel, and Filomarino were being butchered, and Caracciolo hanged to the mast of his own ship? This much is certain, that men thought no more about the institution, and that its existence and very name were forgotten in the great confusion whence modern Italy arose.

And as we stand once more in the little desolate battered villa on the Janiculum, and look again at the portraits of Crescimbeni, of Perfetti, of Gorilla, and of the beautiful Faustina Maratti, of their many nameless companions, mouldering unnoticed on the bare, stained walls, Ave feel even more powerfully than before how deep a gulf separates us from those times, so near to our own, yet so long forgotten, when the Academy of the Arcadi I'cpresented the whole literary life of Italy.

THE MUSICAL LIFE.
THE MUSICAL LIFE.

We go doAvn the Strada San Donate, tlie noblest street in noble old Bologna; we issue out of its lofty arcades in front of the tall red brick church of San Giaconio, pass by the side of its time-worn marble lions, and ring, hard by, at a little blistered door, all scribbled over with music notes. The door creaks, swings back on its hinges, and lets us pass into a little black lobby, illumined by a flickering, sputtering shrine lamp; we clamber up a dark rugged well-staircase, past an open kitchen, and come to a landing. A confused sound of instruments and voices meets us, for the pupils of the music school are at their lessons; Ave push back a heavy leathern door, and enter a vast, lofty, desolate hall, on whose brick floor our steps resound as in a chm-ch. The practising pupils are not here, nor is any other living person besides ourselves; but all around is a croAvd of dead musicians, members of the once famous Philharmonic Academy, in purple and lilac, and brocade and powder, who look down upon us from the walls. Only here and there do we recognise some well-known figure— Handel, majestic in blue plush and a many-storied peruke; Gluck, coarse, bright, and flushed, in a furred cloak; Haydn, pale, grey, Avillow-like, bending over a meagre spinnet; Mozart, sweet and dreamy, with the shadow of premature death already uptm him—; around them are a host of others, forgotten and unknown, their contemporaries, their masters, their friends, their rivals, and perhaps their successful rivals. Very solemn and quaint they mostly are, those ladies with prodigious beribboned liay-cocks on their heads, those fiddlers in dressing-gowns and periwigs, those prim chapel-masters seated by their harpsichords, and those dap^jcr singers with one hand on their music roll and the other on their sword-hilt; very solemn and quaint, and almost droll, but not witliout something that awakens sadness. There is sadness in the dignified thoughtful composers, looking as if the world still rang with the sountl of their music—music not heard for a century; there is sadness in the dandified singers, whose names have long been forgotten, but whose eyes are upturned and whose lips are parted, as if they still thrilled and delighted those that have been dead a hundred years: it is a world of feeling extinct and genius forgotten,

p2 '

a world separated from ours by a strange indefinable gulf. Yet amongst these forgotten nameless figures there is one who can procure us a glimpse into that world: opposite us hangs the portrait of a man in the brocade gown of a doctor of music; thin, sharp, with a shrewd, kindly, humorous face. Our fellow-countryman, Dr. Burney, can yet introduce us to some at least of the forgotten musicians around us; of all his contemporaries he is the only one who does not look down on us in silence.

Let us quit for a while the old desolate hall, hung with the portraits of the Philharmonic Academicians; and descend into the cosy broAvn library, with its shelves of books and manuscripts, its glass cases of quaint lutes and viols, and its Venetian chandelier shining opal-tinted in the sunshine, which slants across the little cloister court^ and gilds the red brick of the adjacent belfry. Here, among heaps of time-soiled scores and bundles of faded letters, and with a subdued hum of music entering by the open windows, we can sit and turn over the leaves of the battered volume which chronicles the musical tour through France and Italy made in the year 1770 by Charles Burney, Doctor of Music.

Charles Burney is scarcely remembered now-a-days except as the father of one of the earliest and most brilliant of female English novelists; but long before Evelina and Cecilia were written, at a time when the future Mdme. d'Arblay was looked upon as a mere ordinary little piece of living furniture in the house in Poland Street, her father was well known as one of the first of English musicians, as a man of great literary attainments and of great social charms, and as belonging to the most brilliant coteries of the day. Although by profession nothing beyond a mere music-master, and without pretensions to an elegant or even very comfortable style of living, Burney had a very large circle of acquaintances, not only among literary and scientific notabilities, but among people of much higher rank and station than his own, Avho were pleased to know him and pleased that their acquaintance with him should be known, for Bm-ney was a man who was acquainted with everyone worth knowing, thanks to his character, his talents, and a certain sincerity and sunniness of nature which attached everyone to him. Born at Shrewsbm-y in 1726, and entrusted during childhood to mere country-folk, he had been early apprenticed to the celebrated composer Arne, Avhose teachings were restricted to making him drudge as a coj^yist, so that the young man owed nearly all he learned to his own indefatigable activity while in this bondage. From it he was released by Fulke Greville, a high-born fop and wit, who took him into his private service, but less as a teacher than a companion. This position,

wliile tlirowin,'," tlie yoiitli into tlio dissipated circles to which his patriiii belonyod, at the same timo nffnrdcd him opportunities of hocoming acquainted with persons of social and literary standing-; and such was Burncy's happy character that he obtained all the advantages without any of the disadvantages which Mr. CJreville i)ut Avithin his reach. A charming and highly intellectual young wife confirmed his tendencies towards domestic life, and towards literary and social culture; and every succeeding year saw him extend his reputation and enlarge his circle of friends. Nothing perhaps im])resses us more with his winning character than the perfect confidence and afiection of all his children, and the constant tender admiration of his daughter Fanny—an admiring enthusiastic affection, not unlike that of Madame de Stael for Necker. But Burney was as great a favom-ite abroad as at home. Among the earliest of his innumerable friends was Garrick, who would show off all his powers of mimicry for the delight of the little Burneys; the accomplished and unfortunate Crisp, to whose conversation Burney probably owed much of the superior cesthetical education he displayed; and Mason, the friend of Gray, and author of Cai'actaciis, whom, together with Thomson of the Seasons, Burney had come across in the earliest part of his career. Reynolds, who loved money, painted Burney's portrait out of mere friendship; and Mrs. Thrale hung it up at Streatham. Goldsmith sought eagerly for the acquaintance of the doctor of music; while Gibbon, Bruce, Bm"kc, Sheridan, Captain Cook, Murphy, Boswell, and a host of other celebrities, flocked to the parties in the house which had once belonged to NcAvton. But of all Burney's friends none perhaps was as hearty and truly appreciative as Johnson:

"Mrs. Thrale," Avrites Madame d'Arblay, "was lamenting the sudden disappearance of Dr. Burney, who had just gone to town, sans adieux; declaring that he was the most complete male coquette she knew, for he only gave just enough of his company to make more desired. ' Dr. Burney,' said Mr. Murphy, * is indeed a most extraordinary man. I think I do not know such another. He is at home on all subjects; and upon all highly agreeable, I look upon him as a wonderful man!' ' I love Burney!' cried Dr. Johnson, emphatically; * my heart goes out to meet Burney. . . Dr. Burney is a man for everybody to love. It is but natural to love him. ... I question if there be in the world such another man, altogether, for mind, intelligence, and manners, as Dr. Burney.' "

In this prosperous condition of his affairs. Dr. Burney, who, it must be remembered, although a wit and a friend of wits, was by]n'ofession merely a music-master, conceived the idea of a great work on his art—a general history of music, such as had never been Avi-itten before, and could never be written except by himself, by the man who had heard more music than any other, who appreciated it better, and had the friendship of all the most

distinguished composers and performers. To this plan lie devt)ted all his leisure time and all his spare money. Ho made extract after extract, bought volume after volume and manuscript after manuscript, and every hour missed liy a pupil Avas, according to Madame d'Arblay, given to his History. Indeed, what would not he done for an all-engrossing work by a man like Burney, who as a boy had tied a string to his toe that he might be waked by a companion in the street and begin his studies at daybreak, and Avho as a young man had learned Latin and Greek while plodding through the mud of Lynn Regis on his mare Peggy? Very soon Burney became dissatisfied with the materials for his History Avhich ho could obtain in England from books and conversation; ho wished to give his work the benefit of every kind of information, and he at length conceived the plan of visiting France and Italy. "In hopes," he wi-ote, "of stamping on my History some marks of originality .... I determined to hear with my own ears, and see with mine own eyes; and, if possible, to see and hear nothing but music." " There Avas something so spirited and uncommon," writes Madame d'Arblay, " and yet of so antique a cast, in these travels or pilgrimage that he had undertaken in search of materials for the history of his art, that curiosity was awakened to the subject, and expectation was earnest for its execution;" and, consequently, well supplied with letters of introduction, and encouraged by general approbation, Dr. Burney set off for Italy with a light heart at the beginning of June 1770. On Tuesday, June 13, Dr. Burney arrived in Paris. He had been there twice before, was well acquainted with its sights, people, and music, and therefore stayed only as long as was required to seek for materials for his work in the public libraries. Dr. Burney appears to have had that high admiration for French writers, and that smiling slight contempt for the French people, which distinguished well-educated Englishmen of his day. Like them he had read the Enci/clo^Je'die, and Voltaire, and Rousseau, and all the other philosophers, without that religious and national hostility and dread which the succeeding generation felt for them. Like most of his travelling countrymen he had noticed the French lower classes, horribly oppressed, miserably poor, and invincibly lighthearted and civil, dancing, bowing, and making witticisms in torn, tarnished clothes, as gaily as if there had been neither taxes nor corvees, nor rack, nor gibbet. He had looked at this strange people without any of the fears and hatred which they were later destined to inspire. The coming revolution had not yet cast its shadow before it. In the eyes of foreigners the Encyclopanlists were not yet atheists and corrupters ; the lower classes were not yet doma--gogues and murderers. All in France was quite safe and pleasant: there were philosophical marquises disbelieving in moral law, while Avaiting for old age and neglect to take to devotion; ministers, who gave delightfidly courteous audiences to insignificant travellers and sent troublesome pam-

phletoers to tlio Ijastillo ; t'lcre were ,i,'ay tattered vai^abonds likeLa Fleure. and cliivalric outca*t.'« like tlie Kni,<;-1it of St. Louis wlio sold pasties; tliere was the whole fantastic world of Yoriok-—aniusincf, charming', d(\si>ieable, and porf(>ctly harmless. Dr. Burney went to the public libraries, walked in the streets crowded with the FtteDieu processions, and on the Boulevart, "which i« a place of public diversion without the gates of Paris. It is laid out and planted ; at the sides are coffee-houses, conjurors, and shows of all kinds. Hero, every evenin.q: during- the summer, the walks are crowded with well-dressed people antl the road with spl(>ndid equipa^-es." Here also people danced minuets, allemandes, and contre-danses when the weather was warm. He went to the theatre and saw comedies exquisitely acted, and operas most vilely sung. He went to the Abbe Arnaud, who bad written much in favour of Italian music, and to M. Gretry, who was trying to bring it into fashion by his own example, and with them Burney lamented to his heart's content over the vileness of French music; for Arnaud's books and Gretry's compositions, though read and heard throughout the country, seemed equally inefficacious to make the French abandon their own atrocious music.

Burney also went to several concerts and operas, thinking that some inq)rovement might have taken place since his previous visits to Paris, and also from a conscientious determination to hear everything, good or bad. and to try once for all to find something enjoyable or commendable in French music. " Those wlio visit Italy for the sake of painting, sculpture, and architecture," writes Burney, " do well to see what those arts afford in France first, as they become so dainty afterwards that they can bear to look at but few things which that kingdom affords; and, as I expected to have the same prejudices or feelings at my return about their music, I detei-mined to give it a fair hearing first." How strong a prejudice already existed in the Doctor's mind is shown by the very precautions he took to remain unprejudiced; indeed it was preposterous to think of giving a fair hearing to French music; for, besides the musical taste of every Englishman of that day being exclusively Italian, it was a fact universally admitted and proved by experiments on the unsophisticated minds of Greeks, Hurons, and Polynesians, that to enjoy French music it was not sufficient to bo a savage but it was necessary also to be a Frenchman. Why the French opera from the time of Lully to that of Gluck should have been a musical abomination incomprehensible to all other nations, it is indeed difficult to explain, except by the fact that all stagnant things corrupt. The French, like the English and the Germans, had originally got tlioir music and their opera from the Italians, but, unlike their neighbours, they liad refused to submit to the constantly progressing Italian taste, while they themselves remained incapable of improving what they had been incapable of producing. Music out of Italy was a delicate exotic, and the

French planted and cultivated it among coarse and tawdry plants by •which it was soon crushed.

When Cardinal Mazarin introduced the Italian opera into France it was in tlie monstrous condition inseparable from times of growth and transition; the dramas were badly constructed, the poetry languid and quibbling, the music harsh and pedantic; no great school of singing had as yet arisen, and the chief attraction of the performance consisted in scenic displays and pantomime wonders, which were pushed to an incredible point. The French never dreamed of altering the opera in any of these essential points. While the Italians gave a new shape to the drama, eliminated all the extraneous elements of machinery and dancing, and cidtivated singing and vocal composition to the utmost, the French, relying entirely upon their own powers, never attending to what was being done in Italy, merely petrified the uncouth and meaningless forms of the opera of the seventeenth century. Musical progress there was none; on the contrary, the greater the distance from the original importation of the opera, the worse it became; the more insipid were the plays, the more extravagant the scenic shows, the more iincouth the music, the more insufferable the singers, and the more satisfied was the public. La Bruyere and Vauvenargues spoke with admiring complacency of what was styled la machine^ of the transformations, the flights through the air, the apparitions from underground, the enchanted castles and palaces in the clouds; St. Evremont and Bourdelot proudly contrasted the ranting, screaming, barking, drawling performance o their countrymen with the smooth and brilliant execution of the Italians, which they found utterly devoid of pathos and fit only to make people gape or to send them to sleep. The most polished Paris audience would turn with satisfaction from a tragedy by Racine or Voltaire to an opera by Campra or Rameau; from the exquisitely dignified declamation of a Baron or a Lecouvreur to the screeching and howling of a Gros or a Delcambre; in short, French music seemed invincible. Gray, who accompanied Walpole to Paris in 1739, has left a long description of a French opera, in which, after detailing the ludicrously vapid subject and the eternal ballets, he concludes as follows: " Imagine all this transacted by cracked voices trilhng divisions upon two notes and a half, accompanied by an orchestra of hum-strums, ... des miaulements et des hurlements eff'royables, melees \'7bsic) avec un tintamarre du diable: voila la mnsique frangaise en abregce" (sic).*

However, as even Frenchmen must travel and find something to admire in foreign countries, a suspicion began at length to spread that French

* Compare Goldoni's .account, which we translate from his Antohiography: " I kept waiting for the airs, the music of which woukl, I thought, have at least amused me; when, behold! out comes the ballet again, and concludes the act. I,

music was not quite so perfect, and Italian music not quite so atrocious, as had been hitherto thought; men of talent and fortune began to seek for Italian scores and to write pasquinades on French operas. An Italian comic company was encouraged to perform in Paris Pergolesi's charming musical farce La Serva Padrona, which immediately awakened the enthusiasm of all who were inclined towards Italian music and the frantic indignation of the partisans of the French opera, and inaugurated a war of pamphlets and epigrams which lasted full a quarter of a century. But French music was not so easily routed. Frenchmen like the President de Drosses went to Italy, heard the Faustina, Senesino, Carostini, all the greatest singers of the day ; brought back volumes and portfolios full of songs by Hasse, by Pergolesi, and by Leo, which were handed round in Paris, copied, and performed by self-sufficient amateurs ; but, after having recovered from the first shock of hearing once more their national music, the travellers would gradually become half reconciled to the French opera. Or else a great Italian singer, like Caftariello, would be summoned to Paris by the Dauphine, and Grimm, "Diderot, and hundreds of others would go into raptures and burst into tears at his performances in the Royal Chapel; but scarcely had he left France when his frantic admirers would turn half complacently to the howlers and screechers of the Concert Spirituel. A vast amount was said and written to prove that Italian music was the only sort fit for civilised beings, and a constant lamentation was set up as to the difficulty of introducing it into France ; yet never did it enter the head of any one that it was as simple to establish a regular Italian opera-house in Paris as it had been to do so long before in London, at Vienna, nay, even at Lisbon and at "Warsaw. The French talked and wrote in favour of Italian composers and singers, but neither'the President de Brosses, nor Grimm, nor D'Alembert, nor Arnaud, nor Diderot, nor any of the warmest partisans of Italian music, ever dreamed of introducing into France tlie Italian style of musical drama, nor the exclusive and passionate worship of the human voice which formed the mainspring of Italian nmsic. They wanted to retain their own national style and just varnish it over with Italian gloss; they wanted the singer to remain subservient to the composer, the composer to the poet, and the poet to the stage mechanician; and at the same time they

thinking that the whole act had been without a single air, turn to my neighbour for explanation on the jioiut. He liegins to laagh, and assures nie that the act I have heard contained no less than six airs. ' How? I am not deaf.' It turns out that I had taken all the airs for an endless recitative. A miiuite later out come three actors, all singing together: this was meant for a trio, but I .again mistook it for a recit.ative. In short, all was l)eautiful. grand, magnificent, excepting the music. When the curtain had fallen, all my acquaintances asked me how I had liked the opera. The .answer bursts out of my lips: ' "Tis a paradise for the eyes, but a hell for the ears !' "

wanted wliat they called Italian music; a proof that, as Barney affirms, they never understood what it really meant, and that they were in reality fighting about mere names. The only French writer of the day who really imderstood Italian mi:sic was Rousseau, and, because lie did, he understood also that his fellow countrymen would never understand it. Of this Burney had ample proof at the Concert Spirituel or concert of sacred music in the Louvre, the only kind of musical diversion which the godly Louis XV. would tolerate on festivals : the performance began with a chorus by Lalande, of which the greater part seemed detestable to Burney, but was " much applauded by the audience, who admired it as much as they did themselves for being natives of a country able to produce such masterpieces of composition and such exquisite performers." Two able Italian instrumentalists were less agreeable to the public; " nay, I could even discover by the countenances of the audience and their reception how little they felt such a performance." Poor Madame Philidor, who only attempted to sing in the Italian way, and who could not be accused of succeeding in the attempt, was scarely better treated; but Mdlle. Delcambre, " who screamed out Exaudi Dens with all the power of lungs she could muster," was much admired, and when the concert concluded with a grand chorus, which surpassed all the clamour, all the noises Burney had ever heard in his life, he saw, " by the smiles of ineffable satisfaction which were visible in the countenances of ninety-nine out of a hundred of the company, and heard, by the most violent applause that a ravished audience could bestow, that it was quite what their hearts felt and their souls loved." Yet these were no longer the days when Lully and Rameau had ruled supreme. Rousseau had written his Lettre sur la Musique Franqaise; Grimm and Arnaud had pasquinaded French composers; Diderot's daughter, when Burney visited her, played only Italian music, and all the fashionable people declared themselves the warm admirers of Pergo-lesi and Galuppi. " It is not easy," writes Burney, " to account for the latitude the French take in their approbation, or to suppose it possible for people to like things as opposite as light and darkness. If French music is good and its expression natural and pleasing, that of Italy must be bad; or change the supposition, and allow that of Italy to be all which an imprcjudiced but cultivated ear could wish, then the French music cannot give such an ear equal delight. The truth is, the French do not like Italian music: they j^retend to adopt and admire it, hut it is all mere affectation.^'

Burney was perfectly correct in saying that the French never really liked Italian music. They never obtained or tried to obtain it genuine; and, so far from its ever being thoroughly adopted in France, the French lost their exclusive worship for Lully and Rameau, made a step forward from the point at which they had been at the beginning of the eighteenth

century, ami liegan to enjoy Italian music only wlieii it was offered them by Gluck cunningly ting-eci Avitli French declamation; and they entirely abandoned their national composers only when Italian music was beginning to decay, when it had ceased to be purely Italian, and had mingled with what remained of the original French style, in the days of Cheruliini, Salieri, and Spontini.

The violent feuds between Gluckists and Piccinnists, which broke out in Paris a few years after Burney's visit, have indeed led some persons to believe that there must have been intense musical life among the French, and that they really possessed an Italian school of composition ; but such a notion is totally erroneous. The French cared nothing for music itself, but they seized hold of it as a subject for dissertation and dispute. Gluck and Piccinni were equally unappreciated by them, and were valued only as affording occasion for a war of pamphlets, epigrams, and vaudevilles, such as was waged upon every other subject and upon no subject at all. The French were in that strange state of mental over-excitement in which scientific discoveries and drawing-room jests, social laws and charlatans' nostrums, became objects of the same engrossing and feverish attention; and music, to which they never listened, but about which they were always talking, was merely another intellectual bauble which amused and excited them for a-while, until Mesmer and Cagliostro took its place, and until all artificial subjects of interest were swept away by the Revolution. With respect to the Italian school of music, it never took root in France, and indeed the first superficial varnish of Italian elegance was imparted to French music by Gluck, whose wild theories of dramatic expression, joined with his aversion to the supremacy of the voice, made him sympathise to a certain extent with the declamatory and unmelodious school of Lnlly and Rameau; whereas Piccinni, bent, like eveiy true Italian composer of his day, solely on perfecting purely musical excellence, was utterly unable to amalgamate his style with that of the French, or to produce any effect on the latter. That this is true, and that the utter musical stagnation of which Burney complains continued in the midst of the most violent theoretical discussions, is proved by Mozart's letters, written from Paris in 1779, when the Gluckist and Piccinnist squabbles were at the highest: " What irritates me most," he writes, " is that these Jlerren Franzosen have improved their taste only to the extent of enduring to hear good music as well as bad. But to expect them to perceive that their own music is bad— eyheiLeihe! And such singing! Oimel If at least French women would let alone Italian airs, I might forgive them their squalling; but to hear good music spoilt is intolerable."

Again: " If at least there were a place here where people had cars and hearts to appreciate music, where they understood a little about iimsic,

and had a little good taste; but with resjiect to music, I am amoiig cattle and beasts (

Vieher und Bestien).'^ Lord Mount Edgcumbe also, -who visited France in 1780, found French music insufferable, and French taste so little improved that Paccliierotti, the most refined and pathetic of all the many exquisite singers of his day, was wholly unappreciated there.

The French, however, continued quite proud of themselves, and protested (and still perhaps protest) that if French music was not perfect, which they could not readily admit, it yet possessed great excellences, without which the Italian school must necessarily have remained incomplete. This was already the style of talk in the time of Rousseau, the first Frenchman who flatly denied that French music had any qualities which the Italians need desire; and these pretensions became such an article of national belief that it is right they should be examined carefully, as well as the answers of their contradictors.

There are no Italian accounts of French music,* for the Italians who travelled avoided hearing it, and those who stayed at home did not even know, as Rousseau remarks, that there was any French music which differed from theirs. Our authorities, therefore, are mainly English and Germans, and Frenchmen themselves, who often confessed individual faults of their music, while refusing to admit its general inferiority. The first and most important fault found by foreigners is that French music is old-fashioned; that, while Italian music has rapidly improved, French music has remained utterly stagnant since the end of the seventeenth century; that the same operas, forty, fifty, or sixty years old, are constantly being repeated, while in Italy ten or fifteen years suffice to render an opera obsolete; and that, even if new operas are composed, it is always in the same traditional style and with the same servile imitation of Lully, Lalande, and Rameau, whose Italian contemporaries have long since been laid aside. "It is wonderful," writes Burney, speaking of the Za'ide of Royer, which he had just heard, " that nothing better, or of more modern taste, has been composed since; the style of composition is totally changed throughout the rest of Europe; yet the French .... have stood still in music for thirty or forty years: nay, one may sssert boldly that it has undergone few changes at the great opera since Lully's time— that is to say, in one hundred years. In short, notwithstanding they can both talk and write so well and so much about it, music in France, with respect to the two great essentials of melody and expression, may still be said to be in its infancy." What we next hear is that the music was not

* Except that of Goldoni, who resided in France for more than twenty years. He refers to about the year \lCt'>, and, althougli unmusical by nature, his opinion is interesting as being that of a man accustomed to the best Italian music.

only olJ-fashioued, but luid, .iiul most sliamefully performed. French singing was proverbially abominable : the French, as we learn from Eoussean, knew only one sort of upper voice, the soprano, raised to the most unearthly j)itch; and they replaced the contralto, so lovingly cultivated by the Italians of the eighteenth century, by a sort of falsetto tenor, of a most nasal and disgusting artificial tone. These misplaced voices were further ruined by being produced either purely in the head or in the throat, no such thing as a real chest-voice being known in France. They were totally undisciplined in the simplest and most essential qualities : they had no swell, no proper shake, no real agility and neatness of movement—above all, no portamento, that is to say, no art of moving from one note to another without cither hopping or dragging, no art of beginning and finishing a phrase; in short, no art of singing. All this was replaced by the most violent vocal contortions, shrieks, howls, gabbles, and scpialls; by the most lamentable drawling, and especially by certain movements, called indiscriminately ports de voix, which, according to contemporaries, were the sourest and most lugubrious graces conceivable. So much for the singers. The orchestra, though very numerous, ■was, as Gray expressed it, one of humstrums ; and Rousseau informs us that, despite its numbers, it produced no effect, as no one knew how to direct it. Add to tliis, that the choruses were bawled in so stentorian a fashion that Burney declares that compared to them the loudest English oratorio chorus Avas a lullaby. As to the com\'7d)ositions, they belonged, as we have seen, with the exception perhaps of dance music, for which the French had natural talent, to a raAV, primitive, and—what was much worse —utterly stagnant style; and the French notoriously possessed neither real, distinctly marked melody, nor real, spoken, Avcll-modulated recitative; both categories, so carefully kept asunder by the Italians, being merged into a kind of awkward, insipid, boorish, continued declamation.

All this the French had to admit wholesale or \'7d)iecemeal, and they had to admit also that in everyone of these points the Italians were as perfect as they themselves were faulty. Yet the French had a loophole of escape: "The Italians," they admit, "sing exquisitely, have first-rate orchestras, compose divinely, but they have no expression. And that is what we, with all our failings, possess to the utmost." But this was the weakest subterfuge, sufficient perhaps for their blind vanity, but which all other nations utterly despised. For by expressimi the French meant the mere coarsest ranting. They could find none in Italian compositions, in the most heroic and pathetic which have \'7d)erhaps ever been written ; a clear proof that they did not feel and recognise true pathos. One of their own light, dissolute rhymesters, Dorat, declared that

11 c'chappe souvent ties sons fi hi doulcur

Qui sout faux pour rorcille, mais vrais pour Ic ca'ur.

But certain it is that French music, to all but Frenchmen, Avas false to the ear, without being therefore just to the heart. Indeed, the constant burden both of l\ousseau and of Burney is that the French did not know what musical pathos meant. Rousseau especially informs us that the chief advantage of French music was that, according as it was sung quickly or slowly (and either suited it equally), it could be made cheerful or melancholy, thus saving much additional trouble ; and that the chief advantage of French, singing was that the performer could slacken or quicken a passage to suit the length of his arms, and the time which it consequently took to stretch them out and draw them in again. What, then, was this wonderful expressiveness of French music ? It was simply, to all appearance, an extraordinary amount of national musical obliquity, and a great deal of theatrical claptrap. A French opera, despite the utter absence of pathos, the horrible monotony of both the poetry and the music—for the first was a mere tissue of the most vapid gallantry and conceits, while the second was a mere succession of trivial, vulgar, and awkward tunes—a French opera was a far more dramatic performance than an Italian one; it was full of ranting and shuffling and screaming and roaring, full in short of all the refuse of tragic representation, of all that is sensational, melodramatic, and unartistic. If therefore French music did eventually give anything to Italian music, it certainly was not musical expression nor musical pathos, which Italian, and not French, music already possessed; it was a quality which could not improve, but only destroy, a work of art—it was the coarsely, falsely emotional. However, a union of the two schools, French and Italian, did eventually take place, to the great advantage of the former, but certainly not of the latter, as some critics would have us believe. But this amalgamation could take place only when both schools were growing feeble, and when the excellence of the Italian was diminishing no less than the execrableness of the French. In France the public was growing tired of shrieking and bellowing, and the romantic movement which began towards the end of the last century was bringing foreign art, as well as foreign literature, into vogue; in Italy, on the other hand, people were growing sick of good singing, and the French revolutionary wars were bringing the two nations into close contact, A third school, the German instrumental School, had meanwhile separated itself from the Italian, to which it Avas originally due, and served further to cement the Italian with the French music. Italian composers, Cherubini, Spontini, and Paer, settled in France, and their works, returning to Italy, diffused the remains of the French style in their country. It is from this moment of union that dates our modern music, born of the disconnected, convulsive, highly theatrical French school, as well as of the perfectly coherent, polished, and eminently musical Italian one. The two elements may easily be

trufcd; they are sometimes equally balanced, but oftener one of them ovenveiglis the other; and, altliongli vc have still got some pure melody ami SOUK' good singing, it is, ^ve fear, easier to recognise in our operas the frantic erics, shrieks, and whimperings; the noisy concerted i)ieces, and the vidgar scenic displays, which disgusted Gray in the works of Ilameau and Campra, than the touching situations, exquisite melodies, and highly i)olished and pathetic \'7d)erf(irmances, which delighted Rou-.>eau in the operas of Pergolesi and Jommelli.*

But this period of union was still far oft' in 1770, and Dr. Burnuy left Paris in unmingled disgust at what he had heard, and j(jurneyed towards Italy in delightful expectation of what he was going to hear. In the provinces music was of course still more abominable than in the capital, for there being no spontaneous musical life in the country, where not imported, it did not exist. At Lyons, however, he met at a cofi'ee-house with a family of which the father and sons played a violin quartet, while the daughters sang. None of the guests at the coflee-house ceased chattering and laughing during their performance, but Dr. Burney was delighted: he heard good music almost for the first time since entering France, and heard it from this family of poor Italian street musicians. It was like a sort of welcome to the country which was at that time the home of music; he accepted it gratefully, and hurried on towards Italy.

H(jw Dr. Buruey got across the Alps he does not tell us. In those days, when Alpine roads were unknown and Alpine scenery unnoticed, a journey of this sort was probably looked back upon as equally horrid and uninteresting, and unworthy, therefore, of being recorded. "We next find him safely arrived at Turin, and settled at the Hotel La Bonne Fannie, round whose rooms some twenty-five years later Xavier de Maistre made many a fantastic journey. And now let us try and place ourselves in the position of Burney, of this intelligent, cultivated, and enlightened traveller of the eighteenth century, on finding himself at length in Italy, the country of countries, towards which he had looked for years, and to visit which had been his dream, as it had been that of so many of his contemporaries. To the mind of an intelligent and cultivated man, Italy was not then what it is now. Its name did not suggest what it suggests to us; it was not the field for the exercise of those faculties which are exercised there in our day. There had been no Byron, no Sismondi, no Lady Morgan, no Iluskin; the generation of Goethe, of IMadame de Stuel, of Beckford, nay, even that of Ann liadclillc, had not as yet

* The Printer suggests that we are mistaken in spelling this composer's uame with two m's, and this certainly is not the usual spelling, The authority for the two w's in Joniniolli ami also fur the two m's in Picciniii (usually written ' riccini') is ISavcrio Mattel, an cmiueut Neapolitan critic, who was intimate with both composers, and who puts the two ;«'s even on Jommelli's epitaph.

appeared. There "was no such thing as aesthetic criticism, as scientific history, as romantic poetry; not even a trace of classical enthusiasm or of romantic awe. Antiquity Avas only just beginning to become a real existence; the Middle Ages were only vaguely supposed to have existed: and as to the Renaissance, it was not known that there had ever been one. Italy was already the great museum of Europe, but its contents had not yet been catalogued and labelled; no one knew what to look at or what to look for, and people ran about in it at random, either seeing the wrong things or nothing at all, or at best only what they themselves could discover in the vast confusion. In a few years, it is true, Goethe would come to revive antiquity in his mind by the help of scenery and buildings, customs, and manners, art and poetry; and Beckford would come and fill his strange fantastic brain with visions of splendour and weirdness, with gorgeous displays of nature and of art, and with fanciful suggestions of terror and mystery. But neither Goethe nor Beckford had yet arrived with romanticism in his company; and the traveller in Italy still belonged to the generation educated in the midst of philosophy and affectation, fed upon Pope and Voltaire, Boucher and Kneller ; poor in historical information, as in poetic fancy, and possessing only a very large fund of good sense and practical wisdom, with plenty of this attendant folly. He came to Italy without prejudices as without enthusiasm, to finish his education or to improve his mind. He was interested in antiques, as historical remains, without much æsthetical appreciation; associating Greek vases with coins of Roman Emperors and with mummy cases; not clearly understanding the difference between Athens and Rome; seeing Hadrians and Faustinas in gods and goddesses of Scopas and Praxiteles, and recognising Brutus and Virginia in bas-reliefs of athletes and amazons. He turned away from Giotto's Tower and Milan Cathedral as barbarous Gothic structures, but went into careful details of Palladio's and Sanso-vino's palaces. He venerated the names of Raphael, Titian, and Michel Angelo, of whose predecessors and minor contemporaries he was perfectly ignorant; but what delighted and entranced him were the fat, languishing sibyls, the dainty dapper angels, the muscular sprawling martyrs of the Bolognese school. The old Florentines and Venetians were certainly very correct draughtsmen and fine colourists, but the traveller of the eighteenth century was above such material merits; he wanted soul, and soul he found to his heart's content in the Caracci, Guido, and Guercino. But he did not go to Italy for mere art; he was too large-minded and universal for that. He examined the cultivation of the fields; he chipped off little bits of rock; he made inquiries respecting the construction of drains and the passing of laws. He investigated into family arrangements and historical legends; he tried to understand the nature of tiiose two strange, mysterious animals the tarantula and the cavaliere serrente;

in short, be took an interest in everytliing, peeped into everything, and judged most emphatically of all things. He did not consider Italy as a thing of the past, a remnant of antiquity, of the ^Middle Ages or of the lienaissance, but as a conntry like any other modern one ; and its inhabitants neither as degenerate descendants of the Romans nor as weird children of the Renaissance. He expected neither heroism nor enthusiasm, nor poisonings, nor bravo-hannted castles, but merely hnman beings very much like himself, only, of course, somewhat inferior to so splendid a type of humanity.

In all these characteristics Dr. Burney was a perfect representative of the educated traveller of the eighteenth century: he was never surprised, entranced, or horrified by anything he saw; he never imagined that he saw what there was not; he looked about bim coolly and complacently. He had, however, two distinguishing peculiarities. He was neither an ordinary stranger nor an ordinary traveller; he had known many Italians in England, mostly, it is true, of the musical sort, whom their countrymen not a little disparaged, although they seem to have given him a very favourable idea of the nation; and lie seems to have felt perfectly at home and at his ease in Italy, more so by far than he had done in France. In the second place, Burney had a distinct object in his journey: he had come on a sort of artistic mission, to collect materials for the work which was the darling object of his life. And this artistic mission was in itself quite different from most others, for Burney had come to Italy not to unite by dint of science and imagination broken limbs of marble into complete and perfect statues, to follow the outlines of frescoes fading away from mouldering walls and to seek for patches of colour under layers of decaying plaster; he had not come to reconstruct a past state of things nor to cherish its vestiges like relics ; he had come to hear music finer, as he believed, than that of any previous time ; to enjoy the fruits of an artistic civilisation while it was yet in its prime, to see a nation to whom music was at that time what sculpture had been to the Greeks and painting to the men of the Renaissance; he had come to deal not with a dead art but with one which, as he says, " still lived."

And he came neither as an ignoramus nor as a student: he had heard Handel's oratorios when Handel himself was at the organ, and Gluck's operas when Gluck himself directed them at the harpsichord; he had heard all the best works of Pergolesi, of Jommelli, of Galuppi, sung by the singers whom the masters themselves had taught, and from whom the masters themselves might have learnt the living musical art; he bad enjoyed all the best of what Italy could give and his object now was to inquire how Italy had been able to give it: he had known Italian music abroad; he wished to know it in its home.

But when Dr. Burney descended into Italy it was the middle of July,

G

the time when the old cities doze the whole long day, when the nobility have gone to tliciv viHas, and the rich burghers run to and fro between their shops and their farms; when the small townsfolk stay sleepily at home, or loiter yawning about barbers' shops and lemonade booths ; when everything is lazy and desultory. At this time no great music was to be heard: the great theatres were shut, the great singers were abroad, the ecclesiastical and secular great folk were far too drowsy to encourage art; the only music to be heard was in the churches during their more ordinary services, in the small popular theatres, in the streets, and in some private family here and there; music which the Italians despised, as their ordinary, every-day, cheap artistic food, but of which Dr. Burney never failed to hear every note, finding it, indeed, delightful and exquisite after what he had heard in France. Music therefore he heard every morning and every evening; in the morning in church, in the evening at the theatre, as he journeyed leisurely through the great drowsy plain of Lombardy. In some one of the churches, thanks to the multitudes of obliging small saints, something could always be heard, and Dr. Burney was so indefatigable and insatiable that even when only passing through a town he would run off, while his horses were being changed and his dinner being cooked, and hear all the monks, nuns, or choristers that could possibly be heard; and when staying in any larger place he would miss no church performance, although dusty scores and illuminated missals awaited him in the public archives; for Dr. Burney, unknow'n perhaps to himself, always cared much more for the music of the present than for that of the past.

In these churches he tells us he never met " much good company," the good company hearing mass in their private chapels (when indeed they had not sent their chaplain to run errands) or in the smart Jesuit churches, where the service was conveniently short, and all the cavalieri serventi stood holding their ladies' mass-book, smelling-bottle, fan, or lap-dog, according to the devotional habits of the day. At the churches to which Dr. Burney went there were only small shop-folk, peasants and artisans, hanging about, staring at their neighbours, saying their prayers, listening to the music for a few minutes, and then walking out; a rather disrespectful manner of receiving the Church's cheap musical gifts; yet even snch listening, repeated constantly, could do more to form people's musical taste than the most strained attention at an opera. The shop-keepers, artisans and peasants, while dawdling carelessly about, imbibed music unconsciously; they became critics, and occasionally one of their sons or nephews, instead of turning shopman or farmer, would turn composer or performer; and indeed nearly all the great

Italian musicians belonged to the humbler, often to the humblest, classes of society. This daily 'church music was usually mediocre in performance; good singers and instrumentalists could gahi far too high remuneration elsewhere to become

attaclied to a churcli, yet every now aiul then Bnnicy Avoukl moot a little choristor destined to become famous or a nun singing like the most refined jn-ima donna. The nuns sang, and sang well; the monks \'7d)liiyed the organ, often grandly and scientihcally, and even in the smaller cliurt'hes the director was a loarnod musician. On the other liand, in the great churches and chapels splendid musical establishments were kept with first-rate performers; every ducal or grand-ducal chajiel possessed at least one great opera-singer; while the famous violinist Pugnani, the groat liautboy and bassoon])layers the brothers Besozzi, and innumerable others, played in the cliurches at Turin, Milan, and Padua. The Maestro (U Capella of a large church was always high in the profession: JommeTlij the greatest tragic composer of Italy, was chapel-master at St. Peter*s> Leo and Caffaro at Naples, Galuppi at Venice, and the famous instrumental composer Saumartini at Milan. Nor were their functions limited to merely directing the performances; they were required to produce several new works every year, and the great church archives of Italy contain numbers of unpublished masses, hymns, and psalms by the greatest composers of the eighteenth century. Besides the usual musical services in cathedrals, and parish and convent churches, there were occasional grand performances even at minor ones, to celebrate the feast of some patron saint or the consecration of some rich nun. Then all the greatest opera singers, the Caffariellos, Manzolis, and Guarduccis, mounted into the organ loft, and a tremendous concourse of people met to hear them; sometimes also, as we learn from Sir Horace Mann, a great musician would have a splendid service performed at his own expense, on recovering from a bad illness or accident.

The music performed in the churches was, as a rule, not very different from that performed in the theatres; for the fact is, that there never has existed such a thing as church music independent of the other branches of the art. There have been various styles of music, one belonging to each epoch, and which have been adapted, one after the other, to all the musical requirements of the time, the church, the theatre, or the room; but there has never been music used solely for the church or for the theatre or for the room. The style of the Roman school of th(! sixteenth century may possibly be more suitable for ecclesiastical pur^joses than any other, we do not deny it; but it is undeniable that this style was the only one then extant, and that Palestrina himself set jirofane madrigals to that very sort of music which is held up as the only sort fit for the church. The eighteenth century also had its style of music, which it used indiscriminately for all purposes, and which has been described as unsuitable to religions ceremonies. Possibly it was not so suitable to them as that of the Palestrina school, but this was no fault of the great masters of a hundred years ago. The art had progressed for two hundred

a 2

years since the days of Palestrina; to ask the composers of the eighteenth century for music such as those of the sixteenth could have given woiild be like complaining that Raphael did not paint like Giotto. They could not have spontaneously produced anything of the sort, and, as to cold imitation, they were incapable of it; for as long as there be a living art there can be no exhumation and galvanising into life of a dead one; so the eighteenth century knew of no Palestrinists, as the Renaissance knew of no pre-Raphaelites. Modern critics—not unlike those who never perceive that Giotto, their idol, was progressing, while they, his disciples, are merely retrograding—modern critics have found fault with the church music of the eighteenth century for not being as suitable to ecclesiastical purposes as that of the sixteenth century; but this fault of the church music of the last century, like the similar one attributed by kindred critics to the church painting of the Renaissance, merely signifies that it belongs to a fally developed and not to an immature art. The form has attained to perfection, the spirit to maturity; it has all the richness and strength of human nature; it is no longer timid and lowly, it is grand and divine; men, according to Goethe's expression, form the picture of the Divinity after their own highest model, as He had formed them in His own resemblance; art is no longer a symbol, it is a form, a thought, a feeling which acts independently and directly. The church music of the eighteenth century is profane, if you will; saints and angels are made to sing like opera heroes and heroines; but what the opera heroes and heroines sing is so pure, so lovely, so noble, that there remains nothing purer, lovelier, or nobler for the saints and angels. These great composers do not, like some later ones, own several styles, one for the gods and goddesses and the other for the Satyrs and Maenads: wherever their art is employed, for whatever purpose it is destined, it is equally noble, not because it is used to express the feelings of Scipio or of St. Eustace or of Harlequin, but because it is their art, which to them is a thing sacred. This being the case, the Italians of the eighteenth century, who set apart no special style for devotional purposes, gave church music all that they gave to all other music, all the richness of device which their art afforded. They preserved the massive choruses on which men like Lotti, Leo, and Durante lavished all their skill of counterpoint; they kept the solemn organ for which Scarlatti had written his grand fugues and on which every composer had learned to play; they kept all the best part of the old, unindividual, unemotional church music; but they added all their own creations, all the individual, emotional wealth of completely matured art; the choral performances were broken by psalms and verses in three or four single parts, performed by the most highly-trained singers, who displayed all their powers of execution and expression; by duets either fugued like the divinely-lovely ones of Pergolesi, or in the freer, more

emotional shape of the opera; by splendidly-moLlulated recitatives, crowned by an air, solemn, pathetic, or florid, sung by one of those great singers whose feeling gave a new soul and whoso fancy added a now splendour to even the most perfect piece. The eighteenth century added also its orchestra, its wind instruments lightly and soberly distributed among the graver stringed ones; and during the hushed moment, when any human voice, be it even that of a Guadagni or a Pacchierotti, would have sounded profane, Tartini or Giardini or Pugnani would take up his violin and break upon the silence of the church.

According to a bad but invincible tendency of which the reader may often liave to complain, we have taken the opportunity of discussing the church music of the eighteenth century in general, when there was no occasion to speak of any save the trifling performances which Dr. Burney attended; keeping our traveller waiting, standing in some dull little church listening to mediocre music; but, alas, we have not the power of introducing our reader into the smallest church, of letting him hear even the meanest performance of the eighteenth century. So, in default of this, we can give him the only thing criticism can give—not art itself, but only a disquisition on it.

As soon as the sun had fairly set and the cool breeze risen, the townsfolk would awake, and having opened shutters, pulled up blinds, and breathed the fresher evening air, they would begin to think of hearing a little music. A little music, nothing grand or tragic, oh, no ! no great singers who required tremendous applause; something simple, easy, and refreshing. So the men have exchanged dressing-gown for snuft- or puce-coloured light coat, and coloured handkerchief for well-combed little wig, and their wives and daughters having slipped on a tidy gown and a coquettish black veil, the population would slowly wend their way towards the comic theatres, pausing just a little to talk to acquaintances, and breathe the fresh air in the white, pearly twilight. In this state of quiet, languid enjoyment, the people would scarcely have given a thank-you for the autumn and winter music—music in her grand, splendid, delicately-w^orked Court dress, led about in state by prince-singers, who wore military orders and bought dukedoms; they wanted music, like themselves, in summer array, music in her most negligent, slovenly attire, wandering carelessly from town to town in company with third-rate singers, vagrant fiddlers, and motley columbines and pantaloons, and yet as graceful and charming, if not as stately and magnificent, as in the serious winter months.

All summer performances were therefore comic, and at small theatres, to which the admission cost a few pence, where people went in and out, made a terrific noise, and listened, and let others listen, only to as much or as little as they felt inclined, it was an amusement for the lower or at

most middle classes, and one which they held very cheap indeed. For, until quite late in the eighteenth century, the Italian comic opera was not only totally distinct from the serious one, but of much lower artistic standing, and its performers Avere a class wholly apart and decidedly inferior. A long comic opera like the Matrimonio Segreto or a semi-serious one like Don Giovanni was equally unknown; there were only short musical interludes of two or three characters, like Metastasio's \. Impresario of tlie Canary Islands or Pcrgolesi's Serva Padrona, intended to be sung between the acts of a spoken comedy; and short musical farces, with plenty of buffoonery and nonsense, like Galuppi's Arcifanfano King of Fools and Leonardo Leo's Cioe. The comic opera, or burletta, as it was called, was a very humble sister of the serious opera, and a near relative of the Italian comedy of masks; it got a share of the musical excellence of the first, and inherited a large portion of the ramshackle, popular buffoonery of the second. Where a singable dialect existed, the comic opera was most often written in it, and the President de Brosses took the trouble to learn Neapolitan in order to fully enjoy Pergolesi's burlettas ; and where the dialect was wholly unmusical the modes of speech of the lower classes were strictly adhered to ; for one reason of the success of the comic opera was its total opposition to the serious one: the more dignified and heroic became the ancient Greeks, Eomans, and Persians of the 02)era sei'ia, the more trivial and farcical became the shopkeepers, sailors, and peasants of the burletta. Baretti, in his book on the Italians, says that comic operas were most often coarse and even gross; and Dr. Burney adds that they were utterly childish and ridiculous ; but Baretti hated all things musical, and never lost an opportunity of throwing undue odium on them, while Burney was accustomed to regard the polished French comedy as the only proper one, and was wholly blind to the merits of the Italian national stage, so that the opinion of neither is very reliable ; and it is probable that the burlettas, although occasionally coarse, had no harm in them, and although fantastic and absurd were decidedly clever. IIoAvever they were strictly popular and lowly, for, although Goldoni wrote a few texts for them in his moments of pecuniary distress, no well-known poet worked regularly for them until the time of Casti, Da Ponte, and Sografi, when the comic opera, in the hands of Mozart, Cimarosa, and Paisiello, had already become the successful rival of the serious one. The performers were on a level with the text-writers; no first-rate singer, male or female, ever deigned to sing in a burletta until quite late in the century; the performers who had been carefully trained ever since their childhood were reserved for the serious opera, more lucrative, more fashionable, more purely musical, where they might stand as rigid as statues and as stupid as babies, providing they could swell and diminish, shake and run rapid divisions, and make long, intricate

extemporary embellishments; they •would have nothing to do with the comic opera, and the comic opera would have nothing to do with them. Occasionally indeed the second man or second woman of the serious opera (in which no one listened to them) would play the serious parts, the two insignificant lovers, in the bnrletta; or a young raw performer would begin his career on the comic stage before attempting the serious one; but such irregular singers were not those on whom the success of the burletta depended. The real burletta performers were men and women of talent, but whom want of voice, want of training, want of ambition, or want of respectability, had wholly excluded from the higher walks of the profession. There were fine voices with insufficient cultivation, and good singers with insufficient voice; but there were likewise brilliant actors, delightfully cheery scapegraces, exquisitely coquettish waiting-maids, magnificently blustering tutors; there was an overflow of life and good humour. Tlie public did not go into raptures and ecstasies about their comic singers as they did about their serious ones, but they liked them and applauded them as jovial friends, and the singers were grateful; they did not sulk when there were no kings or princes or senators to applaud them, they did their best to amuse shopkeepers and vagabonds; they did not show off wonderful rifwrituras and feats of execution, but they improvised a witty answer here, or a comical situation there; parodying, pasquinading, always entering into the fun of the tiling, like that hiifo whom Dr. Burney saw at JMilan, falling on the prompter and thrashing him in default of the actor who played his prodigal son, to the great joy of the whole audience. Many, however, of these inferior singers would have seemed excellent, but for the comparison with the great performers of the serious opera, and Bmney met many who would have pleased on a higher stage, even the worst being better than the best that could be heard in France. The music, on the other hand, was never mediocre, for the great composers of Italy wei'e never so overburdened with money or so sated with applause as to disdain obtaining it by humbler means: the Pergolesis, Leos, Galuppis, and Piccinnis, who were cither positively starving or living in the most modest style, and who had no absurd artistic dignity like their overpaid, swaggering singers, wrote willingly for the comic opera and wrote their best. Nor did they adopt a ditferent style froni that they otherwise employed; for the Italian composers of the eighteenth century, like the Italian painters of the Eenaissance, had only one style, spontaneous and perfect, which, according to the time and the individual, was only more m- less grand, or tender, or gay. The comic opera did not exist in the earliest part of the century,* because the umsic of that time

* Gokloni, Memorie, chap. 35, says, " The comic opera originated in Naples and in Rome, but it Avas still unknown in Lombardy and the Venetian States abont 1735.

was too uniformly grand and solemn; it began to develop only when musical forms became softer and more flexible, and it reached its highest point when they had become so light, graceful, and unheroic as to be positively unsuitable to solemn subjects. But the style of the masters of the last century, which was too spontaneous, too free, too perfect, to be distorted either into the thoroughly tragic or the absolutely trivial, could yet be adapted with more or less success to tragedy or comedy, though always, of course, suiting the one better than the other. The introduction or omission of certain passages, the arrangement of the accompaniment, the choice of the rhythm, of pace and of voice, would alter the style sufficiently, yet without changing its radical nature: Pergolesi was accused of having used the same tune in a piece of his Stabat Mater and in an air of his Serva Padrona, but the melody had been so adapted to each situation that no one would have complained of unsuitableness had it been heard in only one of the two. So much indeed was done by the choice of melodies, of accompaniments and voices, and by the different structure of the whole play, that not only did the comic opera differ totally from the serious one, despite the similarity of the general style, but a complete revolution in musical arrangements gradually developed in the former, which finally upset the latter. For, in the first place, popular melodies, taken from the peasantry, were constantly being introduced into the bur-letta, and thence influenced even serious music, which little by little grew lighter, brighter, brisker, less grand, massive, and studied; the accompaniments at the same time growing more dependent on rhythm and less on counterjDoint, and the more popular and less cultivated wind instruments being introduced one by one into an orchestra which had mainly consisted of strings. Add to this that in the burletta the contralto voice, so dear to the serious composers, especially in men's parts, was completely escliewed, that the principal male part was reserved solely for the tenor, while the bass voice, which in the serious opera was given over to messengers, confidants, and other small folk, appeared, and perhaps to its greatest advantage, in the very effective parts of blustering old tutors and blundering valets. Nor was this all; the comic situations could ill be expressed in the grandly-modulated solemn recitative of the serious opera; they required constant movement and hubbub, and thence the introduction of finales and other concerted pieces where five, six, or seven persons scream and shout and stomi at each other; pieces which the delicate, pathetic situations of the heroic opera excluded, and which, moreover, the despotic serious singers, who had not spent years in constant practice to let themselves be drowned by screaming women and bellowing basses, would never have permitted. Thus there came to exist, not a different style of composition, but a different system of arrangements, in the comic opera; and when the comic opera had risen to the

level of its rival in the hands of Paisiello, Gnglielnii, and Cimarosa; when it possessed first-rate singers, like the charming Coltdlini, the magnificently-comic Casacciello, and the delightful tenor Mandini; when Joseph II. kept comic poets and a comic company instead of serious ones ; then the old arrangements of the opera seria had to give way; contraltos had to be abandoned for brisker voices, tenors were shoved up into important parts, and basses removed out of subordinate ones; recitatives were slashed into, and Curiatius and Pyrrhus, Horatia and Penelope, had to join in thundering concerted pieces, just as the undignified harlequins and columbines of the bur left a had done before. The old opera seria was fused with the old burletta, and, this being done, both expired, leaving a joint product—the modern melodramatic opera.

In 1770 the poor humble little burletta was still far from such triumph: but it was, perhaps, all the purer in its nature, all the more popular, simple, and amusing. Its singers had not yet learned to make rijiorituras like the serious ones; its poets had not yet felt the necessity of introducing deserted, ladies, punished libertines, heart-breakings, murders, and pathos. All was as yet simple, natural, buffoonish, cheap, and jolly. The Abate Metastasio, Imperial opera poet, might smile with contempt at the plays; the virtuosi m peagreen satin and lilac and gold lace might turn up their languishing eyes in horror at the singers; the small shopkeepers and street folk might still shake with laughter on their wooden benches, while the President de Brosses, liousseau, and Burney, could still join in their hearty delight at the bright, elegant music, the droll situations, the easy, off-hand singing, and the inexhaustible humour of the old burletta.

Stepping out of the little cheap theatre. Dr. Burney found music again in the streets—the streets, which, after all, are the pleasantest place in the heavy drowsy summer evenings, when the people loiter about in little knots of threes and fours under the clear blue sky, as clear and as blue, though in so strangely different a way, as at midday. There were bands of artisans, apprentices, shop-boys, marching down the street arm-in-arm, singing, led by a fellow playing the guitar or the mandolin ; and sere-naders coming with flutes and fiddles under windows, which would occasionally open to reward them with a dash of water; and all sorts of similar non-professional music, received by the population sometimes as a favour / \ sometimes as a nuisance. Besides this, in the spacious squares where ' people sat drinking lemonade and coft'ee, where perambulating booths displayed their wares under the flickering torchlight, whore the puppet-show stood surrounded by a ring of eager spectators, there, of course, in the great outdoor saloon of the town, there was music again in plenty— music which the public paid for, feeling that even the humblest professional music is, ceteris panbus, better than that of amateurs. There

were whole families, like the one Biirney met at Lyons, who wandered about, singing and playing in concert, and these perambulating musicians were most often Venetians. They played and sang well, and occasionally a voice might be heard amongst the tables of the coffee-houses which was destined to the utmost vocal glory, like that of the poor untaught girl who was later to be called Banti, the most pathetic female singer of the latter part of the eighteenth century. Bologna possessed in Burney's day a quartet of vagrant blind nmsicians, called the " Bravi Orbi," whom many Italian composers warmly admired, the great and masterly Jommelli always sending for them to])\^y for him. What these people played we are not told; probably favourite opera airs, with just a dash of more popular music. At all events, it was not to them that belonged the really popular songs, for these were the property of the wholly untrained lower classes, workmen, boatmen, fishermen, and peasants, and it was from these that composers like Paisiello learned the rustic, truly pastoral style of some of his pieces; while the vagrant musicians, on the contrary, served to diffuse among the people the more refined and polished styles of composition.

After loitering about a little in the coffee-houses, Dr. Burney would go and end his evening at an accademia, or dilettante concert, in some private house, with Avhose owners he was of course totally unacquainted, but to which he was taken by some musical busybody, whose acquaintance he had made the previous day, and who now treated him as a brother; perhaps some long, meagre ecclesiastic, with immense spectacles on a nose which looked like a pick-axe, wherewith to hew into the depths of musical science; or by some jovial lawyer, who always found time to devote to the Muses, especially when pretty, and who would talk himself purple in favour of this or that composer; or again by a music-master—some still obscure young composer, or some ancient singer who had not provided for his old days—a music-master bound to accompany his pupils on grand occasions, and thankful for the scanty refreshment offered him. By some such individual Dr. Burney would be introduced into the trim little parlour as a distinguished foreigner, a man of universal knowledge, as a glory to England, and an honour to Italy, &c. The company would rise and look with awe at the stranger (perhaps a Milordo —who knows?— are not the English the most eccentric of beings?), the hostess would meet him, curtsey, and express how much her house was honoured, and then the dilettanti would sit down to their instruments, their silken coat-tails neatly disposed on either side of their chair, their well-starched ruffles carefully drawn out; the ladies would rise, smooth out their dresses and aprons, unroll their scores, and the performance would begin, interrupted oidy by a few solemn pauses, during which candles were snuffed, violins tuned, bows resined, and snuff-boxes passed round.

They took things solemnly, these good people, because a hundred years ago musical amateurs were rarer than now, and to be one involved much more responsibility. For among the Italians of the eighteenth century music was at once both more common and more prized than among us; it was a necessity to the greater part of the nation, but it was an art, a]irofession, rather than an amusement or an accomplishniont. All young ladies Avere not taught music; not, as Baretti most falsely and preposterously pretended, because the morals of professional musicians were too slack, but because people had not yet conceived the modern notion of culture, which most often consists merely in giving slovenly cultivation to endowments which deserve no cultivation at all. But where real musical talent existed it was usually made the most of; and it must be remembered that the study of music was at that time far more arduous than in these happy days of classes, piano arrangements, manuals of harmony, and other royal roads to mediocrity. The musical education of professionals, the seven ur eight years spent in learning to sing by men who were to be mere composers; the two or three years spent in learning-composition by those who were to be mere performers; the inexorably complete system according to which one branch of the art could not be mastered without a knowledge of the others; all this reacted on the education of the non-professional musicians: the music which people heard was too good to permit them to endure music that was bad ; the masters were too thoroughly trained to submit to slovenly pupils. Moreover, all was more difficult in itself. Amateurs had not the benefit of pianoforte arrangements; they had to read the full orchestral scores of theatrical music and the figured or absolutely dry basses of church and chamber music; they, like all others, had to learn the difficult science and art of accompaniment which required not only knowledge but natural facility. There were no easy drawing-room fantasies, ballads, or duets ; there were only sonatas, harpsichord lessons, string quartets, cantatas composed of recitative and air, canzonets as difficult in their simplicity as the cantatas were in their complication, canons and madrigals for several voices. There were violins, viols, hautboys, bassoons, violoncellos, harpsichords, but no pianofortes, and that fact alone means a great deal. An instrument very much resembling the modern pianoforte, as distinguished from the harpsichord, clavichord, virginal, and others of the same genus, having been invented by Cristofori, of Florence, at the beginning of the last century, the non-existence of the pianoj'orte as a class (for individual instruments could be found here and there, Farinelli and Count Torre Taxis appearing to have had them according to Burney) means not only that the musical education of that day was free from the influence which the pianoforte necessarily exerts, but that there were circumstances which prevented the instrument from becoming

as common as it lias since. The liarpsicliord, altliongli externally like the piano, was in reality a very different thing, for its quill mechanism, the absence of pedals, and its sharp metallic sound, placed it rather in the category of stringed instruments. Now, viewed as a stringed instrument, the harpsichord had little to recommend it ; its tone was not strong, not peculiarly fine, and extremely monotonous, and the consequence was that people often preferred to it the violin trilie, which was more capable of effect ; and that the harpsichord sank ratlier towards the level of a mere accompaniment. And even when cultivated for itself it had to be cultivated in a totally different manner from the pianoforte; it was too uniform and feeble in tone, and too sharp and unsustained, to permit cither of emotional performance or of that hurricane and lullaby alternation so dear to modern pianists. You could not play a study of light and shade, nor a moonlight fantasia, nor a rhapsody on it, even had such pretentious \'7d)ioces of inanity existed in those days ; you could play a fugue, a gigue, a brilliant scherzo, or an intricate lesson, like those of Handel and Scarlatti, and play them neatly, clearly, firmly, roundly, with a spring and an expression of intelligence and cheerfulness, but that was all you could do on a harpsichord ; and Handel and Scarlatti understood this fact, and turned it to account, as genius turns everything to account. But the violin, the violoncello, the organ, could do much more and better: they could be brilliant or pathetic or grand, and the voice could be all three together ; so the harpsichord was comparatively little esteemed. People regarded it as a respectable instrument, and most great masters, like Porpora, Jommelli, and Pergolesi, wrote a few good pieces for it, but rarely did a composer, like Domenico Scarlatti and Alberti of Venice, devote himself almost exclusively to it, until it turned into the pianoforte and gained a new character, or rather borrowed that of other stringed instruments in the days of Haydn, Clementi, and Mozart. The Italians cared little for harpsichords, and made them badly, so badly that we have been told that when, at the beginning of this century, Clementi returned to Rome, he could barely find an adequate instrument. They niade them feeble and metallic, such as singers and violinists and opera conductors wished them to be ; small, thin, ungainly things, on slender little legs with black keys instead of white, and vice versa, such as you still occasionally meet, faded, yellow, with only a few jangling, melancholy notes left, in old houses where they have not been touched for a century. As to people who went in for execution, tliey might get their harpsichords from England, Germany, or Holland, from Eucker or Droadwood. An instrument like our pianoforte, with a loud, thick, niuffly tone, on which you could execute with considerable disadvantage the music written for other instruments, besides the sentimental and thundering imbecility written expressly for it; with sufficient power of expression to supersede other

instruments, and with power of mecyianical dexterity unlimited enough to ruin itself— such an instrument, such a compromise, could not have existed in the ei,i;litoenth century; and could not therefore usurp all musical])rivilc,s'es, make people lose all notion of adaptation of sound and style, accustom them to unlimited noise and to dubious tune, and foster that wholesale ignorance of music in general which is inevitable where a performer need aim only at mechanical dexterity; arranged pieces, pedals, and tuners, having relieved him from the necessity of learning harmony, of studying expression by means of the voice, and of obtaining a correct ear by tuning his own instrument; where, above all, everything having been done for him by others, he has been educated to total want of individual endeavour.

The dilettanti, therefore, of the last century, were more tliorough musicians than are most of ours, besides having had the advantage of learning, not from teachers who are mere performers who have failed, but very often from first rate composers, Leo, Porpora, Jommelli, Galuppi, who did not disdain by any means to give private lessons. The pupils were usually worthy of their masters, and Dr. Barney heard excellent performers, vocal and instrumental, at the private concerts he attended at Milan, Venice, and Rome, in the dull, bare parlours of the upper middle classes, and in the gm-geously stuccoed and gilded saloons of the aristocracy; for in that day music belonged equally to all classes, being a fruit not of special culture but of general civilisation. Round these dilettanti performers, whether dressed in broad cloth or in embroidered satin, was congregated the far larger class of merely appreciative amateurs, who ^ neither sang nor played, nor composed, but for whose benefit singers, violinists, and composers were produced. Some of these were of the oracular sort, others of the disputative, others of the ecstatic. The oracular ones were old gentlemen, senators, monsignori, lawyers, and doctors, who gave advice to young musicians; and, as the singer Mancini tells us, taught well-endowed but slightly-rigid sopranos and tenors how to move their arms and legs gracefully and expressively, and how (as the malicious Marcello adds) to take snuff and blow their nose without impeding the dramatic action: the disputative were younger men, men of fashion and wit, who discussed musical merit under the hands of their hairdresser, like Parini's young gentlemen, wrote indecorous sonnets against admirers of rival musicians, and occasionally waylaid and thrashed them with sedan-chair sticks; the ecstatics, on the other hand, were mainly ladies, or effeminate cavalieri serventi, descendants, and worthy ones, of those noble dilettanti who sallied out a whole mile outside the town of Bologna to meet the singer Baldassare Ferri, and heaped his carriage with roses, somewhere about the year 1650. In the soberer eighteenth century, when great singers became more plentiful, the ecstatics remainetl

at home, but were none the less ecstatic, the ladies wearing])ortraits of great performers, fainting, like Beckford's Padnan lady, from musical rapture; in short, sliowing their love of music in a hundred absurd fashions, at which satirists either shook their heads like Parini or Gozzi, or laughed like Passeroni and Marcello ; and foreigners looked amazed, and remarked that the Italians had become a nation of children.

It was through such disputative and ecstatic dilettanti that music so thoroughly permeated the life of tlie upper classes ; that, even where it Avas not genuinely enjoyed, it was required as part of fashionable life, and good taste in art became a sort of accompaniment to good taste in dress and deportment. But, as the circles on the water grow fainter as they grow wider, so this general dilettantcism, by which musical culture was extended to the utmost, to even the unmusical, was necessarily comparatively sterile and uninfluential; the really influential dilettanti were of course the active ones, those Avho approximated nearest to the professional musicians. Among these many appear to have possessed much talent and learning, both for the theoretical and the practical parts of the art; and the Italians of the eighteenth century owed two of the best, and one of the very best, of their composers, Domenico Alberti and Emanuele d'Astorga, and the great Benedetto Marcello, to the class of aristocratic amateurs.

II.

Thus Dr. Burney proceeded leisurely through the great plain of Lom-bardy, from Turin to Milan, from Milan to Bergamo, thence to Brescia, Verona, and Vicenza, seeing and hearing everyone and everything ; active, wideawake, observing and criticising; making extracts from dusty books and MSS. on the music of other days; taking down notes on music and musicians of the present. Ah! if only we could obtain a sight of those notebooks in which Dr. Burney kept his journal, of those letters in wliich he told his friends at home of all his doings: those original sketches, taken from true life, and of which the printed work is but the curtailed, polished, enfeebled copy! As we turn over this cold, civil, pseudo-diary, trimmed and clipped so as to give offence to no one, we feel instinctively how much we have lost—what droll anecdotes, what racy adjectives, Avhat humorous descriptions, have fallen victims to the doctor's prudent scissors. In looking up at Buruey's portrait, by Reynolds, we can fancy the ineffable suppressed smile with which this sharp, shrewd, caustic little man, with almost as much rapid perception of the ludicrous as his daughter and perhaps more kindliness of nature, must have sauntered through the Italian musical world of the eighteenth century—a world which, while it

The Musical Life. !)'>

]irnflnpod mnstorpicccs of art cqiial to those of a Phidias, a Raphael, or 11 Miltnii, also produced living figures and eombiiiations of figures worthy of Sterne, or Hogartli, or Hoftnumn—of that Hoffmann ^vho even from far away caught strange glimpses of it, ■which lie handed down to ns in those fantastic stories of beautiful singers, crabbed Kapellmeisters, and nielo-maniacs dressed in coats the colour of A sharp minor. What a series of whimsical silliouettes, of delicately touched caricatures, Dr. Burney might have given us; how he might have shown us all the droll and touching realities of those musicians whom we see only with composed mien and holiday dresses in the])ortrait gallery of the Bolognese Academicians— composers, singers, tiddlers, and dilettanti, in dapper silk and plush and well-powdered wigs, solemn and dignified as if, while they belonged as artists to the unchangeable, eternal Avorld of the grand and lovely ideal, they had not also belonged as men to the ephemeral world of quaint and ludicrous reality, the world of academic pedants, of dandy nobles, of cavalieri serventi, and of harlequin actors; the Avorld of Goldoni and Gozzi, and of Marcello's Teatro di Musica alia Moda.

Throughout Lombardy Dr. Burney had heard only the music which formed the ordinary every-day artistic food of the people; not Avhat they])rized and took trouble to produce, but what they got easily and scarcely noticed, and which was thereby almost more important to the critic. But, if the art which is in common use be good, that reserved for special occasions must needs be excellent; and such art, carefiilly obtained and kept up, not by the lower and middle but by the rich and cultivated classes, nay, by the governing oligarchy. Dr. Burney first met at Padua, the terra firma suburb of Venice. In this c^uiet, straggling town of reedy canals, silent gardens, and faded villas, the Venetians held their great annual fair of St. Antliony, or the Santo as he was styled; when the vast oval space of the Prato della Valle was turned into a little town of booths; where merchants from the East, from Germany, and from Poland, brought their costliest wares, in almost mediaeval fashion, and all the wealth and luxury that still remained in Venice came riotously across to the melancholy old town. Then, as at the other great fairs of Roggio and Lodi, there were new operas performed by the finest singers—as Gray explained to his friend West, who associated only giantesses and gingerbread with the word fair, and could not comprehend this great annual market, where the Republic sold what yet remained of its commercial and artistic products. For these performances of the fair of St. Anthony all who came had of course to pay; but the Republic had its own permanent music at Padua. It spent large sums on the musical establishment of its great, half Gothic, half Byzantine basilica of St. Anthony; it kept up a large band, composed of first-rate performers, and for only four annual performances it gave 400 ducats and the cn^ss of St. Mark, the only decoration the

State possessed, and Avitli which it was wont to reward Ambassadors and Proccuratori, to Signor Gactano Guadagni, one of the finest singers, and the handsomest and most brilliant actor, in Italy, the favourite pupil of Garrick, the famous original Orpheus of Gluck. Guadagni was in no wise tied down by this liberality, and belonged, in the intervals of the i'uur performances, to the rest of the world quite as much as to St. Anthony's; but Padua was the sole possessor, and almost the shrine, of a greater and more famous musician than he. Tartini lived there during well-nigh half-a-century, playing regularly at the Santo, and when Burney arrived there, a few months after his death, the silent city was full of the fame of ,the great violinist, whose dark, puzzled genius and fantastic story fitted well into the framework of the strange medifeval town. Tartini, who was born in Istria at the end of the seventeenth century, and had sj^ent an adventurous youth, had passed the remainder of his long life in quiet artistic routine; composing, playing, teaching, meditating over his art, and writing, surrounded by devoted pupils, and tormented by an insufferably ill-tempered wife ; but in this uneventful existence there was one little speck of romance which shed weird lights over all the rest. Early in the century Tartini had received a visit from the Devil, and had heard the Fiend play the violin more beautifully than even he himself had ever played. Whether Tartini was dreaming or awake during this visit is a matter of small importance, and certain it is that the demon's performance left a deep impression on this whimsical-minded, Petrarch-reading violinist—an impression of weirdness which can be seen not only in his fantastically-beautiful works but in his haggard face, with intense, wildly-staring eyes, as it is portrayed in the gallery of the Philharmonic Academicians of Bologna.

The reputation of Tartini and his career were equally different in nature from that of the great vocal performers of his day, and would have been so even had he not been a very eminent composer and writer on musical science as well as a mere violinist, for the Italians of the eighteenth century placed vocal and instrumental performers on a totally separate, though not necessarily nnequal, footing. Tartini may have had greater talents than, say, Farinelli, and a fame not very much inferior to his; but he could never have had his career, for the greatest, nay, merely the great, singers of the last century exercised a sort of magic which even the greatest performer on the most perfect of human-made instruments never possessed. The singer, besides the immense individual influence due to his being at once the performer and the instrument, had a much larger and more universal audience than the violinist; the first was heard on every great theatre, and by every class of society, while the second was rarely heard out of the room, and that room not a concert-room. For the concert, in our sense of the word, was not an institution of the eighteenth

century, it least not in Italy; music was too spontaneous, too universal, to be conined in any stated place more limited than the theatre or the church; it was not an exotic enjoyment for cultivated gentlefolk, it was a nat.)nal necessity, a necessity as much to the petty artisan, the gondolier, the lazzarone, as to the great lady, the senator, and the prelate; and when uusic was inclosed within the limits of a room it was not because it vas too rare and fine for ordinary use but because it was so common, sc all-pervading, as to become indispensable in private life. The instrumental performer, therefore, who, after a certain eminence had been attained, wculd probably not condescend to jilay in a theatre orchestra, could be hei'.rd by all the world only in the organ-loft of a church, and, if he rejected that, he must be satisfied with playing in private houses and gaining his n-ead by teaching. Thus most of the great instrumental performers became fixtures, tied down to some churcli or chapel, like Tartini to the Santo of Padua; Pugnani and the two Besozzis to the royal chapel at Turin ; only now and then venturing abroad, where chamber music was an exotic, like Giardini in England, or taking service with some royal personage, as Domenico Scarlatti and Boccherini did in Spain. The great violinist, or hautboy or bassoon player, could thus gain only a limited income—Tartini securing 400 ducats for yearly attendance while Guadagni got as much for only four performances—and only an inferior reputation; for, although uilettanti might flock to Padua to hear Tartini, he was never heard or heard of by the thousands of people who might applaud a singer. The life of a musician of this sort was therefore modest, quiet, without the tumultuous opulence of the singer; where he went he was received with respect and list med to with the deepest admiration; but he was not petted by people of fasiiion, idolised by great ladies, and permitted to swagger, bully, and pout Ijike his vocal rival; his life was less brilliant, but perhaps more worthy of jrespect, and occupied in the patient, humble study of his art. '

In a period wf^en music was a natural product, a thing for tlie whole people and only Isecondarily for the individual, that branch of it which essentially belonged to the house naturally followed the progress and adopted the style! of the more universal one belonging to the theatre and the church. As, in the great days of Greek art, the carvings on cameos and seal-rings were ejoecuted in the same grand style as the colossal statues on the fronts of tevmples, so instrumental music was dependent on vocal music, developing Us it developed, and following its changes of style; but, just as the Greelw ptists understood that a small shell or onyx requires a different treat ^nt of details« from that required by a huge block of marble, so the Ital«ans of the eighteenth century also understood that a violin, a violoncello, or a Avind-instrument, must be treated differently from the human voice, an d in accordance with its peculiar tone and volume, and

H

with the nature of the Iniilcling- in whicli it is to be heard. Th« instrumental styh^ was therefore an adaptation of the vocal, within flie strict limits of each particular instrument: no one wrote for the harpsic lord what might equally well have been written for the violin, the violoncello, or the voice, yet the general style had been learned from vocal composition, just as the education of every instrumental performer had begun with learning to sing; nay, if we examine the sonatas even of Haydn, we carnot fail to see how much the most purely instrumental of German composers had learned from Porpora, the greatest singing-master of the eighteenth century.

Burney had come too late to hear Tartini, but, with an artistic piety by no means common in those uncultured days, he went to see his house, and the organ-loft at the Santo in which he was wont to play, and collected eveiy possible relic of his compositions. Having done so, Le embarked m one of the barges, crowded with people returning from the -illeggiatura, and loaded with vegetables and fruit, which, having slowly carried him along between the reed- and willow-grown banks of the Brenta, drifted him across the lagcon, and landed him at Venice on the 4th of August, 1770.

And now Dr. Burney found himself for the first time in a musical centre, where the art was not only a cheap amusement of the people, but a splendidly managed State concern and an enthusiastically cultivated occupation of the upper classes. The street music soon tf^ught him the superiority of Venice over the cities of the mainland : there were guitars, mandolins, fiddles, and voices in the two squares of St. Mirk, among the coffee-house tables and the story-tellers, and their music ^ivas better than any street music elsewhere; there were the gondoliers chanting Tasso, and by night barges full of musicians, like the one on which Goldoni and his merry companions had mounted, fiddling and singing, up the Po towards Pavia; there were serenades on the canals, which to Burney sounded exquisite, and music issuing from the windows of the palace(s; the now silent city of winding canals and fantastic lace-like architecturfi was still full of music, music destined to cease with the destruction of tlae fast crumbling State. Then there was music in numberless churches, from the archaic chants of the Greeks and Armenians to the florid rondoS: and sonatas of the Redentore ajid the Gesuati. Dr. Burney went to SS.: Giovanni e Paolo one morning that the Doge and Council were attending^ mass, and heard the music of the Venetian State, as carefully guarded from corruption and as singular in character as that of the Sovereign Ponti I. The Commonwealth kept its own chapel of St. Mark's, where themusi.chad been directed by a series of the most eminent national composers. ' The compositions performed at St. Mark's on State occasions, and Uhose sung on the Bucentaur when the Doge wedded the sea, all belongcci to the Venetian

school of the end of the seventeenth and beginning of the eighteenth centuries, at the head of wliitti uas the famous Antonio Lotti: madrigals and fugued pieces, elaborate and stately, either wholly without instruments, or accompanied merely by the organ, nnimpassioned and solemn, suitable to the dignity of a great oligarchic State—of Venice, not perhaps as she really was, with her corrupt nobles, spying police, and effete commerce, but as she continued to exist in the imagination even of her own degenerate sons, strong, placid, and venerable beyond all others. And Dr. Buruey, who had heard music enough to make him rather insensible to any save its purely artistic qualities, seems to have received an unaccustomed impression from these performances, and confesses that, he knew not well how or wh)--, they affected him even to tears.

Dr. Burney next proceeded to visit the music schools for girls for which Venice was famous: the Pieta, the Mendicanti, the Incurabili^ and the Ospedaletto. As their names imply, these institutions were originally and really nothing but hospitals and workhouses ; but as the girls educated in them were taught music, and the best teachers were given them, the four conservatori (literally asylums) had gradually become engrossed hy musical interests, until at length girls neither orphans nor beggars were admitted, merely because they showed disposition for the art. Although the public heard of them only as musicians, these girls were being thoroughly educated without any view to making music their profession; as long as they remained in the conseri-atorio, they were permitted to sing nowhere else; comparatively few took to the stage, and the greater part were dowered by the State and married; those who did not, remaining and growing old and amazonian, as Beckford tell us, at their double-basses, French horns, and kettle-drums. Nor did this singular system cost much, for the older girls taught the younger ones, the choruses being stuched under tlie guidance of the foremost pupils, so that the State had to provide only the masters to compose, direct grand performances, and finish the best pupils. But in the matter of masters the Serene Republic was incomparably generous, accepting only the most eminent composers, so that in the course of the eighteenth century the four schools were respectively directed by Porpora,* Domenico Scarlatti, Hasse,f and Jommclli, who taught, directed, and composed for the girls, from the simplest exercises up to the grandest oratorios and the most elaborate masses. And the performers were worthy of their teachers : all the writers on music of the

* The Venetian music-schools of the last century are now rcineniliereil chiefly by the readers of George Sand's great novel, as (/onsuelo is made a pupil of Porpora at the Mimdicanti.

t Niccolo Porpora, born at Naples in ICST, died in 17G7. Domenico Scarlatti, bora iu 1()83, died iu 1757. Adolfo Hasse, born in Saxony about 1700, died in 178:5. Niccolo Jommclli, born in 171-1, died in 1778.

eighteentli century speak with enthusiasm of the performances of these girls, of their voices, of their excellent performance, choral ami instrumental perfection, and of the singular effect produced by the sight of an orchestra entirely composed of women, Avho played in a masterly manner the most difficult solos and the most complicated symphonies. Lady Mary Wortley Montagu, no particular friend to music, speaks with astonishment of the concerts given in these hospitals, where she says she heard finer voices and better singers than the Faustina and the Cuzzoni, who then surpassed all other singers. The President de Brosses and Rousseau soon after mention them with equal enthusiasm ; Beckford, who was a great musician himself, was entranced by what he heard in 1780 ; while Goethe, in 1787, seems to have received a grander impression from these girls' performance than from any music he had previously heard; in short, the fonr charity schools of Venice were one of the musical wonders of the eighteenth century. Of all writers on the subject, Dr. Burney is, however, the most detailed, and at the same time the most enthusiastic. At the j^eriod of Burney's visit to Venice, the two best of the schools, whose respective merit oscillated according to the eminence of the teachers, were the Incurahili and the Ospedaletto, while the Pieta had previously been more famous for singers and the Mendicanil for instrumentalists. At all of them, but especially at the two first named, Burney heard admirable performances : sjilendid voices of every category, whether for agility, expression, or grandeur; excellent orchestras and choruses, which were perfect, although c<jnsisting only of female voices, the compositions being skilfully scored for soprano, mezzo soprano, and contralto, the latter singing at a pitch which the unmusical Mrs. Tlirale called "odd unnatural enough." Dr. Burney went to several rehearsals, and to the small concerts, where, a few friends only being present, the girls played all sorts of vocal tricks, in order to show off their powers of voice and lungs. Of all these various performances Burney has but one judgment to give : that they are admirable, equal, and perhaps superior, to anything that can be heard on a first-rate stage—in short, some of the very finest things which he, the great musical critic, who had known every opera and every singer since 1740, had ever heard.

A great deal, of course, depended on the masters. At the two best schools Burney found respectively two of the greatest of Italian composers, one in vigorous old age, the other in brilliantly promising youth: at the Incurahili, the Venetian Baldassare Galuppi, surnamed Buranello ; at the Ospedalello, the Neapolitan Antonio Hacchini. Galuppi was one of the Italian composers whom Burney most admired, placing him second only to Jonimelli; Sacehini was one of those whom Burney was most to esteem in later years; each belonged to a separate period of musical transition : Galuppi, born 1703, to the transition from the solemn, heroic

style of Lotti, Dnraiito, and Leo, to the deeply and almost femininely pathetic one of Gliidv, .Tonimelli, and Trajetta ; Saccliini, born about 1738, to the period of transition from this latter style to the \intragic, lovely, sunny style of Cimarosa, Paisiello, and Mozart. Each was to cause others to be forgotten, and to be forgotten in hi>! turn, in the rapid changes which Italian music was undergoing ; but Sacchini, being the nearer to us, is probably less entirely forgotten than Galuppi, from whom he was separated by a whole artistic generation.* Galuppi, who was an immensely prolific composer, abounded in melody, tender, pathetic, and brilliant, which in its extreme simplicity and slightness occasionally rose to the highest beauty. He was not a very learned composer, used instruments very sparingly, but when, for instance, he introduced wind instruments, it was with a delicate and deliglitful effect. The purely musical qualities satisfied him, and he defined tlie requisites of his art to Burney in very moderate terms, " Chiarezza, vaghezza, e buona modu-lazione," clearness, beauty, and good modulation, qualities which he himself possessed to a high degree, without troubling himself much about any others. Sacchini, on the contrary, thought much of orchestral fullness and dramatic expression, or, rather, he followed the taste of his time, which was constantly tending to the first and momentarily interested in the second ; yet, with more effort at pathos, he obtained it less successfully perhaps than Galuppi, in whose time it came more spontaneously than in that of Sacchini, when musical forms were tending to the idyllic rather than the tragic. Galuppi, although he lived many years in Russia, always remained faithful to the jiurely musical school of Italy, while Sacchini, seeking his fortunes in France about 1785, adopted to some extent Gluck's dramatic system. The lives of the two composers were as widely opposed as their genius: Galuppi was a model of the respectable modest artist, hving quietly on a moderate fortune, busy with his art and the education of his numerous children ; beloved and revered by his fellow artists ; and, when some fifteen years later he died, honoured by them with a splendid funeral, at which all Venetian musicians performed; the great Pacchierotti writing to Burney that he had "sung with much devotion to obtain a rest for Buranello's (Galuppi's) soul." Sacchini, on the other hand, was most irregular in his habits and luxurious in his mode of life; his dissolute conduct surrounded him with enemies ; his singers were constantly rebelling; he was more than once reduced to almost beggary, and died poor, broken-spirited, and neglected, before he was fifty.f

* ^Ir. Browning's fine poem, "A Toccata of Galuppi's," has made at least his name familiar to many English readers.

f Sacchini had gained the friendship of the great s-ntirist Tavini, who, on his death, mourned him with an ode. Tarini, a very moral man, was totally mistaken

Venice, being the city where music was cultivated at greatest expense, was naturally the one where most was done in the way of music-publishing, nearly all the printed music in Italy coming from Venice. This was, however, very little; nothing compared to what was done in this line in England and Germany; for in the last century music-printing was quite exceptional in Italy. Musical types had indeed been invented * by an Italian, Ottaviano Petrucci of Fossombrone, and much music had been engraved and printed in the country during the sixteenth and the first half of the seventeenth centuries; but gradually, as the musical life developed, as the number of musical productions increased, printing and engraving were thrown aside as too laborious and expensive processes ; it was not worth while, as Rousseau explains, to strike off a number of copies of an opera or oratorio which might be forgotten in a year; for in the]-apid rush forward of Italian music, in the tremendous vortex of new compositions, the work even of an eminent composer was rarely performed more than one season at the same place, especially as it was usually written so exactly to the measure of this or that great singer that where he or she was not the opera could not be performed with any hope of success. The system of copyists, who could produce exactly the number of copies that were demanded, was therefore developed to the utmost; all the Italian operas of the last century existing only in manuscript, while only collections of sonatas or cantatas published by subscription were printed. These copyists, who knew of no such thing as copyright, had a very profitable business of it, although they gave their work very cheap ; for they not only supplied the theatres, and churches, and native amateurs, but were often employed to prepare whole musical libraries for strangers, whom their countrymen expected to bring home loads of the newest Italian compositions. In these cases it was a joke of long standing, already mentioned by Marcello in 1720, and still spoken of by old Italian musicians, that the copyists would sell, as rare works by eminent composers, hotch-potches made up of odd pages of old operas and exercises which the rich Milordi bought up as treasures. However, it must be said in favour of this rather uncivilised practice of copying that much of the music of the last century was written in a way to gladden the heart, compared with our crabbed, stiff type, on the thickest and creamiest paper, in large, bold, elegant characters, which prepossess you in favour of a piece even before you have read it. The paper has now, alas! become yellow and stained, the ink brown and shiny, the loose,

     in Sacchini's character, and praised him for virtues which Saccliini entirely ignored, while taking the opportunity of throwing a little of his usual abuse upon singers, among whom Parini would, however, scarcely have found so dissolute a spendthrift as Sacchini himself. * About 1500.

     uiottlc cardboard bindings give ont a cloud of dust Avlicn you loucli them, but the compositions are full of that divine youth which never fades.

     The private concerts to which Burncy went at Venice were as superior to those he had heard elsewhere as was the church music; he was present at several in the houses of patricians, amongst others in that of the Grimani, and heard excellent performances by persons of the highest rank. One of these concerts was devoted entirely to the works of Benedetto Marcello, some of which a party of ladies and gentlemen performed once a week; and this might be considered as a kind of national and social institution, for the Venetian dilettanti naturally regarded their great patrician composer as a sort of patron saint; and this might well be the case, for Benedetto Mavcello was the personification, the incarnation, of all that was most original and noble in the music of the Venetian oligarchy, uniting as he did the genius of a great composer with the spirit of a noble of the great commonwealth. The younger son of the Senator Marcello and of a lady of the famous Cappello family, Benedetto was born in] 686, one year after Handel, during the efflorescence of Venetian music, and in a highly intellectual and musical house. An old story tells that the young man was recalled from a dissolute mode of life by a fall into an empty tomb, whose slab had given way beneath him. This may or may not be true, but we prefer to think of Marcello, not as the converted libertine, but as the delicate, precocious, ardent boy, from whom his parents had to hide every book, and who, disdaining the servile, mechanical study of music, attempted to learn the art in his own rapid way, luitil a slighting remark from his elder brother, who told the Princess of Brunswick that he was a clever little fellow, and very useful in finding the place in books, goaded him into serious study of the art. How serious that study was, how deep a knowledge of harmony he obtained, is evident from his works—so masterly, so simple, and yet so elaborately finished. And that study was carried on by the side of many others, for Marcello became well known as a writer, nay, even as a writer of verse, and having taken his degree in law he entered the service of the Republic as a judge of the criminal Quaranzia. About 1720 he began his setting of the first fifty psalms, translated into Italian by another patrician, Ascanio Giustiniani. This work was enthusiastically received all over Italy; it became a model for composers, a study for singers, and was commented on by the many musical arclneologists of the day, who compared it with the works of Arion, Terpander, and otlior Greek musicians, of which they knew nothing and about which they were therefore extremely enthusiastic. A few years after the publication of this grand work, the famous composer and wit, whose palace was the meeting-place of all the Venetian musicians and literati, went and buried

himself in the little marshy, semi-ruined Dalmatian town of Pola, at the order of the government, which had appointed him Provveditore there. Marcello set bravely to work at his official duties, employing his dull leisure in composing and writing; but after five years of this kind of exile his health gave way and he was obliged to beg for other employment. The Republic recalled him, and appointed him to a fiscal office at Brescia, but his health, weakened by over study, had been ruined by the malaria of Pola, and after languishing for a few years he died in 1739, at the age of fifty-three. In the last years of his life he had met a girl of very low birth, called Rosina Scalfi, had been struck by her splendid contralto voice, had taught her to sing, and had, as tradition has it, ended by marrying her, although by so doing he incurred the displeasure of the Senate and Council, who by no means approved of such marriages. We are told but little concerning Benedetto Marcello's private life, yet enough to picture to ourselves a grand character, following quietly an ideal of the conduct of a Venetian noble, earnest in his belief, serious in his official work, full of suppressed and unostentatious enthusiasm for his art, going through life with a deep perception of what he owed to the State which had given him social nobility, and to Ilim who had given him artistic genius; yet not without a certain softness and playfulness of humour, Marcello hated and despised every sort of mediocrity, and this he proved in two very different yet very characteristic writings: the one a solemn letter, written shortly before his death, in which he admonished his nephew to live and serve the State as befitted his family; the other a satire, published when he was about forty, in which, while professing to teach how managers, singers, and composers should act in order to please a modern audience, he held up to contempt all that was mediocre in his art.

This little prose vs^ork, entitled // Teatro di Ilusica alia Moda, is not only a great musical curiosity, but, in its style, a literary masterpiece ; not an ordinary satire such as the Italians possess by the dozen, not a pasquinade, nor a humorous display of provincial characteristics, like those of Marcello's countryman Gritti, but a curious mixture of all these, with a dash of the fantastic extravagance of Carlo Gozzi, and a droll simplicity worthy of Addison and Steele, whom, however, it is far from probable that the Venetian had ever read. In a grave, simple, businesslike style, it purports to teach how best to suit the theatrical and musical taste of the day, recommending a series of petty absurdities, interspersed with more glaring follies, and crowned every now and then by a burst of the quaintest, drollest, wildest nonsense; and in so doing it gives a more complete and more completely developed picture of the motley theatrical life of the time, certainly not as it was, for absurdity never was so amusing, but as the artist, the idealiser of nonsense and extravagance, would conceive it;—not of the liiglicr artistic classes, wliich in all times must needs be serious and manly, but of the lo-wer ones, in wliich all the folly of the profession and of the time bursts out unmitigated—classes whicli afforded Goldoni'and his imitator (inimitable himself) Bografi the most delightfully comic characters and episodes, as in the Impresario delle Smirne of the former and the Convenienze Teatrali of the latter; but which Marcello alone viewed as a whole, as a cycle of humorous absurdities, as the heroic world of grotesque folly, and which he alone treated in an epic spirit, showing us all its heroes and heroines, laying bare all their feelings and displaying all their various actions, making us witness all the complications and collisions of their several whims and requirements. For there is a perpetual struggle in this grand world of the Teatro alia Moda, a battle of conceit, avarice, imbecility, and servility, between the singers and the composer, the composer and the poet, the wliole company and the manager; and Marcello, its Homer, brings us into the midst of the strife—among the swaggering, bragging singers; the threadbare, cringing, and shuffling \'7d)oets ; the fantastic prime donne, with their dialect-jabbering mothers, and their retinue of parrots, lapdogs, monkeys, and admirers; the stolid, ill-educated composers, complacently plagiarising, curtailing, lengthening their operas; the self-important bear performers, the pushing figuranti decked in their companions' clothes; the whole jostling, screeching, bellowing, tossing warfare of behind the scenes. And to each and all Marcello lays down the law, quietly teaches his part in the general scuffle, regulates and systematises the universal folly. The poet gets his lesson of cringing impudence ; the composer, of exacting slovenliness; the singers, male and female, of wild conceit and artistic inanity—precepts of which we can give but the following short specimens.

The starving poet, the patchcr together of operatic imbecilities, must declare : " That for his part he has never deemed it necessary to read the ancient writers, since the ancient writers never deemed it necessary to read the moderns. He must secure the assistance of some influential person, cook or valet, agreeing to share all dedication fees with him, who will teach him all the names and titles to be put on the dedication. He must exalt the family and ancestors of his ^la^cenas and be profuse in such expressions as mxinijicence., generous soul, &c., and finding nothing to praise in the great personage himself (as is frequently the case) lie must explain that he refrains from eulogies for fear of offending his modesty. Fame, with her hundred sonorous trumpets, will re-echo his immortal name from one pole to another. He will conclude liis epistle with the declaration that, by way of showing his profound respect, he kisses the jumps of the fleas of the dogs of his Excellency." He will, moreover, write a dissertation on tragedy and poetry in general, quoting

Sophocles, Envipides, Aristotle, Horace, &c., and adding that all good rules must " bo set aside to meet the requirements of the corrupt time, the absurdity of the theatre, the extravagance of the composer, the indiscretion of the singers, the susceptibility of the hear, of the figuranti, &c. He must not fail to give the usual explanation of the three unities of the drama, place, time, and action; the place being such and such a theatre, the time from two hours after sunset to six, and the action the ruin of the manager." The composer must be very humble towards everyone, standing Avith his hat off before the singers, and showing every possible degree of politeness towards the hQSi¥,i\\e figuranti, and the candle-snuffers; but he is to maintain his station with the poet, " ordering him to put in such and such metres and syllables, insisting on the poem being legibly copied, with lots of commas, semi-colons, notes of interrogation, &c. although in his composition he is to pay no attention whatever either to commas, semi-colons, or interrogations."

The singers, male and female, are to keep up their dignity above all things, "never listening to any other actor; saluting the people in the boxes, joking with the orchestra, &c., that people may clearly understand that he or she is not the Prince Zoroaster but Signor Alipio Forconi; not the Empress Filastrocca but Signora Giandussa Felatutti ... If the singer plays the part of a prisoner, or slave, he must take care always to appear well powdered, with many jewels on his dress, a very high plume, nice shining sword and chains, which latter he is to clatter frequently, in order to awaken compassion in the audience ; the prima donna must always raise one arm, then the other, constantly changing her fan from one hand to the other; and if she perform the part of a man she must always be bi;ttoning one of her gloves, must have plenty of patches on her face, must very frequently on entering the stage forget her sword, helmet, wig," &Q,. The seconda donna " must always insist on the poet making her come out before the priina donna, and when she has received her part she must count the words and notes in it, and if there be less than in that of the prima donna she must insist on the poet and composer giving her the due number of words and notes, as she must never be inferior to her in the length of her skirts, the amount of paint and patches, in her shakes, embellishments, and cadenzas, protectors, parrots, owls," &c.

These lamely translated quotations can give but a very poor notion of the wonderful talent of the Teatro di M-usica alia Moda; it lies in the details, in the subordinate figures, actresses' mothers, protectors, teachers, scene-painters, bear-performers, pages, &c., and in the ludicrously grave incidents which arise between them; in the completeness and drollness of the whole picture; and, such as it is, Marcello's humorous talent might be envied by his fellow-countryman Goldoni. And in all this Benedetto Marcello is always perfectly gentlemanly, never gross, never buffoonish,

never bitter; looking down upon the absurdities of tlie profession with the delicate and amused contempt of a patrician who is above the squabbles of professionals, and of a genius who is above the disputes of mediocrities. For Benedetto Marcello was much more than a mere wit, than a mere high-bred critic ; to the spirit of a noble amateur, who could permit liiin-self all sorts of artistic vagaries, he united the genius of a great composer who could deal with every sort of material. His (Jilettante\^ fancies, learned and fantastic, which no professional could permit himself, raised suspicion in the minds of professional critics, among whom we grieve to find the usually candid and appreciative Burncy, who was inconceivably blind to Marcello's merits ; but these fancies and oddities were controlled by unerring instinct. Marcello might score his pieces for strange combinations of voices, leaving only a solitary contr.alto to cope with three or four tenors and basses, but he would make that contralto soar grandly above them ; he might continually change measure, key, and pace, change recitative for air and air for recitative, but with these abrupt alternations he would produce a splendid and harmonious effect; he might go into the port, into the synagogues, and into the Armenian churches, and imitate the strange, nasal, barbaric chants he heard there, but he would use them as the groundwork of choruses of extraordinary beauty and grandeur; he might be as odd as he chose, he could never be otherwise than great. For Marcello not only lived at the precise time when Italian music was in its full youthful strength and grandeur, but he had the peculiar endowment for the musically sublime. His works afford examples of many sorts of composition for single voices and for many voices; of the simplest slightest melody, and of the most complicated fugued style ; of the tender and the florid; yet they resemble each other by a peculiarity which it is difficult to define—a certain, if we may say so, impersonal character: they seem to express not so much human emotions due to human circumstances as the impressions which a poetical mind might receive from nature—impressions which, though vague, are embodied in the most distinct and artistic shape, somewhat in the same way as the vague divinities of nature took plastic forms in the conception of the

Greek people, yet without losing something characteristic wliich betrayed their origin. What we meet in Marcello's works seem impressions of the sea, of the sky, and of the moonlight, with all their solemnity and stillness and vastness, sweet or austere. A sort of pantheistic nature-worship is suggested by liis great psalms, which raises them far above the more emotional and dramatic church music of other composers. Wliile his contemporaries gave the loveliest musical form to the human emotions, Marcello seems to have musically embodied man's mysterious sympathies Avith inanimate nature. This could only be done by a man placed, like Marcello, high above professional requirements, unaffected by fashion, and able therefore entirely

to follow his own natural dispositions. Marcello wrote mucli church and chamber mu?ic, the remains of which now lie mouldering away in archives and lumber-rooms, even as Giorgione's frescoes mouldered away patch by patch from off the Venetian palaces ; his psalms only have been published and republished, and are still known to the more studious among Italian musicians; but they alone suffice to show how groat and original a composer is due to the Venetian aristocracy, which, despite corruption and sloth, was yet the only remaining institution of the Italy of nobler days. Of the distinguished men which it produced Benedetto Marcello was the last great and characteristic one.

Dr. Burney left Venice about the 18th of August, and proceeded direct to Bologna, which was one of the principal stations of his musical pilgrimage. It could not indeed afford what Venice did; it had not the great musical establishments of the latter, nor anything of its musical life, but it was eminently the studious town of Italy, and was therefore the home of the more purely erudite and abstract part of music. The rich Bolognese nobles, more intelligent and less frivolous than the Venetians, cultivated music even to a high point; the great Teatro Comiinale, which the famous Bibbiena had just built, was admirably managed by the Senate; the deputation of patricians who had the care of the great Gothic church of S. Petronio stinted neither trouble nor money to obtain first-rate performers on each recurrence of the feast of the patron saint; all this, and a good deal more, would have sufficed to place Bologna in the first rank of musical cities, but it had, moreover, a peculiar walk of musical activity in which it was supreme. The town of universities and academies naturally possessed the society which dispensed the highest musical honours, and the man who had penetrated deeper than all others into the mysterious depths of musical science and history—the famous Philharmonic Academy, and the not less famous Padre Martini. The Philharmonic Academy was the highest standard in Italy, because it was purely and rigidly musical; it accepted, indeed, the patronage of royal personages, but it would not open its doors to the fashionable and professional mediocrities who crowded all similar institutions. It was as democratic and suspicious as any mediaeval commonwealth; its president, or principe, reigned only a year, and was elected only after many disputes; it accepted as members only those who had undergone the severest examination in musical science; and we know Avith what exultation the young Mozart passed through the ordeal of being locked up alone in a room and developing the theme given him, and how fond his father was in after-years of telling people that Wolfgang was a Bolognese Academician. There were consequently no inferior men in the Academy, and all the most eminent composers and singers belonged to it : the composers and singers whose quaint faded portraits no^v hang, forgotten and

unnoticed, in the former refectory of the convent of S. Giacoino Maggiore, converted by Napoleon into the present musical school. If a stray traveller go there now, it is not for their sake, but for the sake of Kossini and Donizetti, who, while passing to their lessons, may sometimes have stopped, looked wonderingly at their predecessors in powder, brocade, and satin, have thought for u moment how frail ami unenduring a thing is musical fame, and then gone on themselves to join the number of those who in their turn will be neglected and forgotten.

Of course Burney did not fail to go to the Philharmonic Academy, which later honoured him with membership, but his lirst thought at Cologna was to run to the Franciscan monastery of S. Francesco, and deliver the introductory letter to I'adre]\lartini given him by Gretry, for the famous monk was not only the most learned theoretical musician in Italy, but was himself busied with a vast history of music, of which the first volume had appeared some twelve years before. Giambattista Martini was the most eminent type of a peculiar class of musicians which had swarmed in Italy ever since the end of the sixteenth century ; the class of musical humanists, or, if we prefer, of scholarly investigators into the science and history of the art, as distinguished from its practical and sesthetical sides. The humanists of the Renaissance had been exclusively busied with the literary remains of antiquity, and it was not till music began to replace the plastic arts in the general interest that the new category of musical humanists could arise ; men who had inherited all the blind enthusiasm for antiquity of their literary predecessors, but who, caring really little for literature, and having a smattering of counterpoint and mathematics, devoted their thorough knowledge of Greek, Latin, and Hebrew, and their unwearied inglorious patience, to the subject of ancient music ; ransacking every classic author for allusions, copying bas-reliefs of musical instruments, trying to decipher ancient systems of notation ; attempting in short to understand the unintelligible. Many of them, of course, firmly believed that they understood how to produce music like that of Pythagoras and Anaximenes, as was the case with the unfortunate little humpback Gabriel Xande, who pei-formed a genuine Pyrrhic dance before the jeering court of Queen Christina; and with those noble Florentine gentlemen of the end of the sixteenth century who thought they had reconstructed ancient tragedy on their theatre in the Palazzo dei Bardi, when they had in reality invented the modern opera. Those who could not aspire to performing ancient music made up for it by most furiously abusing modern music, like Doni, Kircher, and a host of others ; so, while modern music was rapidly developing in the hands of empirical students, of composers and singers, who gradually refined and enriched the musical elements they had received from the people, a number of scholars, men without voice,

fingers, or tiilent for the art, gravely condemned everything that did not suit their notions of ancient music. Of course they coukl neither prevent nor direct tlie growth of modern music, but so blind was the worship of antiquity—antiquity, we need scarcely say, neither understood nor appreciated—that the critical and scientific world bowed down before their verdicts. While Scarlatti,* Pergolesi, Leo, and Jommelli, were bringing the art to the highest point of excellence, while the whole Italian nation went into raptures for its great composers and performers, treatise on treatise was published to prove that modern music was low, immoral, and totally without the miraculous powers of ancient music; and these treatises were read, commented on, and rarely, very rarely, refuted. D'Alembert scarcely dared to suggest that, after all, ancient music was a mere name ; Metastasio thought it prudent to write an immense commentary on Aristotle's Poetics, to prove that ancient tragedy was exactly the same thing as modern opera; men of original thought, like Arteaga and Eximeno, always maintained the superiority of ancient music; and Sacchi, a very judicious critic, whose musical ideal was the rather xm-antique Signor Farinello, declared that ancient music nmst have been better than modern music since ancient sculpture was better than modern sculpture—the very reason, to our minds, for its being inferior; while only now and then a sturdy dilettante, a lawyer or doctor like Saverio Mattel, would boldly enter the lists in favour of modern art, driven to this extremity by the perverse and insolent pedantry of the musical humanists.

To this class Padre Martini undoubtedly belonged, but he joined to the bigoti'y of other scholars so much learning, musical and mathematical, so much candour and gentleness, and so much self-abnegation towards his art, as to neutralise it in great part. People might think him prejudiced and infatuated, but they were compelled to view him with respect. Padre Martini had an intense aversion to the then existing Italian music: to him, who possessed far less musical talent than musical science, it seemed frivolous and superficial; he attacked Pergolesi for not having written his exquisite Stabat JlTater in the more scientific fugued style of the sixteenth century ; and when one day a young man desiring his advice had very skilfully developed a theme given him to test his knowledge, and had subsequently informed him that he was Niccolb Jommelli, engaged to compose for the Bolognese opera, Padre Martini burst out into lamentations that so fine a genius should be Avasted in composing operas. Jommelli, whose peculiar excellence happened just to lie in dramatic expression, used to speak very highly of his obligations to

* Alessandro Scarlatti, born about 1650, died in 1725. Giambattista Pergolesi, born according to recent accounts in 1710, died in 1737. Leonardo Leo, born in

1694, died about 174

).

Padre Martini as to the first scientific musician in Italy ; but added that lie h;ul but little real musical genius, although he wished to direct that of others. To Burney Padre Martini was a most interesting person, as he had written more on the art than any other Italian, and possessed the largest musical library in the country ; a library of which the most considerable part had been made him a present by the famous singer Farinelli, who, after having had the most wonderful career which a musician ever enjoyed, may have looked with a sort of mixed compassion and envy on the perfect contentment which the poor old monk enjoyed among his books and MSS.

This Cavalier Don Carlo Broschi, surnamod Farinollo, was in fact a much more interesting person to Burney than poor good Padre Martini, despite ail the learning stored up in his head and in his MSS.; nor was Burney at all singular in the vague curiosity with which this great singer inspired him. Even unmusical travellers arriving at Bologna between 1760 and 1780 would, if they had credit among the aristocracy, try and get presented to him like the Abbe Coyer; or, if they were less fortunate, like La Lande and Dupaty, would question their fellow-lodgers and the townsfolk about him, so as to be able to put down a sentence or two in their diaries about the Cavalier Broschi's history or present circumstances; for Fari-nello, or, as the English, including Dr. Burney, called him, Farinelli, had had a most extraordinary social career, which, magnified by time and ignorance, and fused with his immense musical fame, surrounded him with that species of mysterious effulgence which curious persons are always trying to see through, even at the risk of seeing something far smaller than they imagined. He was eminently one of those figures which leave a deep impression on the popular imagination, an impression which for a long while grows stronger in proportion as the reality is removed further away. His voice, it was universally acknowledged throughout Europe, had been infinitely more voluminous, extensive, and beautiful than any other that had ever been heard before or since; his musical talent far more versatile and astonishing than any other; in short, the whole eighteenth century was unanimous in placing him alone and far above all its other great singers, his predecessors, contemporaries, and successors; and musicians, as the eminent singer Mancini emphatically writes, regarded Farinelli not so much as the most brilliant member but rather as the tutelary divinity of their profession.* Carlo Broschi,f one of a family of shabby-genteel musicians, had been launched into the theatrical career about 1721, when a mere boy and still the pupil of the famous Porpora, and had immediately become famous under the schoolboy nickname of Farinello, due to the protection of some dilettanti called Farina, and which, after the easy-going Neapolitan fashion and the habit of contemporary musicians, he continued to be called by for the rest of his days. The Italians and the Germans lavished every species of honour and adulation on him, for in those days singers were paid much less in money than in the wildest enthusiasm. There are prints representing Farinelli seated among clouds in the midst of allegorical figures with preposterous draperies and preposterous inscriptions: a long, slim, sober youth, looking on with the most absolute indifference at tlie puffy-cheeked Fame blowing her trumpet, and the creasy little Cupids pelting him with roses: no bad allegory of the perfect self-command and modesty which the great singer preserved amidst the most exaggerated prosperity. All the Italian poets, good, bad, and indifferent, wrote vapid, turgid sonnets for him: amongst otliers the very talented Tommaso Crudeli, destined to end his days imjjrisoned for atheism, Avrote a couple of odes for this musical divinity. In one of them the poet, in despair at the thought of his going off to England, calls upon Cupid to detain him in Italy; to which Cupid answers that the plan is impracticable, since he cannot help following him where-ever he may think fit to go, across the sea, or across the Alps. In this glorious way Farinelli de|)arted from Italy, young, and at the height of popularity. When he returned twenty-five years had elapsed ; he was elderly, broken in health and spirits; he had been sent home ignominiously by the new King of Spain, Charles III., and ordered to fix his abode at Bologna, the place he hated most in the world. During those twenty-five years his fellow-countrymen had been constantly receiving vague and wonderful reports concerning him. He had gone to Spain, cured Philip V. of melancholy madness by the magic of his voice, kept Ferdinand VI. alive by the same supernatural means, become omnipotent at Court, been made prime minister, and, people added, had governed the country like another Solomon; all of which extraordinary pieces of information were duly registered by historians and writers on music, who have handed down to posterity the fame of this miracle. It was indeed a miracle, and, like all other miracles, could be explained satisfactorily only by one fact, that it had never taken place. Not that it was groundless ; on the contrary, it was merely the popular exaggeration of what few people at the time could thoroughly understand, namely, that a great singer had gone to Spain, had pleased poor old, dull, duped Philip by his voice, his intelligence, his good French, and his good nature, and had gained much infiuence over him ; that Philip's successor, Fcrdiuand, had liked and esteemed him still more, and that thus he had insensibly got to possess very considerable political power. Such a position as this was dififioult to define, and consequently easy to exaggerate; the story was in itself a strange one; people made it much stranger, the glamour of Farinelli's

musical fame lieighteiiing the effect and inducing them to add on all sorts of fanciful colouring; for, whenever humanity has a chance of tasting the uncommon and inexplicahle, it takes good care to season and si)ico it to the utmost. Thus there came to exist a sort of popular myth of Farinelli, in which the singer appeared much as he does in the pageantlike portrait by the crotchety harrocco painter Amigoni: colossal, dark, uncanny, mysterious, standing out sharply and strangely in his white mantle of Calatrava from a vapoury, lurid background, filled with vague forms of elves and genii. But only eliminate the additions made by popular fancy, the strange, weird lights and shades, and see him through an ordinary medium, and you find yourself in the presence no longer of Amigoni's sphinx-like demi-god but in that of an ordinary man, very amiable, very intelligent, very incapable of being a prime minister, such as you may see Farinelli in the smaller portrait belonging to the Bolognese Philharmonic Academicians, in which a book, a walking-stick, and two dogs, replace the theatrical paraphernalia of the large picture. Yet, after all, the reality is almost more curious than the fiction; Farinelli never cured Philip's madness, he never became prime minister, he never governed Spain, as even well-informed people like the Margravine of Anspach and President Dupaty affirm, but his residence at Court is none the less singular from the sole fact that never was there a person less made to be a royal favourite than this favourite of two kings, and never was there a man less capable of profiting by Court hifluence than this man, whose influence nobles, ministers, kings, and emperors were continually trying to beg, steal, or buy. For Farinelli cared neither for money nor for titles, cared nothing for political power, which he felt incapable of wielding and which he was incapable of selling; he was proud of being a singer and afraid of being a political agent; yet, while childishly mistrustful of all Avho flattered and courted him, fearing and despising their aims, he was as childishly confiding in those who treated him with coolness and ingratitude, remaining unshaken in his devotion to the Queen—a vain, avaricious woman, w4io used his influence for her own selfish purposes while making him believe she was a saint—and maintaining with all his might the minister Ensenada, a clever rascal, whom he imagined to be the noblest of philanthropists, and to save whom from well-deserved ruin he risked everything, even after being convinced of his gross treachery towards himself. This is how we see Farinelli: not in the high-fiown panegyrics of Lombard! and Grossi, but in Sir Benjamin Keane's despatches from Madrid. All the romance is gone, but there is something nobler than romance in this man, who was neither a genius nor a wizard : modest and self-respecting in the most corrupting position, imselfish and forgiving amidst baseness; something which makes him appear like almost an idyllic hero among the artificial, worthless people around him. Farinelli

I

had lost his credit at Court, and paid for it by exile from Spain nn the accession of Ferdinand's half-brother Charles—a wanton act of injustice, due, in all probability, to old Elizabeth Farnese, i\\Q. new King's ruother, whose influence over her husband, Philip V., Farinelli had considerably usurped, and whose tool he had declined to become. He had been living near Bologna about ten years when Dr. Burney arrived there, spending the dull last years of his life in a desultory, intellectual fashion, seeing a vast number of celebrities, teaching his nephews, writing innumerable letters, singing, composing, and taking part in the easy cheerful life of Bolognese senators and professors, always serviceable and generous, except in undeserved praise, which was exactly wherein his contemporaries were most lavish. He came to meet Dr. Burney at Pacbe Martini's monastery, and the Englishman visited him several times at his counti-y-house, which Bolognese tradition still points out in the fields near the Reno. Dr. Burney, although a trifle awe-stricken by the dim halo of royalty which surrounded the old singer, experienced strongly that singular attraction, due to manner, voice, and unmistakable goodness, which Farinelli seems to have exerted over everyone, making men's hearts open instinctively to him, they knew not why or wherefore, and in which lay the real explanation of his otherwise inexplicable career. When, therefore, Dr. Burney took leave of Farinelli, whom he had met only twice or thrice, he felt, he tells us, quite sorry and melancholy, as if in parting with an old friend; and nearly thirty years later, when the great singer had long been dead, and Burney was himself grown old, and forlorn, and sceptical, he looked back to this visit, and declared that, of all the celebrities he had ever known, none had inspired him with more liking and respect than the Cavaliere Broschi Farinello.

Dr. Burney left Bologna after a week, and proceeded towards Florence, crossing the

Apennines wholly unconscious of the delightful Radcliffian thrills of horror which Mrs. Jameson and Washington Irving were destined to render so popular; indeed the writers of the eighteenth century are so perversely cool and comfortable about the Apennine passes that you might almost imagine brigands and ghastly inn-keepers to have formed part of the travelling paraphernalia of the romanticists of our century, by whom they were introduced into Italy, together with circulating libraries and English groceries. Florence was not a particularly musical town in the musical Italy of those days : it had neither the inexhaustible musical life which in Naples bubbled up spontaneously from the lowest depths of society; nor the carefully cultivated, splendidly dowered art belonging to the Venetian nobles. Although it had done much for music in the sixteenth century, when the opera took rise in 'ts court pageants and learned academies, Florence had been passive ever since, submitting to imported taste, listening to Neapolitan, Venetian, and Umbrian composers and

singers; for the one great master whom Florence produced, Chcrubini, was still a mere child, and attained to maturity in France, at a time when the musical civilization of Italy was dissolving and spreading over other countries. But Florence, with its thriving agriculture, its comfortable laws, its easy fortunes, its mild little intellectual stir, with all that it still retained from greater days, and with the addition of the levity introduced by the Austro- Lorenese Court—Florence in the eighteenth century was the place of places for fashionable dilettanteism. It could no more have produced a Marcello or an Alberti, than a Pergolesi or a Durante, but it produced a groat number of small dilettanti, half nobles, half burghers, who sang and played and quarrelled and went into ecstasies: a public of rapid, intelligent, if rather superficial a\'7d)preciation. There was first-rate music in the fashionable churches, where all the best singers and fiddlers performed; * there were innnmerable parties in private houses, where, alternated by chit-chat and improvising verses and erudite discussions, Dr. Burney heard great performers, like the stentorian soprano IManzoli and the famous violinist Nardini. The Anstro-Lorenese princes were themselves, of course, very musical—musical in a humdrum, paternal way, as they were in all things : as, for instance, the Archduke Ferdinand, the son of the then reigning Peter Leopold, who would summon his chapel musicians any day or hour to perfonn with him one of those many operas and symphonies which he kept neatly bound in gaudy German paper with the titles written in the middle of droll pictures, " Vorstellung einer vornehmen Assemblee in einem schonen Saale," and so forth, intended to be cut out for children's pasteboard theatres; childish-looking volumes, half vulgar, half pathetic, Avhich have rarely been opened these eighty years.

The Florentine aristocracy had the fashionable melomania to almost as great an extent as the Milanese. The Italian nobles of the last century built their theatres by subscription, forming themselves into a sort of academy, each retaining a certain number of boxes, and all retaining the right to discuss the choice of the performers or of the delegated manager. At Lucca, where the aristocracy was accustomed to mercantile and political business, the theatre was under the direct management of the Senate, and there is a droll account in Beckford's correspondence of the solemn visit of expostulation paid by the Gonfaloniere and the Anziani to his friend the great singer Pacchierotti, on acc(junt of certain cold-taking excursions with the author of Vathek, about wliich they vociferated and gesticulated

* There is scarcely a minibcr of the Monltore ill Toxcana of a huiulred years back which does not contaiu a notice of some such performance, registered in company with the noble weddings, royal presents, monster births, miraculous cures, and occasional falls into wells and ajioplcctic strokes, which consoled the Florentines of those days for receiving but little political news, and that little about six weeks or two months old.

" as if the safety of their mighty State depended on them." This system of course infinitely increased the ah-eady existing musical hustle and squahble; preference for this or that composer or singer implying not mere abstract enthusiasm, but palpable advantages for him, and the amateurs were constantly coming to blows about their favourites. A curious instance of the jiassionate interest taken in musical matters by the frivolous Florentines of the eighteenth century may be seen in Sir Horace Mann's Correspondence. The British minister was so infected by this very un-British mania that he kept informing Horace Walpole, who cared nothing for music, how this and that theatre at Florence was managed; how such and such a singer had perfonned, how such a virtuoso had treated his rival; how such a prima donna had been dressed as Penelope; and giving him regular bulletins of the condition of his favourite Gizziello: what medicine he had been given, how many times he had been bled, what the doctors said, and so forth.

Dr. Burney found the attention of the Florentines engrossed by a musical phenomenon which had excited universal wonder throughout Italy, but which, we believe, he shrewdly suspected was a mere fair-booth wonder, destined to come to nothing : it was a boy of thirteen or fourteen, a weazen, childish little creature, who played the harpsichord astoundingly, had composed an opera, and was being courted by everyone. Of course Dr. Burney held his peace on the subject: since Signor Farinelli had thought fit to encourage the boy, and the Poj)e to give him the Golden Spur, and the Improvvisatrice Gorilla to write him sonnets ; since the people would make a fuss about the creature, and send him bouquets, fruits, and ribbons, and cry " Evviva il Maestrino! " why let them, there was no harm in it; but as to him, Dr. Charles Burney, he maintained certain doubts as to the possibility of infant prodigies coming to any good, and especially in the case of this little Signor Volfango Amedeo, son of M. Mozart, Vice-Chapelmaster of His Serene Eminence the Prince Archbishop of Salzburg.

On his way from Florence to Rome, a dismal six days' journey. Dr. Burney stopped at Montefiascone, near Viterbo, in order to visit an old acquaintance, the singer Guarducci, who, according to the vocal fashion of the time, had in his old days taken to him his peasant family, left far behind during his brilliant career. Guarducci was a very eminent performer, extremely refined and expressive, and cei-tainly also exceedingly ludicrous in aspect, if we nuxy believe the Bolognese print, in which his fat and flabby countenance peers out from beneath an immense antique helmet. He is forgotten like all his rivals ; nor should we have mentioned him had he not suggested a few remarks on the singers of the eighteenth century, which we can make at our leisure while Dr. Burney's

chaise is slowly rmnbling through the Umbrian fields and oak-woods, southwards towards the valley of the Tiber.

The singer was a niuch more important personage in the musical system of the eighteenth century than he is now-a-days. He was not merely one of the wheels of the mechanism, he was its main pivot. For in a nation so practically, spontaneously musical as the Italian, the desire to sing preceded the existence of what could be sung: performers were not called into existence because men wished to hear such or such a composition, but the composition was produced because men wished to sing. The singers were therefore not trained with a view to executing any peculiar sort of music, but the music was composed to suit the powers of the singers. Thus, ever since the beginning of the seventeenth century, when music first left the church and the palace for the theatre, composition and vocal performance had developed simiiltaneously, narrowly linked together ; com]ioscrs always learning first of all to sing, and singers always finishing their studies with that of composition ; Scarlatti and Porpora teaching great singers, Stradella and

Pistocchi forming great composers ; the two branches therefore acting and reacting on each other so as to become perfectly homogeneous and equal—homogeneous and equal because, in this national, spontaneous development of music, unwarped by critical speculation, the art tended to perfect balance ; tended to satisfy, not an abstract ideal, but an irresistible mental craving, the craving to hear music, and the best music that could be heard. Now music is a twofold entity, consisting of composition and performance. To unite the two halves in one individual would have been to prevent either frtjm duly developing ; to subordinate the one to the other would have been to produce an ill-balanced whole, and therefore to frustrate the attempt to reach what was wanted. The two branches were therefore given over to separate individuals, equal in talent, in education, but different in function, and the collision between whose equal powers constituted the full, strong artistic life of the day.

The singer, therefore, was neither a fiddle for other men to play upon, nor a musical box wound up by mechanism. He was an individual voice, an individual mind, developed to the utmost; a perfectly-balanced organisation ; and to him was confided the work of embodying the composer's ideas, of moulding matter to suit the thought, of adapting the thought to suit the matter, of giving real existence to the form which existed only as an abstraction in the composer's mind. The full responsibility of this work rested on him ; the fullest liberty of action was therefore given him to execute it. Music, according to the notions of the eighteenth century, was no more the mere written score than a plan on white paper would have seemed architecture to the Greeks. Music was to be the result of the combination of the abstract written note with the concrete voice, of

the ideal thought of the composer with the individual personality of the performer. The composer was to give only the general, the abstract; while all that depended upon individual differences, and material peculiarities, was given up to the singer. The composer gave the unchangeable, the big notes, constituting the essential, immutable form, expressing tlie stable, unvarying character; the singer added the small notes, which filled lip and perfected that part of the form which depended on the physical material, which expressed the minutely subtle, ever-changing mood. In short, Avhile the composer represented the typical, the singer represented the individual.

To perform such a work, to bear such a responsibility, the singer had to be produced almost like a work of art; the physical powers had to be developed to the highest point, the mental powers had to control them to the utmost, the whole had to become so balanced that no physical movement could be made without the direction of the mind,* and that no mental movement should be without its physical expression. This was the aim towai'ds which singers and singing-masters constantly strove, the ideal which, when, attained by an individual, gave him the undisputed supremacy of a Farinelli or a Pacchierotti. To attain it, merely to approach it, was the labour of years—patient, self-sacrificing, intelligent labour on the part of both master and pupil. It could not begin too early, it could not continue too long. The singers of the last century began to learn how to produce and steady the voice before they were ten; they continued studying how to render it supple and docile not only up to their beginning their career at seventeen or eighteen, but long'^afterwards; they went on refining their style, selecting their ideas, all their lives; and then, after ending their career, they might say, as the old Pacchierotti said to the young yet unknown tenor Rubini, " Our art is too long for a lifetime : when we are young we have the voice, but do not know how to sing; when we arc old we begin to know how to sing, but we no longer have the voice."

Few, very few, of course, ever attained to this ideal, but it was so high a one that the

Avhole level of the art was raised, and mediocrity itself became excellent; for in this attempt to reach perfection of development and balance every good quality was encouraged and every bad one eradicated to the furthest power of the individual; hence those many incompletely gifted, yet extremely excellent, singers, who had partially filled up

* Stendhal, M'ith his keen nrtistic sense and sentimental jargon, has expressed this in the style of his day: " Ce grand artiste (Pacchierotti), qui ne s'ctait jamais permis un son, un mouvement, qui no fut calcule sur le besoin actuel de I'ame des anditeurs;" a great artistic triumph turned into a preposterous hysterical calculation; yet Stendhal knew what he meant, although few of his readers can say as much.

natural deficiency by unwearied study, like the Bolognese Befnacchi,wlio, witli a bad and weak voice, still became one of the most perfect singers of his day ; and the more modern Marchesi, who, with a prodigious voice and but little taste, was yet tempered down into a highly refined performer; hence also those innumerable others who, with neither much voice nor much talent, were forced by the weight of tradition and of universal requirement into very considerable excellence.

The composer remained a comparatively abstract creature in the eyes of the Italians of the eighteenth century ; they applauded him, indeed, vehemently, but. once the opera over, he was rarely to be met except in specially musical houses and among others of his profession. It was the singer who awakened personal enthusiasm, and who became the musical idol of society at large; and, as the male singer was at once more respectable and more thoroughly artistic than the singing actress, it was he who had all the social advantages of the art for himself. He was received with open arn;s in every house ; all his impertinence and caprice were tolerated; when he sang people remained silent and breathless, and occasionally fainted and went into hysterics ; when he ceased the applause Avas perfectly frantic ; everyone possessed his printed portrait with Latin distichs, Cupids, laurel-wreaths, &c. ; the ladies wore miniatures of him, sometimes four at a time ; all the wits of coffee-houses and lecture-rooms wrote sonnets in his honour ; nay, the very writers who had held him up to derision were forced to join in the general enthusiasm. All the travellers in Italy tell the same story, and foremost of them the President de Brosses, whose love of scandal was highly and not unreasonably gratified by these demonstrations. The singer, meanwhile—usually a mere lad at the commencement of his career, of the lowest extraction, and who had hitherto led the hardest, dullest life of musical routine—was placed in the most trying situation, and if the sudden change from the rusty cassock, the scanty food, and abundant blows of the conservatorio, to fine clothes, lacqueys, fashionable dinner-tables, and great ladies' flatteries, did turn his head and make him an intolerable, capricious, swaggering coxcomb, it was less his own fault than that of society at large. But the satirists of the eighteenth century, embittered by this musical infatuation, by the insolence of individual singers towards themselves, above all by the comparison between their pecuniary and social circumstances and those of the singers, fell upon the virtuosi with implacable rage. Parini denounced tlie singer as a base and ungrateful upstart, as a corrupter of morals; Passeroni abused him as a conceited imbecile; Baretti roared tliat of all living creatures the singer was the most abject; Marcello, Goldoni, and Sografi, were more successful in their attempts at depicting him as an absurd, jolly, cowardly, bragging puppy—more successful because they produced genuinely humorous, and therefore really valuable.

pasquinades. But delightfully droll as are the Signor Alipio Forconi of Marcello, the Carluccio of Goldoni, and the Giuseppino of Sografi, it is clear that they represent only the most inferior class of performers—the small fry, which in every profession is almost equally worthless; the really great artists entirely escaped the satirists' hold; neither Marcello, nor Goldoni, nor Sografi can show us one of them ; we see them occasionally in memoirs and letters—modest, honourable, and intellectual, spending their time among books and friends, often the intimates of men like Motastasio, Zanotti, Winckelmann, and Canova; we see their portraits, gentlemanly and intelligent, among those of the Bolognese Academicians ; and we feel convinced that the dignity in which the vocal art was then held necessitated in some measure the dignity of the artist; for it must be remembered how much intelligence, feeling, and refinement, how much honest, patient striving after excellence, was required of the singer, and how much the possession of such requisites argues in favour of those who possessed them.

The eighteenth century required such a development of singing; it deemed it absolutely indispensable; and in that day of artistic strength and riches, the genius spent in an extemporised vocal ornament which was never transmitted to paper, in the delivery of a few notes which lasted but a second ; the genius squandered in the most evanescent performance, the memory of which died with those who had heard it—all this seemed no waste, and indeed it could well be afforded; but when we read of it—we, who can only read of it—we feel an undefinable sense of dissatisfaction, a wistful dreary sense of envy for what did not fall to our lot, and of pain at the thought that all that feeling, all that imagination, all that careful cvdture, has left no trace behind it. In turning over the leaves of memoirs and music-books we try, we strain as it were, to obtain an echo of that superbly wasted vocal genius ; nay, sometimes the vague figures of those we have never heard, and never can hear, will almost haunt us. And of all these dim figures of long-forgotten singers which arise, tremulous and hazy, from out of the faded pages of biographies and scores, evoked by some intense word of admiration or some pathetic snatch of melody, there is one more poetical than the rest — for all such ghosts of forgotten genius are poetical — that of Gas-pai'o Pacchierotti, who flourished just a century ago.* For in those that heard him he left so deep an impression of supreme genius, of moral and intellectual beauty, that even now we cannot read of him without falling under a sort of charm. In the pages in which the writers of the day speak of Pacchierotti there lies, as it were, a faded, crumbling Hower of feeling, whose discoloured fragments still retain a perfnme that

* 1750—1824,

goes strangely to the imagination; so that \vc almost fancy that wo ourselves must once, vaguely and distantly, have heard that Aveirdly sweet voice, those subtle, pathetic intonations. Home such occult charm, acting after a century, there must bo, for no story, no romance, is connected with this singer that could explain the interest he awakens. We catch a glimpse of him once or twice in Bockford antl Btondhal's books, we see him oftenest in Madame d'Arblay's Diary— a gaunt youth, with plain features, but which would light up with a look of genius; proud and shy and silent, but bursting out sometimes into a strange impassioned sort of prose-poetry, beautiful and grotesque, such as children and jjoets appreciate ; ardent and patient, learning English and Latin and Greek witJi passionate eagerness, loving his own art with iiitense, never-satisfied enthusiasm ; a curious whimsical character, always in pursuit of some indefinable excellence ; equally at home in Dr. Burney's parlour in Poland Street, in Mrs. Thrale's garden at Streatham, and in Daddy Crispe's hermitage at Chesington, an unexpected figure by the side of Johnson, of Burke, and of Reynolds; comprehended by very few, liked by all, and especially, with a singular romantic, sisterly sort of affection, by that most sharp-witted and sharp-tongued little Fanny Burney, who, years later, when he was dead, and she an old woman, declared, that had Pac-chierotti not been a singer, he must certainly have been a poet, without perceiving that the secret of his influence lay in his being both together. Strangely enough, by a curious accident, we got yet another glimpse of this singer—the glimpse, as it were, of a ghost. For rambling one day through a quiet corner of Padua—where the rows of gloomy porticoed streets have gradually thinned, and the town seems insensibly to grow into the open country, green with budding vinos and corn ; whore you are met by bends of the sluggish, verdure-garlanded canal, which reflect faded Palladlan villas, and by tracts of desolate gardens, with only mutilati>(l statues and rows of undipped trees, to mark their former avenues,—in this remote corner of Padua we stumbled one day into a beautiful tangle of trees and grass and flowers, separated from the grand cedars and magnolias of the Orto Botanico by a bend of the Brenta, and were informed by a gardener's boy that this garden had once belonged to a famous singer, by name Gasparo Pacchierotti (of whom your Excellency has perhaps heard ? Why should we, why should anyone ?). The gardener led us into the house, a battered house, covered with creepers and amphorre, and sentimental inscriptions from the works of the poets and philosophers in vogue a hundred years ago— beautiful quotations, which, in their candour, grandiloquence, and sweetness, now strike us as so strangely hollow and melancholy. He showed us into a long narrow room, in which was a large slender harpsichord, the harpsichord, he informed us, which had belonged to Pacchierotti, the singer. It was open, and looked as if it might

just have been touched, but no sound could be drawn from it. The gardener then led us into a darkened lumber-room, where hung the portrait of the singer, thickly covered with dust: a mass of dark blurs, from out of Avhich appeared scarcely more than the pale tliin face—a face with deep dreamy eyes and tremulously tender lips, full of a vague, wistful, contemplative poetry, as if of aspirations after something higher, sweeter, fairer —aspirations never fulfilled but never disappointed, and forming in themselves a sort of perfection. This man nmst have been an intense instance of that highly-wrought sentimental idealism which arose, delicate and diaphanous, in opposition to the hard, materialistic rationalism of the eighteenth century ; and the fascination which he exerted over the best of his contemporaries must have been due to his embodying all their vague ephemeral cravings in an art which was still young and vigorous ^to his having been at once the beautiful soul of early romanticism and the genuine artist of yet classic music.

Some faded scores, a few passages in memoirs, a grimy portrait, are all that remains of Gasparo Pacchierotti; yet, slight as are these remains, they have sufficed to do that in which many far more important might have proved inadequate : to bring us vaguely and drowsily into the presence of a man forgotten since the days of our great-grandfathers; perhaps because Schiller may after all be right and

Wer den Besten seiner Zeit genuff gcthan, Der hat gelebt fiir calle Zeiteu.

Whither have our fancies carried ns ?—The garden at Padua, the harpsichord, the portrait—are none of them present. Pacchierotti, so far from being a mere faint recollection, is as yet a scarcely noticed reality, an obscure youth with undivined talents. Dr. Burney has never yet heard his name, and, little dreaming that eight years hence a new world of music is destined to be revealed to him V)y this singer, whom he is so passionately to admire, the Doctor of Music is now jolting along the hiffh road to Rome, in the mouth of November 1770.

III.

In the eighteenth century, as in the sixteenth, Rome was sterile of art and artists, but it was once more the market to which were brought the productions of other provinces. As the town of Italy where men of all nationalities had most met, where every period of history had left the greatest trace, where everyone found most to suit his taste—as the huge centre of eclecticism—Rome was at once unable to produce anything herself and able to absorb all that was produced elsewhere ; for great works of

art arc born of a i;iiigle locality ami a single period, but are destined for the whole World and all time. A hundred years ago Rome was a mnsical centre; it alone had preserved the music of the sixteenth century as a sort of relic, and the living music of the eighteenth was poured into it on all sides. The nobles, ignorant and pedantic, were as infatuated for musicians as they had been forty years before for writers, with the addition that the former Avere tidier, better mannered folk than the latter. The princes of the Church, immensely ostentatious, thought fit to collect and keep singers (when obtained cheap) as well as antiques. Perhaps they could no longer afford to keep private chapels as a hundred years before, when Milton and Evelyn were at Rome; but they had numbers of musical proteges, whom they flattered with dinners, for whom they intrigued with foreign theatre directors, as the great Alessandro Albani disdained not to do, and by whose means they could get up sacred, though tolerably profane, operas in their palaces, as Metastasio's godfather Ottoboni did at the Cancelleria. The smaller priesthood hunted about everywhere for poor and modest young men of talent, who composed oratorios and masses for their shabby little churches and schools. The middle classes, an easygoing, independent, rather indolent set, with the intelligence, cynicism, and good humour of Pasquino, were so many born critics; the opinion of shopkeepers and shopkeepers' wives, who heard music from morning till night, was important; that of doctors, lawyers, and secular priests, paramount. The enormous class of indescribable half-lay, half-ecclesiastical creatures, poor, witty, disreputable, called ahati; adventurers, scholars, poetasters, filled the pits of the theatres, where they reigned supreme; they, in their rusty black cloaks and horse-hair wigs, bearding the scarlet-robed cardinals and be-ribboned grandees in the boxes. For they were a most intelligent and pugnacious lot; quick at epigram and pasquinade, always ready Avith smart sayings, sonnets, and unripe apples, wherewith to express their several states of mind. Behind these youngsters were the graver wearers of black : physicians, jurists, chaplains, and secretaries, respectable old gentlemen who had published unread treatises on the music of the ancients, on the opera. Sec. ; slow and reserved in judgment, inquisitorial and paternal. These two classes supplied the total absence of musical journalism; their disputes at coflfee-houses, their disquisitions in drawing-rooms, constituted the a^sthetical life of the people; their combined impertinence and dignity, rapidity of perception and solidity of judgment, kept all in check; cardinals and nobles could not gainsay them; when they had cried errivn to a singer the]iroudest princess could not shut her door to him, although he be a lout and a coxcomb. When they had thrown tomatoes at a composer, the Pope himself could not engage him. This critical tendency, due to constitution and social

arrangements, was considerably increased by an absurd regulation forbidding women to perform on any stage in the Eternal City. When the opera originated, as when the drama took its rise in Greece and in England, it never occurred to anyone that women might rationally perform women's parts ; their introduction was an innovation which gained ground slowly, despite prudery and jealousy: the Italian Church could not object to dramas, nor damn actors, as did the Gallican Church, because the Italian drama had originated in monasteries and prelates' palaces; but the Italian Church did set its face against female performers, and this original disapprobation remained expressed in the regulation above mentioned, a regulation made early in the seventeenth century, and which the priests of the eighteenth were too unoriginal, rather than too moral, to revoke. Consequently, all the female parts were performed by men or boys, to the great delight of Goethe, to whom the performances of a black-beai'ded young man, as Goldoni's Mirandolina, seemed a return to the days of Roscius. At the opera the women's parts were performed by boys, who looked the parts amazingly well, as Burney, Brosses, Goethe, and Miss Berry inform us, and as all can believe who have seen the Tuscan peasant lads playing Armida and Bradamante on their rustic stage. Now not only did the exclusion of women, who were often handsome and invariably coquettish, render public appreciation purely artistic and coolly critical, but the youth and comparative immaturity of these boys rendered their critics singularly sharpwitted and practical; these lads were brought rather to finish their musical education than to be applauded; their masters came less to gain money by them than to sound public opinion; and the audience reproved, and approved, and corrected timid schoolboys in a manner which would never have been tolerated by men and women of confirmed style and settled reputation. The Roman public, therefore, was not only critical to an intense degree, but highly paternal, and with paternal freedom and vigour did it administer the intellectual rod to singers, composers, and teachers. It was a well-established fact, recorded by Gretry, that when an opera or performer had once been approved by the Romans it must succeed everywhere else, and, when a man was applauded elsewhere, shrewd people would say " Wait till he has been to Rome;" for Rome was the inexorable judge—inexorable, yet discriminating, for, when it approved of a composer but not of a singer, it would intersperse its hissings with " Bravo Maestro ! " or vice vei^sa; and when it discovered any touch of plagiarism it would cry " Bravo Galuppi!" " Evviva Piccinni!" in the middle of an opera by Signor Bimolli or Maestro Bcquadro. Therefore the greatest composers deemed it an honour to live among the Romans, even with the small stipend of chapel-master of St. Peter's or St. John Lateran, and it is touching to see with

wliat candour the great Jommelli sent Padre Martini a copy of a medal, showing his eflfigy adorned witli donkey's ears, with which the Romans liad honoured liim.

Vet even tlie Ivonians were not always infallible. At the foot of the riiieian, where its laurel and rose hedges first begin, there stand, or rather did stand a short time since, the four walls of a burnt theatre—an empty dismal shell which still gave its name to the adjoining Vicolo d'Alibert, close to the Via ^Nlargutta, the street full of the incessant hammering and chipping of sculptors. This burnt-out shell is that of a theatre far older and more illustrious than S. Carlo or the Scala, the so-called Teatro delle Dame, built by an equerry of Queen Christina, a certain M. d'Alibert, whence its other name of Teatro Aliberti, This Teatro Aliberti, and not the Tordinone or the Argentina, which have replaced it, was the principal Roman theatre of the eighteenth century ; Metastasio wrote his plays for it; Porpora, Leo, Durante, Ualuppi, Jonimelli, all the great composers of the day, composed for it; and it was there, if we may believe tradition, that when one evening the great Pacchierotti was playing Arbaces, and when, not hearing the usual instrumental bars which filled up his recitative, he tui'ned impatiently to the orchestra, exclaiming " What the devil are you about?" that the composer, from his harpsichord, answered simply, " We are crying."

Well, to return to the one instance of Roman injustice. One day, in the year 1735, the performers of the Aliberti brought on to the stage an opera called the Olimpiade, the work of a young pupil of a Neapolitan music school. He was only twenty-five, with a delicate, feminine, almost Raphael-like face, and a fragile, sickly person. He had comj)osed an opera or two and some church and chamber music with great success; his name was Giambattista Pcrgolesi, of Jesi in the March. This opera, the Olimpiade, was his last and dearest work; in it he had done things that no other composer had done : it was a masterpiece, marking a new era in music. Now it so happened that, from some reason or other, the good Roman critics were out of temper that night: they hissed the opera off the stage, and one of them threw an orange at the head of the composer, who sat directing at the harpsichord. The opera was suspended, and next day news came from the rival theatre of Torre Argentina, that another new opera, the Nerone of Duni, had been enthusiastically received the very evening of the fall of the Olimpiade at the Teatro Aliberti. Duni, who was a good man or a very bad one, came to his rival and condoled with him on the ill-success of his work. The Olimpiade, he said, was far superior to his own Nerone; the Romans were the stupidest people on earth: he was furious with them for their bad taste. " Son frenetico con questi Romani." Poor Pcrgolesi made no answer; he returned to Naples and to his work there, but he would never again write for the stage. He wrote

his splendid cantata Orpheus, and some church music, but then he fell ill; his reverse had utterly broken his spirit, and with it his frail constitution. His friends took him to Torre del Greco, the place where consumptives are sent to revive or to die; he got worse and worse, but continued to work at the Stabat Mater, for which, in consideration of his had circumstances, he had already been paid. The price was eight scudi, about thirty-five shillings, and Pergolesi was too honest to give an incomplete work in return for it. He died in 1736, one year after the fall of his Olhnpiade, leaving the Stabat finished and a divinely perfect work. People heard of his sad end, were sorry, made amends; two years later his house was already shown to strangers; the Olimpiade Avas performed for years and years all over Italy, in England, in Germany, nay at the very Teatro Aliberti; it was considered a masterpiece, one of the few that withstood changes of fashion, and Pergolesi was acknowledged all over Europe to have been perhaps the greatest Italian composer of his day. The Olimjyiade is truly a beautiful work, but the Stabat, written on the young man's death-bed, is a still finer one, and is recollected even now.

Naples, the last of the stages of Dr. Burney's musical pilgrimage, was also one of the, if not the, most important of them; for, if Italy was regarded as the musical country of the eighteenth century, Naples was universally considered as the most musical town in it. And this was but natural; it was at Naples, that, so to speak, modern music, as distinguished from the old choral music of Rome, Bologna, and Venice, had originated; it was there that, towards the middle of the seventeenth century, music had ceased to be symbolical, liturgical, and scientific, and had become human and humanly excellent; there that composers had listened for the first time to the rude, sweet inspirations of the people; that the art had been brought back to revive, as it were, in the fresh air, to drink in the strong-life-giving wine of popular feeling, after its long imprisonment in churches and schools, where it had dragged on a weak existence, starving on mere science. This new movement, doubtless very slow and imperceptible, became strongly marked by, and inseparably united with, the figure of the great elder Scarlatti. Born in the middle of the seventeenth century, when the purely contrapuntic style of Palestrina's successors was still predominant; when the opera was a mere puppet-show, sometimes literally performed by puppets; when melody was feeble and unsteady, and recitative stiff and ill-modulated, Alessandro Scarlatti had died about 1725, when Porpora had brought the art of singing to perfection; when Marcello and Durante had developed tlie free church style to the utmost, when Vinci and Leo were rapidly carrying tragic melody and tragic recitative to the highest point; and if we seek for the link between these two generations, for the men to whom the inmicnse progress is due, the

luaynificent figure of Scarhitti is ulono vi>ibl(>, tlirmviiig all luimblcr ones into shade. For Scarlatti was i-ssciitially one of tlios(> iiicii destined to aeliieve a great movement; hold and original, but never, as Gluck was, beyond the limits of possibility ; upsetting readily, but only as much as he could rebuild; innovating rajndly, but because carried on by the tide of universal feeling; always following instinct, never following theory. He was the strangest of strange modulators, the most pertinacious cx-presser of the words, the most wholesale adapter of popular themes; trying all, and nuiking his works a wonderful, splendid, grotesque medley, full of untold wealth of harmony, of melody, and of expression, riches which required onl\'7d- to be singled out, purified, and recast by others.

All the musicians of Italy flocked round him: Porpora, Durante, Leo, Vinci, were his personal jnipils ; Kaiser and Stefani carried the Italian style, inaugurated by him, to Germany, where it helped to produce Handel, Hasse, Bach, Graun, in their turn constantly receiving new grafts of it from the works of the Italians themselves, brought to the north by singers like the Faustina, Senesino, Farinelli, and Carestini, pupils of Scarlatti's pupils. The influence of Scarlatti's school, and the consequent musical supremacy of Nai)lcs, persisted for two generations ; Pcrgolcsi, Jommelli, I'iccinni, Sacchini, and an immense number of great singers, diflused the fame of the Neapolitans all over Europe. Rousseau, the only really great and fascinating writer on music of the day, told the young musician to go to Naples as to the head-quarters of his art, in that famf)us article on Genius^ in which he poured forth lava-like eloquence to singe and wither up French music. All subsequent travellers mentioned Naples in the same fashion, some, like La Lande, deferring all accounts of music till they arrived there; and Dr. Burney, who knew better than any other man what Naples had done for music, arrived there with intense expectations. He had taken care to be provided with the means of fully enjoying the musical wealth he expected to find; he brought letters for Jommelli, for Piccinni, For the Ambassador Lord Fortrose, and for the later too famous Sir William Hamilton. The latter received him most cordially ; his wife, not the terrible Lady Hamilton of the year '99, but an amiable and accomplished woman praised by all travellers, was herself a great nmsician, and at her house, and at that of Lord Fortrose, Dr. Burney met several eminent musicians, amongst others the singer Calfarelli, or more properly Caffariello, who had been extremely famous for his voice, talent, beauty, wit, and immeasurable insolence, which latter he had vented on all the greatest personages in Europe.

Dr. Burney then went to see Piccinni, who was at that time about forty, very well known all over Italy, reckoned among the most eminent of living composers, but by no means yet raised to that pitch of importance which lie was soon to obtain in Paris as the rival of Gluck. Piccinni had

special talent foi* comic music; his Buona Fiyliuola, written to a text of Goldoni's, had been applauded everywhere, and he did more than any composer of his day to bring about the gradual transition to the softer, brighter, less tragic, more richly accompanied style, which, twenty years later, was to attain to perfection in the hands of Paisiello, Cimarosa, and, most resplendently unheroic of all, Mozart—a transition which consisted in a gradual change of the musical forms, which became lighter, smaller, more tripping, more twirling, less massive and simple; in a gradual development of the rhythmical accompaniment, hitherto almost unknown, which was to culminate in Cimarosa and Mozart's delightfully buoyant rondos, and to degenerate into Rossini's machine-like crescendos; in a gradual breakiiig-up of the melody and sharing it with the orchestra, which was permanently endowed Avith those wind-instruments which had till then been reserved for very special occasions. Piccinni was at the head of a change in the art, a change which captivated the public at large, but which a few individuals regarded with suspicion and aversion, growling out, like Mattel, that music was losing its dignity and worth; that it was growing effeminate and frivolous. Nor were they entirely Avrong; but in losing one set of good qualities it was gaining another, and classic music could not enter into its last and most brilliant phase without leaving its earlier, more sober, and solid ones. The idol of this austere minority was Niccolb Jommelli ; not that he was theoretically of their opinion, for in this lies the main difference between Jommelli and the other great composer whom he resembled almost like a brother, Gluck: Jommelli was essentially a practical artist, paying no heed to theory, indolent, placid, following only his instinct; nor did he, who was the most amiably candid of men, underrate Piccinni, or abuse the movement which Piccinni represented, as did his partisans ; but he held aloof from it, because he had no sympathy with it, because he was incapable of going along with it, because he was essentially a survivor of a previous generation of composers. Jommelli, who was born in 1714, the same year as Gluck, lived for about fifteen years, between 1755 and 1770, at Ludwigsburg, as Chapel-master to the Duke of Wiirtemberg; and this long stay in Germany, though not longer than that of many another Italian composer, gave rise to the legend that his style underwent a process of Teutonisation. When he returned to Italy, the Italians seem to have looked on him with a degree of suspicion, and his works seem to have struck them as strange; a circumstance which, to the minds of German critics, evidently proves that Jommelli had ceased in some measure to be Italian. But this theory is founded on a misconception, and has grown, thanks to national vanity. Jommelli underwent no change during his absence, but his countrymen did; he brought back from Germany only what he had carried thither, but when he brought it back it was already

so out of date as to seem almost a novelty. The public had changed, not he : the admirers of Leo, Ilasse, and Pergolesi were dead or dying out, and in their stead were men who were gradually getting accustomed to the fast-developing style of Piccinni, Sacchini, and Sarti, composers much younger than Jommelli, and who had scarcely been boys in the time of his immediate predecessors. To Jommelli this new style, with its broken-up melody, its easy modulation, its light, brilliant ornaments, its strong rhythm, its wind-instruments constantly used and used in the same fashion as the others; all this easy, lightly pathetic music seemed trivial, effeminate, undramatic, and meretricious. He resisted the new style to the utmost, intensifying in so doing all the peculiarities of the old one. The lighter and less serioiis became his contemporaries, the more solemn and tragic became Jommelli; and the more they dealt in wind instruments and slightly tripping rhythms, the more vigorously did he adhere to his violins and the more varied and complicated became his accompaniments. The public listened with as much awe as a Neapolitan public could muster; Jommelli's undisputed fame and undeniable genius enforced it, but all the same the public was not satisfied; it instinctively disliked Jommelli's efforts to stem the onward movement: it was vexed by his composing solemnly where another would have composed lightly, by his putting few instruments where another would have put many, by his writing solid passages where the singers wished to improvise flimsy ones; add to this, that the performers, vocal and instrumental, were unaccustomed to his music and incapable of performing it, not because they were inferior, but because they were capable of performing something else. Jommelli's works were less and less liked: some people said they were hard of perfomiance and comprehension; others, as Bnrney tells us, that they were written for the learned many and not for the feeling few; others still, as Mozart heard, that they were old-fashioned. At length things came to such a pitch that when, in 1773, Jommelli offered the public his opera of Iphigenia, which contained many extremely beautiful things ; many, like the great duet between brother and sister, which might have been composed by Hasse or Pergolesi, and nothing that indicated that forty years had elapsed since their day—when Jommelli thus pushed his resistance to extremes, the opera broke down in the performance, the audience grumbled, the Government ordered another to be performed, and Jommelli, having returned the price of his opera to the manager, entirely abandoned the profession. 8ome years later he wrote his last work, his great Miserere, and died, honoured but not appreciated, in 1778. The old style died with him. In 1780

Sarti wrote his GiuUo Sabiiio, ^lozart his Idomeneo; Cimarosa and Paisiello reigned supi'cme; the comic opera gave laws to the serious one, and classic tragic music was buried for ever.

K

Dr. Buruey paid a visit to Jommelli, whose peculiar genius, at once so elevated and so sweet, so full of that solemn, intense tenderness which he shared with Gluck, the Englishman admired immenselj'. Jommelli had made a very considerable fortune, as the fortunes of composers then went, and lived comfortably enough, married, but childless, a well-educated, quiet, highly benevolent, very indolent man; immensely stout ever since his youth, not unlike Handel in face, and, according to Metastasio's account, " liking to saunter at his ease and indulge the laziness of his well-fed body "—a placidity and self-indulgence which probably prevented him from becoming, like Gluck, a would-be reformer, and kept him satisfied with following his own ideas and letting others follow theirs. He received Burney very well, and invited him to attend the rehearsal of his new opera Demofoonte, which he was then putting on to the stage of S. Carlo. Burney went, not only to the rehearsal but to the performance of this opera, the last by Jommelli which was either well performed or at all successful, and at the same time the first serious opera which the Doctor had heard since his arrival in Italy, where the burletta • alone sufficed during the summer and autumn.

An Italian serious opera was in those days a very different thing from what it is now—different in its object, different in its production, different in its natm'e, answering to requirements iinlike those of our own time, and regarded in quite another manner. In the second half of the eighteenth centiu-y music had run through an untroubled course; it was still young, still vigorous ; it grew and altered spontaneously and insensibly by the same vital force as a child grows into a youth; it had not required any artificial treatment, any doctoring at the hands of theorists, for it had never given signs of decrepitude ; and if it had occasional maladies it got over them quickly and imconsciously. It had not yet grown old, and the public had not yet grown tired of it; men did not yet require dramatic effects or psychological interest, for they could still obtain pure beauty; they did not ask for distinctly marked characters, for historical pictures, for mythological allegories; they asked only for music. Greeks, Romans, Persians, Chinese, and Indians, the heroes of Homer and those of Ariosto, were all made to sing in the same Avay, because there was only one way, and that the proper one—just as the ancient heroes and samts of Eenais-sance painters are all dressed in the same nondescript delightfully inaccurate fashion, because that fashion was the most becoming one; the historically valuable and artistically worthless being left to later and more critical times. The object, then, being to have music, and only music, people began by discarding every irrelevant, and subordinating every additional motive. Now in a time of artistic life the best art must always seem to be the newest ; the art is in motion, the \'7diublic with it ;

there are no received classics because there is no perceivable decay; performers suit their style to that of composers, or rather it grows with theirs, and if they were thoroughly suited to the old they would be more or less unsuitable to the new. The consequence was that in the eighteenth century no opera lived more than a few years ; others folljwed it, as good, but in a different style; and in the immense bustle of new productions and new styles there was very rarely time to revive an old one. An opera was therefore almost invariably new—either newly composed or newly imported—and there was no such thing as a repertoire. Every great toAvn had yearly one or two operas composed expressly for it, and one or two imported from elsewhere. When the opera was newly composed it was composed for a given set of singers already engaged; the composer bad, as it were, to take their measure, and there was no such thing as writing for an abstract soprano, tenor, or bass, and then trying to fit the part so written (and such a fit must often be bad) on a concrete one; an opera was written for such or such a performer, in order best to display his or her peculiar excellences. Of course, in proportion as it fitted them it was also unsuited to others, for, as we have already remarked, the individuality of the singer was highly developed ; it was therefore usual that an opera should be performed only by its original performers, who, so to speak, kept its copyright, and very often kept its composer bodily; thus all the most popular serious operas of the eighteenth century were indissolubly connected with some great singer— the Artaserse * of Hasse with Farinelli, the Recjolo of Jommelli with the Mingotti, the Orpheus of Gluck with Guadagni, the Quinto Fahio of Bertoni with Pacchierotti, who sang it at Venice, at Florence, at Lucca, at Vienna, in London, everywhere. To attempt a part written for another was to throw down the glove and pretend to equality with him or her ; such audacity was generally severely punished by the audience ; and when, for instance, the Italians permitted Pacchierotti, Marchesi, and Rubinelli successively to sing Sarti's Giulio Sabino, it was for the pleasure of comparing their three greatest singers, of pitting them against each other, and for the attendant pleasure of street riots and coffee-house fights.

Two points, then, are established : the opera must be new, or at least new for the place ; and, secondly, it must have been composed expressly for the principal performers. The consequence was that each theatre could scarcely prepare more than one opera each season, as the performers and audience both required to be perfectly familiarised with it; the same opera was therefore performed twenty or thu-ty successive times, and then

* Basse's Artaserse, 1730; Jommelli's Jicgolo, 1750 ; Gluck's Orplim», 1764 ; Bertoni's Quinto Fahio, 1780.

k2

l^acked off to another place. Moreover, as the music was all and everything, the music alone was required to be new, while the words were as old as possible ; every composer of the eighteenth century had set nearly all Metastasio's plays, and most of them twice, thrice, or even four times. The plays were beautiful, the public knew them by heart; so much the better, it enjoyed them here and there, and gave its main attention to the music; that was novel, and full of unexpected turns and twists, whereas everybody knew since his childhood that Zenobia was not to be killed by her husband, that there was poison in Artaxerxes' cup, that Megacles was to be married to Aristea after all, that Timanthes was not Dirce's brother; and was consequently highly indifferent to the sudden explosions of wrath, the attempts at assassination, the alarming oracles, and similar stage business which would otherwise have absorbed its attention. Thus the play was of but little account, the music was everything ; but gradually, as the audience became acquainted with it, parts of it also began to pall on the hearers : the pieces belonging to the secondary parts began to be but little heeded, and when the thirty or forty performances were drawing to their close; when the public—which had started with a thorough knowledge of the play—had become heartily sick of the connecting scenes and the subordinate parts; only five or six pieces were attended to, the audience paying visits, playing at cards, talking, making an intolerable din during the remainder. But let only the prima donna or the^^rmo ^Lomo come forward, especially if she or he be a Gabrielli, or a Marchesi, or a Davidde, and the whole theatre becomes as silent as a church : woe betide those afflicted with colds or coughs ! As the Venetian Majer informs us, they become an object of universal hatred. The crowd listens breathless to the great recitative, to the duet, the trio, the air, to the rondo, that crowning glory ; they have heard tliem thirty-five nights consecutively, and each night twice or thrice, but they never tire of them:

how could they, since each new performance means a new intonation, a new ornament, a new variation—nay, sometimes a perfectly new reading of the piece ? the great singers having become positively incapable of singing a thing twice alike, and sometimes entering the stage with three or four totally different renderings in their head from which to select on the spur of the moment, as Farinelli had done, as Pacchierotti did, and as old, old people can still recollect Velluti, the last of vocal autocrats, to have done before Rossini came and said, " Lascia fare a me." * Then the audience became breathless, ecstatic; then amateurs.

* An intelligent German traveller, Rehfues, who was in Italy about the year 1800, gives the following information concerning the rifiorltiire of the famous Luigi Marchesi, who left the stage just about that time. It is all the more curious as ilar-chesi was famous rather for voice, agility, and dramatic power, than for imagination,

like Stendhal's friend, would gently slip off tlieir shoes, and throw first one, then the other, across their shoulder, in silent agony of delight.

Foreigners were amazed at this strange mixture of utter indifFeroncc and utmost rapture, of loud-voiced inattention and breathless attention; the Germans especially, who took all their pleasures as duties, and all their amusements as tasks, cried out that assuredly the Italians must be the most unmusical, the most una^sthetical, the most unconscientious of nations; but, many years later, a German and an a^sthetician, Hegel, vindicated the Italians, pointing out to his countrymen that only the unmusical will give intense attention to every detail of a play—to every note, will be equally interested in the important and tlie unimportant, and be so merely because they are really interested in neither; while the genuinely musical will heed only what is worth heeding; an important lesson, unfortunately unnoticed in our days, when people rarely reflect that art demands not volitional attention but instinctive appreciation; that when an art is of spontaneous growth it is enjoyed as men enjoy outdoor nature, freely, independently, carelessly; and that the Greeks of the days of Pericles, and the Italians of the time of Leo X., could enjoy Athens and Florence in a less pedantic manner than we do, for whom works of art are rarities and the beautiful a mere study.

The opera was the product of requirements different from those of our times; it was therefore a different thing in itself. In the days of Jomnielli it was, it is true, undergoing a gradual change, or rather it was beginning to be affected by that organic change in the art itself which was to complete the evolution of classic music; but the change was as yet slight, and, above all, the change was solely in the music. The peculiarity of the opera of the last century was, as we have said, that it was essentially classic, as Hegel uses the word: that is to say, that the principal aim was a purely artistic, as distinguished from a dramatic or psychologic one, and that the principal interest lay in the musical form. The play was there to suggest the music, not the music to illustrate the play; the play corresponded to the capabilities and requirements of the music, and gradually changed to suit its changes. Now the music of the first seventy years of the last century, although thoroughly developed in point of modulation and of melody, had not yet attained to full rhythmical and orchestral maturity; the fact is, that the great vigour of modulation and melody excluded much rhythm and sonority, and that the uniform, more or less mechanically-marked, rhythm, and the volume and

like his rival Pacchierotti: "Man hat ihni manchmal in Opcrn nachgeschricbcn, aber, trotz ilcr oftmalioen Wiederholung tier nchniliclieu Stiickcn, waren seine Vcr-

iinilcrungen uuaufliorlioh verschicdcu. Mcin Freund S in L besitzteinc solche Sammlung" (of rifioriUire and cadenzc taken down during the performance).

variety of sound, were employed in proportion as the modulation became weaker and the melody less massive. Now as long as rhythm and sonority were in this undeveloped state there was no possibility of anything beyond the air, or the double air called a duet, besides the recitative and the chorus; for the concerted piece, where a lot of small snatches of melody are caught up and carried along by the general rhythm, could not exist as long as the rhythm was undeveloped; and as to fngued pieces, where the parts follow each other and cross and combine in a regular and intricate fashion, they were kept solely for the church and the room, as being unsuitable, from their methodical and artificial construction, to the expression of dramatic situations-. The consequence was that all the action of the play was transacted in recitative, mostly unaccom]:)anied, and that melody and orchestration were reserved as the expression of mere emotion; of the result, so to speak, of the previous action, not as the expression of that action itself. Nor was this peculiarity at all considered as a disadvantage, for people instinctively recognised, that, while in comedy the interest lies in the joint action, the hubbub and tussle of several characters, the interest of tragedy lies in the emotion of the single characters, emotion more or less solitary althougli subject to be influenced by the emotion or action of others. While, therefore, rhythmical concerted pieces were gradually being employed in the burletta, the personages of the serious opera stood, musically speaking, alone, or at most in groups of two or three, as the figures stand, sharply defined and separated, in Greek frescoes, from the mere want of that general rhythm of the accompaniment which would press them together, tie them up in balanced groups, as the figures in modern painting are united by means of perspective and effects of light and shade. The personages of a serious opera anterior to 1775, not excepting even those of Gluck, who, despite his efforts at dramatic expression, never hit upon that rhythmical arrangement which, in the humblest burlettas, was already making the music follow the action— the personages of the old serious opera stood united together by a mere recitative, like so many statues on a Greek temple: as isolated, but also as individually perfect; for their very isolation caused them to be seen closer, to be appreciated more minutely than are the combined figures of a painting, where one hides the other, and many are lost in the deep shade, where you cannot immediately tell wliose is that head or whose that drapery; this close scrutiny forced both composer and performer to aim at the greatest perfection, at the greatest harmony between the feeling and the expression, at the greatest grandeur of outlines, at tlie greatest finish of details.

The art was jesthetically mature, though, perhaps, like Greek sculpture, dramatically as yet undeveloped; the songs of the Italian and German masters up to the time of Paisiello and Cimarosa are so many single artistic

.i^'oms, oadi in its own stylo ; like the Ginstiniani Minerva, the Amazon of Polycleto, the Discobolus of Myron, the Faun of Praxiteles, tliey lose notliing by boin.s;' removed from their niche, from that connecting franie-Avork of recitative, itself grandly simple. We, who have enjoyed Hh' wondrous musical pictures of Mozart, wliere form molts into form and group succeeds group, united by the light and shade of the accompaniment, we moderns should truly not bo satisfied with those series of perfect solitary gods and goddesses and demigods of the operas of Handel, of Per-golesi, of Jommelli, of Gluck; but the men of the eighteenth century were, and if we consider what splendid and lovely forms those wei'e we need not compassionate their ignorance.

Dr. Burney hoard another now opera at Naples, a little burletta called Le Trame per Amove, by a young man named Giovanni Paisiollo. Burney had never before heard of him, but he was delighted with this little farce, so full of life, of easy melody, of coquetry, of passages so simple and easily remembered; and perhaps the Doctor was not without an instinct telling him, that, while an old artificially maintained style was dying out in the full pomp of Jommelli's opera at S. Carlo, a now power in music was rising up with Paisiollo's burletta at the shabby little Teatro Nuovo, a power which was destined to triumph before ten years were out, and whicli, while it for ever precluded the pi'oduction of a Judas Maccabcsiis, an Olimpi'ade, or an Orpheus, would give the world a Matrimonio Segi^eto, a Marriage of Figaro, and a Don Giovanni*

After Jommelli's new opera—for only lazzaroni and low folk as yet deigned to notice Paisiello's—what most attracted Burney's curiosity in Naples were the famous music schools : SanV Onofrio, the Pieta dei Turchini, and S. Maria di Loreto, which, like the four conservatori at Venice, had been founded towards the close of the sixteenth century, and had afforded gratuitous musical education to boys and young men as the Venetian ones did to girls. The difference in the sex of the pupils constituted the only main difference; but it was a very important one, for, whereas the girls mostly married and disappeared into private life, only a very few becoming professionals, the boys developed into the most

* The comic operas of this school are tolerably iu keeping with the requirements of onr day ; the Matrimonio Scgrcto of Cimarosa (born 1749, died 1801), and the Jiarhierc di Sir'KjIia of Paisicllo (1741-1810), have both been performed in Italy (the latter shamefully and without any success) during the last two years; but the serious operas of the same day, the Orazi of Cimarosa, the Pirro of Paisiello, the Clcmcnza di Tito of]\roznrt, arc entirely inconip;itil)lo with our present (good or bad) opera habits, on account of the absence of action, the incoherent effect produced by light and idyllic music (suited to comedy), adapted to very tragic words, and partly also the chief male part being written, as in all serious operas of the 18th century, for a soprano or contralto voice, a habit extending to Kossiui's day.

famous composers and performers in Italy. In the Venetian schools, therefore, music was regarded as an accomplishment forming part of a liberal education, while in the Neapolitan conservatori it was taught essentially and almost exclusively as a profession. Now as Naples had, during the first half of the eighteenth century, been the focus of Italian musical life, its music schools had necessarily become most important in the history of the art. The elder and greater Scarlatti had taught in them; Porpora, Leo, Durante had been educated and taught there, themselves forming such pupils as Pergolesi, Vinci, Jommelli, Piccinni, and 8acchini; while at the same time a great proportion of the finest singers of the day were trained under their care, as the immense heap of vocal exercises, from the most rudimentary to the most complicated ones, by all the great Neapolitan masters, abundantly proves. The music schools of Naples were consequently far more important, if less cm-ious, than the Venetian ones. Who could tell how many embryo geniuses there might not be among those sallow little urchins, promenaded about by twos, like seminarists, in their coloured cassocks and sashes and symbolical leading-strings? What wonderful voices might not be resounding in those dreary, whitewashed convent-like rooms? What new musical glory might be developing in those schools, so venerable for their memories of past splendour? iSo Dr. Burney naturally thought, and impatiently asked leave to visit these wonderful establishments. But the Neapolitans somewhat damped his ardour; they looked modest, and hummed and hah'd about their conservatori, while Jommelli and Piccinni, who had themselves been educated in them, shrugged their shoulders and warned the Englishman not to let himself be run away with by his expectations. All this Dr. Burney interpreted as mere modesty, true or false; as the indifference of men long accustomed to musical supremacy, or as the peevishness of the praisers of past days. He visited the conservatori S. Onofrio, S. Maria di Loreto, the Piettl dei Turchini, each and all; went over every part of the establishment, listened to every class, vocal and instrumental, and followed the pupils to their public performances at churches and convents; did all, in short, which can be done by a man who cannot well believe his own senses, and tries to wake out of a sort of nightmare. No, it was all of no avail; there could be no delusion, no mistake; it was as clear as day, visible, audible, undeniable, irrefutable, that in not one of the conservatori of Naples could there be discovered a talented composer, a fine-throated singer, a well-taught instrumentalist, a single piece of good music. The schools where Scarlatti, Porpora, Durante, and Leo had taught,—where Pergolesi, JommeUi, Piccinni, Caffariello, Gizziello, all the greatest of Neapolitan composers and singers had learned, —those famous unrivalled schools were now filled with ill-taught, untrained mediocrities; composers without originality, singers without voice; mu-

sicians as raw and inferior as a musical country and a musical time could well produce.

What could it mean ? asked Bnrnoy. Did the State g'ive less money to the maintenance of the establishments? No. Had Nea])olitan masters migrated elsewhere ? No. Was there any rational explanation of this extraordinary decay ? No one could afford any. The more philosophical doubtless remarked that sucli plionomena are inexplicable, being, in the good language of the eighteenth century, so mtawj freaks of Nature. But the additional experience of a century has taught us moderns that Nature is the least freakish, prankish, or whimsical of creatures ; but, on the contrary, the most matter-of-fact, economical, and practical of beings ; and it has also shown us why the Neapolitan schools had become sterile. The reason was simple: they had produced enough ; they had done their work ; they might cease to exist. A very ungracious mode of proceeding; but Nature, in her wise niggardliness, by no means shrinks from unkiiid-ness. She had used Italy, and more especially Naples, and in Naples most particularly those three schools, as the mechanism by which music was to be made to traverse the second great phase of artistic life, the classic one, the one during which the art is no longer subordinate to some exterior aim, like the religious aim, as in the phase rightly designated by Hegel the symbolical; and when the art has not yet gradually been diverted to some other likewise unartistic aim, such as those of dramatic effect or scientific suggestion, as in the third or romantic stage; the second phase when art exists literally for art's own sake; when men ask it only for the beautiful; when it stands in full independence. Now this classic phase— being in fact merely the time when art has become capable of interesting by its own sole force, of riveting attention without borrowed aids, and before it has become unable thus fully to satisfy the mind Ijeginning to require artificial and foreign stimulant—this classic phase requires a peculiar combination of circumstances. Like some splendid plant, it needs for its efflorescence a peculiar atmosphere, a peculiar temperature; like the plant, also, it requires that its roots should be in one spot and should strike into the lowest layers of soil: " Et quantum vertice ad auras a?therias, tantum radice in Tartara tendit;" it must be spontaneous, national, and poi)alar; it must be born of period, of a nation and of every class of that nation ; it must grow naturally, freely, unconsciously, because it must grow in the most favourable of circumstances. Such a phase is of short duration—short, at least, when we think that an art lives not years but centuries. In ancient Greece it lasted some three hundred years; in the Renaissance barely fifty; in its last instance, the one we have been treating of, scarcely five generations of artists, from Carissimi to Cimarosa.* In 1770, the classic period of

* Carissimi died in 1672; Cimarosa in 1801.

music, the period of music for music's own sake, and of perfectly spontaneous national growth, was fast coming to a close; music in this sense classic had only one more stage to pass through before gradually declining into romanticism; the stage represented by Mozart, Cimarosa, and Pai-siello. Now Paisiello was already nearly thirty, Mozart was fifteen, Cimarosa eighteen; the minor masters, Guglielmi, Sarti, Sacchini, were still older; the men and women who were to perform for these masters were also well nigh mature. The younger musicians, therefore, yet children in the conseri'atori, were destined to activity about the year 1800, exactly the moment when classic music melted into nothing, when Italy ceased to be spontaneously creative; they were to be those weak and barren composers, those slaves of first sopranos, as Hoffman called them, of whom Zingarelli, Paer, Pavesi, and Portogallo were the gloriously inglorious leaders; they were to be those abnormally wretched singers, mere apes of former styles, who were destined to bring Italian song into disrepute and to call forth Eossini's sudden abolition of all vocal licences; in short, they were to be the men employed by fate to publish to the whole world that truly classic music was dead, that the real artistic energy of Italy was well nigh exhausted, and that it was time for romanticism to arise, to render art cosmopolitan, eclectic, and to restore its influence by making it appeal to men's love of excitement, of the new and of the scientific. Some persons, nay many, nay perhaps most, from that moment date the real existence of music, at least of the music which will last; and Hegel, we know, distinctly said that music was essentially a romantic art, which only means that it thrives best when not cultivated solely for its own sake, and that it is most valuable in the days when composers aim at scenic effects and philological distinctions; when they build up their works out of the fragments left by various preceding generations, to the accompaniment of a chorus of critics; when art is born spontaneously nowhere, but exists equally artificially everywhere; when, therefore, composers who are putting together forms originally created by Italians talk loudly of German music, and Italians, who have learned all their newest tricks from Germans, cry out that foreign music should be banished; when, in short, criticism and eclecticism are playing at the game of original creation. Perhaps this may be the case, perhaps cultured people are right to like only the music of their cultured century; we do not dispute it; all we can say is that with these cultured days and this eclectic music we have at present nothing to do, for with them ends what we have been trying to reconstruct—the musical life of Italy in the eighteenth century, as Dr. Burney saw it one hundred and ten years ago.

Of all this strange movement in the future Dr. Burney of course never dreamed; and he left Naples for England, highly delighted with Italian

music, unable to explain that odd little decay in tlie conservator), and little guessing that in forty years all that musical life would have vanished, all that musical supremacy would have ceased, and that the works of Mar-cello, of Jommelli, of Piccinni, of Galuppi, nay, even of Paisiollo and Cimarosa, would have been thrown aside by generations asking for a new spirit in art, for more vehement emotions and more violent sensations.

We shut the old, brown, calf-bound volume of Dr. Burney's musical tour, and lay it down on the oaken table. The evening sunlight, rosy and golden, is gilding the red brick belfry of S. Giacomo Maggiore, the grass of the quiet little cloister court, the brown fittings of the cosy library of the Bolognese music school. We tie up the bursting portfolios of old prints, we replace the ill-sewn, musty-smelling music books on their accustomed shelves ; we close the cardboard box of yellow, shrunken letters, and we take our leave. In going away we pause a moment in the vast, vaulted, desolate refectory, where our steps re-echo as in a church; the grey twilight is slowly filling the place, and from out of it faintly appear the rows and rows of portraits: Marcello, stately and sad in his patrician robes; Jommelli, heavy and bowed ; Farinelli, strange and weird in his knightly mantle of Calatrava; Pergolesi, sweet and mom'uful; and the many others, more forgotten thaii they, dignified composers at their harpsichords, dapper and sentimental singers holding their scores, men and women in plush, and satin, and powder, and buckle wigs, once famous, now forgotten. Dimmer and dimmer do they grow in the twilight, till they melt into the colourless imiformity of the walls.

We turn away, descend the dark tortuous staircase, cross through the black lobby Avith its sputtering shrine-lamp, and pull the iron bar of the creaking door.

Outside there is the pearly light of evening; the old bricks of the Gothic palaces glimmer with rosy hues, and at the end of the long row of dark arcades is the purple and golden glory of the sun setting over the green plain of Lombardy. There is rumbling of carts, and clicking of tinkers' hammers from beneath the old leaning towers, and clanking of officers' SAvords, and clatter of glasses, and strum of guitars, and laughter from the open coffee-houses; but we pass heedlessly through the bustle of the summer evening, threading our way almost mechanically through the crowded streets, silent and absent, our thoughts still bent upon that dead, forgotten world of art, which has faded away, even as the last streaks of crimson arc now fading in the grey evening sky.

METASTASIO AND THE OPEEA

METASTASIO AND THE OPEKA.

On the 28th of January, 1750, the Abate Pietro Metastasio, Imperial Court Poet of Austria, scribbled off in a letter to the Cavalier Broschi, court singer and royal favourite of Spain, a page of mock biography, beginning thus: "In the eighteenth century there lived a certain Abate Metastasio, a tolerable poet among bad ones."

The Abate Metastasio was in high spirits that day ; he had just received a present of snufl", chocolate, and quinine; he had been given hopes of obtaining some hundred doubloons of pension, and he had heard that the Queen of Spain declared him to be the greatest poet of the age; a conjunction of agreeable things which made him bm-st out into a dithyramb of frolicsome nonsense crowned by mock humility, by the supreme drollery of calling himself a tolerable poet among bad ones.

The notion was certainly a very funny one, and certainly must have made everyone laugh very much; yet, by a strange irony of fate, this judgment, scribbled in a moment of bufibonory, is the very one which the future was destined to pronounce over Pietro Metastasio, expressed with the would-be leniency of candid criticism. For the fame of Metastasio has undergone singular vicissitudes; the Italians of to-day mention his name with a contemptuous smile and a contemptuous shrug, often with a rhetorical mixture of pity and taunt, of stinted praise and restrained abuse; yet scarce a hundred years ago that name was famous tliroughout Europe, adored in Italy; those much-reviled works were in every man's memory, in many men's hearts, and on all men's shelves. Metastasio was petted by kings and empresses and popes, and looked up to like a sort of prophet by his countrymen; while Voltaire, the sneerer at all things un-French, said that he was greater than the Greeks, equal to Corneille when Corneille was not declamatory, and to Racine when Racine was not insipid; and Rousseau, the denouncer of false sentiment and pastoral lyrisni, declared that he was the only living poet who was a poet of the heart.

Wiisj. .^ itastasio unworthy of the admiration of tlie n.nst'- * ' t t'the c(nitemiit of flip iir('<oiit? A +

while his century admired him for what were sometimes faults, our own times yet oftener despise him for what are in truth his merits ; the ei.yhteeuth century praised him because he belonged to the eighteentli century, which was often his misfortune; the nineteenth century derides him because he does not belong to the nineteenth century, which is most often his advantage. Metastasio was great because he wrote not tragedies but operas, at a time and in a country in Avhich the opera was the dramatic form spontaneously created and appreciated by the whole nation, while the tragedy was the dramatic form artificially elaborated and eclectically enjoyed by a few men of letters; because he never shrank from the faults which were inherent in the style which belonged to his day, and strove only after the beauty which it could afford, instead of pruning away inevitable defects and seeking for unattainable merits like his great rivrd, the fastidious, faultless, pleasureless Alfieri; Metastasio was great because

/ \ his position as court poet placed at his disposal the best tragic actors of his day, its singers, while Alfieri, the disdainful amateur, was forced to seek his Brutus and his Antigone among the harlequins and columbines of the comic stage; Metastasio was great because, being himself weak and characterless, his unerring instinct, his psychological imagination, was free to create the most varied and well-defined types, while Alfieri made his men and women only a curtailed and lifeless copy of his own , strong self. But music, as it became more boldly multiform, mangled

V Metastasio's plays, and finally wholly rejected them, so that at length they disappeared from every stage in Italy. The position of Court librettist at Vienna became a source of contempt and hatred when national liberty and independence were once more sighed for. The feebleness of Metastasio's own nature, when once known to the public, raised against his Avorks a suspicion of effeminate hypocrisy; in short, the causes of his true greatness, of his deserved fame, became in time the causes of neglect and scorn, both totally undeserved and perfectly unintelligible neglect and scorn, which will last till criticism shall have taught us that a mean man may be a greater poet than a noble one, and that a faulty product of a whole time and nation is more valuable than a faultless fabric of eclectic refinement.

I.

One evening in the summer or winter, no one remembers which, of the
year 170'j, two wearers of the grave black cloak of priests and scholais
the Abate Gian Vincenzo Gravina, of Hellenistic and legal fame, and
famous also for his revolution in the Arcadian Academy, and 'ns friend
^ic I>orenzini, were strollin.i^- about in th >f

Eome, when tbey perceived a crowd collected in the Piazza dei Cesarini, between the bridi^e of S. Angelo and the Farnesc Pahice. On approaching, they found that the people were collected ronnd a little boy, who, perched upon a curbstone, was singing extemporary verses. The child was pretty, his voice was beautiful, the verses followed each other with singular facility. Gravina and Lorenzini remained standing and listened, and were moi-e and more astonished at the ease and grace of the improvisation. The boy, on his part, perceiving the scholarly gentlemen who had joined his audience of artisans, beggars, and street children, turned towards them and extemporised some lines of thanks and of excuse; thus he continued to sing his verses and they to listen. When he had ceased and the crowd had dispersed, the two literati called the boy to them, and asked him who he was and what he did. His name was Pietro Bona-ventura Trapassi, son of Felice Trapassi, druggist and macaroni-seller in the neighbouring Via dei Cappellari; he was eleven years old, having been born on January 6,1698, and had two sisters and one brother. His father had sent him to a day-school, where he had been taught reading and writing. Gravina was struck with the child, and bade him come next morning to his house in Via Giulia, over the Chapel of the Soffragio. Then the two scholars went their way, while the boy ran home to tell the good news.

Felice Trapassi, descended from an honourable family of Assisi in Umbria, had served as a private in the Pope's Guard, ostensibly composed of Corsicans, but recruited in reality among the riff-raff of all parts of Italy; he had been a thrifty man, and, on marrying a Bolognese called Francesca Galasti, he had set up a little shop of flour, maccaroni, oil, drugs, tallow-candles, soap, and that curious variety of things designated by the Romans as White Art. He had, by some means or other, probably the patronage of some great cook or valet, obtained the inestimable honour of having his younger son nominally carried to the font by the very handsome, dissolute, and art-loving Cardinal Pietro Ottoboni, nephew of a preceding Pope; but, beyond permitting his name to be entered in the parish register of 8S. Lorenzo e Damaso, his Eminence appears to have done but little either for father or son. Felice Trapassi was therefore much pleased at the expectation of some small present which the rich and learned Gravina would doubtless make his boy. So the next morning Pietro Trapassi was dressed in holiday clothes, and sent to the house of the great jurist and scholar. The Abate Gravina was still better pleased with the little poet, so pleased that either then or soon after he asked Felice Trapassi to give him the boy that he might educate him as his son. Gravina was rich, learned, and famous; his offer opened the way to a far higher career of fortune than could be dreamed of for his child by the ex-soldier and druggist; ho accepted.

L

This is tlie authorised narration of the strange chance which turned Pietro Trapassi into Pietro Metastasio, a druggist into a poet; it is probably not absolutely correct, bul. yet relatively true, compressing into one or two striking scenes what was certainly a naatter of days and weeks, possibly even of months. The Abate G ravin a, though only nominally a priest, was unmarried, his sole near relative being his old mother; he had a number of pupils, young men and boys, whom he was preparing for a legal or classical career; it is probable that he had at first merely admitted Pietro Trapassi to some of his lessons, and that gradually and slowly, as the boy developed in undoubted talents, he took him into his house and adopted him as a son; for he likewise took charge of the education of Felice Trapassi's elder son Leopoldo, less gifted and less insinuating than his brother. Be it as it may, Pietro Trapassi had not yet completed his twelfth year when he was entirely settled in Gravina's house, lodged, fed, clothed, and taught by the famous man. Giovanni Vincenzo Gravina was between forty and fifty, a tall, spare, handsome man, prematurely bent and pale from study and from discontent; among the dull, benevolent, cringing pedants of his day he stands out almost like the ghost of some old humanist of the times of Poggio or Valla. He had the intense, blind, sterilising love of antiquity of the men of the fifteenth century, their boldness restrained by servile imitation, their scepticism, their bitterness, and their inordinate and morbid vanity; the people of his time, even his most intimate friends and warmest admirers, thought him disagreeable and eccentric; the rest of the literary world looked upon him with susj^icion and aversion, and pasquinade and calumny were showered on him. He hated all things modern, and, like the Hellenists of the Renaissance, was discontented even with his own name, which he changed from John into Janus.* The name of his two pupils, the druggist's sons of the Via dei Cappellari, offended him beyond measure, and he lost no time in seeking a Greek equivalent or approximation to the plebeian and modern Trajmsso, The substitute he hit upon was elegant, scholarly, sonorous, well fitted to become famous;—it was Metastasio.

The name represented the fact; Pietro Trapassi, the son of the Ai^te Bianca dealer, had entirely ceased to exist; there remained only Pietro Metastasio, the adopted son of the greatest of Roman jurists. To the Via dei Cappellari the boy never returned except on a visit; his brother was permitted to be present at his lessons, and thus remained somewhat of a companion; but from his father, his mother, and his sisters, he became

* Gian is a common Italian contraction for Giovanni, especially when followed by snch a name as Vincenzo, but that Gravina took it deliberately is evident from his styling himself, in his own Latin, not .lohannes but Janus.

daily more alienatod. Ho lived in a i)leasant Ixmse, ato off Gravina's handsome \'7d)latc, studied out of costly books, dressed elegantly as a little])riest, and associated with the well-born, or at least well-('ilncat(Hl, lads whom Gravina was bringing up. He was taken to literary assemblies in the houses of nobles and prelates; he had the honour of improvising before cardinals and princesses; he was handsome, brii^ht, winning; everyone approved Gravina's choice in adopting the little poet. His career lay ready mapped out: he would become a great scholar and legal authority like his master, exercising poetry only as an elegant pastime. Gravina would push him on in the law, he would take orders, become auditor of the Rota, pontifical advocate, prelate, cardinal, wli(» knows what ? It was a splendid present and a splendid future, but it had its drawbacks. The child, taken out of the society of his old conn-ades th(> street-boys, restrained by the trammels of unaccustomed gentility, decorum, and study, crammed with book pedantry by a protector impatient to enjoy th(> fruits of his munificence, stiftened in the society of literary celebrities and academic dignitaries, shown off as a poetical wonder before every highborn or learned idiot who asked to hear him, was living in an intellectual hothouse, and undergoing the most intense intellectual cultivation, in order that he might sooner burst into Hower and gratify his [»atron's vanity. He was growing into a pale, stunted, priggish piece of precocity, vain and conceited from the general applause, timid and depressed from the sense that such applause was the price required by Gravina, who had adopted him mainly as a means of satisfying his greed for praisje. Metastasio was declining in bodily and mental health when Gravina was suddenly called by business to his native Calabria, whither he conducted his dear, precious, stunted, applause-obtaining pupil. Passing through Naples he could not resist the desire of showing off Metastasio before the many legal and scholastic celebrities of the place, among whom, perhaps unnoticed, and contrasting strangely with the complacent and prosaic commentators on the Pandects and St. Thomas, was the great Vico, seeing dimly, chaotically, with the half-mad enthusiasm of a proj^het, that great field of philosophic history which Montesquieu and Herder were first to open to us. Before these great men, great men mostly long forgotten and not worth remembering, Gravina made Metastasio improvise eighty stanzas at a sitting, and then left Naples triumphant.

But Metastasio was exhausted, and when they got to Calabria it was necessary to leave him there, less to study than to recruit his strength, under the care of Gravina's cousin Grcgorio Caroprese. at a place called Scalea. After the dark Via Giulia, the narrow Roman streets, the dismal academic rooms, Caroprese's house struck Metastasio as a sort of paradise; sixty years later he spoke with vivid pleasure of the little room in which the breaking of the sea against the rocks had lulled him

T. •>

to sleep, of the boats in which he had rowed about, of the boys with whom he had studied, of his teacher's little dog, of the good old Caroprese, the gentle and amiable pedant, who would jestingly teach him logic and amuse him with optical and chemical experiments; a world of study, serene and happy, so different from the dead classic world of Gravina, in which nothing lived save bitter vanity. And even Gravina had to relent; he had to cede to the remonstrances of the charming blue-stocking sister of Prince Pinelli di Sangro, of that strong, warm-hearted, intelligent woman, to whom, when she had become the Princess Belmonte Pignatelli, Metastasio was to owe so m\ich ; he forbade Metastasio ever again improvising a line,—a great sacrifice from a man who had seen him improvising with Rolli and Perfetti, the most famous of extemporary poets, and had heard him complimented by the pompous old humpbacked Pindar Guidi. Gravina also moderated the study of Greek and Latin; he forbade all scribbling of verses ;

he was beginning to see that his desire for immediate success might lose him the pleasure of his pupil's final triumph. Still the life in Via Giulia was much the same; the same studies, the same academic amusements, the same solemn philosophic banquets, the same lectures, the same squabbles, inuendoes, satires, and other literary violences; while Gravina grew more bent, more pale, more sickly, more consumed by unsatisfied vanity and bitterness as his great Arcadian schism came to nothing, as his adherents abandoned him for his rivals, as his tragedies remained unsold at the booksellers, as his satirist Lodovico Sergardi became fiercer and fiercer, and even his friend Martello jested blandly over poor, learned, intelligent, eloquent, conceited, ill-tempered Gravina's eccentricities. Gravina was also intellectually difficult to deal Avith: broad as were some of his views, and intelligent as were some of his criticisms, he was often narrow-minded, not in accordance with the ideas of his times, but in obedience to a captious character. Antiquity was his idol, but antiquity cramped and warped by his appreciation, antiquity rather negative than positive, stiff, cold, subtle, as suited the scholar who hated everything the world enjoyed, who despised love, and scorned women, in his bitter revolt from the pomp and gallantry, the effeminate pastoralisms, of the dying seventeenth century. The Italian language he found Aveak, the Italian poets childish—Ariosto alone found grace in his eyes; Tasso/ he abhorred and tried to annihilate by praising his stiff rival Trissino. Gravina was constitutionally in contradiction with his times, and his conceit and obstinacy rendered him doubly contradictory. " You must concur in every one of his opinions ; praise him, and he will love you like a son," wrote Martello about liim. During Metastasio's boyhood, wliilo Gravina looked down upon him in undiminished majesty, before he luul had opportunities of comparing his judgments with those of others, and testing his likings by his own; while he was but a poor little feelingless,

idoalloss scholar, Metastasio probably rogardod Gravina as a god : be concurrod in his judgments spontaneously, unhesitatingly, and blindly.

It was in this stage of liis intellectual existence that Metastasio wrote his first work, the play of Giufttino. The story is that he worked at it at night, fearing his master's displeasure, and that Gravina discovered the manuscript only when completed. This may be, but the play is written distinctly in Gravina's shadow: the story is taken from the Italia Liherata of his favourite Trissino; the action is so to speak none; the speeches are immeasurably long, pompous, and dull ; the choruses, the best i)art of the performance, are painfully copied from the moralising lyrics of antiquity : it is a tidy patchwork, made up by a boy who sees only the shell of the antique, to whom Seneca is as strong as Sophocles, and Lucan as grand as Homer; awe-stricken before the Elzevir and Aldine classics, pleased with the polish and sentiment of the courtly French, utterly without experience of character and passion ; thinking he understands and admires, merely because he has never felt the true nor seen the beautiful. Such is Giustino. Gravina was pleased with it, got it approved by his friends, and finally had it printed, probably after it had benefitted by his revision.

This was Metastasio's attitude towards Gravina when still a boy; did it not undergo a change as the boy grew into a young man ? Did not the Armida of Tasso, with whom he became acquainted in some clandestine way, seduce him from allegiance to dull old Trissino ? Did not Lope and Calderon, devoured in stealth, open a world of movement and passion unknown to Seneca and Gravina? Did not some opera or mask comedy, which he saw muffled up and hidden in the pit of the AUberti or Palla-corda, give him a glimpse of sjilendour and humom-, of living art as opposed to dead erudition ? DitI not some face he may have seen, some word he may have heard, suggest that the world contained other things besides Aldines and Elzevirs, that there was more than was known of by the omniscient Gravina? Surely all this must have happened; surely as Metastasio grew up, and c[uestioncd others and questioned himself, some doubt, some sneer, must have crossed his mind respecting his master's dogmas; surely he must have begun to feel that reaction against the antique, that distrust and aversion of its pedant-expounded masterpieces, which to the last prevented his seeing more than a barbarian in iEschylus and an obscene jester in Aristophanes. And then, did he cease to praise Gravina ? Did he fail to concur in all he said ? No, for Gravina loved him like a son to the last. When we thiidc of Gravina's character, of Gravina's ideas, and of Metastasio's position of total dependence upon him, we are inclined to think that the accident which made Metastasio's literary greatness possible rendered almost inevitable the pusillanimity of his life, (ira-vina's education taught Metastasio not only a hypocritical love for an unlov-

able man,but a cowardly acceptance of opinions not his own. A great benefit may ennoble a strong nature, which can be both grateful and independent; it can but degrade a weak character, leading it to servility or ingratitude.

Gravina's worries and bitternesses, his total humiliation in his contest with his stupid rival Crescimbeni, the ill-success of his literary undertakings, the inuendoes of enemies accusing him of irreligion and what not, finally determined him to leave Rome and to seek for success at Turin, whither he was invited by the King of Sardinia. But it was too late: his constitution was broken down, and he died unexpectedly, prematurely, humbling himself before his adversaries in his last moments, and regaining while dying the sympathies he had disdained during his life. To his old mother he left all his Neapolitan property ; to his beloved pupil Metastasio all the remainder of his considerable fortune.

Metastasio wrote off several letters, telling, in a half stilted, half trepidating style, the death of his master and his good fortune ; he paid Gravina's little accounts, arranged the legal affairs, gave the materials for an obituary notice to one of Crescimbeni's Arcadians, wrote a solemn, constrained, obscure, but not unpoetical elegy on the death of his master, and read it among general applause at the meeting of the Arcadian Academy; and then, having performed his duties, looked round him.

Here he was, the penniless son of the druggist, suddenly in possession of a house, furniture, much valuable plate, a fine library, three lucrative hereditary offices, several bonds of Neapolitan investments, the whole amounting to upwards of 15,000 scudi, about 4,000/. It was a good fortune for a man of letters, and more than enough to secure a successful legal career. But Metastasio was only twenty; the idea of further drudgery displeased him; he had, four years previous, taken the minor orders requisite to hold ecclesiastical benefices, and he determined to obtain some employment about the Pontifical Court, and while waiting for it to amuse himself. So Metastasio, very young, very handsome, very clever, entered the world of the frivolous, gallant, though ecclesiastical, city. He was successful: he pleased everyone; he Avas witty, tender, elegant, a poet, and moreover a rich one; he led the life of a smart secular priest, going to balls, theatres, villas, throwing his money about lavishly in every sort of dissipation save gaming, from Avhich his])lacid, timid nature shrank. He was a favourite with ladies of all ranks, for whom he wrote such pretty affected pieces of gallantry as his canzonet, " Gia riede Primavera," * and the two graceful cantatas in which he offered snuff and chocolate to candid nymphs in hoops, ribbons, and long stomachers. His godfather, the handsome Cardinal Ottobini, whom he so strangely re-

* Exquisitely set, sixty years later, by Paisiello as the lesson-piece in the Barhiere M Siviglia.

sembled in effeminate f^ood looks, introduced him to the great occlosi-astical world,—

ostentatious, worldly, immoral, and insincere,—in which he hoped to make his way by dint of smiles, flatteries, and bribes.

Thus tliin,<^s went brilliantly in the midst of amusements, gallantries, and applause; but the ecclesiastical situation was not forthcoming, and after a couple of years, on examining into his finances, Metastasio found them in a deplorable condition. The hope of a sinecure was gone with the money that could buy it; the certainty of steady advancement in the law had been trifled away in idleness; friends and protectors vanished, creditors began to rise up, flirtations became subjects of jealousy; Rome grew hateful to Metastasio; he was sick of dissipation, fearful of want, longing for change. He sold the house, plate, and most of the books, and set off for Naples, Gravina's home and the home of legal pursuits; poor, but determined to work, somewhere in the year 1720.

As he had received only the beginning of a legal education from Gravina, INIetastasio apprenticed himself to a distinguished Neapolitan lawyer, called Castagnola, as whose clerk he began to work. This Castagnola was a hard, sensible man of business ; he had heard of Metastasio's idle life in Rome, of his reputation as a drawing-room poet; he probably expected but little real work from the young man, and, by way of keeping him to his studies, he extorted a promise that he should completely abstain from any reading or writing of verses. Metastasio, afraid of poverty, tried to follow his employer's advice; but a little poetiy he did write, probably behind his back, a canzonet to the pretty young daughter of the famous philosopher Vico, of which Castagnola could not be expected to hear; and a long grandiloquent poem, stately and sweetish, full of gods, goddesses, and little chubby Cupids, after the style of the Bolognese painters, for the marriage of his noble patroness the Princess Pinelli di Sangro with Prince Belmonte Pignatelli, a necessary piece of civility of which the gruff lawyer could not possibly complain. Metastasio did not like hard work, he did not like the law, he did not like his employer; his temperament required light and elegant work, and pleasant easy-mannered people; still, he continued, for, although lazy and self-indulgent, he was the most prudent, the most excessively prudent, of men.

One day in the year 1722 a servant of the Viceroy of Naples, Prince Borghese of Sulmona, brings word that his Most Plustrious Excellency desires to speak with the Abate J\Ietastasio, clerk of the Advocate Castagnola. Metastasio, in an agony of surprise and curiosity, hurries to the Viceroy's palace and waits for the mysterious communication. The Viceroy appears, receives the young man in the most flattering nianner, tells him that he has had the highest reports of his poetical powers, probably from the good Princess Belmonte and uer family, and

asks Metastasio whether lae will undertake to write a short play, to be sung on the birthday of the wife of the Emperor Charles VI., then still King of Naples and Sicily. Metastasio is taken aback, hesitates; he has, it is true, written several such pieces in his days of prosperity in Eome, the Galatea, the Endymion, and others; he feels that he can succeed; but he has had experience of the vanity of a poetical career. He fears to displease his employer, Castagnola, by so flagrantly breaking his promise; he dreads being dragged from his dull but solid profession into the unlucrative, demoralising habit of writing verses. He would like to accept, but dares not. The Viceroy inquires into the reasons of his hesitation; the young man, emboldened by his condescension, explains his dilemma. Is that all? In that case all is well; his Excellency gives him his solemn word that not a living soul, not even the composer, the performers, no, not even the printer, shall know the authorship of the proposed piece ; Metastasio may go and obey his request wath perfect tranquillity of mind. So Metastasio takes his leave and goes home. During the daytime he copies in Castagnola's office, and only at night, when the sulky un-poetical lawyer is asleep, does he venture to work at the play. At length it is finished. Metastasio carries it to the Viceroy, and receives from him fresh protestations of secrecy and two hundred ducats; and then awaits, hidden and safe in his legal den, the reception of his work by the public.

II.

Metastasio's new. work. The Gardens of the Ilesperides, was what people in those days called a setx'nata: a sort of dramatic cantata destined to celebrate a marriage or a birth, a sort of poetical decoration for a grand entertainment. When, in the first half of the seventeenth century, the opera was first transported on to a public stage, the serenata remained in the palace, as the oratorio did in the cloister, the two minor developments of the musical pageant of which the opera was the highest, most altered form. While the opera, rej^resented on a large theatre before every class of society, required a distinct dramatic action, well-defined characters and situations, and above all rapidity of movement,—the serenata, only half acted and sometimes not acted at all, in a hall or on a terrace, before an assembly of great folk coming from a wedding, and waiting for a ball or a supper, remained what the earliest melodrama had been,—a tissue of long §|jeeches, of refined conceits, of florid descriptions, like the pastorals of Tasso and Guarini, and the masks of our own Elizabethan and Jacobian poets. While the opera turned to account all the heroic deeds, great love, great murders of antiquity, the serenata required only the slightest mythological theme. In the opera Orestes was torn

by remorse, Cleopatra stormed and imprecated, Ca?sar strutted and bullied, Greek queens calumniated their step-sons, and Persian satraps poisoned their kings on the bare boards before the roughly-daubed scenes; in the serenata Galatea and Proserpine, Endymion and Paris, sauntered about placid like shades in Elysium, sweet and dapper like china shepherds and shepherdesses, grandiloquent like dedicatory letters, among the real shrubs and flowers in a palace, among the trimmed hedges and triton fountains of a garden, a sort of well-bred, languishing, love-sick Olympus come to entertain the greatest folk in the country with their conceits and their roulades, their cooings and their cadenzas. Metastasio's serenata is a serenata like every other, only much better. Venus and Adonis glide about in the gardens of the Hesperides something between the flabby chalky divinities of Guido and Albani and the peruked and furbelowed heroes and heroines of an heroic ballet; they sigh and weep, and smile and glow in phrases borrowed from .4?»m<a and the Pastor Fido; they move in a pastoral world made up of recollections of Theocritus and Virgil, and impressions of formal, artificially sweet French gardens; they are at once unnatural and lumbering like a decorative stucco, and finickiiigly finished like a fan-painting ; they are among the latest products of the dying seventeenth century, the century of nepotism, ofv^ conceits, and of Bernini, when art has fallen to the level of upholstery and poetry has sunk to the level of dedication writing. Still the Orti Esperidi has great merit: beneath the upholsterer there is an artist— beneath the dedication vrriter a poet; the play is good in as far as a bad style will permit it.

And good it was found liy the audience, who heard this graceful nonsense accompanied by the solemn, manly music of the early eighteenth century, so droUy unconscious of the discrepancy; better still did it seem to those who read the book, prettily ornamented with barrocco vignettes; the verse was so good, so clear, so elegant in that time of slovenly inflation, there was so unmistakable a poetry in the midst of the conventional flourishes, that people began to talk about it and to ask who was the author. The composer asked, the actors and actresses asked, the noble ladies and gentlemen asked; but the Viceroy kept his promise, and it was of no avail. The mystery increased the general curiosity ; every one tried to discover the author; some wrote to the Custode Generale d'Arcadia, but he knew no more than they; it was all in vain. The most curious of all these curious people was Signora Marianna Benti, wife of Signor D(mienico Bulgarelli, commonly called La Bomanina, who had sung the part of Venus in the mysterious play. She had been particularly struck with the piece, and had piqued herself on discovering the author. She made inquiries in all quarters; she threw money about freely; at length she found a clue to the secret: a servant of the Viceroy informed

her that a certain young man, a clerk of the lawyer Castagnola, had had several private interviews with the Viceroy just at the time that the performance was proposed, that he had moreover sent to the palace various rolls of manuscript at the very moment that the play began to be learnt. The Romanina immediately commissioned a friend, who knew Castagnola, to obtain her a piece of his clerk's handwriting, while she, on her side, borrowed from the printer the manuscript of the play. Comparing the two manuscripts, and putting facts together, the ingenious and pertinacious lady ascertained to her complete satisfaction that the author of the Gardens of the Hesperides was in short no other than the Abatino Metastasio. But she was not satisfied; her final triumph required that the fact should be confirmed by the author himself. So she induced some friends to take an opportunity of bringing Metastasio to her house without letting him suspect her discovery.

Signora Marianna Bulgarelli, commonly called La Romanina, was not only one of the most famous Italian actresses and singers, but was well / known as a singularly respectable, well-educated, and intelligent woman, whose house was an intellectual centre, Metastasio, therefore, could not resist the invitation. He was taken to one of the Romanina's receptions, which was crowded with poets, composers, singers, lawyers, travellers, and the more intelligent nobles. She was no longer young, and had never been beautiful, but she was dignified yet lively, insinuating and clever, one of those women who, without inspiring love, can gain a great ascendency over an intellectual man by the strength of their will and the warmth of their sympathies. She received Metastasio with every degree of courtesy, made him feel very happy, and then suddenly asked him whether he was or was not the author of the Orti Esperidi; the question was so unexpected and so direct that Metastasio was forced to confess that he was. The Romanina had gained her point; now that her curiosity was satisfied she might have ceased to care about the poet. But Metastasio had pleased her; he was young, handsome, soft-mannered, and clever; and perhaps the very effeminacy, the absence of strength of character, which was written in his fair smiling face, rendered him attractive to her. She bade him return to her house, and he did so, finding himself for the first time in his right element. But the Romanina, much as she got to like Metastasio, had, by her thoughtless curiosity, put him into a dangerous position. In a few hours all Naples knew who was the author of the serenata, and the Advocate Castagnola heard it but too early. He was a hard and imperious man, and took Metastasio's breach of faith and subsequent dissimulation all the more ill that he had not before doubted of his implicit obedience. Of the serenata he did not condescend to speak, but began to treat his clerk with the most insulting gruffness. Metastasio cowered before his unspoken anger, and waited

that it slioulil consume itself, wliile lie vcsumod his work with greater assiduity, and treated his employer with greater deference than ever. But the lawyer became daily more un])leasaut, and his house intolerable to Metastasio; in the evening he would go to the Romanina's receptions, and seek consolation in the literary and musical company around her, but after some time Castagnola's ill-will and desire to get rid of him grew too strong to be borne. Metastasio appeared at the Romanina's depressed and disconsolate ; she and her husband, whom we see only as her shadow, pressed him to say what ailed him, and the poor fellow, utterly broken-spirited, told the story of his promise, of its violation, and of Castagnola's Avrath. Perhaps the Romanina was sorry, perhaps she was glad ; at all events it was evident that her indiscretion had been the proximate cause of Metastasio's losing his employer's good will, and finally his employment also. Her advice was decided: " Leave that detestable Castagnola; there are lots of other lawyers in Naples; another employer will soon be found; meanwhile, get out of his house as soon as possible, and come to mine till you be settled." The obedient husband re-echoed her energetic invitation. Metastasio hated Castagnola's office, he liked the Romanina's drawing-room: the offer was in itself too tempting; the determined temper of his friend entirely broke through any resistance on the part of his prudence. Metastasio was weak, ceding to people with strong likings and dislikings whenever fear, stronger than any human will, did not command him to resist by means of flight. The Romanina did not give him time to hesitate, but dispatched her husband to Castagnola's to see that Metastasio took his leave, and to have his luggage instantly transported to her own house. So, shielded by Signor Domenico Bulgarelli, Metastasio faced the furious Castagnola and meekly departed from the lawyer's hated habitation.

Once fairly established at the Rulgarellis', Metastasio seems to have forgotten all about the necessity of finding another legal employer, or, at least, to have postponed the matter indefinitely. For the moment he was comfortable and happy; the Romanina could afford to support him for awhile, and neither she nor her husband was in any hurry to get rid of him; he could on his side earn a little by writing more screnatas and more bridal compositions, now that the Orti Esperidi had given him a name. All was well. The Romanina, no longer young, childless, fast coming to the close of her professional career, centred upon him all tlie energetic interest, all the passionate affection, of her intense nature; that she did so was her pride, and she disdained to hide it. Some people smiled and whispered at this adoption of a young and handsome man by a woman herself not old nor ugly; but to their inuendoes neither she, nor her husband, nor Metastasio, would give any attention; that he was

her lover she scorned to disprove, she to whom he was more than a lover, more than a son, a suddenly found object of an intense and headstrong devotion such as other women of her character have given to some political or social object. Her strength and breadth of character strengthened and widened, at least for the time, the timid and narrow character of Metastasio; her generosity ennobled as that of Gravina had debased him, because the one was noble and the other mean. She was a large-minded woman, strongly educated, with clear ideas—best of all, with strong sympathies; she matured Metastasio's mind, and raised it above the pastoral insipidities which had been his admiration. She was a great, simple, masterly singer, above all a grand actress: in her Metastasio first saw the incarnation of the artistic Avork which was allotted to him; in her society he was first led into the world of art in which he was to create.

Round the Romanina centred that great musical life which existed at Naples and Venice in the early eighteenth century. It was a very different world from those hitherto seen by Metastasio; from the crabbed wooden decrepitude of the world of erudition, from the hopeless formal ossification of the world of plastic art, from the artificial and sterile exuberance of the world of poetry. Many things, blighted by the great catastrophe of the sixteenth century, had faded away during the seventeenth, and died grotesquely at the beginning of the eighteenth,— erudition, painting, sculpture, lyric and epic poetry: but some things, dormant in the Renaissance, had quickened and grown unnoticed during the great lethargy of the seventeenth century,— Italian tragedy, Italian comedy, and, above all, Italian music. And now music arose, in its first fresh life, as painting had done in the days of Ghirlandaio, Mantegna, and Signorelli, grand in its very adolescent roughness, chai-ming in its very immaturity, magnificent in its concentrated not yet unfolded strength. At the beginning of the eighteenth century music had no past, only a rich present and a richer future ; it had none of the academic classicalities of the v effete plastic arts, no models, no rules, no pedants, no originals, no threadbare inheritance of importance, nothing false or borrowed. Its artists were simple, earnest, cheerful ; not dreaming of artistic dignity, conscientious, self-unconscious workmen, as have been the artists of eveiy living art. Despised by the academic painters with their mouths full of classic forms and their brains empty of thought, despised by the erudite poets who revived Pindar and Anacreon by means of scissors and gum-pot, perhaps they were a little awe-stricken before the dignified dotage of other arts, and half ashamed of their infatuation for their own adolescent unrecognised art, but satisfied with themselves, happy in the obscure consciousness that they were alive, the art and themselves, and that, the same life filled those who listened when they played or sang. Such were

these musicians upon whom we now look back as upon primaeval giants. And Metastasio met them, sympathised with them, was infected with the life of their art, and put it into his.

We may picture to ourselves those musical gatherings in the Bulgarellis' (house: tlie two or three bleak rooms furnished in the heavy Italian imitation of the heavy Louis XIV., red and black and gold, the flourishy Flemish prints on the walls, the dim mirrors set in dim glass, Metastasio's solemn little collection of parchment-bound classics in a corner, the tables covered with the nicknacks of the great actress's admirers and with her new friend's books and papers; the whole pale with the light of the Avax caudles and drowsy with the scent of the fading nosegays brought back from the theatre; the rooms filled with a motley noisy crowd of old composers, in solemn perukes and beribboned shoes, of dapper literary pricstlets redolent of bergamot and sonnets, of shy young composers conscious of threadbare coats and unapjjreciated genius, of youths foreign and queer, come from the Marches, from Bologna, nay from Germany and Spain, to study music; of beautiful actresses in long embroidered stomachers and cushioned hair, of comic actors, Scaramuccias and Coviellos, only just stripped of their parti-coloured garb and black masks ; a loud-spoken, jovial wurld, jabbering Neapolitan and gesticulating terribly, half serious and fierce, half light and buffoonish, always moving, acting, performing, overflowing with rough artistic life. And in the midst of them, moving rapidly from group to group, made room for respectfully by all, the energetic yet almost regal Eomanina, intensely interested about everything and everyone, constantly active about something, encouraging, reprimanding, ordering about, assigning to each lii> business, as befits the queen of that world. Yes, we can see her moving about in hor rustling brocade and trailing velvet, going from the great singer lolling about the har\'7d)sichord, his fat, sentimental face half hid in his curly wig and lace frill, one fat bejewelled hand thrust into his satin doublet, the other playing with his music roll, accustomed to be adored, and waiting dawdlingly for adoration, an affected puppy wlien speaking, a grand and inspired artist when singing ; from him to some obscure fair-haired young man, stammering broken Italian with German absurdity, sent to Naples by the King of Poland, called perchance Adolf Hasse, and ten years later, by these Italians who are now grimacing at him, " the dear, the adorable Saxon "; and from him the Romanina will go up to the great Alessandro Scarlatti, father of the Neapolitan school, old, gouty, and occasionally peevish; she will bend over Iiis arm-chair, asking after his beautiful sweet-voiced daughter Flamminia, after his son Domenico, great on the harpsichord, now at Rome or at Venice; she will make him feel happy and almost young again. She will lead up to him a grave handsome man, in

patrician black, introduce him to the old master as his Excellency Signor Benedetto Marcello, a great dilettante and composer from Venice, and the noble will bend humbly before the plebeian, as a pupil before a master. Then she will dive into the crowd of young students of the Conservatorio, exchange a word, hurried but earnest, with the impetuous but gentle Leonardo Leo, with the sedate scholarly Durante, with the smart and fiery Vinci, till she finds the burly, sarcastic ^orpiora, greatest of cantata composers and singing-masters, and will ask him jestingly whether he is satisfied with his new pupil, the Abate Metastasio. The Abate Metastasio, handsomer and bi-ighter beneath her glance, laughs and vows he will sell all his benefices and turn prhno tenore and make a fortune. The Romanina leaves them, and turns towards a boy of sixteen or seventeen, too tall to be hidden behind the stumpy Porpora, struggles with his shyness, drags him along on her arm in affected gravity to the harpsichord, pins him down, all blushing and protesting, and cries out that since he cannot be got to sing alone he must sing with her. She strikes a few notes and sings, while all become breathless, the boy hesitatingly beginning, till, seeing him absorbed in the performance, her own dexterous voice completely drowned by the immense splendour of his, the Eomanina stops and lets him run on alone in endless intricate passages, unconscious of the crowd, till at length he is interrupted by the universal shout of admiration, "Bravo, Farinello! " Metastasio jumps up, runs to the harpsichord, seizes hold of the boy, and cries, " I am honoured by this applause ; we belong to each other, we are fellow pupils, twins, born together for the world, you in song, I in verse. Remember it in later years, adorable twin brother! "

From the men who met at the Romanijia's house, from Scarlatti, Por-pora, Leo, Durante, from the many great singers whose names ai-e now forgotten, from the very mediocrities of that musical world, Metastasio learned his place in art, learned to co-operate in what, to the enlightened and cultured of the day, probably seemed a mere huge incongruous monster, at best but a sort of sublime puppet-show, but what was in reality the real artistic form, musical and dramatic, slowly elaborated by the whole Italian people, the assemblage of the finest gifts of a whole civilization, the masterpiece of the eighteenth century as the chryselephantine colossus was of antiquity; in which there were indeed unsightly frames of wood and grotesque clamps of iron and trumpery additions in stucco, but which was yet in tlie main of dun gold and creamy ivory, and was formed in dignity and loveliness—the Opera.

III.

The opera was a necessary product of Italy ; it existed in germ in the \y very essence of the Italian language; it developed by the very pressure of Italian culture. True tragedy, as it existed in England and in Spain, \vas perhaps impossible in Italy, with a language which naturally took musical inflexions, and with a people who naturally sought for artistic pleasure. The language fell into regular cadences hostile to the fluctuating accent of emotion; the people desired definite and artificial forms incompatible with the upheavings and wrenchings of tragic action. The Italians wrote and acted many a tragedy, from the mediaeval Ezzelino of Mussato down to the Merope of Maffel; but these tragedies were works of imitation, due to the feeling that what had been done by the ancients must needs be repeated by the moderns; they were not the product of a national craving which insisted on being satisfied. They were written, performed, applauded, and published, one after the other, in rapid succession, but they never called into existence a permanent stage ; they were the works and entertainment of academies and erudite courts—the people outside neither desired nor noticed them. Construct them with the utmost care, write them with the greatest eloquence, declaim them with the greatest intelligence, it was all useless; neither the verse of Poliziano and Tasso, nor the skilful recitations of academic actors, nor the ingenious stage mechanisms of Peruzzi and Palladio, could make tragedy a real necessity, a real pleasure, to the Italians. Humanists and erudite courtiers might be faintly interested in such performances, but the townsfolk cared only for their carnival mummers, gods, goddesses, virtues, shoemakers, and pastrycooks, singing dialogued couplets on their cars; and the peasantry cared only for their maggio actors, for their raw lads chanting on stages of planks and bedsheets the stories of saints and paladins;—nay, even the very courts themselves, when not hampered by learned advisers, cared only for their pompous anomalous festivals, in which knights fought for enchanted ladies, sirens and tritons swam across villa ponds, and Flemish or Flemish-taught musicians sang madrigals inside the flanks of cardboard monsters. Thus, on the part of the burghers, the peasants, and the nobles, we see the desire for an artistic form far more artificial than the mere recited tragedy. This form, this fusion of drama, music, and scenic effect, will be crudely elaborated by the upper classes, saturated with humanism and false chivalry, a weak and uncouth anomaly, with not much vitality in it; but once born, once seen, it will be eagerly grasped by the peo^^le at large, it will be vivified by popular feeling, and it will develope in fair growth as a product of the Avhole nation. The opera is not the court pageant, not the street mummery, not the village play; it is the court pageant developed ami transformed by the influence of those classes whose

vague hankerings find their imperfect expression in the street mummery as seen in the carnival song, and the village-play as exemplified in the maggio.

In the second half of the sixteenth century, while the plastic art of the Renaissance is dying away in decorative imbecility, music becomes an ever more important accessory in the festivities of courts,—music which, during the century dividing Josquin from Palestrina, has attained to a partial but in itself wondrous perfection; a perfection of symmetrical design and interwoven colour like that of the limited but subtly-finished art of the East. At the magnificent wedding of the Grand Duke Francesco dei Medici with Bianca Cappello there were, together with tournaments, pageants, verse reciting, and scenic shows, long musical performances, complicated pieces set in learned contrapuntic mazes by Strozzi and Peri, sung by men and boys trained as carefully as those for whom Palestrina was composing in Rome. A few years later, at other court V feasts, we meet music even more developed; choruses sung to pastorals like those of Tasso and Guarini, players and singers on the stage sitting round the harpsichord, viol, lute, and fife in hand, as we see them in the concert pictures of Niccolb Abati and Leonello Spada. And in one of these pictures a musician has left the harpsichord and is pacing the boards, plumed hat in hand, with solemn gesture. Is he reciting, or is he singing? Is this a rudimentary opera or merely a play interlarded with concerts? This is the ever recurring question concerning the mixed performances, ^^ dramatic and musical, which took place in the late sixteenth century. We are told that there was music, we see that there was declamation; but were the two separated and merely juxtaposed, or had they already amalgamated? Were those verses merely spoken and those choruses only sung, or had the first timid modulations been noted under the single declaimed parts? The plays with harlequin and pantaloon with which Orazio Vecchi amused the Lombard cities, the pastorals written by Rinnuccini for the marriage of Henri IV., are still of this anomalous sort. And the indecision is inevitable; the music must have been limited to the choruses until slowly, imperceptibly, the single parts had disentangled and separated themselves from the great woof of harmony, Avhich, until the beginning of the seventeenth century, existed alone in its balanced complication. For during the Middle Ages music had been but a unison, a faintly rhythmical, almost formless chant; and during the Renaissance, while in the hands of the great Flemish and Hispano-Flemisli composers, of whom Palestrina and Gabrielli were the last, though Italian, representatives, music existed only as a harmonic structure, as a sheaf of wondrously-combined sounds, ■ learned, sublime, wonderful, but miindividual, unemotional, unmelodic, and unrhythmic. When this sheaf of harmony had been perfected and handed over from the erudite North to the artistic South it was gradually, timidly

looseiiod; the Italians severed and extracted one part from the other; made the separate parts—imheard-of wonder!—stand alone in trcpidating awkwardness, bnt stand alone, individnal, independent, freed from the association Avhich stiffened and weighed them down, free to develops individually, to become one of the two great divisions of modern music: noted declamation or melody, recitative or air.

Men had wished to enjoy that music which they had heard in palace and church in their own hoiise; they had suul;- one of the parts of those splendid cimibinations of sound, and had sought for the other ones on their viol, their lute, their virginal, trying to reconstruct the great vocal fabric. But they had destroyed it; this single human voice would not let itself be bound together with the voice of the wood and of the string as it had let itself be fettered with the other human voices. It leaped up, broke loose, and giddily followed its own course; a strange, wild course, from which it returned, trembling and terrified,'seeking the shelter of the instruments. But independence once tasted was never forgotten; the single voice had learned the existence of a world of music whose doors had been closed to the compact harmonic groups; it had learned that it had the strength to move and work by itself. Henceforward the single voice is the main musical interest: to train it for long sustained quiescence, for rapid movement, becomes the Avork of the age, of the seventeenth century, which is to music as the fifteenth century had been to painting: the century of innovation, of awkwardness, of timid grace, of over-bold attempt, the predecessor of perfection. The instruments have become the servants of this new master of the art, ofthis individual voice: they nmst prepare its advent, wait for it, sustain it, give it time for repose, receive it back after its triumphant jonrnoyings. But what shall this liberated voice do? Shall it travel in regular and cunning mazes, in definite and peifect circles and arabesques, or shall it follow l)oldly in the free, varying steps of the spoken word ? Shall it sing or shall it declaim? At first and for a long time the answer is difficult: it does both and neither. Accustomed but little to its liberty, uncertain of its powers, uncertain of what is in store, it feebly attempts both to sing and to declaim; nay, sometimes, in its foolishness, it tries to imitate its servants, the violins and fifes; worst of all, it still seeks safety in the shadow of its servitude, and would when free do what it did when imprisoned in its harmonic shackles.

The song or air, the melody, in short, necessarily originated in the attempt to reproduce with one voice what had hitherto been done by several; the recitative necessarily suggested itself simultaneously, for as one singer left the chorus and sang alone, it naturally occurred that he might sing the verses intended for one part; and, as the blank verse of this narrative or dramatic part neither suggested rhythm nor definite

M

sliape, it was noted in a sort of approximation to the speaking tone. The story goes that recitative, as this noted declamation came to be called, was invented by certain Florentine gentlemen, the poet Einnnccini, the /composers Peri and Caccini, who met in the house of a Bardi, Count of / Vernio, to discuss the music to which the ancients had sung their choruses: instead of reproducing ancient tragedy they invented modern opera. It may be so, but as music had long been on the stage, although only as chorus, the attempt to reduce the inflexions of the speaking voice within musical limits must have been made all over Italy at the end of the sixteenth century, independently and simultaneously, because the same causes prevailed everywhere. But for a long while there is, strictly speaking, neither recitative nor air: the poetry is written Avithout sufficient distinction of metre, the instrumental part is still too rudimentary, the voice still too untrained. There is neither enough melody nor enough declamation; musical form and prosody are alike confused, and even in the Avorks of Monteverde, the greatest Italian composer of the early seventeenth century, we can scarcely distinguish the music which can be sung from the music which must be recited. / His setting of Rinnuccini's lament of Ariadne on

Naxos contains, in its rich and pathetic modulations, the germ of the great art of the Pergolesis and Jommellis ; but Ave cannot define it as either air or recitative: it is not an air, because it is too unsteady in rhythm, too unadmitting of a real, formal accompaniment; it is not a recitative, because it reproduces too little of the inflexions and punctuations of speech to be freely declaimed.

But this double product of the enfranchisement of the single voice, recitative and air, confused and rude though it was, was at once recognised and fostered by the Italian people. The musical drama almost banishes the recited pastoral off the court stages; it penetrates into church and cloister in the form of oratorio, it is dragged about from town to toAvn on the cart of Pietro della Valle, Thespis fashion; instead of chapels we now begin to hear of singers. Milton and Evelyn, travelling in Italy about 1630, meet everyAvhere great t-irtuosi, Leonora Baroni (the heroine of Milton's Latin verses), Lauro Vettori, Baldassare Ferri, artists trained from their earliest childhood, and Avhom the whole nation honours with ^ poems, flowers, p)resents, and triumphal processions. Meanwhile, on all/ ' sides, theatres have sprung up at EaiiC, at Parma, at Venice, at Rpme;, very different from the little theatres hitherto erected in palace halls; yimmense stages, fit for the most magnificent scenic displays; immense houses, in Avhich the voice resounds as it never did in a church; galleries on galleries, capable of holding thousands of spectators; for now the whole nation,—nobles, merchants, artisans, gondoliers and lazzaroni,— have discovered what they want and insist upon being admitted.

But this rapid development is necessarily very unequal, anomalous.

This musical drama, wliicli the Italians have instinctively called ^Hhe work." gives scope to too many and various arts: the already matured arts,— architecture, mechanic and pantomimic art,—obtain more than their due share from the yet imperfect arts, poetry and music. The plays are ill constructed, uncertain mixtures of the historical and the mythological, ^-^^ patchv^orks of lyric verbosities and cold conceits, interlarded with stupid mask-buffooneries; the music is still awkward and unfinished: timidly modulated, ill punctuated, frigid recitative; imperfectly rhythmical, ponderous, indefinite melody; accompaniment added at random, without perception of its real place and poAver ; the singers are rather coarse and over-exuberant, fond of rough vocal gymnastics, with but little care of general effect or of finish. On the other hand, the remains of the pageant^g-rt of the Renaissance crowd the stage; there are continual changes of scenery, iumiense displays of horses, camels, elephants, armies; transformations into wild beasts, into birds, into plants ; enchanted palaces rising out of the ground or dissolving into thin air; chariots drawn by winged serpents, heroes carried off on the backs of dragons; Tartarus, Elysium, Chaos, nay, as in Beverini's opera at Venice, nothing short of the Creation of the Universe. This was the condition of the opera about the middle of the seventeenth century, when (a suggestive fact) the Cavalier Bernini, the Michelangelo of Barrocco art, built a theatre, painted the scenes',' hewed the statues, wrote the play, composed the music, and sang and acted the pi- incipal part himself; when flourished Carissimi, the striver after elaborate simplicity—Cesti and Cavalli, sweet and pathetic in their very con-strainedness; when Italy, which had long been ceasing to impose artistic fashions on the world, gave Europe her last artistic creation, made it recognise her latest supremacy—the supremacy in music. Mazarin had introduced the opera into France, witTi Italian words, Italian music, and Italian singers; but the French soon rebelled from foreign domination, had plays constructed on the tlien existing Italian model by the coxcombical, pastoral, sugary Quinault; music composed in the Italian style by Lully and Lalande, and singers trained according to Italian rules; an attempt to be at once imitating and original, pupils and masters, which speedily ended in turning the French opei*a,—words, music, and performance,—

into a European laughing-stock. The opera had early been carried to Germany: Schiitz and Staden had tried to TeiTtonise it even in the days of Monteverde, but the attempt failed in monotonous, allegorical, contrapuntic frigidness, little suited to the coarse German middle classes; but the Italian opera, with Italian poets, Italian or Italian-taught composers, and Italian singers, took root in every one of the Frenchified German courts. At Vienna, an Italian court poet was kept expressly to ^^ furnish libretti; at Dresden, Munich, and Hanover, the bes^talian music could be heard; even at Teutonic Berlin a great singer and composer,

M 2

J

164 Metastasio and the Ojjera.

Pistocclii, was kept, althougii his music accompanied tlie movements, not of real actors, but of waxworks; even the Archbishop Moritz von Thun, prince of the little mediaeval Salzburg, had an opera called Avininio performed at the end of the seventeenth century, as we learned from the soiled MS. lying on his Eminence's beautifully inlaid ebony and ivory harpsichord, silent for nearly two hundred years. Italian singers and compositions began to be imported into England in the days of Charles II., Davenant and Purcell attempting to do in English what Quinault and Lully were doing in French; and the opera, first of mixed language (Niccolini singing Italian and Mrs. Toffts English), but finally entirely Italian, was definitely established in the reign of Queen Anne. The opera was recognised as a production of Italy, and a production for which all the other nations were clamorous.

Meanwhile, as the seventeenth century drew to a close, music, in the hands of Alessandro Scarlatti, of Bononciui, and of Pistocchi, was rapidly maturing: melody was solidifying into strong, clear forms; recitative was expanding and growing bolder and more elastic; accompaniment was becoming fuller, more meaning, taking a certain reciprocal importance; singing was developing in wonderful perfection, perfection of superb delicacy and vigour. And as music moved so the poetry to which it was to be linked had to move also, and before their growing importance scenic shows and mimic performance were to give way. Silvio Stam-piglia. Court poet of Leopold I., and Domenico David, Venetian playwright, began to disband the transformations, the enchantments, and other shows of the old opera; to turn out harlequin and pantaloon; to eschew flimsy mythology for serious historic subjects; to give to their opera texts the proportions and dignity of tragedies; while at the same time the composers began to require less rhetoric and more passion for their recitatives, more simplicity and metrical clearness for the airs; and the singers began to insist upon being given the place and the work due to their respective voice and importance. Thus, little by little, thanks to the pressure of the public, to the conflicting claim of authors, composers, and singers, the opera was moulded into a definite shape, as we first see it in the hands of the first true opera poet, of the predecessor of Metastasio, the Venetian Candiot Apostolo Zeno.

The literary activity of Apostolo Zeno, who was born in 16G8 and died in 1750, was mainly during the last years of the seventeenth and the first of the eighteenth centuries, while occupying the post of Poeta Cesareo or Imperial Opera Poet to Joseph I. and Charles VI. He was a very learned man, a philologist and antiquary, according to the ideas of those days; poetical gifts, in the sense of fancy and metrical talent, he had next to none, and no power of conceiving character; but he had great instinct for the dramatic, for well-tightened action, for simple plot, for effective scenes. What he conceived he executed firmly, strongly, ^vithout losing time in rhetoric and pathos, sketching rapidly, clearly, harshly, Avith much ease and evident satisfaction in his rough, curt work. Pathetic speeches or even avowedly pathetic scenes he ignored, interesting ami moving the audience rather by the tragic earnestness, the very hard decisiveness of the situations. A forgotten writer, left even in the eighteenth century merely to patchers-up of libretti, never read by the public, and now found only on the shelves of public libraries, yet when read giving an impression of power, of solid art, reminding you somewhat, at once for worse and for better, of Corneille; a man with little to please and amuse, but occasionally, as in his Lucio Papirio, with something that rivets and impresses. Though no poet, and not pretending to be one; though dry, cold, hard, inharmonious, and freely plagiarising, Apostolo Zeno is what the Trissinos and Cinthios, the Contis and Maffeis, the whole herd of Italian tragic writers, were not, a true artist, because, unlike them, he is working at a living and national art. Zeno did not give the melodrama its shape, he merely compressed it firmly into the form required by the development of music; he merely defined the necessary tendencies which had begun to exist with the very birth of the opera.

The opera, as elaborated by Apostolo Zeno and perfected by Metastasio, is not a classical production like the French and Italian tragedy, constructed according to supposed Aristotelian precepts and in avowed imitation of the antique: it is, in the same sense as the plays of Shakespeare and Calderon, a romantic product, born unnoticed by the learned and suffered to grow up unmolested by them, and only given an outer semblance of classic correctness when already fully and individually developed. It is the double product of the musical revolution of the early seventeenth century, melody and noted declamation, woven into dramatic shape with the addition of scenic display. These three items,—melody, recitative, and mimetic and mechanical show,—are its three originally most important parts; poetry is thought of only later, and must bend to suit them. The opera is first for the ears and eyes, and only subsequently for the reasoning faculties. It is the exposition, or the supposed exposition, of a story by means of music, and action, and scenery; words and their recitation (the staple of the pseudo-Greek drama) are added only from the necessity' of defining the story and giving words to the music. The words, therefore, are such as the scenic display, above all as the music, requires them. Now how do they require them ? What dramatic forms do they elaborate ? In the very first place the scenic part entirely rejects the famous unity of place: the object of the mechanician is to change the scene as often as he possibly can, so that the poet has to satisfy Aristotle's commentators (if he care to satisfy them at all) by the shallow excuse that "the

^

various places are all sufficiently near each other to be gone to and from in the course of twenty-four hours." This violation of the unity of place carries with it a real, although not avowed, violation of the unity of time; and this unavowed violation of the unity of time induces an unblushing violation of the unity of action. For as the scene keeps shifting, and the actors appear now in a wood, now in a palace, now in a temple, there is absolutely nothing to tell the audience whether the scene in the wood takes place the same day, week, month, or even year, as the scene in the palace; and as there is thus no perception of limits of time; as no one clearly knows when the various actions take place, there ceases to be any objection to introducing half a dozen various actions interwoven with each other,—plots, counterplots, murders, remorse, vengeance, mistakes, recognitions, complications enough for years and years of human life. Thus, instead of a correct tragedy according to Aristotelian precepts, we obtain an exceedingly loose and complicated play virtually setting all three unities at defiance. And since so many plots and events are compressed into one jjiece, since the action is not one, but none in particular, why not give up the Aristotelian canon of going from good to bad and bad to worse,—why not satisfy the noble lords and ladies assembled to celebrate a wedding or birthday, and the citizens and artisans come to enjoy their Carnival or Ascension amusement, and neither at all wishing to be moralised,—why not satisfy their craving for pleasant impressions by making the play progress from bad to better, or at all events wind up cheerfully? Why not? Here, then, is another piece of corrupt heresy: happy endings are substituted for dismal ones, even as in the harrowing Measure for Measure and the ferocious Fnenteorejuna of Lope de Vega.

Thus far the necessity of the scenic display has forced the opera out of the old pseudo-classic groove; the requirements of the music will push it into full romantic eccentricity, and the claims of the performers will give it the finishing touches needed to make it what the good critics of the eighteenth century called it—a monster, seductive or ridiculous. The music which developed on the stage was reducible to two forms, recitative and air. Besides the noted declamation, the one-voiced melody, there existed, until the full development of rhythm and instrumentation in the last quarter of the eighteenth century, only one really distinct musical form, the fugue or madrigal, inherited from the sixteenth century. For in default of that general rhythmical movement which could swing along the various parts, and of that instrumental mixture which could solder them together, as in the concerted pieces of the time of Paisiello, Cima-rosa, and Mozart, there was no choice except between letting one part (or one chord as in the choruses, where all the voices move together at regular intervals) move alone, or making two or more parts move together by that system of reciprocal balancing and pushing invented

by the cunning harmony of the Renaissance, and brought to perfection in the fugued choruses of Handel and Bach, in the fugued duets and trios of Marcello and Pergolesi. But the opera had from the earliest rejected the fugued concerted piece as too formal, too scientific, too difficult of execution, and too deadening of action on the stage; so, until the appearance of the rhythmical or symphony-like concerted piece of the late eighteenth century, it entirely dispensed with concerted music, which was left to the church or the room. There was as yet no way of making several voices sing together in a manner not unfit for the drama, so the voices were left to sing each in turn, and to meet only in recitative, except in the case of the simple chord-like chorus and in that of the duet, which was merely two airs juxtaposed and crossing each other at one or two points, two voices singing mainly alone, and only for a short time at the third or fifth. So the musical elements were virtually recitative and air.

Obviously the recitative was used in all scenes of action, altercation, and fluctuating feeling, for it was free, changing, impetuous as conflicting emotion; obviously, also, the air was used when a person was left to speak alone, or when a feeling had become perfectly homogeneous, for it was single-voiced, consistent, and defined as the ruling emotion of an individual. The bulk of the play, therefore,—the whole action, the whole friction of characters and collision of interests, all that makes the piece move on,— is given up to recitative; the superadded pieces, the lyrical similes, the solitary outpourings of feeling, all that is stationary in tlie play, all this is the domahi of melody. Their functions are defined and separate; their requirements are distinct and their influence opposed. The recitative, the approximative noting of the speaking tones, the musical expanding and ennobling of speech, requires, first of all, that speech be speech, and chooses, therefore, that poetical form which is most like prose, freest, least hampered by metre and rhyme, richest in various combinations of l)hrase, in long, short, broken, sustained periods—blank verse. And of this blank verse recitative requires that it be clear, to the point, chary of involutions which perplex the musician, hostile to set phrases, to figures of rhetoric, to oratorical lengthiness, to far-fetched graces, which condemn him to monotony of modulation because they are monotonous in spoken expression. Various, brief, clear, simple, abrupt, passionate,— such is the blank verse which is required for recitative ; no oratorical splendour, no stilted majesty: Seneca and Seneca's Italian imitators, the French poets who made Augustus and Athaliah speak like Bossuet and Boiirdaloue, are here no longer models; the librettist must strike out a new path, pushed onwards by the musician.

These are the requirements of recitative; those of melody are still greater. In the first place melody abrolutely requires lyric metres, metres totally

unlike thnt of the recitative—short, regular lines, rich in rhj'thm and rhyme, strongly marked, compressed into the most definite shape; strophes which both as wholes and as parts shall suggest well-marked musical phrases. And these short lyrics must be as lyrical as possible. They must be as absolutely homogeneous in feeling as is the music in plan; they must be worked up into arabesques to correspond with those of the voice; they must move towards a climax like the melodies to which they are set; they must, in their briefness, contain lines, half-lines, epithets, ejaculations, which the composer can detach, displace, and repeat and re-repeat as often as the melody may require; they must consist of metaphors, of similes which may be dwelt on and brought round again in new forms, which may suggest some imitative accompaniment, some particular vocal grace; above all, they must be manifold, offering the composer as many different rhythms, as many different moods and shades of mood, as possible; they must be by turns solemn and long-stepped, sighing and pathetic, tripping and cheerful, abrupt and passionate, brief or lengthy, in order that every sort of melodic form may be displayed. The lyrists of the Middle Ages and of the sixteenth century, the Petrarchists and followers of Bembo and Tasso, with their monotonous tinkle of sonnets, their vague, languid, turgid drawl of canzoni, can teach the librettist nothing; the ancients, with their curt metres, but their convoluted, inextricable sentences, can teach but little. The librettist must again follow his own devices, under the directions of the exacting-composer.

The scenic mechanician has forced the opera into being a play without real unity of time, place, action, or plot,^.an eccentric performance, crowding together all manner of events, and ready to move from bad to good as easily as from good to bad. The recitative has forced it to put all the action into blank verse, simple, uninvolved, curt, varying, impetuous, passionate, unoratorical, and unlyrical. Melody has forced it to interlard this blank verse with lyric strophes of intensely lyrical feeling and form, strongly marked, singable, metaphorical, various as various can be in metre and style. The opera is already a monster, setting Aristotle, Tris-siuo, and Castelvetro at defiance ; romantic, mixing blank verse and rhyme, dramatic and lyric, plain-spoken and metaphorical. Thus far we ^have seen the influence of the decorator and the composer on the poet, an influence which drives him to distraction, makes him^violate all rules, and, instead of a worthless piece of imitation, makes him create a new style, homogeneous and natural. There is yet another influence, that of the performers.

These performers are singers; they are, first of all, so many voices of various pitch, which have been trained from infancy to every sort of vocal gymnastics; whose respective importance is a purely ffiusical one. A

natural law of music makes the highest pitched voice invariably the most important; the singer with the highest voice, therefore, is inevitably the principal performer. Now, the highest voice necessarily suggests relative youth ; the principal part is, consequently, almost always that of a youth. And the emotions proper to youth, and best suited to high-pitctied voices, are the tender ones; the hero and heroine are, therefore, invariably in love, love passionate, melancholy, or solemn, but love of some sort; the harsher passions being left to the lower voices, so that ambition, patriotism, vengeance, and such like, fall to the inferior performers and become subordinate to that main love interest as the lower voices are subordinate to the upper. The poet has thus to develops to the utmost youthful characters and feelings, and to make love and the misfortunes of lovers the chief interest of his play. In this the ancient Greeks and Romans, who understood dramatic love only as a family virtue or a family crime, the love of Alcestis or the love of Phsedra (both too monotonous, the one in resignation, the other in fury, to give full scope to music), can be of little help; nor can their Italian imitators; still less the French dramatists, to whom young people are most often puppets, like Severe in Polyeucte, Curiace in Les Horaces* Xiphares in Mitliridate, and Aricie in Phedre, and for whom love is a mere insipid stuffing and bolstering for more violent and tremendous passion. The Spaniards, Avith their jealous husbands, seduced maidens, duennas, and poignards, as in Lope's play about the Infanta Dionysia and Caldcron's Alcalde of Zalamea, are almost equally useless. The poet who has created Eomeo and Jessica, Imogen and Helena, is unknown to the Italian librettist of the eighteenth century: the development of youthful character, the development of love interest and story, must be done by him.«elf unassisted. Further, the singers are voices; they are easily fatigued, and when fatigued are worthless; they insist upon having their parts distributed in a way to equalise the work. Again, being voices trained to various cunning artifices, they insist on displaying them all. Each principal part requires at least four airs of four distinct characters : a graceful, easy air, but not easy to sing (ai-ia di mezzo carattere), a pathetic air (cantabile), a speaking or dramatically active air (aria par-l(inte), and a passionate, florid air \'7baria di brarura). The inferior jiarts are not on any account to get anything as interesting as the superior parts, and they are to get less, the ultima parte getting only one air, and

    • In 1790 Cuiiarosa wrote his beautiful Orazi c Curiazl to a text of the comedian Sografi. The phiy is absolutely modelled on Corneillej_tragedy, witliout any additions or omissions". But who is the principal performer? Horatius, the murderer of his sister, as in Corneille ? No; Curiutius, who in Corneille is a mere doll; and why? because Curiatius, having to sing love duets with Orazia, must be, according to the habit of the day, the soprano, while Horatius must be the tenor, and consequently less important.

    that insignificant. Two airs of the sanae metre and character must not succeed each other, and two performers having the same sort of voice must not be made to sing in succession; claims in reality extremely moderate and rational, but which the writers of the eighteenth century declared monstrous, and v^hich, while taking the opera more out of the mould of the tragedy, completed it by balancing and co-ordinating _ its parts.

    Such was the musical drama of the early eighteenth century; a thing born of scenic displays and concerts, cherished for a century by the whole nation, moulded into a romantic, wholly original shape, by the requirements of scenery, music, and singing. Such it was, defined and regular in form, in the last days of the reign of the too-much forgotten Apostolo Zeno; an original, elegant, well-balanced, dignified, and wholly national form of art. The music to which it was linked was in high perfection, a perfection of solemnity, of heroic strength and grandeur; of ample and impetuous recitative, of majestic and solemn melody : the music of Lotti, of Handel, of Caldara, of Marcello, of the great composers of the first quarter of the last century. The singers who performed it were deeply scientific, trained in the schools of Pistocchi and Scarlatti, supreme in graduated and sustained solemnity, in powerful and well-marked rapidity ; magnificent in broad and dignified recitative; those heroically strong contraltos and solemn sweet sopranos for whom Handel composed his Rinaldo, his Giulio Cesare, his Admeto, his Flavio; among them superb actors and actresses, statuesquely fine in gestui-e, like Vittoria Tesi, the Romanina, Senesino, Carestini, and that Cav. Niccolino of whom Steele said that his gestures were as noble as those of an antique, and Addison, in the days of Betterton, that he wished all

English actors would take him as a model.*

* Steele's account of Niccolini is very quaint:—" Siguor Niccolini sets off the character he bears in an opera by his action as much as he does the words of it by his voice. Every limb, and every finger, contributes to the part he acts, insom uch that a deaf man might go along with him in the sense of it. There is scarce a beautiful posture in an old statue which he does not plant himself in. . . . He performs the most ordinary action in a manner suitable to the greatness of his character, and shows the prince even in the giving of a letter or the dispatching of a message. ... I have seen him enter alone at the remotest part of the stage and advance from it, with such greatness of air and mien as seemed to fill the stage, and at the same time commanded the attention of the audience with the majesty of his appearance."— Tatler, No. 115, Tuesday, January 3, 1709. Steele, be it remarked, had no musical sense, and abominated operas. Addison, in the Spectator (in which there is another eulogium on Niccolini's acting), has a very droll story of this singer's encounter with a lion, in the opera of IJydaspes, who roared in high Dutch to a figured bass, and, being when off the stage a tailor, claMed open the hero's doublet in order to make work for himself in his other capacity. Niccolini's voice was a low contralto; Handel wrote for him his fine part of Rinaldo.

Well-balanced, strong-, solemn, heroic, is this opera of Zono, of Cal-dara, of Handel; in these qualities it can gone further. Let it be perfect. Metastasio, Pergolesi, Leo, Jommelli, may arise.

IV.

In the year 1723 the Romanina got Metastasio engaged to write the text of the opera in which she was to perform the following Carnival. The subject chosen was Dido. The treatment was talked over between the friends, perhaps also with the composer Sarro, and with the Cavalier Niccolino, the greatest actor in Italy, so warmly admired by Addison and Steele, and who was to play ^neas. The Romanina conceived, we are told, one of the most original scenes. That the dramatic conduct of the play, the masterly rapidity of the action, were due to the influence of the great actress, is more than probable. Dido has faults, and in plenty; there are many tedious scenes, tiresome disquisitions, action springing from nothing; and ending in nothing; but it has a something, a simplicity of language, a swiftness of movement, an energy of passion, which show a new style and a master. The manly, generous, but lukeAvarm ^neas has the ease and dignity which Steele has described in Niccolini; a simplicity and modesty of gesture which yet fills the mind, because it is broad and elegant. Dido has a proud drawing herself up, a sweeping impetuosity of passion, a grand draping as it were of the part, whether calm or excited, in which we can recognise what the Romanina must have been,—in her scornful humbling of Jarbas, in her pretended indifference to ^neas, in her pitiful clinging to him, above all, in the splendid scene where, abandoned by all—dauntless, despairing, and bewildered—she hurls her death as an evil omen on the path of ^Eneas, and precipitates herself into the crashing ruins of the burning palace. In all this there is something almost superior to Virgil, superior as are the ample modulations, the concentrated accent of a recitative to the natural, but confused and feeble, intonation of mere spoken words.

Metastasio wrote not only the tragic play itself but wrote also two little comic interludes, according to that illogical jumbling fashion which prevails whenever an art is adolescent. After the curtain had fallen upon the intensely tragic Romanina Dido upbraiding the stately and statuesque Niccolini ^neas, it rose upon Signora Santa Marchesini, as a]irima donna, quarreling with the stage tailors about the length of lier train, and interrupted by the arrival of a famous buffo as Nibbio, a ridiculous manager from the Canary Islands. Metastasio had no true comic talent, yet these interludes are droll enough—caricatures of the very tragedy that they relieve, caricatures of the wrath and faintings of just such a queen as Dido, caricatures of just such airs, with tremendous

nautical, botanical, meteorological similes: roses, rainbows, gilliflowers, copper kettles, lions, tigers, lobsters, cold fowl, &c., as Benedetto Marcello recommended to opera poets of the year 1720, and as Metastasio himself made by the dozen—caricatures of the impresario, of the prima donna, of the audience; turning of everything into ridicule fearlessly, from the certainty that as soon as the tragedy was resumed people would weep as much at the originals of the caricature as they had laughed at the caricature itself.

The success oi Didone Ahbandoiiata vfas prodigious; it was immediately set by all the principal Italian composers, and performed on all the l^rincipal Italian stages. It was printed and reprinted. To the composers it offered a musical perfection, an elegance and variety of blank verse and rhyme such as had hitherto been wholly unknown. To the actors it gave an intensity of movement to which they were unaccustomed, to the public in the theatre, and to readers in the closet, it revealed a completeness of character and action, a height of pathos and passion, such as Apostolo Zeno could never have conceived. And from that moment dates the end of Zeno's reign, the commencement of that of Metastasio. Dido is iri some respects a mature, a perfect work, showing a complete mastery over the subject, an unerring instinct of the treatment. It is a simple, strong, correct blow, correct perhaps because it is the first that is struck. It is satisfactory because it is limited, because it does not aim at much, because in it Metastasio does not attempt to do more than a third of what can be done by him; because the plot is simple, the action evident, the characters and passions concentrated, and given ready made by Virgil. The plays which succeeded Didone are woefully inferior as wholes; they are as unsatisfactory as Dido is the reverse; they are confused, insipid, exaggerated, disagreeable, from the sense that the poet is at a loss how to proceed. They are often ridiculous in inanity and artificiality: in Cato in Utica, Csesar at one moment threatens Cato with Roman hardness and terseness, at another talks Petrarchesque sonnets at Cato's daughter ; in Semiramide Riconosmtta, Semiramis, pretending to be her own son, is made the judge in a dispute for the hand of a Bactrian princess, is recognised by a lover who had tried to drown her on a pretence of infidelity, and who consequently gives up the Bactrian princess, and refuses the cup which she oflfers her three suitors. The Hyrcanian prince, who, thinking his favoured rival would accept the cuj), had put poison in it, has it offered in turn to him, and is sorely puzzled what to do. . . . And thus for three acts of interminable complications. In Alessandro ?te//e/?irf2e, Porus pretends to be one of his own generals, carries messages to and from himself, and offers to betray himself into the hands of Alexander, in order to catch the latter. In Siroe, a princess, wishing to avenge her father on the tyrant Chosroes, dresses as a man,

becomes his favourite councillor, urges him to every degree of injustice towards his son, in order to make that son, who loves her, the instrument of her vengeance. Tlie son refuses; is accused of conspiracy, cannot clear himself without accusing her, and so on. In Artaserse, the hero, accused of regicide by his father, and unable to disculpate himself, is let out oF prison by the king, his bosom friend, and thus comes up just in time to crush a revolt, by means of which his father intended to depose the king and liberate him. There is so much action, so much plot, so much heroism, so much lyrism and love-making, so much blundering and recognising, that you get wholly indifferent to everything, to these eternally agitated men and women, and to these everlasting theatrical strokes—the very good qualities of the plays, the real passion, real pathos, real poetry, increase the impatience with the confused whole. Yet the Italian public did not grow impatient, and was not dissatisfied with these plays. Nay, it was better pleased with them, in their imperfection, than with Dido in its perfection. And the Italians were right. They instinctively recognised that the very inequality, the very languor and exaggeration of these later works, was the result of a development of Metastasio's genius ; that his uncertainty arose from striving after new effects; that the faults arose from the attempt to seize new beauties; that the want of proportion was the effect of growth. He was expanding the style, seeking its limits, fumbling for its characteristics; every fault corresponded to a new merit. If he was over-lyric, he was striking out lyric beauties; if he was over-complicated, it was because he was more varied and inventive; if his action was precipitate, his passion accumulated, and his movement jerky, it was because his action had become more rapid, his passion more concentrated, his movement freer; if he was swaying between the example of the French and of the Spaniards it was because he was absorbing some of the qualities of both. There cannot be another Dido : it must for ever remain his best nnless it be followed by very different works. And if Dido be Metastasio's best, Metastasio will never be Metastasio, the Metastasio of Achille, of Demofoonte, of the Olimjnade, of Eegolo. He will be but a better Zeno, forgotten hke Zeno. Thus, despite the bungling work of these plays, they were far more successful than Dido. They were newer, more original, contained more elements of greatness ; irregular, but great beauties, like the roughly but grandly sketched Cato, far more Roman and more dramatic than Addison's mild platonician ; like the two slightly executed, but powerfully conceived characters of Siroes and ^tius—noble, arrogant, boastful, passionate—like the beautifully pathetic situation of Arsaces in Artaserse, judged and condemned by the father whose crime he expiates, but dares not reveal: beauties also of lyric expression, of metrical originality and power, of brilliantly conceived plot and action. In Dido, Metastasio is

drawing correctly, with mastery, after the antique; but he can do more than copy the antique, he can compose whole pictures, balance large groups, manage cunning lights, combine splendid colours. He has now left the antique; he is sketching confused groups, blurring strange colours—no matter, he is learning his true work.

Almost immediately after the successful appearance of Dido, the Ro-manina, her husband and Metastasio, left Naples for Rome. Metastasio's brother, Leopold, was employed to look for a house, and bought or hired one in the Corso, between Piazza del Popolo and S. Giacomo, not far from where, some fifty years later, Goethe was to finish his Iphigenia in the palace oj)posite Rondanini's. To settle in Rome was equivalent, on the part of the Romanina, to retiring into private life, as ecclesiastical lu-udery would suffer no woman on the stage. Marianna Bulgarelli's career was over; her future interest in life lay solely in Metastasio. She was more devoted to him than before. She took into her house not only himself,—young, famous, and agreeable, and whom she idolised,—but what was very different, his whole family: an old man, who, however worthy of respect, was but an ex-soldier and a small ex-shopkeeper; an old and broken woman, ignorant, illiterate, accustomed to hobble about with a kerchief on her head, and an earthenware brazier under her apron, much honoured by the company of the neighbouring housekeepers ; a couple of girls, perhaps a little less homely, but probably not much more cultured, very like those whom the Romanina may have seen, gaudily tricked out, eating pumpkin seeds and oranges in the highest part of the theatre; and finally Metastasio's elder brother, Leopoldo, well educated and well-bred, but lazy, peevish, and perpetually dissatisfied. But they were Pietro Metastasio's family, and for Pietro's sake, for the sake of his fair and Avinning present, his dimly splendid future, for the sake of her passionate devotion, the Romanina,—intellectual, cultured, a great artist, accustomed to the society of men of rank or of talent, a proud, though self-made woman,—made these people her companions daily, hourly, and for as long as they chose to stay. These good people must have felt rather odd in their new position; they must have said and done things which made the Romanina's grand visitors look at each other and smile. Was the Romanina vexed ? Probably not. She may have smiled and tried to set all right and make everyone comfortable, but the elegant little Abate Metastasio, in his dapper black dress and a little white wig, with his soft, dignified manners, may sometimes have turned aside—crimson or livid— to hide his shame and disgust at some droll blunder of his father, or mother, or sisters. Yet, saving such little mortifications, his life was pleasant enough. True, here in Rome everyone knew about Gravina, some about the arte bianca shop, and there were all the Trapassis to tell their own tale. But living in this rather strange fashion in the house of

an actress, surrounded by the haruni-scai'um theatrical world, risen from the mud and living strange lives, Metastasio got a sort of devil-may-care feeling, and thought less about proprieties and dignity than before, for Metastasio's preoccupation throughout life was to come up to the notions of those who immediately surrounded him. And the life in Rome was pleasant in its way. There was no further thought of the law: Metas-■ tasio was to gain his bread writing texts for the opera. What he earned was spent on bread only metaphorically, since he and his lived off the Romanina, but it was a pleasant pocket-money for his little vanities and amusements, of which there were plenty. There was much company in the house, and always amusing, literary, and theatrical folk, who would talk, brag, and had many and various adventures ; young idlers, clever and agreeable, jovial men of the middle classes, who cared more for music and jesting than for their shops and offices; light ecclesiastics, gallant and cynical; occasionally also some traveller or passer-by.

So they lived in Rome during the winter, Metastasio writing his plays and looking on, while the energetic Romanina drilled the boy actresses of the Aliberti theatre; teaching them how not to trip up in their skirts, how to hold their fans and fold their arms, all extremely droll, no doubt; and generally instructing everyone, from Ihe prince of Persia in his fair wig, immense plumed helmet, and gilt manacles, down to the pages and senators and other dummies. Then the excitement of the final performance: the pasquinades, the applause, the triumph; the Carnival amusements, with the windows crammed full of friends; the riderless Barbary horses rushing down the Corso ; the stream of masks harlequinading along, throwing up flowers and sweetmeats, amidst a rain of plaster comfits and of witticisms ; the waxlights lit, and snuffed out, between street and Avindow; the yells, giimaces, quips and cranks, and everything that is childishly, barbarously amusing.

Then, during the dull Lent, some oratorio or sacred opera to write for this prelate or that, some wheedling of ostentatious princes of the Church, as Metastasio never entirely gave up the hope of ecclesiastical proferment, wishing, as was quite possible in the Rome of those days, to dine off the altar and sup off the stage'; to live in the house of an actress, surrounded by theatrical riffraff' and adventurers, and still to hold some sanctimonious office—clerk of the Inquisition, secretary of the Congregation of the Index, treasurer of the Propaganda Fide, or something similar.

And perhaps, too, there were walks in the spring, lazy strolls in the violet-grown dells of the Villa Pamphili and beneath the inky holm-oaks of the Borghese. Yes, there must surely liave been such : the cantatas which Metastasio Avi-ote about that time prove that he was not always on the pavement of the Corso and the boards of the Teatro Aliberti. Id. these charming little pastorals of a page or so, of which the gruff and

sarcastic Porpora set the blank verse in pithiest, lightest recitative, and wrote to the rhymes the sweetest, brightest melodies, wreathed with delicate cadences, starred with crisp turns and sparkling little shakes, in these cantatas of Metastasio's there is an element of truth which there was not in the Endymion or the Gardens of the Hes\'7dierides —there are no patches of Virgilian or Theocritan colour, there is no sweetly insipid perfume of Tasso and Guarini; Thyrsis and Chloe, Philenus and Irene, the shepherdess who is invited to go on the sea, fretted by the moonlight; the shepherd who dreams that he sits on the brink of the well with his beloved, and starts up awake at the appearance of his rival; the youth and the nymph who are caught by the shower and take refuge in the cave: all these bright, graceful, actively feeling and moving little figures, are neither real rustics like Lorenzo de' Mgdici's immortal Nencia, nor yet dainty Dresden ladies and gentlemen, with flowered bodices, long waistcoats, powder, and crooks. They are something betwixt and between, embodiments of impressions received neither from the fields and woods nor from the clipped avenues and terraces of a garden, but from the sort of Elysian ruralness of those sweet, solemn Roman villas, where the horses graze beneath the red-stemmed pines, where you tread on a carpet of lilac anemones and starry daffodils, where the bays meet overhead, and the water trickles over the maidenhair of the broken fountains, where Arcadia seems real, Ai'cadia neither of dusty pedants like Crescimbeni's yonder on the Janiculum, nor of porcelain beaux, like that of M. de Florian, but an Arcadia of your own, according to your own heart.

In the scorching Roman summer there were the little open theatres, where Pulcinella and Coviello jabbered the Neapolitan dialect, which Metastasio preferred to his own stately Roman, and where hairdressers' apprentices and coffeehouse waiters played great ladies and sly waiting-maids. Later, in the pestilential autumn, there were villeggiaturas at Albano and Frascati, with long games at cards, noisy midnight Avalks, and singing and laughter to heart's content. Every now and then there was even some longer excursions to Bologna, Avhere the bufifoonish, jolly men of science flocked round the Romanina and Metastasio; to Venice, where the Dido was received with rapture; where they met old Neapolitan friends, Porpora and Vinci composing, and Metastasio's adopted twin brother, Farinello, singing, no longer a boy, but the greatest, most brilliant, most versatile, most magnificent of singers, living in a sort of permanent apotheosis. At Venice also they met the Saxon Hasse and his famous, beautiful wife Faustina, staunch friends in later years, and destined to set and sing Metastasio's verses into popularity all over the world. And at Venice a famous rococo painter, by name Amigoni, later destined to paint the finest scenes for Metastasio's plays, put the poet into a half realistic, half allegorical picture, with himself, Farinello, and the

Faustina, to whom he might have added her husband Hasse; with these three Metastasio was to be indissohibly connected, though going through life in different countries; while increasing their individual fame, constantly contributing each to the other's triumph; they were young and hopeful, fit to be painted together. The Eomanina Amigoni did not dream of putting into his picture : she was gradually becoming a thing of the past.

But meanwhile time was going on. All hopes of ecclesiastical preferment had vanished; the price of each of Metastasio's new dramas was fixed at 300 scudi (about 60/.) ; their success was certain. All was going well, but all was limited: more new plays, more 300 scudi, more applause, he knew it all by heart, and it probably began to pall upon him. Such a smooth, straight road, down which he could see for miles, was depressing him; he would fain have turned a corner, at the risk of whatever might appear round it. Perhaps, also, the sense of dependence iipon the generosity of the Eomanina began to weigh upon him; perhaps he was weary of being so constantly thought of and cared for; weary of being the sole thought of a woman who no longer sufficed for him. He was what people in those days called imprudent, and she was a prudent Avoman—he imprudent, safe in her care; she prudent in her absolute devotion: the words sound like an irony. Imprudent he was, in the sense of following his whims, of ceding to his passions, and the Romanina was prudent in trying to restrain a weak, selfish man. Perhaps she would have had him more manly, stronger, more capable of restraint, able to repress all but some huge folly like her own, more like her own self—blind to the fact that had he been like her she could not have felt towards him as she did, nor he have been what he had become to her. There were petty quarrels, the more frequent because Metastasio brooked interference less, now he was tired of dependence. There were worse than quarrels, worse than anxieties: Metastasio, from fault or weakness, got himself into a predicament which placed him at the mercy of enemies. This is all his biographers dimly hint, speaking vaguely of his " frequent visits to a person for whom he had a polite partiality," of " regard towards her family forbidding further explanations;" of calumnies spread; of a lawsuit threatened, and suppressed by the influence of a friendly cardinal; of the matter not ending till the mysterious person had "jjreso stato,'" which can mean only one of two things, marriage or the cloister. Whatever the matter was it must have been scandalous, judging by the extreme anxiety shown by Metastasio to suppress all discussion on the subject, as in his letter written to Cardinal Gentili, written some years later—the most abject humiliation, the most painful knee-kissing, the most pathetic entreaty for hel\'7d) which could be extorted from a man who

N

has let himself slip into a disgraceful position, who cannot defy calumny, and sees safety only in complete silence. Altogether, the pleasant life had become embittered.

Did the Romanina notice it ? Surely. But she did not become angry. She let Metastasio suggest to his old protectress, the Princess Belmonte Pignatelli, that he was anxious for change, for a less precarious position; that—ah, were it only possible ! if only—but he had no thought of it— if he might obtain employment at Vienna, in case Apostolo Zeno, the Court poet, should require assistance. The Princess Belmonte repeated the insinuation to her sister-in-law, the Countess Althann, widow of the favourite of the Emperor, and herself at one moment his flame; then the matter was left to itself. The suggestion worked its way. On September 27, 1729, Metastasio received a grand letter from the Austrian Embassy, a letter whose aspect and seals must have made him turn white and red, and the Romanina tremble and sicken. It was from Prince Pio di Savoja, one of the Emperor's lords-in-waiting, and said that the universal applause excited by Metastasio's poems, and the appi'obation awakened in the august Emperor, were the reason for which his Majesty desired to oflfer his service to the Abate Metastasio, on whatever terms he might mention; that Apostolo Zeno, the present Court poet, wished for no other companion, and that, as soon as an answer in the affirmative was received, money would be forwarded to cover the expense of the journey from Rome to Vienna.

Metastasio was astounded, not at the proposal, for which he had been sighing, but at the rapid fulfilment of his dearest wishes. His biographers tell us that the letter put him into terrible perplexity; that he could not resolve to leave his dear native city, his dear father, brother, and sisters, his dear benefactress; that, without uttering a word, he placed the letter in the Romanina's hand; that she was overjoyed, chid him for his coolness, laughed, joked, and saluted him Poeta Cesareo. Alas! the pretty little story must be apocryphal: the post had been long coveted, the indecision long settled, the Romanina's sacrifice had long been made; and an answer, joyfully accepting the offer, and suggesting 4,000 florins as annual stipend, was despatched the very next morning. Presently came Prince Pio's reply: 4,000 florins were deemed too much; would the

Abate Metastasio accept 3,000, and a hundred unghei^i for the travelling expenses? The Abate Metastasio most humbly and gratefully accepted. He begged time to settle his affairs in Rome, to provide for his family (already provided for by the Romanina), to put an opera on to the stage, &c.; all would be completed by Lent, and in Lent he would start.

All was completed by Lent. His family was to remain with the Bul-garellis; Leopoldo was to continue at the bar; the Romanina was to

teach the singers of the Teatro Aliberti how to perform his pieces; he was to go, become rich, great, who knows what? And in a few years he would obtain a holiday, and pass it in Rome; or they should all come over to Vienna—why not? It was not so melancholy after all; only a little twinge at parting, a little sickness of his too feminine sensibility, a few tears, and then all would be over; once off, all would be merry as ever. But would it be merry for the Eomanina; for her who was going nowhere, who had no future, and was to lose the present? Metastasio wept, and wept copiously, we may be sure, and then sprang cheerily into his postchaise. Marianna Bulgarelli parted from him with a smiling face, and words of hope and encouragement; but when he was gone there I'emained in her poor life a void, a darkness, cheered up only by the hope of seeing him again.

V.

Charles VI. of Austria, King of Hungary, Emperor of Germany, King of Naples and Sicily, sovereign of the Milanese, Caesar Ever August, was a very stately and splendid sovereign, surrounded by very solemn magnificence. True, the Austrian house was beginning to be the football of Europe; his father and brother had been brow-beaten by Louis XIV.; he himself had been turned out of Spain by the little imbecile Philip V. True, he was on the point of losing Parma and Naples, and could with difficulty cope with his rebellious electors ; true, his daughter was to be ignominiously deprived of the empire by Charles of Bavaria, and to be buff"eted about by Frederick the Great, Augustus of Saxony, George II., M. de Choiseul, and Madame de Pompadour; true, the Austrian finances were deplorable, the Austrian people ragged and ignorant, the Austrian armies ever defeated; true, he was a pompous empty pate: true, most true, yet Charles VI. was surrounded by a halo of glory, an aureole of victory, a dim majesty of Roman imperialism. And he knew it. He felt the necessity of a degree of holiness, of solemnity, of magnificence, such as only the heir of the Caesars could assume. His court, his capital, were full of prudish gallantry, of fiivolous devotion, of ostentatious bad taste, of majestic brutality, of imbecile bigotry : a mixture of French elegance and levity with German coarseness and heaviness, Spanish solemnity and vacuity, Hungarian pride and love of display. Oriental splendour and misery, and Italian love of art. Feudal courtiers kept musical chapels and d)-ank fifty sorts of wine at dinner; Jesuits built plaster beribboned churches; ladies were publicly and solemnly asked to appoint their lovers; men who had struck priests who had insulted them were promenaded through the town in sackcloth, holding expiatory

N 2

candles; heretics were slaughtered in Silesia; Turks were dreaded on the Danube; the Empress and her ladies amused themselves with archery meetings where jewelled Cupids were shot at; the people amused themselves with seeing robbers and murderers racked and broken on the wheel; there were grand circus games, where bears were baited, bulls torn to pieces by dogs, and horses ripped open; German comedies, where Hanswurst and Kasperl said and did all that is filthiest; and Italian operas, where heroic contraltos and idyllic sopranos sang virtue and clemency to exquisite music: of that strange medley of refinement, brutality, pomp, vice, and bigotry which constituted a German Court of the early eighteenth century, that of Vienna was a perfectly balanced specimen: less vicious than Saxony, less brutal than Prussia, but as dignified, splendid, and bigoted as any. And in this Olympus, with his feet on the heads of Magyar and Bohemian nobles, of German mercenary generals, of Italian and Spanish princes, of Occidental and Oriental magnates, was throned Charles VI. Ever August, with his confessor behind liim, his humpbacked, velvet and diamond clad dwarf on the right hand, his gouty, grave chapelmasters, and plump, wistful singers, on the left. Like all of his family, a mongrel, without sympathy for any nationality, Charles VI. was too much of a German lout to be a successful Spaniard, too much of a Spanish grandee to be a satisfactory German; he had suffered too much from France to endure anything French in dress, language, or manners; so, on the whole, he inclined towards being Italian in all that he could be. And, while as a German, a Spaniard, a Hungarian, Charles VI. was but a huge, pompous puppet, twitched by the various European stringholders into attitudes the droller for his very gravity, as an Italian he had his fine side in his sincere passion for music and his truly intelligent cultivation of it. He was a good j)erformer, a tolerable composer, an excellent critic, though, as artistic sovereigns iisually are, rather jealous of supreme merit. His two chapelmasters, Fux and Caldara, were somewhat ancient and pedantic, innovating genius rather disconcerting Caesar's musical habits; but he also employed more modern and fashionable composers, like Lotti, Porpora, and later Hasse. He would have liked to compose his operas and to sing them in person, but the sense of Cajsarean dignity restrained him. He did the next best: he made all his dependents learn music; he sent his little Archduchess, Maria Theresa, on to a miniature stage when she was still an infant, and made her sing duets with Signor Senesino when she was already Grand Duchess of Tuscany; he had operas performed by his chamberlains and ladies of honour ; he accompanied Farinello on the harpsichord, and well-nigh gave singing lessons to the greatest of living singers; he had long interviews with his chapelmasters, and presided at every sort of rehearsal. He squandered the money of his poverty-stricken country on wonderful

performances in the open air, where the choruses were sung by a hundred distinguished singers ; on operas in the Favorita gardens, witli astounding scenic shows and naval battles, like the one seen by Lady ^Mary Wortley Montagu, which cost 30,000/.; he kept comi)anies entirely composed of celebrities, like the Tesi, the Faustina, Carestini, Senesino, Lotti's wife, and the like, of whom a single one was enough to sustain the great theatres of Naples, Venice, or Rome. For the sake of his operas also he kept Apostolo Zeno, a Cretan Venetian, one of the most distinguished literati and humanists of the day, who received 4,000 florins for one or two dramas, and who was assisted by another playwright, Pariati, at a salary of 2,000 florins. And for the sake of his operas Charles VI., on Apostolo Zeno retiring from active service, had called from Italy its greatest dramatist, the young Abate Pietro Metastasio.

The honour of being the servant of so great and splendid a sovereign was too much for Metastasio's feelings; he himself wrote home that, although he had prepared himself for the event, the presence of Ctesar Augustus entirely overpowered him. It was at the palace of Laxemburg. The gentleman-in-waiting introduced the poet into the room and left him on the threshold. Metastasio made three most humble bows, one at the door, one half-way, and one before the Emperor, and went down on one Icnee before the immense and monumental monarch, not, as in his pictures, in a breastplate and laurel crown, but in walking dress, a three-cornered beaver on his majestic peruke, leaning against a table, looking very serious indeed. " Rise, rise," said Caesar, and Metastasio, in faltering tones, began the speech he had probably composed before his departure from Rome, which sounded thus: " I know not which is the greater, my joy or my confusion, at finding myself at the feet of your Ca^sarean Majesty. This is a moment for

Avhich I have longed ever since my earliest years, and now I find myself not only in the presence of the greatest monarch of the world, but even in the glorious capacity of a servant of his. I know the obligations of this position, and if the loss of a great part of my blood could make me a Homer I should not hesitate to become one. I shall, however, do my best to supply my want of talent, sparing neither attention nor fatigue in your Majesty's service. I know that, whatever the degree of my incompetence, it will always be less than the infinite clemency of your Majesty, and I hope that the position of poet to Caesar may give me that merit which I cannot hope from my talent." Charles VI. listened patiently, and as he listened his countenance became more serene (why should it have ever been otherwise?), and then he answered: "I was already persuaded of your ability, but lam now further convinced of your good manners, and I do not doubt that you will satisfy me in all my Cffisarly service; nay, tliat you will force me to be satisfied with you," The Emperor stopped, waiting to see whether

Metastasio had any request to make; he begged permission to kiss Cfesar's hand, but Ca?sar laughed and shook hands friendlily with him. " Dehghted by this demonstration of affection," writes Metastasio, " I squeezed Caesar's hands in both mine in a transport of pleasure, and gave it so sonorous a kiss that my most clement master could not but perceive that it came from my heart."

We may smile at this scene, at this ludicrous crawling speech of the poet, at the solemn mien of the Emperor, at the transports of joy and the overwhelming sense of honour with which the greatest of Italian writers received the stinted, ungracious civility of this pompous Ceesarly jackass ; but we must remember what royalty was in those days, what a halo, what a glory, what holy splendour sun-ounded it; we must remember that the Bold Bavarian had not yet snatched the imperial crown ; that Frederick the Great, with his shabby clothes and democratic manners, had not yet brought Austria to the last gasp ; that Maria Theresa had not yet made herself cheap to everyone, from the King of France's mistress to the smallest vice-chapelmaster of Salzburg ; that the Holy Roman Empire, that mysterious inheritance of the Caesars, that link between Augustus, Charlemagne, and modern times, was still intact; and that this pompous jackass, this dull, crowned music-master, was its incarnation, and as such stood on a mental pedestal, in a mystic niche, which could be approached only with awe and trembling. Metastasio was in no respect superior to his age, which was servile; nay, his temper made him improve even on the servility of his day; so Metastasio was extremely happy, and there was a more interested reason for his satisfaction. If he had offered to shed his blood in order to write better plays for Caesar, if he had squeezed Cesar's hand with such transport, if he had given it such a sonorous kiss, it was not merely from abstract loyalty and abstract servility: the post of Court poet was, in his eyes, a golden door to a vaguely-splendid career of Court favour. And why not ? The Emperor, constantly busy about his operas, his oratorios, his cantatas and serenatas, had frequent opportunities of noticing his theatre poet, of talking with him, of making him his intimate. Metastasio's predecessor, Zeno, who had left Vienna just before his arrival, had been most remarkably honoured by Charles VI.; he had been treated with the most astonishing familiarity, had been made the Emperor's companion, his friend, his crony, had been given opportunities of obtaining a splendid position at Court, if he had not been too great an old fool to seize his advantages. And if Zeno, an old, simjDle, crabbed scholar, caring and knowing only about parchments and books, without a presence, without manners, without desire to please, could have gained so much of Caesar's affection, what might not be done by a young, handsome man, by an acknowledged genius, a man of the finest manners, the most delicate tact, the most insinuating conversation, who hungered for imperial condescension, and could give such heartfelt and sonorous kiases ? Ah, yes, Metastasio would captivate Cassar as he had captivated Gravina and the Romanina.

Meanwhile he looked around him in this new world of Vienna, this world of mongrel feudalism, of heraldic hierarchy, in which people were judged of by their quarterings; so different from his own democratic Italy, where servility was unprejudiced and practical, the only inequality being that between those who could confer favours and those who could accept them. Metastasio did not know a word of German, any more than any other foreigner of the eighteenth century, to whom the language was a mere guttural jabber fit for drunken postillions and half-witted alchemists, but not for polite lips or polite ears. But this ignorance, although it was of no hindrance in conversing with chamberlains, maids of honour, and similar civilised people, was a great disadvantage when coping with Viennese servants and tradesfolk, especially where there was not much money to facilitate comprehension. Metastasio, therefore, ingratiated himself with a fellow-countryman, Signor Niccolb Martinez, a Neapolitan of Spanish origin, and interpreter of the Papal Nuncio. He had long lived in Vienna; his wife knew how to deal with Germans ; both he and she were pleasant, reputable people, just rich enough to have a comfortable home, just poor enough to be glad to share its comforts with a man who could pay for them. So Metastasio took up his abode in the Martinez's apartment, up a great many stairs, In the Kohlmarkt Street, and arranged his occupation methodically, as was his habit, and as was easy for a man who had always been taken care of by others.

It being a pious Court, he began his day by going to mass at the Capuchin church; then he wi'ote his plays, then he went about paying his visits, all with the regularity of clockwork. He thought to captivate all the Viennese magnates with his handsome face, his discreet wit, his delicate scents, his elegant, subdued dress, his perfect balance of good ([ualities. And so he went his round of visits. But the Austrians seem to have been rather cold towards this plebeian Italian poet, without quarterings, without ancestors, with nothing but talent, and without a voice, which was the only thing tliat could make these blue-blooded feudal grandees tliaw towards an inferior; for a singer, like a spaniel, a horse, a dwarf, was one of those inferior beings which could be fondled without indignity. But Metastasio was only a poet, that is to say, something very like a valet: being the Emperor's poet, he had indeed a place in the hierarchy, not as high perhaps as that of the Emperor's chief butler, or chief groom, or chief dwarf, but he had a place, and one which must be recognised even by those who, instead of writing verses for Caesar, had the supreme honour of handing him his wig, and buckling his garters. Beyond such a frigid recognition of Metastasio, things appear

scarcely to liave gone; and Metastasio ever after hated the Austrians, especially the ladies, seated solemnly over their samplers, from which they would raise but a supercilious glance at the poet. Metastasio's good looks and graceful speeches were unremarked by all this blinking, lisping, half-deaf Viennese pride ; but they made a conquest, and an important one.

Do you remember the Countess of Althann, to whom, as to her sister-in-law, the good Princess Belmonte had applied on Metastasio's behalf, and through whose influence the post of Poeta Cesareo had been obtained for him? To her, as the source of his good fortune, as the relative of his former patroness, as the greatest of Italo-Austrian great ladies, Metastasio immediately turned. She had perhaps seen him once or twice at Naples, where her husband had been Viceroy at one time; she knew all about him through the Princess Belmonte ; she received him very well, and he, rejected by the Austrian grand folk, solitary and discouraged, threw himself at the feet of this, his only hope. Marianna Pignatelli was a very great lady indeed, both by birth and by marriage; her late husband, John Michael III., Count of Althann, had been the chief favourite of Charles VI. She herself had long been, and perhaps still was, the Emperor's chief flame—honours in a German Court, where every infraction of the morality of lower folk was sanctified by its title, badge, and place in the hierarchy. She was very rich, had beautiful possessions in Moravia, and moreover was extremely influential and venerated at Court. She was an intellectual, liberal-minded woman, not indeed (being an Austrian by marriage) as jovially familiar with writers, composers, and singers, as her warm-hearted sister-in-law, the Princess Belmonte, could be in unceremonious, undignified Naples; but appreciative, encouraging, gracious to talent, whatever its number or jjaucity of quarterings. Metastasio's works she admired, his compa^ny she enjoyed. For the Countess Althann was probably weary at heart: weary of her grandeur, weary of the Court routine, weary of the empty-brained people with stars on their breasts and keys on their coat-tails, who formed her society ; incapable, from Italian birth and education, of taking an interest in the squabbles for precedence and for footstools, which occupied the court; incapable, from character, of feeling attachment for these pompous male and female Court dolls. Moreover, she was ceasing to be young; forty was fast approaching, and, as it approached, her famous beauty, her famous fascinations, were vanishing. Charles VI, may still have been jealous, but he probably had long ceased to be in love; she was turning into a neglected dowager, without much interest in life. At that moment appeared Metastasio, young, good-looking, witty, broad in opinions, delightful in manners, an Italian, a genius or very nearly, and ready to see her young, beautiful, fascinating, all that she had been; ready to adore

her discreetly, luimbly,—raising- his eyes upon her only enough to show her that ho wished to do more but dared not. She was delighted with him, with his respectful love : she encouraged him. That she was amiable, clever, charming, is probable ; that she was rich, powerful, his only resource and hope, is certain. Little by little he made his way with her, not foreseeing perhaps what did happen, that the great lady ceded completely to him, became his slave, his mistress—most wonderful of all, his legitimate though secret wife ; that he should have foreseen this is scarce possible; but in the Countess Althann he saw an ally, a protectress, who might push him on in this dull stupid Court, and help him even more than the sonorous kisses on the Emperor's hand.

And meanwhile it was pleasant; Ctesar was distant and Olympic indeed, but benign ; the Empress was encouraging ; the archduchesses adorably gracious ; one play succeeded better than the other; with time and patience he might still obtain as much notice as Zeno liad done, and he would know how to set it to profit. And the Countess Althann would help him on. . . . All went well. In the winter he went daily, as was the duty of a respectful cavaliere servente, to amuse his noble protectress while she was having her beautiful hair curled, pomatumed, and powdered, and again in the evening when she received her friends. There were long chatty games at cards ; music, with Hasse and Caldara to play the harpsichord, and the Faustina, Farinello, or himself, to sing, and pleasant talks with condescending ministers and diplomats. In the summer there was the visit to the Countess in Moravia, the long strolls through the woods, the rambles gun in hand, everything familiar and charming. But there was not comjjlcte peace in Metastasio's mind while he shulfled his cards, talked gaily, and listened to the music : something began to worry him. He had found a delightful protectress here at Vienna,—a beautiful, accomplished, rich, powerful and loving Mari-anna ; but there was another IMarianna, the one he had left in Rome.

The Romanina had permitted him to leave her; she had supported the parting with fortitude, she had been happy in the thought of his hapi)i-ness. But once away, her mental eyes were never turned from the direction in which he had gone; she attended to household matters, to the wants of hei- husband, of Metastasio's father, brother, and sisters; she directed the performance of his plays at Rome : all went on as usual, but her thoughts were far away, straining to see through the space that separated him from her, straining to see him, to follow his actions, to live in his presence. Much she doubtless supplied by her own fancy, working upon the scanty facts contained in his letters. But he did not tell her enough of himself and of his doings. Why not ? Perhaps because, wearied of long tutelage, he was vaguely vexed by her attempt still to keep him in her sight, under her supervision. He wished to enjoy his liberty,

to account to no one for his actions, to be independent, and independent she woukl not permit him to be. His letters (Heaven knows how much pruned and revised by those who published them) are at first affectionate, dutiful, but with a sort of hurried affection and quickly despatched duti-fulness. There is no lingering over this sort of talk with the distant one, no fond entering into such details as could make her see him; it is all very proper, grateful, civil; he feels bound to write so many times a month, but he hurries over his lettei', and sends it to the post with a pleasant sense of accomplished duty. The Romanina, intensely sensitive. —all eyes, ears, imagination in what concerns him,—is dissatisfied : she wants more details ; she complains of briefness, of reticence; he answers with greater briefness and reticence, and also with a little impatience, filling up his letters with moral reflections—moral reflections to her who is hungering and thirsting for love, for something that may enable her to be in his company, at least in imagination. She becomes suspicious, jealous ; imagines he is purposely concealing what he is working at, complains, accuses. Metastasio, with the impatience of a slightly niffled stoic, resigns himself to complaints which, he says, have become as regular and inevitable as fits of quartan ague; forgives her, becomes more brief, more general. The Romanina has been very good to him, dear, generous soul, but she is too ridiculous, too exacting towards a young man in his position; well, she is an evil, with her eternal suspicious epistles at regular intervals; but it must be borne. Meanwhile he goes to the Countess Althann, sees her hair dressed, reads her his poems, basks in the sunshine of so great a lady's aff"ection.

But the Romanina cannot take things so philosophically; she has no future, no present; she has only a blank, a void, an immense bitterness to live upon. And were they not to meet ? Was he not to return to Rome after a few years ? Does he ever allude to that, the ungrateful wretch ? Was there not a talk of her joining him in Vienna? He has forgotten that. But she has not. Join him, and how? Under what pretext ? How leave her house, her husband ? How undertake such a tremendous journey, not of days but of weeks ? Has not the Emperor a chapel, does he not engage all the greatest Italian singers ? And is she not a great singer—a great one among the great ? The poor passionate creature forgets that she is old, that she has long left the stage, that she has refused engagement after engagement. She thinks only of seeing him again. Let him get her engaged.

Metastasio is terrified at the idea. Engage her, an old woman ? Never. There is no danger of that, indeed. But if she knows there is no chance by this means, who can tell whether she may not sacrifice house, husband, all, and come to Vienna, openly, avowedly to see him ? He trembles at the thought. What, to be claimed by her, as her protege,

her adopted son; Heaven knows what! By an actress, a singer, a mad woman, without sense of decorum or prudence, in the face of the whole Court, of the Emperor, of all his friends and enemies! To be made the laughing-stock of this prudishly gallant town ? And the Countess of Althaun! "What will happen if she, the proud great lady, whose property he has become, sees him claimed by another woman, a plebeian, a stage woman ? She who thinks him entirely hers, who never dreams of his having been defiled by less noble patronage ; and the Romanina, who thinks that he lives solitary and faithful to his gratitude, finding him the acknowledged pet of another woman! What may not happen? Good heavens! the earth will open beneath his feet; his hopes, his career, all be engulfed, and he be left to shame and misery.

No ; the Romanina must not, shall not come. But the only means of preventing her is to let her continue in the hope that she may; to delude her into fancying that he is Avorking for her, lest she take the matter into her own violent hands. Oh, wise young diplomatist! sagacious reader of the human heart! Expert manager of life's stage ! How admire thee enough? Alvisi, thy biographer, is too delighted with thy ingenuity, and expatiates on it: " He loved her sincerely ; he did not let a post-day pass without giving her the most lively signs of affection, but he took care not to satisfy her. He managed things so that the hope should not be extinguished in her, while he abstained from taking any steps to obtain what she desired. The most exquisite policy did he use in the matter, so as neither to disgust Marianna nor to risk any imtoward concatenation."

Exquisite policy! And what sensibility, what consideration for Mari-anna's feelings, as well as for those of the Countess I A troublesome game, but beautifully played; nay, almost a pleasure to play it. But the most dexterous player cannot play against Fate. Fate would have it that Marianna, wearied, suspicious, became exasperated at the delay; that some singer or composer, returning from Vienna to Italy, dropped an incautious word about the Countess Althann .... Metastasio played well and long, but Fate could not be wearied. "What happened ? We do not know. Suddenly, in the year 1734, a letter comes, a black letter. Metastasio falls as if stricken. He can no longer conceal his feelings. He is ill, very ill; cannot go to Court for months; remains at home for weeks, till at length the Countess Althann, alarmed, throws dignity and decorum overboard, and rushes to him, up the three pairs of stairs, into his rooms at the Martinezes. All we are told is that Marianna Bulga-relli, commonly called the Romanina, was dead. Around this fact there is a great stillness, a great darkness. But in the stillness circulate faint, A'ery faint murmurs; in the darkness are visible dim outlines of things which frighten us The mm-murs cannot be completely comprc-

bended, the outlines cannot be distinguished, yet there remains a terrible something, a legend made out of these confusedly interpreted vague sounds and sights ; a legend which now, after 150 years, would scarcely be understood, but merely suspected, had not a great philologist, a seeker for curious myths of all sorts, registered it in his common-place book. There it stands, hard and prosaic, in the common-place book of Gotthold Ephraim Lessing, Librarian of Wolfenbuttel, in its alphabetical place, among notes on antique medals, extracts from mediaeval MSS., memoranda on hydraulics, old German ballads, &c.

"Metastasio. —In his youth he was called Trapassi. Finazzi tells me that the Didone Abbandonata, performed for the first time in Venice in the year 1725, contains to a certain extent the story of Metastasio himself and the Romanina, the most famous of then flourishing Italian singers. The Romanina had fallen in love with him, and when M. was called to Vienna she wished, shortly after, to follow him. But Meta-statio feared lest she might occasion annoyances to him in Vienna, and might damage his reputation there, as she was married to a certain Bulgarelli, a poet and musician. So he obtained an order from the Court, which was sent to her half-way on her journey, forbidding her entering the imperial dominions. The Romanina became furious, and in her first rage tried to kill herself, and wounded herself in the chest with a penknife. The wound was not mortal, but she died soon afterwards of grief and despair,"

The Romanina was not married to a poet and musician; J\Ietastasio may never have been in love with her ; she died full four years after his settling at Vienna; Didone was written ten years before her death; orders to prevent people entering the imperial dominions were not granted to Court poets for the mere asking; the asking for such an order was not the simplest or least com].)romising step a man could take. The myth is a myth, full of incongruities and absurdities as all myths are; but myths do not originate out of nothing: they are distorted phantoms, too hideous for reality, but which haunt and avenge.

Metastasio staggered under the news of this death, so sudden, so opportune, so unexpected, perhaps also so horrible. So Mariauna was dead! She who had so long stood in his way was removed ; the letters of which he had been so sick had come to an end ; the suspicions and accusations would never again be renewed; the journey to Vienna, which had so terrified him, would never be carried out ; that dreaded encounter would never take place; he had been fighting for his honour, his safety: they were no longer in peril. He had almost hated the Romanina, and now he loved her again. Oh to be chidden once more, to dread her again, to risk all from her arrival! anything rather than that she should be dead; gone, gone in wrath at his ingratitude ; gone before he could have made

amends (as he had doubtless intended to do) for the cruelty to which he imagined he had been driven by circumstances ; gone before he could have loved her again and been grateful to her once more! And even in her anger, in her moment of death she had forgiven him, had loved him, provided for him, made him heir to all her fortune after her husband's demise. This generosity was too much; this money was too loathsome to him ; he had fine and generous instincts and ideals when selfishness did not frighten him out of them. He did not hesitate for a second, but wrote otf to his brother, in answer to the news of the Romanina's death and of the inheritance, a quiet, manly letter, but intensely remorseful and sad:—*' In the agitation caused by the sudden blow of the death of poor, generous Marianna, I have not the strength to write at length. I can only say that my honour and my conscience persuade me to renounce the inheritance in favour of her husband. I owe the world the rectification of a great mistake, namely, that my friendship for her had its foundation in interest or avarice." . . . Then he gives instructions concerning the legal measm-es necessary for the transfer; he conjures his brother to keep on good terms with the Romanina's husband, all calmly and briefly, but at the end his grief bursts out:—"But poor Marianna will not return, nor can I hope to console myself, and I think the rest of my life will be insipid and melancholy. May God help me and give me the force to keep up, for I do not feel it in me."

Metastasio, the least Quixotic of men, had done a Quixotic thing. Neither honour nor conscience nor any feeling towards Domenico Bul-garelli required his giving up the inheritance, for Bulgarelli was to have the interest of the capital all his life, and there was no reason whatever why the Romanina's fortune should not go to her friend after her husband's death, rather than to some person, unknown in all probability to herself, whom Bulgarelli might choose as heu-. Metastasio was merely depriving himself and his of a capital of 1,500 crowns without any real necessity or reason. But he was sacrificing the money not to Bulgarelli, not to justice, not to appearance, but to the memory of the Romanina, to his own ideals, to his own feelings. Let no financial advantage mar the perfect grief at his benefactress's death; let him not accept a gift from her to whom he had been ungrateful. ., . He had been mean, cruelly mean; hard fate (no doubt) had forced him to ingratitude ; now, freely, spontaneously, he would be generous, self-sacrificing ; it raised him out of his humiliation, it did him good to wipe out by the generosity which was of no use the meanness which had killed.

After this Mctastasio's grief became milder and more bearable; he had the pleasure of looking back at the past with tender regret; he could freely love the Romanina, freely vent his gratitude towards her, praii^e her, talk of her, now she was dead. Of an easily moved disposition, the

mention of the Romanina's name ever after brought the tears into his eyes—tears of sincere affection and admiration, which he coukl shed even in the presence of the Countess Altliann, who was doubtless much moved by the grief of her dear friend, and who may even have cried a little over this generous woman who had done so much for him, and who was safely removed far beyond all jealousy. Thus ended the romance of Metastasio's life, and with it his youth, and soon after his hope and his genius.

VI.

Metastasio's genius, and with it the musical drama of the earlier eio'hteenth century, attained to perfection only after his arrival at Vienna and after the year 1730. This date represents the maturity of the composers who were to be his fellow-workmen, in the same way that Bononcini, Caldara, Scarlatti, Lotti, and Keiser had been the fellow-workmen of Apostolo Zeno. Although the general forms both of the drama and of the music remained the same, the early works of Metastasio, of Leo, of Vinci, and of Hasse represented a change: an attempt to obtain greater flexibility, greater variety, intensity, and delicacy of form and effect. A younger, subtler genius was entering the forms left by the older masters, and as it moved, expanded, and altered, it also discomposed their solid dignity. Metastasio was not the mere equal of Zeno, as Vinci, Leo, Hasse, and Pergolesi were the equals of their predecessors,—he had from the first an immeasurable superiority of talent; yet the first works of the younger poet, like those of the younger musicians, are far less satisfactory than those of the older: both poet and musicians obtain new and beautiful effects of movement and pathos at the sacrifice of the former dignity and completeness, at the expense of alternate insipidity and jerkiness. Gradually the change is completed, the new genius and new style are matured, discrepancies and awkwardness disappear, the various qualities coalesce and harmonise, the excrescences are absorbed. Already in Artaserse, vfrittcn in 1729, there is less vacillation of purpose ; in Adriano the leading character is fuller and more conspicuous; in Demetrio, Avritten in 1731, the unity of plan and the development of situation are almost perfect; in Issijrile, written in]732, the unity of plan is disturbed, but the action greatly strengthened;—these are all imperfect works, but they balance and correct each other's imperfections. The period of perfection begins in 1733 with the Olimjn'ade, followed at intervals of six months or a year by Demofoonte, La Clemenza di Tito, Acliille in Sciro, and Temis-tocle, and it is closed in 17-10 by Altilio liegolo, after which masterpiece there is nothing but imitation and inferiority.

As the opera was an artistic form, distinct and different from tragedy,

so also Metastasio was a difterent sort of poet from Shakespeare and Lope de Vega, from Corneillo and Racine; as the opera was a combination of two very distinct mnsical forms, recitative and air, so also Metastasio was a poet of two very distinct categories: a dramatist and a lyrist. But here we must note a difference: the opera, in its duality, belonged half to the poet, half to the musician; they were subservient to each other by turns: in the recitative, the musician, composer, and singer helped the poet, worked to give his verse the strongest, most artistic expression ; in the air, the poet helped the musician, laboured to give him, composer and singer, the greatest scope for free melodic invention and execution. The notes of Pergolesi, the intonations of Farinello, were of first-rate beauty in the recitative, but its real absorbing interest was the words of IMeta-stasio; in the airs the rhymes of Metastasio were often of first-rate beauty, but the real, absorbing interest was the melodies and harmonies of Pergolesi, the swells, and runs, and shakes of Farinello. Metastasio's real greatness does not lie in his lyrics, beautiful as is sometimes the sentiment, perfect as is always the expression, deft as are invariably the metre and rhyme; these lyrics are even more incomplete Avithout the music than would be the notes of the recitative without the words; the notes of the recitative would be vague, formless, meaningless without the words; but the lyrics are wholly diflferent without the music. For the music entirely changes the character of the lyrics: those little strophs, which look such ridiculous appendages at the end of scenes, whose brief metre and recurring rhyme jar so painfully with the sustained blank verse, which are read off with a rapidity out of all proportion to the time required by what precedes ; those little strophs are altered, enlarged, transposed by the composers, expanded into broad musical phrases Avhich coalesce perfectly with the musical declamation of the blank verse ; their component parts are arranged and repeated in different fashions, their metre is widened, their rhymes veiled; they take as long to sing as two or three scenes of blank verse do to declaim. Those tripping, skipping rhymes, which seem, when read, such absurd vehicles for pathos or passion, are made by the composer into sustained and intense lamentation, or impetuous and whirhnnd-like invective ; those little comparisons of flowers, seas, ships, storms, skies, &c., which read so insipid and tiresome, are turned into exquisitely graceful melodies, into rich and florid songs, during whose performance poet, words, rhyme, and metre are forgotten in pure musical enjoyment.

Further, as the opera was performed by voices, of which the highest pitched and therefore most important ones suggested youth and youthful feeling, Metastasio diverged from tragic writers by the immense importance he was forced to give to love. There must be love between the ^jrimo 1107110 and the jmma donna, else how obtain a satisfactory duet between them ? And e\^en ■where, as in Themistocles and Regulus, the real hero is not the high-voiced youth but some graver father or adviser, on whose patriotism or revenge the real interest depends, even then an additional interest, a love story, must be created for the priino uomo and the prima donna, who by musical right, and despite dramatic suitability, remain the most important performers. Nor is this all. An action, and a complicated action like that of Metastasio's plays, cannot possibly be carried on by merely the three principal characters ; other characters are required to complicate the threads, another young man or young woman is required to bring about the jealousy or the sacrifice in which consists the pathos of the situation, not to speak of the confidants required to give and receive information. Thence arises a second couple of young people, the secondo uomo and seconda donna, who have to make love respectively to the jyrirna donna and the jmmo uomo in order to produce unfortunate complications, and who, in the intervals, when they must come forward in order to let their exhausted superiors take breath, can find no other employment than again making love with each other. This inevitable subordinate love is inevitably uninteresting: it has been created not for its own sake but for the sake of the other love ; a second pair of lovers cannot be made to go through the selfsame scenes of tenderness and rage as the first pair, and, as the musical recitation of the play forbids any mere exchange of witticisms, any fanciful flippancy such as Shakespeare gives to his second pair of lovers, to Jessica and Lorenzo, Nerissa and Gratiano, Beatrice and Benedick, this subordinate love-making of the opera is mere namby-pamby cooing and sighing, weak sonneteering, fearful trespassing into the ground of pathos and passion reserved to the jjriino uo7no and prima donna.

Moreover, the difference between recitative and ordinary speecli induces a radically different conception of character from that of the ordinary tragedian, iRecitative, drawing its existence from the inflexions of the speaking voice, starves on rhetoric and dies miserably for want of feeling. Long descriptions, disquisitions, logical propositions, involving no alteration of mood, supply no intonations to recitative ; what it wants is feeling, fluctuating and rapid. The consequence is that Metastasio entirely eschews everything like speechifying for its own sake; if his men and women speak it is because they feel. He accustoms himself to think not so much how people would speak but how they would feel. He cannot conceive one interlocutor waiting quietly while the other discourses ; the very internal emotions, which in reality find no vent in words, but only in looks, are noted and treasured by him, are communicated to the audience by means of those continual apartes, those exclamations, oh Dio! Stelle! Dei! &c., which seem absurd and womanish in print as long as we suppose them to be spoken, but which are most effective in

recitative, as the expression, by artistic licence, of what is merely felt, not said. Metastasio could not have conceived Cinna sitting calmly listening to Augustus's eloquence; to his mind, Cinna would have bounded up after the first sentence: he could not have imagined Theseus listening quietly to the narration of his son's death; in his Clemenza di Tito, which is in the main the same situation as Corneille's Cinna, the principal scenes are totally different. What interested Metastasio was not what Titus said, but what Sextus felt; and into Sextus's feelings he dived, bringing them out with wondrous perfection of gradation, from the first terror of finding himself before his betrayed benefactor, in the line

Oh voce che piombami sul cnore

through the stages of sickening and dizzy fear, the agonised hesitation, down to that passionate explosion of feeling, that sweet though anguished flood of tears, with which the traitor sinks down overwhelmed by the generosity of the betrayed :

■ Oh Tito, oh mio clementissimo prence, &c.

To conceive an emotional situation, to develope it, gradually yet swiftly, marking each step, each movement, even as a musician would develope a theme, this was Metastasio's aim and his glory. To obtain opportunities for such development was his constant thought; he was for ever seeking for pathetic situations, he loved to crowd them together. The subjects treated by the ancients and by the French did not satisfy him, they were too meagre for him. He would take the main situation from half a dozen plays and poems, and work them into one plot, combining together in his Titus the Cinna of Corneille and the Andromaqne of Racine; weaving together Sophocles and La Motte, Ariosto and Racine, Lope and Herodotus, and then, in the prose argument prefixed to his play, referring the reader with grand vagueness to Strabo, Pliny, Sanchoniathon, anyone ; as romantic as Shakespeare or Calderon, while thinking he was correct and classic as Maffei.

As a writer of opera texts, Metastasio was much influenced by music and musicians; he had none of the sense of discomfort of ordinary libretto writers; he enjoyed writing for music, being a musician himself and a passionate lover of the art. He was intensely fond of Hasse, who set most of his operas, and between whose very delicate, graceful, and pathetic music and his own verse there was a strong affinity ; of Jommelli, closely resembling Gluck, he was an immense admirer; himself an excellent singer and somewhat of a composer, he was at his ease in the musical element and moved freely in it. Instead of the contempt and hatred of such writers as Gasparo Gozzi and Parini, he felt a liking for singers: he recognised their artistic value, sympathised with them, made friends with them, and was repaid for his friendliness. He did not write for

o

abstract performers: his actors were before him, and he wrote to their measure. They were indeed singers, biit the early eighteenth century, with its immense development of recitative, was rich in singers with dramatic talent, which required only to be directed. Some of these singer actors and actresses were really great: intelligent, energetic, handsome, and with a natural dignity of gesture which was increased by the dignity of vocal recitation; and Metastasio let his conception of a part be influenced by the individuality of the performer. Thus, in his Dido and -/Eneas we can see the Romanina and Niccolino ; in his passionate proud -(Etius we can recognise the superbly strong and florid Carestini; in some of his princesses the charming, soft Faustina Hasse, in others the Amazon-like, majestic Vittoria Tesi. The charming part of Megacles in the Olimjnade —of whom Argene says, " Avea bionde le chiome, oscuro il ciglio . . . gli sguardi lenti e pietosi—" was suggested by a beautiful young pupil of Porpora, with fair curls and femininely soft brown eyes, Felice Salirabeni, who afterwards represented Achilles disguised as a girl on Scyros in a way which astonished Metastasio himself: " The part is made for him "—he wrote to his brother. " I have trained him with great care, and he has succeeded so perfectly that the opera will not have half its effect where he cannot perform it."

Under the influence of composers and singers Metastasio received the finishing touches requisite to make him a romantic poet: it was impossible to conceive correct tragic folk, solemn Greeks and Romans like those of Corneille, Racine, Maffei, and Alfieri, in the midst of this strange and motley vocal world of the eighteenth century: of these women dressed as men, and boys dressed as women, in powder, velvet, rose-coloured doublets, hoops, jewelled helmets, immense feathers, many-buttoned gloves, and every eccentricity of cut and colour ; of the soprano and contralto heroes and heroines, quarrelling and making love in richly modulated recitative, with fiddles to mark the cadence and hautboys to play the ritornellos, sighing their passion or threatening their anger in magnificently melodious airs with fugued accompaniments, or in wondrously subtle and flimsy woofs of swells and runs and curling turns and luminous shakes. A distinct race of beings, as distinct as the euphu-istic, fantastically dainty young men and girls of Shakespeare, as distinct as the grotesquely wonderful masks and Kings of Hearts of Gozzi, was necessarily created under the influence of the proud beautiful music of the Hasses, Leos, Pergolesis, and Jommellis.

And they had not time to be ceremonious and stilted, these opera heroes and heroines: they were called into existence too rapidly for that. There was no thought of the Imperial theatre poet first writing half a dozen plans of a play, then working out one in prose; then versifying the prose, then turning the diction into correct Tuscan, as did the fierce and

energetic Alfieri : the plays were ordered and had to be produced at once, to be ready by a certain day, to be ready for representation,—-poetry, music, scenery, acting, everything; nay, once, in the case of Achilles on Scyrbs, the performance had to take place eighteen days after the play was ordered of the poet. Metastasio had to dash down an argument on a large sheet of paper, make memoranda of the scenes and stage business, and begin scrawling ofif verse after verso, song after song, while the messenger waited to carry each page to the composer, at whose door another messenger Avaited to carry each piece to the singer; and then Metastasio had to be present at the ■prima donna's house at the rehearsal of the second act, and to clamber on ladders and teach the mechanicians where he wanted the temple, porticoes, and ships of the first act; while the third act was only taking shape in his brain. Beset by composers, singers, scene-painters, mechanicians, there was no time to take down the dictionary of the Crusca; the people had to speak, not Tuscan, but Roman, and sometimes familiar Roman, such as Metastasio himself spoke; luckily the pedants were forgotten in the bustle.

And now, having followed Metastasio in the composition of his play, having seen all the requirements and restrictions due to music and scenery, seen the poet surrounded by the odd figures of the eighteenth-century vocal heroes and heroines, writing under the influence of eighteenth-century music, hurried by copyists, mechanicians, messengers, chamberlains; having watched him at his work, we would fain see the production f-when completed, witness the performance of one of .his operas. But we cannot. The wonderful Favorita Theatre, with its open-air stage extending into real avenues and thickets, may indeed still be standing, but long abandoned and decayed; the scenery may still be lying in some lumber-room, but blackened and tattered ; the music of Caldara or Hasse mav still be contained in some mouldering music-book, but long silent; the voices which declaimed the verse and sang the songs have long died away and been forgotten ; of this combination of arts, of this splendid and delicate and complex work, fostered by a whole nation for a whole century, there now remain only ruins, memories, and the volumes containing Mctastasio's plays. We cannot scientifically reconstruct, nor fancifully evoke a vanished form of art; we can only take up and examine what yet remains of it; these plays, which are not a whole in themselves, but only a part of a great whole, of the opera of the eighteenth century.

Of these plays three may be considered as representative : the Olim-pmde, of the year 1733, for the delicately-sketched youthful characters and pathetically-developed situations; Achille in Scire, of 1736, for buoyancy, swiftness, and impetuosity of action; and Attilio Jiegolo, of 1740, for sustained simplicity, solemnity, and grandeur of situation.

o2

Mctastasio tells us in his preface tliat the subject of the Olimpiade is taken from Herodotus; in reality the story is but slightly modified out of the Orlando Furioso: the scene is in Elis instead of being in Paris, the tournament turns into the Olympic games, Charlemagne becomes Clis-thenes King of Sicyon, Bradamante his daughter Aristea, beloved by a Greek, Eoger called Megacles, and by his bosom friend and benefactor, Lycidas, who is made Prince of Crete instead of Prince of Constantinople. The original chivalric colour of the story is never wholly lost: the Olympic games, despite their choral processions and olive wreaths, retain something of the mediaeval tournament; Megacles, Greek wrestler and runner though he be, acts with the punctilious sense of honour of a paladin; Aristea is more of an Erminia or Isabella than of a Briseis or Iphigenia; antiquity and chivalry, Ariosto and Herodotus, are fused, and out of their mixture is produced a something perfectly original, situations and characters neither classic nor mediaeval. Megacles arrives at Olym-pia obeying the summons of his friend Lycidas, who has saved his life, and who claims the fulfilment of his promise of gratitude ; he arrives in the very nick of time; he must hasten and enroll himself among the competitors in the games which are about to take place, enroll under the name of Lycidas ; there is not a moment to lose; all shall be explained on his return. He goes and returns. Lycidas explains the plot. The prize of the Olympic games is to be Aristea, the daughter of King Clis-thenes ; Lycidas is in love with her ; he has no chance of winning her in the contest; his friend Megacles, a repeated victor in the games, shall win her for him. Megacles is struck dumb; to the eager, hopeful words of the flippantly passionate Lycidas he answers confusedly ; he staggers, he begs to be left to repose before the games begin. This Aristea, this prize whom he is to win and to hand over to his friend, is his own long

hopelessly beloved ; he can possess her and he must not keep

her ! He will keep her; but what of Lycidas, who loves her, who hopes only in him, for whom he had sworn to sacrifice his life ? Is he to refuse him this, the first, the only gift ever asked ? Honour and gratitude vanquish; yes, he will conquer Aristea; Lycidas shall possess her, and shall never know at what a price his happiness is bought. If only Aristea can be prevented from knowing the real victor, if only she can be led to Lycidas without thinking of Megacles; if only her presence be avoided; before her what would become of his resolution? All would melt away. At this moment he is interrupted in his thoughts; he turns round ; it is Aristea herself ! Megacles ! and is it he himself, the long-beloved, and yearned and wept for in vain! Has he at len,gth heard his poor Aristea? Yes, he has come, and how opportunely! Oh happy love, happy past griefs! But why is Megacles so silent, why does the colour

come and go in his face, why doos he not look np ? Has he not come to win Aristea ? He has. Then why this confusion and sadness ? She understands it all ; some one has made him doubt of her fidelity ; frankly, cheerfully, she sweeps aside the idea; he has been and will ever be her only love ... he has for ever been in her thoughts. But why does he not answer? Why does he smother exclamations of grief? Listen: does he believe her to be faithful? As faithful, is the mournful answer, as beautiful. Is he not going to win her ? He hopes it. Has he still his former valour ? He thinks so. And will he not conquer ? He hopes it. If it is so, will she not be his ? From Aristea, clinging lovingly, but anxiously to him, Megacles tries to sever himself; the recitative becomes melody, the exquisitely simple touching melody of Pergolesi's duet, " Ne' giorni tuoi felici;" he bids her remember him in the happy days to come; she asks him the reason of these strange, sad, words ; he'begs her, weeping, not to speak; she entreats him to explain; the words of the one, the silence of the other, are intolerable; she sees him in grief without imderstanding its reason; he struggles with suppressed jealousy; both join in complaining of their cruel destiny; a solemn, deeply pathetic passage, of doubt and boding evil, which closes the scene.

The Olympic games come to a close, and Megacles, under the name of Lycidas Prince of Crete, is the victor. King Clisthenes crowns him with the olive wreath, while the chorus sings an ode; and then the prize, the beautiful Aristea, is led forward. Megacles pretends that he is suddenly called back to his father in Crete, and begs Clisthenes to intrust his bride to his friend iEgisthus, who is, of course, no other than the real Lycidas. Lycidas, light, eager, impulsive, is impatient to discover his love to Aristea; he urges Megacles to explain all to her. Megacles asks to be left alone with the princess, much to the surprise and annoyance of the unsuspecting Lycidas, who retires. Once alone the ordeal begins. Aristea throws herself into the arms of Megacles, rejoicing at their final happiness; to her words of love and joy he answers only with enigmatic sadness, trying how to break the terrible news to her. Is he in earnest or jesting ? she knows not what to think; sadly, tenderly, solemnly, he begins to explain, and, as he speaks, vague fear seizes her. Has she not often said that what she most loves in him is his spotless honour, his gratitude and generosity; would she still love him if he had become ungrateful to his benefactor, perjured to the gods, false to his promise ? And how can Aristea ever conceive such a change in him ? Let her then know that by becoming hers Megacles will be all this : ungrateful, deceitful, perjured. And he tells her the story, his promise to his benefactor, of the Cretan prince's love, of the plot by which he is to win her for his friend. What! he has fought for another ! he would consent to

lose her, he would have her sacrificed ! Mcgacles, half broken in purpose, revives; he begs her, as she loves him, to enable him to do his duty, to crown his sacrifice, to love his friend as she has hitherto loved him ; he calls upon her generosity and heroism . . . but Aristea will hear nothing of this; she sees only that she is to lose him, that all her hope, all her future is gone, that her happiness is shattered; generosity, heroism, what is all that to her ? The resigned, quiet Magacles determines to be brief; he cannot face her despair and wrath; he bids her farewell, the last farewell. The last! Aristea is struck down by the sudden blow; he is leaving her already. Go he must, and, if he go, better at once ; she would detain him in vain ; he goes; and overcome by grief she falls down insensible. Megacles hastens back; this sight entirely breaks his resolve ; he kneels down by Aristea, tries to revive and comfort her. This is a piece of accompanied recitative, set magnificently even by so late a master as Cimarosa. He calls her in vain ; he will stop, she shall be his wife, anything rather than see her thus ; but she does not revive. "What shall he do ? can he leave her ? leave her thus? and, if he remain, what becomes of his honour, his gratitude? What will Lycidas say, and the deceived Clisthenes ? At least he will delay the going. Delay ? it will be this agony again ; what shall he do ? the sighing violins and viols are the only answer. Better go. Farewell, his beloved, his hope, lost for ever. The instruments echo, Lost for ever. May the gods watch over her and give her the happiness he has lost: a passionate, lyric burst of almost melodious declamation, borne upwards by the instruments. Lycidas, where is Lycidas ? Lycidas comes; has Aristea heard all ? but what does he see ? what is the meaning of this ? Hastily, impatiently, Megacles answers ; a sudden grief has overcome her; involuntarily, he is angered by the unconsciousness of Lycidas, his unconsciousness of all the tragedy that is going on. " And thou leavest me ?" says Lycidas. " I go," answers Megacles, " ah, think of Aristea." Alas, what will she say when, reviving, she finds him gone ? Lycidas, attend; and these last instructions glide from recitative into slow, gently heaving melody, the exquisite melody of Pergolesi—" If she asks what has become of me, tell her I am dead." But a thought strikes him, a deep, passionate thought, which makes the melody stop, and expand solemnly. " All, no, do not give her such sorrow for me. If she asks after thy friend, answer her only, ' he went hence in tears,' and the accompaniment breaks in low, tremulous sobs; then, while Lycidas hastens to succour the still fainting girl, Megacles bursts out in one last, rapid, wild outpouring of grief at losing his beloved, and hurries away. Aristea revives, calls upon Megacles, and recoils in horror on recognising a stranger instead of her beloved. "Where is Megacles?" "Gone," answers Lycidas quietly; "but I, thy love, thy husband, thy Lycidas,

am here " Lycidas, is he Lycidas ? she cries, starting to her feet; and Megacles has left her! Where is the justice of heaven if the gods leave such villany unpunished ? What ails her ? What has Megacles done ? asks the perplexed Lycidas. Does she ask for revenge ? She shall have it, she shall have all and everytliing from him. From him ! Aristca bursts into impetuous song, broad, majestic in its very passion, the masterpiece of the great master Leo. Away, out of her sight! He is the cause of all her wretcliedness, of all her misfortunes ; let him never hope for love or forgiveness from her; his sight will for ever be hateful and monstrous to her. But all comes right at last, after many complications, attemjited suicides, and murders; the tender and vehement Aristea is united to her Megacles, wonderfully sustained in quiet, tender, resigned affection, for Lycidas is discovered to be her brother, a long-lost sou of Clisthenes, and returns to his former love, Argene.

Achilles on Scyros is far better constructed than the Olimpiade, or rather it is not constructed at all. It is an organic, spontaneous, perfect growth, scene developing insensibly out of scene, and action out of action, unbroken by oracles, recognitions, or murders, unhampered by the second pair of lovers ; a beautiful and swiftly moving whole.

An oracle having declared that Troy cannot be taken without the help of the young Achilles, Ulysses, despatched by the Greek chiefs, arrives in the island of Scyros, where Achilles is said to lie hidden by his mother Thetis. While waiting for the succour promised by the king Lycomedes, Ulysses remarks, among the damsels of Deidamia the king's daughter, a certain Pyrrha, whose strange beauty, martial expression, vehement manner, and passionate love for the princess, lead him to suspect that she is the object of his search, disguised in woman's clothes. He takes every means to make sure, to elicit some unmistakable proof; while, on the other hand,

Deidamia, in love with the disguised Achilles, does all in her power to prevent the discovery. Achilles, swayed alternately by martial instinct, by shame at his disguise, and by love and fear of losing Deidamia, is for ever on the point of discovering himself, and for ever restrained from so doing. At length Ulysses, fully persuaded that Pyrrha is Achilles, resorts to an artifice which shall force him to disclose himself. Lycomedes, King of Scyros, is banqueting with his guests, and Ulysses describes in eloquent terms the preparations which are everywhere being made for the Trojan expedition ; and as he speaks he watches the supposed Pyrrha, standing near the princess Deidamia, listening eagerly, forgetful and agitated. " All Greece," says Ulysses, " has risen like one man; the cities are emptied of their inhabitants ; decrepit old men drive on their sons with envy; the very children and maidens bm"n to join the fight, and the wretch wliom some hard necessity holds back accuses Heaven and thinks himself hated by the gods."

Deidamia, terrified at PyrrLa's strange demeanour, calls her, chides her lover for his want of prudence. The king bids Pyrrha take her lyre and sing to entertain the guests; reluctantly, and only at Deidamia's bidding, Achilles acquiesces. He sings in bitterness of love and his cruel power, which takes pleasure in degrading the wisest and bravest, in degrading men and gods ; in making Jove himself assume the shape of beast and bird; and after all this requires the victim to kiss his chains, to praise his shame and servitude. In the midst of the ode, Achilles is interrupted by the arrival of the servants of Ulysses, bearing presents to the king of Scyros. Lycomedes and his friends admire the purple apparel and costly vases, the princess the gems and ornaments: the eyes of Pyrrha are fixed upon the swords and shields and lances. " Ah! " exclaims Achilles, " what splendid arms !" " Resume thy song, Pyrrha," orders Deidamia angrily. At that moment there is a great clangour of arms, a noise of strife; all rise in surprise. Areas, the confident of Ulysses, rushes in, calling upon the chief to stop a contest which has arisen between his followers and those of Lycomedes. The noise grows louder; Lycomedes hastens to the scene of the fray with his friends, Deidamia runs to hide in her chamber; Achilles remains, trembling with martial rage. Fire runs in his veins, a mist rises up before his eyes, he can contain himself no longer. " To arms ! " he shouts, " to arms ! " But he stops, he perceives the lyre in his hand, the lyre, his only weapon. He dashes it on to the ground, seizes a sword, and rushes forward, heedless of his woman's weeds, with the magnificent impetuosity of the Pompeian fresco. At that moment Ulysses, who has been watching him unobserved, advances, takes him by the hand, and salutes him as Achilles. Terrified at the discovery, the son of Thetis recoils; but Ulysses embraces him, and tells him that it is too late for more dissimulation. Come, he will lead him to glory ; Greece awaits him alone; Troy fears only him. Achilles, overjoyed, follows him, but stops. " And Deidamia ? " " Deidamia ! he shall return to her more worthy of love." " And meanwhile? " " And meanwhile, while the whole world was on fire, he would remain hidden on Scyros ? What would posterity say ? That Diomede, Ido-meneus, Ajax, had broken the walls of Troy, and divided the spoils of Hector: and what was Achilles doing ? Achilles, robed in woman's weeds, lived ingloriously and feebly among the maidens of Scyros, slumbering to the sounds of other men's exploits. Ah, let this never be said! Let no one see him again in this garb. See, does he recognise himself? " and as Ulysses raises the shield as a mirror, reflecting the youth in his disguise, Achilles tears his dress in wrath, and cries out for arms. And Ulysses leads him oft", quivering with shame and rage. As they go they are met by Nearchus, to whose care Thetis had confided her son, and who tries to stop the supposed Pyrrha. Achilles shakes him off, bids him never again pronounce that shameful name; but then, when Nearchus asks wliat is to be said to Deidamia, he turns round. Toll her that he loves her, that lie leaves her faithful, that he will return ere long; a beautiful tender air, quite in kcei)ing with the character. Nearchus, dreading the anger of Thetis, hastens to Deidamia, and tolls her that Ulysses will carry off her lover unless she prevent it. Meanwhile Ulysses is leading Achilles to his ships, and admiring the young hero, in his shining armour, rejuvenated like the serpent which has shed its skin, and twists and untwirls proudly in the sunshine. At last, says Achilles, he fools himself ; but like a prisoner whose chains have been struck off he still doubts of his freedom, the shadows of his prison are before his eyes, the sound of his fetters still in his ears. Ah, when Avill he see the shores of Troy? He will wipe out the stains on his name; the indignities of Hcyros shall be erased by his sword; he will bury the remembrance of his shame beneath that of his glory. " And Thetis thought to hide him from the world!" exclaims Ulysses; and the recitative bursts into a grand and vehement air, rolling and storming with its splendid simile of the fire bursting out of a volcano and rushing in destruction over the land. The ships come up to shore, and Achilles is about to cross on to one of them when Areas runs up, hurrying their departure: " Deidamia," he whispers to Ulysses, " pursues them." '• What has happened? Whence this haste ?" asks Achilles. " The King of Scyros," answers Areas, " has heard of our departure, and may attempt to prevent it." "Prevent the departure of Achilles? Is he then the slave of Lyco-medes? " " Away! let us not be detained," urges Ulysses, well knowing how dangerous a foe pursues them. But Achilles refuses to move; he will await Lycomedes and show him that he is no prisoner. Instead of Lycomedes arrives the infuriated Deidamia. She stops before Achilles, and they remain a moment in silence; then she bursts out in complaints of his perfidy; he would ansAvcr, but Ulysses stops him. " If thou speak, thou art lost," he whis])ers. But Achilles cannot listen in silence to her passionate accusations; he must, he will answer; he explains that he loves her, but that he can no longer remain in shame on Scyros ; he must follow Ulysses; he has dreaded her grief, her tears, he has fled from her because he loves her ; but go he must. Deidamia feigns rosignatinn; she confesses that he is in the right, that his disguise was shameful, that his love was weakness; yes, he must go. But give her a day, only a single day more, let not the blow be so sudden ; can he refuse it ? Achilles does not answer, but remains Avith downcast eyes. Will he not give her a day ? What thinks Ulysses ? Ulysses answers with scornful indifference, "Achilles is master of his actions; let him go, or let him stay. But he, Ulysses, must go at once ; if Achilles wait, he will leave him behind." Achilles knows not what to answer.

" Well ?" asks Deidamia, "resolve." "I would remain, but wliat of Ulysses ? " " Resolve," cries Ulysses. " I would go, but what of Deidamia? " " I understand," cries Deidamia, " thou wouldst go; go, unfaithful wretch !" To go, or to remain? which shall he do? Deidamia no longer begs him to stay ; no, she sees that it costs him too much ; she asks but one last gift : since she must die, let it be by his hand; let him begin his deeds of war on her ; he will go, unhampered ; she will die happy, dying by his sword! The half-serious comedy touches Achilles; he bids her not speak thus: "Ulysses, I cannot go, it would be too cruel." " So I see," answers Ulysses, " farewell," " I ask only one day's delay," begs Achilles. " Oh ! that is more than I can afford. I must hasten to the Greek chiefs, and tell them what noble deeds are wiping out Achilles' shame; what grand amends he makes for the idleness of Scyros, what trophies he is raising." " Valour is valour," answers Achilles, " it is not lost in a day." " Valour! " cries Ulysses, " do not speak of it. Strip off those arms. They are merely a weight to Pyrrha. Ho! bring tlie hero's gown! He has sweated too long beneath the helmet." " I Pyrrha! oh gods ! " and Achilles becomes ready to go. " Thou leavest me? " asks Deidamia. " I must." " Already?" " The delay is fatal to my honour;

farewell, Deidamia; " and he mounts resolutely on to the ship. Deidamia, left alone, bursts out with furious grief; calls upon the gods to avenge her; her ghost shall haunt him everywhere, and bring him to his death. But no; alas, whose fault is it? Could Achilles remain for ever? If some one must pay the penalty, let it be the miserable Deidamia ; she has lived for him; for him she will die. And overcome by grief she sinks inanimate. Achilles sees it, pushes aside Ulysses, who would vainly restrain him, springs from the ship, and runs to her side; and calls her, and tells her he will stay. "Areas," says Ulysses, " the battle is lost; let us cede for the moment, and then we will try other arms; " and he hastens to Lycomedes, persuades him to give his daughter to Achilles, and postpones the departure till Achilles can go to Troy, leaving behind him his bride. Thus ends Achilles on Scyros; not a tragedy, but rather an heroic comedy of intrigue and love.

Attilio Eegolo, on the other hand, is pure tragedy, with a more than tragic, almost religious solemnity: in it there is no crime, only a grand self-sacrifice; there is no plot, nothing but the gradual action of the hero's influence on those around him; the whole interest depends upon the resistance of Regulus against his own friends, his final triumph over their love and their veneration. The play opens with tlie daughter of Regulus, Attilia, stopping the consul Manlius as he descends the stairs of the Capitol, and apostrophising him in favour of her father, a prisoner at Carthage. This scene is magnificent in dignified impetuosity; Attilia neither begs nor threatens, she demands assistance with a consciousness

of justice, of greatness, which places her, the supplicant, far above the man who is supplicated ; every word, every burst of passion, means a gesture, and a gesture of infinite nobility. Manlius, secretly jealous of the heroism of Regulus, is disconcerted, left without an answer. At that moment the news comes that Regulus is in Rome, brought thither by the Carthaginian ambassador, come to ncgociatc peace or an exchange of prisoners. Regulus has sworn to return to die horribly at Carthage if the treaty be rejected. All Rome is ready to accept any terms for the sake of liberating him; his friends await with joy his speech before the Senate, sure that all will be granted. Regulus is introduced before the Senate in company with Hamilcar, the Carthaginian envoy; he pauses a moment on the well-known threshold, " Wherefore does he stop ? " asks Hamilcar, " Is this place unknown to him? " " I was thinking what I was leaving, and to what I am returning," answers Regulus, and the instruments, taking up the phrase of recitative, re-echo his thought. Hamilcar reminds Regulus of his promise, of what awaits him if the treaty be rejected ; Regulus will fulfil all he promised. Hamilcar exposes briefly the conditions of peace, and waits foi- Regulus to second the proposal. And Regulus speaks : Carthage desires peace on condition of retaining all her conquests; or, if that be refused, at least an exchange of prisoners; the advice of Regulus is to refuse botli. Every one is in astonishment; he holds firm, he desires to return to Carthage. Manlius, jealous of the sacrifice which raises his rival, tries to prevent it; Regulus has pointed out that the deliverance of Roman prisoners, broken to every ignominy, and the giving up of a number of warlike Carthaginians in retuini, will be fatal to Rome. Manlius answers that mere utility is not the only question, that Rome must think of what is honourable, and honour requires gratitude to Regulus. For the first time Regulus loses his usual moderation of tone. Does Rome wish to show gratitude towards him? Let it avenge him then. The barbarians have thought that he would betray his country from cowardice, urge acceptance of the treaty from fear of returning to Carthage. This outrage is worse than any torment they have inflicted; let Rome avenge him. Arm, hasten to tear from their temples the Roman trophies; do not sheathe the sword until the enemies be crushed. Let Regulus read the fear of Roman anger in the faces of his murderers; give him the joy of seeing in his dying agonies that Carthage trembles at the name of Rome. The Senate vacillates, but Regulus has not yet conquered; his children stir u\'7d) the people to protect him from himself; the Senate decides that an oath extorted from a prisoner is not binding; the Carthaginian envoy himself, moved by the sight of such greatness, offers to let him escape. There is yet a long struggle against violence of passion, from which Regulus, simple, determined, finally issues victorious, causing all, by the calm weight of his purpose,

to cede and make way; his children he silences into obedience ; the Senate he shames into more rigid honour; the treacherous Hamilcar he chides with disdain. The Senate and his family permit him to go, the Carthaginian galleys await him on the Tiber, but the people of Rome refuse to let hira pass to his death, and a struggle begins between the Consul wishing to open a way for Regulus and the Tribune ordering the crowd to refuse the passage. The Consul tries to explain, but the crowd drowns his voice with the cry, " Regulus shall stay." At this moment Regulus appears, and on his appearance there is a sudden silence. Regulus shall stay, he cries, and does Rome wish his dishonour? The Tribune answers that Rome wishes to strike off his chains. " Without them," Regulus answers, " I am but a perjured and fugitive slave." But the augurs have decided that the oath of a prisoner need not bind. Regulus rejects such pretexts for bad faith as worthy of the barbarians. But what Avill Rome do deprived of her greatest citizen? Regulus answers gravely, firmly, but with a moment of enthusiasm. He is old, and has served his time, he can no longer be of use to Rome, fate offers him a glorious end, let him not be defrauded of it to die in obscure infamy. Let not the Romans think differently from himself; down with the rebellious arms; as a friend he begs; as a citizen, exhorts; as a father, he commands. The arms are lowered and the crowd silently opens to let him pass. At last he can go. He bids Hamilcar ascend on to the ship; he will follow. He stops once more and turns round to the silent, solemn multitude:

Romans, farewell. Let this the last aclieia Be worthy you and me. Thank Heaven, I leave, And leave you Romans. Oh preserve unstain'd The mighty name, and you will thus become The earth's sole arbiters, and the whole world Will be for Rome. Ye deities that watch Over this sacred soil, ye who protect JEneas' breed, to you I now entrust This race of heroes; and on you I call To guard this soil, these roofs, this city wall. In them for evermore let glory, faith, And braveiy dwell. If to the Capitol Malignant stars now threaten evil fate, Here's Regulus, oh gods; and he alone Shall be your victim, and upon his head Let all the wrath of Heaven be discharged, But Rome uninjured . . . What ye weep? . . . Fai-ewell.

The plays of Metastasio are neither fashionable pieces of pseudoclassic
^ work, like those of Voltaire, nor eclectic works of classic imitation, like
those of Alfieri; they are a national, spontaneous form, evolved by the
artistic wants of a whole nation. And this being the case, Metastasio's
men and women are neither eighteenth-century gentlemen and ladies, with togas and chitons slipped over their brocade coats and silk embroidered stomachers, talking the talk of eighteenth-century drawing-rooms in majestic theatre language; nor are they conscientiously reconstructed Greeks and Ivomans, draped in imitation of the antique and speaking on the pattern of Thucydides and Tacitus, uncomfortably fearful of taking up modern attitudes or uttering modern sentiments. They are something quite apart, born neither of contemporary manners nor of classical study, but of the peremptory necessities, the irresistible suggestions, of a great and living art. If we would know the origin of Megacles, of Aristea, of Achilles, of Attilia, and of Regulus, let us turn over the scores of Per-golesi, of Leo, of Handel, of Jommelli, and we shall answer: They arc the oflspring of the music of the eighteenth century.

VII.

There was nothing now to compromise Metastasio, nothing now to impede his complete success at Vienna. But the success did not come: the Emperor approved of his dramas and gave him a lucrative fiscal post in the Neapolitan States; the Archduchesses took lessons of him in Italian and declamation, and were adorably civil; made him sit in their presence, and gave him a snuff-box ; the Countess Althann took him publicly into her favour, and, it was rumoured and believed, gave him her hand; but beyond these isolated successes things would not go. Neither the approbation of the Emperor, nor the favour of the Archduchesses, nor the love of the Countess Althann, obtained for him any higher position than that of Court poet, any influence beyond that over singers and composers and theatre mechanicians. He held, in short, the self-same position lie had held in Kome ten or fifteen years before, only gilded with Court titles and hampered by Court restrictions ; he was, as then, nothing beyond a mere writer of libretti; instead of three hundred scudi a play he received three thousand florins a year; his employer was an Emperor instead of a manager; his public came to the Favorita Theatre by Imperial invitation, instead of entering the Teatro Aliberti for so many bajocchi; it was all far smarter, loftier, more splendid, but also far less hearty. The Austrian magnates, caring nothing for poetry, only superficially conversant with Italian, took far less interest in his plays than did the shabby priestlets, the shopkeepers, and the populace of Rome, who understood and were pleased with everything; the very signs of approval were forbidden in the august presence of Ca?sar, and a successful masterpiece was heard frigidly, silently, without even the excitement of a little cabal and pasquinade. It was all very distressing and narrowing for a poet: he heard

of himself as of a great genius from the letters of his friends in Italy; here, in Vienna, he was merely a functionary, an Imperial servant, who, in virtue of imperial perfection, must needs be as good as possible. There was no outlet, no future; all was dull, as dull as at Gravina's, as dull as just before he was called from Rome, with the difference that he had then been on the steps of the ladder, and was now on the top without hope of getting higher. Csesar had approved of his plays, and had kept him persistently at a distance in his appointed place as playwright. For Cajsar, surrounded by etiquette and suspicious of all attem\'7d)ts at being circumvented, was the last man to encourage such forward loyalty, such enterprising devotion, as Metastasio had from the first displayed. Old Apostolo Zeno he had indeed taken into his confidence, because he felt that he could do so without fear of compromising his dignity, because he knew that this childlike, amiable pedant knew and thought of nothing beyond his books, was blind to any advantages to be obtained from such intimacy; because he could find a sort of friend, something far too simple and pedantic for a courtier, in the good Candiot dramatist; but this young, pushing, wheedling, flattering Abate Metastasio was not a person to be encouraged: his kisses on the Imperial hand were too sonorous, his humility was too humble, he was seeking for favour. Charles VI. kept him at arm's length.

To this failure of his Court career were added vexations concerning his brother in Rome. The transfer of the Romanina's inheritance, so useless, so foolish, so unconscientious, towards her desires, had borne its natural result. After a few years Domenico Bulgarelli, her husband, had taken it into his head to marry again. Leopoldo Metastasio, furious at the notion of the Romanina's property (over which he had never ceased to groan) being left to Bulgarelli's second wife or possible children, was violent to prevent the marriage. But Bulgarelli, now wholly independent, snapped his fingers at Leopoldo, and In-ought home liis new wife ; Leopoldo, an ill-tempered, unreasonable creature, never ceased complaining; the new wife objected to such a household; and finally, after a deal of quarreling, Bulgarelli gave Metastasio's family to understand that he could no longer live with them. Thus the comfortable household, once presided over by the Romanina, was broken up; Leopoldo and his father and sisters sought another abode ; Metastasio was called upon to suj^ply additional money, and was constantly worried by the lamentations and recriminations of his brother, who hated having to work. Metastasio, who had never been very fond of his brother, was weary of his ill-temper. He began to write rarely and sharply, and froni that time, perhaps, dated the common saying at Vienna, that Metastasio particularly begged never to be informed whether he had any live relatives.

Still, he had the occupation (not the amusement, for he protested that

he hated writing) of supplying plays for the Imperial Theatre. But this also ceased. In 1740, ju?^t as ho had finished his Reffitliis for the Ent-poror's birthday, Charles VI. ate that momentous dish of mushrooms which, according to Voltaire, set Europe on fire—and died.

The pompous melomaniac Ctesar had had the power, the power of tradition and habit, to keep the Holy Roman Empire together. As soon as he was dead, Bavaria, Prussia, France, Spain, all suppressed enemies, were lot loose upon his daughter and her husband. The danger was not that which had disturbed the pomp of Charles VI. Not merely a long-protracted war with the Turk in the distant East, not a rapid campaign of French and Sardinians against the Imperial possessions in Italy: it was a war at home against the very existence of the house of Austria. Those \ were the heroic days of Maria Theresa, when young, handsome, with a somblanco of legality on her side, without troops, without money, with nothing but her indomitable courage, her unblushing cunning, her aspect of conjugal and motherly devotion, and the entliusiasm, personal and traditional, which she aroused, when this strange, picturesque figure had to fight it out with the whole dull, sceptical, Machiavellian world of rococo conventionalities, and at last came out victorious.

But patriotism was not a growth of the eighteenth century, nor was active loyalty; and least of all did it exist in Metastasio, Ho, who had made Cato, Themistocles, Regulus, speak, and speak with superb breadth »-of intonation, was but little moved by the political cataclysm. What most affected him was its extreme discomfort to himself; what his sensitive feelings shuddered at was the suspension of salaries, the cessation of theatrical amusements, the extreme dulness and disorder of the Court; he felt mentally and morally chilly in this great storm, and thought more of the petty ailments it caused in himself than of the immense dangers and miseries which it brought to others. He felt himself neglected by everyone, he was mortified at the Empress-Queen being constantly surrounded by generals, ambassadors, ministers, and such like, and never glancing at him; he shrank into a corner by the side of the Countess Althann, and moped, and began to think that he had some mysterious nervous disease.

When the peace of Aix-la-Chapelle settled matters, when Maria Theresa was thoroughly reinstated in her imperial position, when Austrian finances began to be set right, and the Viennese Court was reorganised, Metastasio was already an elderly man, a hypochondriac, an idle routinist, without the desire or the power to work. His ambition was dead, his desire for power and fame was dead; he was beginning to be purely passive, livipg on the past, caring only to secure a future as safe as the pr* sent, dreading change, excitement, incapable of great joys, seeking only tir trumpery pleasures. The peculiar nature of his position had forced him, when a certain level was once attained, to become stationary, and his character was such that to be stationary meant to be stagnant. He had no interest in life beyond himself, so that himself once provided for he ceased to have any at all; egotism so absolute as to refuse thoughts and action to any exterior aims or objects must needs grow into a passive scepticism, / and finally into hypochondriac cynicism. Metastasio had no enthusiasms, political, religious, or personal; no love for any idea whose triumph would be his triumph, no passion for any discovery which would be his discovery; he had not even a pleasure in the movement of society, and of things in general. The eighteenth century was sterile of political or religious enthusiasms; political and religious forms were both too utterly dried up and crumbling ; but it had intense social and scientific Utopias, hopes of reform and perfection in which even the most timid, even the most fi-ivolous, joined; but Metastasio had neither of these. He found it, as he himself declared, more conducive to peace of mind to accept dogmas than to examine them; yet he expressed every degree of aversion to over-zealous belief; he saw the way the century was going, he even foretold great convulsions, but he neither rejoiced at the movement nor regretted it: he was never astonished, never moved. In the days of active reform, of philanthropy tinging even the most frivolous and corrupt, of reactionary disgust warping even the noblest, in the days of Beccaria and Filangieri, of Baretti and Gozzi, Metastasio remained wholly indifferent.

Nor did any interest in his own art absorb his energy; be worked unwillingly, like a cobbler at his shoes (according to his own words), and for the works of others he did not care. The ancients he had learned to hate at Gravina's; about the French and Spaniards he was lukewarm; Mosu Racine, as he called him, seemed a prig, and Corneille a ranter; he would not decide between Ariosto and Tasso, and cared probably but little for either; Dante he mentioned with deprecating respect. Voltaire's books he bought, with Voltaire's praise he was pleased, but he did not even attain to the point of saying, with Parini, that he was too much praised and too much blamed. About contemporary Italian literature he was equally indifferent; the verbose magnificence of Frugoni he disliked but praised, because Frugoni was court poet at Parma; the comic genius of Goldoni he probably admired, but mentioned coldly, because Goldoni was a heretic in the eyes of the upholders of the old Italian stage. The only intellectual concern about which Metastasio displayed any genuine feeling was music; nor did he perhaps ever show so much abstract interest as when he entreated the composer Jommelli not to change his style, or when he groaned with the famous singing-master Bernacchi over the decay of contahile singing. It was the same with his social relations.

^ At forty-tv o he made it a point never to dine out ; he shut himself out of general society, seeing only the people who went to the Countess

Althanu; and those who, from curiosity or business, came to hinr on 8uudays; lie hail four or five friends whom be saw daily, almost liourly, and with whom he went through a perfect social routine. He met Count Canale, the Sardinian minister, and a Canon Perlas, regularly three times a week to read Horace, and when they had finished they began again at the other end. He kept up correspondences with people like the Princess Bclmonte and a certain Filipponi, whom he had not seen for years, whom he was never likely to meet again, and with whom he had no news to interchange, from the simple fact that they had ceased to have any common interest and almost any mutual friends. Add to this that he was getting apprehensive about his digestion, his nerves, his health, and complaining of mysterious symptoms which no one could see. Thus, towards 1750, Metastasio was getting mummified. He had weakened his body by over-much care; he had hampered his actions by rules of conduct; he had stultified his genius by routine and indifference; he had weakened his affections by constant and stupefying familiarity within a narrow circle; he had compressed his whole life, and was beginning to suffer by the compression.

About this time he took a step, almost the last ever taken by him : he contracted a new friendship which elicited the last works which came from his genius. The Emperor Charles VI. had, by way of augmenting his salary, given him the post of Treasurer of Cosenza in Calabria, an office which could be farmed out for about three hundred scudi a year. Scarcely had he received his first payment when war broke out between Austria and Spain. Don Carlos, son of Philip V., seized the Neapolitan States, and was made King of Naples; all the Austrian officials were replaced by Spaniards, and Metastasio remained, as he expresses it, with his commission as Treasurer of Cosenza ready to be made into a bag for sugarplums or into curling-papers. This loss became the more serious when Maria Theresa began to suspend the payment of his salary; and he endeavoured to recover his post by means of representations to the Neapolitan Government, and by every sort of influence, through cardinals, ambassadors, and ministers, all in vain. The King of Naples would not hear of any sort of indemnity. But the treaty of Aix-la-Chapelle having put an end to the hostile relations between Vienna and Madrid, Metastasio bethought himself of applying to the most powerful person, after the King and Queen, in all Spain, to l)on Carlo Broschi, Knight of St. lago and of Calatrava, who had been the greatest of Italian singers under the name of Farinello. Metastasio had known him in his happy Neapolitan days, when Farinello had been brought to the Romanina's by his master Porpora; he had liked the boy, and playfully dubbed him twin-brother ; he had met him later at Rome, Venice, and Vienna, the most indisputedly great among the great Italian singers, an intelligent, hand-

p

J

210 Metastasio and the Opera.

some young giant. Metastasio had liked him still better and continued to call him twin-brothei-, for he was rich and courted, and there was no reason for thrusting him away. Then Farinello had left the stage and gone to Spain, where, during the long time of war and interrupted communication, Metastasio had lost sight of him. During those years a most extraordinary phenomenon had taken place, and when the poet again heard of his singer friend it was as the omnipotent favourite of Philip V,, of his successor Ferdinand VI., and of his Queen; as a maker and un-maker of ministries, constantly beset by grandees, governors of provinces, ambassadors, and ambassadresses, and to whom even the immortal Maria Theresa wrote curiously civil little notes.

That this unexpected recognition of his old acquaintance, of the most unlikely person in the whole world in the very position, only infinitely more defined, more magnificent, more astonishing, which Metastasio had probably dreamed of for himself when he kissed the Emperor's hand with such vehemence; that this realisation of his dreams, a realisation so concrete and undoubted, but in the person of another, gave the poet a pang, left in him an aching void, is most probable. This was the living commentary on his own failure at court, this success of a man so totally different from himself. Metastasio, who had looked upon his employment, upon his art, upon his fame, as merely so many steps to imperial favour; who had sought for new friendships and rejected old; who had laid himself out to please, to flatter, to wheedle ; who liad been frantically loyal and sublimely groveling for the sake of court influence, had been superciliously passed over, coolly and majestically pushed aside into his allotted place ; and meanwhile his old acquaintance, without a thought beyond his art, his friendships, and amusements, perfectly satisfied with his musical fame, taciturn and haiighty (after the manner of singers) with his superiors in rank, bluntly ingenuous in his words, stalking through life without a look or a bow for any save his friends, this unambitious, vminsinuating, self-satisfied singer, had become the most important person at the Spanish court, without any sacrifice of dignity or convenience. But Metastasio was not envious where envy could obtain nothing. Farinello had been more fortunate than himself (owing to that perversity of faith of which he was the particular victim); the best thing to do was to try to turn this unjust good luck to profit. So he wrote to his old acquaintance, reminded him of old Neapolitan days, exposed the lamentable story of his treasurership of Cosenza, called him his dearest tivin brother, and waited for an answer; suspecting, however, that the Cavalier Broschi might no longer care to bo reminded of the days when he was still Farinello; that he might think Metastasio an intolerable claimer of friendship and assistance, that he might politely send his twin-brother to the devil. The answer came. Farinello was overjoyed at the

resumption of acquaintance, overwhelmed by the lionour of still bein^ the twin-brother of the author of the Olimpiade and of liegulus, immensely coniinunicative, from friendliness, rather than from vanity, about his life in Spain, his friends, his relatives, the bad Spanish doctors, the beautiful Spanish ladies—everything. He had already been to the Queen ; he had already written to the King- of Naples; he had got the minister Ensenada to make special applications for indemnifying Meta-stasio's loss; he was willing to do anything merely to enjoy the pleasure of Metastasio's letters. And, if matters went well, would his great twin-brother write him some poems ? He wanted this, that, and the other.

Metastasio was delighted ; a little of his friend's grandeur had fallen upon him. He was the Benjamin of a favourite </?fasz-minister, if not a favourite himself. Farinello kept writing, one letter more affectionate than another, offering his services, sending immense presents of chocolate, of vanilla, of snuff—such exquisite snuff—with which the poet regaled the haughty Austrians, informing them from whom it came ; losing no opportunity of boasting of his friendship with so great a personage. The Austrian grandees opened their eyes; this was a new view of Metastasio. They all had brothers, cousins, friends, whom they wished should bo recommended at the Spanish court; would Metastasio intercede for them ? I\Ietastasio graciously granted the request, mentioned the app'licants to Farinello, adding that they were wholly unrecommendable, but that some civil excuse must be given them. The favour was conferred without hurting the poet's conscience. Metastasio was beset by noble toadies for his friend's patronage; he looked modest and joked over it, but he enjoyed it vastly; enjoyed having generals, ambassadors, and magnates asking him, ** Signer Abate, when are you going to write to your twin-brother? " His heart dilated when Prince Belmonte asked for a letter of introduction from him; when Cardinal Migazzi begged him to speak well of his brother to the great singer; when Esterhazy embraced him in the street, and thanked him for his recommendation ; when the mighty Kaunitz himself desired him to ask whether the Cavalier Farinello was still as partial to him as in former days.

In the return for all this second-hantl influence Metastasio wrote ff>r Farinello some of his last, but most charming, cantatas: and one day sent him a packet containing the words and music of the famous, most famous canzonet: "Ecco quel fiero istante." It was the last work that came from Metastases genius; all "aFEer it was the result of practice and dexterity. Perhaps it did more for Metastasio's popidarity than all his dramas put together; it was set and reset by every composer, translated and retranslated into every language ; it was not \'7d)assionate, not very sincere; it had not the great merits of the best of his works; but it was

p 2

liappy in conception and execution, complete, spontaneous, perfect as only small and inferior things can be. The people of the eighteenth century made sure, in their blindness to the difference between real emotion and artistic emotion, that Metastasio himself was the hero of the poem; that the l^angs of separation were his. But Metastasio was far too true an artist, far too cold a man, not to feel that neither he nor his love-stories could find a place in poetry; the Countess Althann was too prosaic for artistic representation ; the Romanina had been too tragic ;

he must deal only ■with ideal passions. " You will find it very tender," wrote Metastasio to Farinello, as he sent him the canzonet, " but do not do me the injustice of supposing that I am in love; you know whether I am capable of such

f imbecility." And Metastasio, the poet of the heart, whose works were being sighed over by all the lovesick people in Italy, was speaking with perfect sincerity. Love was all very fine in novels and on the stage, but a man of his experience of life was far too wise to make himself happy or wretched about other people: emotion was far too dangerous to the digestion, not to speak of its danger to one's social position,

Metastasio had begun his correspondence with Farinello in hopes of being helped back to his treasurership of Cosenza; he had continued it for the satisfaction of being the friend of a man in power, for the satisfaction of being asked to obtain favours for grand folk; still when he wrote immense letters in which he deluged the singer with affection, called him his dearest, most adorable, most incomparable twin-brother, he was not insincere nor wholly interested. Farinello pleased him beyond measure; the mixture of a supremely great singer and of a supremely powerful favourite, of titles and money and reputation, was enhanced in Metastasio's eyes by the addition of a strangely upright and amiable character. Metastasio, as a prudent man, had an eye for rank and fortune; but Metastasio as a poet, as the creator of ideally noble figures, had an eye also for fine characters; he was a connoisseur in Tituses, and Farinello had something

'a of the Titus in him. It pleased the poet's ideality to hear of his friend's spotless honour in the midst of a court (Metastasio had written so many fine lines against courts and courtiers), of his perfect modesty, of his self-respecting frankness, of his generosity to his detractors, of his indifference to money and titles, just as it pleased Metastasio to hear how Farinello was present at the King of Spain's council, how the Due de Duras and his wife used to beset and wheedle him every time they could; how, as Beckford expresses it, he was in the habit of drilling sojDranos and tenors on one day, and ambassadors and ministers on the next. To Farinello, on the other hand, Metastasio appeared as a sort of little divinity; the singer, despite his intelligence and prudence, was eminently gullible, impulsive, magnifying the good, closing his eyes to the bad ; obstinate, unconvincible of error. A fervent Catholic, profoundly per-

(

suaded of the graciousness of the Madonna and of the saints, though boldly rushing into danger of damnation by his friendship for Antichrist in tlie person of the atheist poet Crndeli, Farinello was ever ready to add to heavenly more earthly objects of devotion, to make a Madonna out of the amiable mean little Queen of Spain, and a saint, an apostle, out of the philanthropic but unscrupulous minister, Ensenada. Metastasio, with his passionate eloquence, his magnificent tirades about virtue, his infectious nobility of sentiment, appeared to the singer something super-naturally beautiful, whose letters were a heavenly gift and a sign of grace. The whispered story of the Eomanina's death Farinello had probably never heard; if he had he would have indignantly refuted it, have treated it as an infamous lie, even with the proofs before him. Metastasio was the greatest of poets, the noblest of men; a divinity before whose shrine no sufficient amount of chocolate and snuff coiild ever be deposited. Metastasio jogged on through life without a mistake, without ever being a dupe of anyone save himself. Farinello, even while this whimsical, flattering correspondence continued, was agitated by troubles of which his friend never dreamed ; the combat between reality and fiction, between the dupe and the deceivers ; the long, bitter struggle to keep in power his friend Ensenada, despite his insolent ingratitude and his unpopularity, and at the same time to serve the Queen, Ensenada's mortal enemy; the struggle to conciliate what to him seemed opposed, but equally generous, plaijs, which were in reality equally mean and false. Ensenada was a saint, and must be kept in office; the Queen was a saint, and must be helped. Ensenada pretends that he is in reality opposing the dangerous alliance with France; that he accepts the order of the Saint Esprit and the French money only to gain time to mature relations with England. Meanwhile he is plotting with Choiscul; everyone in Spain suspects it except Farinello; the proofs are put before him, he refuses to believe in Ensenada's treachery. Ensenada, seeing that his case is hopeless, merely laughs at his credulity, and insults his good faith. The minister is taken, condemned; the Queen is frantic for revenge. Farinello betrayed, derided, rushes to the King, begs, implores, threatens; Ensenada is let off with mere banishment from court, despite the Queen, who would see him a beggar, a prisoner—best of all, see him dead. In the midst of outward splendour and power, Metastasio's poor twin-brother was but a pitiful dupe, pulled hither and thither by foolish generosity, without real power, and without much real happiness.

Metastasio would have acted differently,—Metastasio the prudent, the self-restrained, who had prevented the Romanina from coming to Vienna, who had crawled on the ground before Charles VI., who was so far beyond any imbecility of love. Yet let us not be too hard upon Metastasio. We have had to show bim as he has appeared to us, always selfish, often

servile, sometimes ungrateful, meanest in action wlien noblest in words~; but, while showing him thus, we must show also the almost irresistible influences which degraded him. Between him and his friend Farinello there lay an immense difference, far greater than that between a man cold and timid and a man warm-hearted and rash ; the difference between a poet and a singer, between an artist who has a market and an artist who has not. It was easy for Farinello to be independent and self-respecting; sure from his earliest youth of money and applause, knowing that as long as he had a voice he had the means of subsisting anywhere without need of protectors ; it was needful for Metastasio not to be servile and timid, knowing, from his youth, that his existence depended upon the favour of Gravina, of the Romanina, of the Emperor; knowing that without a real literary public his writings could support him only inasmuch as they gained him protection and offices: if the singer offends the Emperor, no matter, he will go to England, to Spain, to Venice, and gain as much money and obtain as much credit; if the poet displeases the Emperor, or the Emperor's friend the Countess Althann, or the Emperor's lacquey, where else will he be sure of a pension for life ? In England ? No Italian poet is kept. At Berlin, Dresden, or Munich ? He may get five hundred florins at most. Is he to return and write plays for tlie Teati-o Aliberti, at three hundred scudi a piece, and be left to starve when he can write no longer? The singer in the eighteenth century had a paying public, the writer had not; the one lived off his talent, the other off his servility; that is why the singers of the eighteenth century, like Caffariello and the Gabbrielli, insulted Kings and Empresses ; that is why Italian poets of the eighteenth century, like Metastasio and Frugoni, crawled before ministers and chamberlains. In Goldoni's plays the singer is well fed and insolent, with a fur coat and jack boots; and the poet is hungry and humble, in a ragged doublet and broken shoes. A false economical position implies a false social position, and a false social position implies personal degradation.

In 1755 Metastasio lost the Countess Althann. She was an old woman; she had even grown-up sons ; she had been his for twenty-five years; yet there had been to the last something of the flavour of romance, rather than of the staleness of domestic life (stale at least to a mind like his), in this connection with a woman who was his wife and was not, who lived under another roof, who bore another name, Avho remained his superior in rank, whom he treated in public with a sort of deference and courting devotion. " I have never been in greater need of the assistance of a real friend like you," wrote Metastasio to Farinello, " and you, without knowing it, have given it to me in your last most affectionate letter, whose kind words have proved to me that I am not left in a desert now that we have lost our very dear Countess of Althann," This was

not a shock, not a violent grief like that at the death of the Romanina; it "was a dull sense of forlornness, of being, as he says, in a desert, which made him stretch forth his hand to a man whom he had not seen for so long, who was so far distant, and whom he would probably never see again.

There is a portrait of Metastasio painted about this time, of which an old copy belongs to the Arcadian Academy : he is seated, half reclining on a sofa, one arm over its elboAV, as if aboiit to add a word to the manuscript on the table by his side; short, fat, rather languid and bent, not sickly, but delicate and lazy in body ; the large head is raised, but the high wide forehead, the imaginatively turned brows, are weighed down and materialised by the lumpish aquiline nose, and the long square jaw, imbedded in double and triple chins; the long slit mouth is smiling sweetly, the eyes are lit up with humour, the heavy cheeks are dimpled, yet there is a melancholy, an absence of animal spirits, a something which tells you that this face is but a living mask, the muscles of which will easily give way, the eye grow dull, the mouth droop, the jaw drop, the whole collapse into vacancy. There is no strong life in the man, though there is a flickering semblance of life : he is amiable, bright, whimsical, humorous, can tell anecdotes well, can make a witty repartee, can seem the very ideal of cheerful old age, when in company or when writing his letters, which is but another way of being in company; but he becomes dreary and apathetic when alone or with his intimates. People compliment him on his looks, on his activity in mounting the stairs, on his clear voice in singing, on his bright eyes and pink and white complexion, which, against his white wig, makes him look like a pretty old lady; but he shakes his head, complains of a mysterious nervous disease, of attacks of trembling, of flushing whenever he gives his attention to anything; he calls it a hysterical condition, clearer still, hypochondria, confessing, without perceiving it, that he has the vain weak nervousness of indolent, over-pampered women ; the ridiculous depression of broken-down, idle old men; he dreads motion, change, activity, all that can cure him. In reality, what ails him is mental and moral enmii.

This Vienna of the third quarter of the eighteenth century is an intolerable place: lifeless, or living only a mean little life. Nothing goes on of any importance: wars are carried on on all sides, sometimes against the English, sometimes against the French, no matter which; they are no subject of excitement; the Austrian Empire is perfectly safe, falling always on the right side. When beaten, making allies of the victor, always ready to tack and veer so as to avoid tempest and meet a mild little breeze. The victories are those of allies, and inspire no heroic joy, like those of yonder Frederick sung by Eammler, Gleim, and Kleist; the defeats arc also those of allies, and produce no great convulsions, no terrible ruin like those in which the splendid Polish court of Dresden crashes down; a

Te Deum is ordered, or a Eequiem with prayers for better luck, both sung by the cheapest possible singers. There are lots of processions in the streets, lots of seizures of books at the custom-houses. This town, which is neither German, nor Sclav, nor Hungarian, nor Italian, is sleepy and indifferent. The court is dull and miserable: the Emperor Francis, mild little busybody, useful conjugal dummy of the Empress, keeps the accounts of the expenses, pares and scrapes, farms out the court-balls to those who will pay most (by giving least hghts and refreshments), collects the cheapest singers, after much haggling, for the court theatre, makes all as stingy and shabby as things can be, till the blood boils in the breast of Leopold Mozart, Vice-

Chapelmaster of Salzburg, who turns away in loyal shame at such a capital, in which there is not money and movement enough to afford any chance for his little phenomenon Wolfgang. The Empress, the heroic Maria Theresa, is shut up with the dear Minister Kaunitz, scheming to marry off as many as possible of the many archduchesses who are now, by way of philosophic education, sweeping their rooms and making their beds, growing up ignorant, unbridled, ready to become Carolines of Naples, and Amelias of Parma, or at best, if of nobler fibre, Maria Antoinettes; plotting to get duchies for some of the many archdukes, who are at present learning carpentering, until, grown into Josephs and Leopolds, they quarrel with their mother, visit the King of Prussia, sweep out Jesuits, and make up for years of servility by bilious, headstrong reformation. She is keeping a shrewd look-out on European affairs, watching for the moment when she must drop her allies and toady her enemies, when she must make friends with the cynical, sneering Frederick, with the philanthropic murderous Empress of Kussia, with the poor inflated King of Poland : when she is to write to Madame de Pompadour beginning, " Ma princesse et cousine;" and in the intervals of this powerful political game she appears proud yet modest, simply dressed, surrounded by an effaced husband and stultified or rebellious children, a picture of maternal and conjugal perfection, in church, or reviewing the good pandours of Trenk; she weeps at the sight of a poor widow, gives her her own breakfast, sighs over her inability to relieve distress ; she raises herself to a majestic height of virtue, and Avrathfully exiles to Moravia, to Hungary, to Transylvania, any unlucky lady against whose reputation there has been a whisper. A heroine in the eyes of those good English far off, a saint in those of the lower classes, Maria Theresa was but a queer mixture of virtue, of unscrupulousness, of prudery, of bigotry, and of cynicism, for those who see and had her in sight. For a poet, a poet dealing especially with tragic and idyllic character, nothing could be worse than to be thus constantly in the presence of such a sovereign—a sovereign too who, for the sake of the past, had to be called glorious. She was, after all, a heroine, a Semiran^is, this Maria

Theresa; but wliat an unhernic heroine, what a prudish, bigoted, insult-swallowing Semiraniis ! She was a disheartening sight, making humanity seem petty and shabby in her very greatness. And, such as she was, jNIetastasio was forced to see her, forced by proximity, by his own rajjid, unerring judgment: if he could have seen her as slie was not, but should liave been; if he could have been duped, his self-respect, his good faith, his fiiith in goodness, would have been saved: but Metastasio was by nature cool, critical, sceptical; he could not see a saint in every friend, a Madonna in every patroness, like his twin-brother Farinollo; the very saints and Madonna in heaven did not awaken his enthusiasm, and as to seeing them on earth ! he was too shrewd and frigid for that. He could not believe, he could only accept dogmas; he could not be blind, he could only shut his eyes; he could not delude, he could only perjure himself; he was kneeling before altars in whose miracles he did not believe, and kissing relics which he knew to be no better than the refuse in the dustbin.

And Metastasio, cut out from all life in admiration and belief, had no real life in lower things: he could not, like Goldoni, be satisfied with a little amusement in looking at street squabbles, and a little excitement in l)laying faro for a scudo; he could not consume his energies in editing classics and writing pasquinades, like the two Gozzis ; he could not be filled with ineffable pleasure while improvising a stanza over a bottle of maraschino, with a great lady in a new Paris hat opposite, like the gay old rhymester Frugoni; he could not dilate with holy rage while scourging vice and folly like Parini; he was too selfish to take pleasure in anything concerning others, too delicate of mental fibre to take pleasure in mere coarse enjoyment and coarse warfare : he took pleasure, therefore, in nothing, or, at best, but a feeble pleasure in trifles.

In this numbing of all his faculties from disuse, two, the most developed, still kept a little sensibility; his vanity and his benevolence could still be tickled. The little notes with which the Empress occasionally testified her remembrance he treasured up with delight; the gold (or gilt?) candlestick with the lampshade which she gave him, bidding him " Take care of his eyes," he displayed and talked over with rapture. So much for his vanity. In 1759 he met his former teacher, the composer Porpora, a man often vainly assisted, vainly pushed into comfort, hopelessly spendthrift, quarrelsome and disreputable ; Porpora was old, forgotten, without employment, without money, and applied to Metastasio for assistance. Metastasio wrote off to Farinello a long letter, a masterpiece of pathetic eloquence. " We are bound by every duty to help poor Porpora," he urged ; " he is a man, and we are obliged to assist our fellow-creatures; he is of eminence and a friend; he is old, and a small pittance will save him. I shall be personally obliged to you for saving me the pain of seeing the wreck of

a man Tvlioni we have respected from our early youth," and so on ; but the letter is too fine a piece of writing: a few dollars, a little endeavour to obtain Porpora employment, above all, a little perception that a really kind man like Farinello required only to know of distress, would have been better. Metastasio's benevolence is too abstract.

The very same year, 1759, Ferdinand VI. of Spain and his Queen died, Charles iCsucceeded, and Metastasio's twin-brother fell from his greatness. A year of terrible suspense, of sickening attendance upon a miserable, loathsome maniac, as the King of Spain became after his wife's death ; of melancholy watching the defection of one friend after another, and the daily diminution of importance, had been at length closed by disgrace, by unexpected banishment from the country, by finding himself suddenly alone, severed from old connections and habits, powerless, with -out voice or youth, reduced to nothingness ; and all this had smitten down Farinello : the strong, cheerful, warm-hearted giant had been broken by the fall as a man weaker in body and temper would never have been. Metastasio, so to speak, hastened up, took him by the hand, looked into his face with the smile of a friend; and the rapid, unhesitating, thorough act of friendship was felt and never forgotten. His letters on this occasion are full of that tact, of that right balance between cordiality and reticence, between the desire to console and the fear of appearing to do so, which can come only from singularly delicate moral fibre. Farinello could no longer be useful to Metastasio ; he could serve neither his avarice nor his vanity; he had lost all influence, but he had not lost his handsome fortune, his social standing nor his good name, and he could in no way endanger Metastasio. And Metastasio, so far from being a mere toady to influential people, was singularly disinterested and sincere where he could be with safety: he would have been the most grateful and generous of men had he not sometimes been afraid.

So Metastasio continued his life of idleness and indifference, writing a play or a copy of verses when absolutely required, but nothing good; withdrawing more and more from the world, complaining more and more of his health, never going to the theatre, to court, or to any party. While the man was thus fading away, his fame was growing daily. His works had been printed and reprinted in all parts of Italy; they were translated into French, English, German, Spanish, and even into modern Greek; he was read in mud villages in Portugal and in wood villages in Russia; to foreigners he represented the whole sum of Italian poetry since Tasso. Voltaire, in his preface to Semiramis, praised him up to the skies, with the usual addition of a little depreciation of Italy, operas, and everything that was not French and Voltairian; Rousseau praised him up to the skies pretty well everywhere, with less critical acumen and backbiting. He had been made a member of every possible academy; medals were now being

struck in his honour, and sent to hini; even the arch-heretic Baretti, who trundled about the world calling all established celebrities the most shameful names, wrote a splendid rhapsody on Metastasio, ending that he was truly a poet for Kings and Emperors (even Baretti, being an Italian of the first half of the eighteenth century, could find no higher praise than that). Letters poured in from all parts of Italy, delightfully candid in their obtrusiveness, letters from authors sending their works (which were always pronounced to be excellent), from learned men propounding their theories, from young men asking for a rule of conduct, from young ladies confiding their aspirations and affections. Everyone in Italy had read and re-read Metastasio's works to such an extent that they felt quite intimate with him, persuaded themselves that they knew him most thoroughly, and that it was quite natural to confide everything to so omniscient a creature, just as they might lay all their ideas and troubles before the busy but hopelessly intruded-on Madonna and St. Joseph.

That Metastasio was the best, wisest, happiest of mortals, seemed evident, even to the people who, like Hir Nathaniel Wraxall and Dr. Burney, came into his presence on Sunday mornings. He looked so rosy, so cheerful, so placid, such a picture of rewarded philosophy and virtue ; surely he must be the happiest of mortals. He was not particularly happy, and perhaps took a pleasure in being so as little as possible: to be wretched was at least some little excitement in this monotony. His intimate, the Canon Perlas, with whom and Count Canale he went on year after year, jogging dully through the classics, wrote to some one (whom we are not told) that " Metastasio is universally considered the happiest of human beings, but in reality no man is more unhappy than he. Since the death of the Countess Althann I have been his confidant; I know his woes, and if I could tell how great they are I could greatly diminish your present grief," &c. Strong words. Heavy woes, heavy enough to make those of other men seem light; no man more happy than he ! We pause before this awful announcement. But no, we cannot be made to condole, to pamper Metastasio's sickly sentiment.

And Metastasio, in his old age, was not quite alone. The Martinez family with whom he lived were kind and deferential; nor was this all. About 1769 appears for the first time (from out of a convent or school ? we know not whence) a third Marianna, a girl of singular intelligence and great cultivation. She was called Martinez, the sister of Joseph Martinez, then the head of the family ; but she was also called Metastasio's pupil, his niece, his adopted daughter. Was she the daughter of tlie poet ? Perhaps she was; perhaps she was not. She seems to have come into existence already grown up, We never see her except as a very mature young lady, with the self-possession and independence of a spinster. Metastasio, who had little paternal instinct, but a great, cool liking for

intellectual women, especially not too old (charming nymplis, as he called his blue-stocking correspondents), took much pleasure in Mavianna Martinez, in perfecting her education, in making her into a sort of female self. She had great musical talents, which were cultivated to the utmost. A poor young scholar was got at a great bargain to teach her the harpsichord and composition in return for board and lodging: he, in his threadbare coat, had the honour of sitting at table with the Abate Metastasio, listening solemnly to the great poet's words ; he often spoke of it later when he had become more famous throughout Europe, and, having received an Oxford degree, was called Doctor Haydn. Metastasio taught Marianna Martinez to sing; he sang beautifully himself, as befitted a pupil of Porpora and of the Romanina, and the intimate friend of Hasse, of the Faustina, of Farinello, of Jommelli; and Marianna turned out an exquisite singer, in the most noble and delicate style of the early eighteenth century, which was then being fast forgotten ; so that Dr. Burney had no words to express his admiration of her. She was a good linguist, spoke German, French, English and Spanish, admirably, and was altogether a most admirable young lady. But withal a little cold: why did she not cure Metastasio's melancholy? Why did she not marry him and cheer him by the sight of children? Perhaps she cared but little for this amiable old hypochondriac; perhaps he cared for her only as a pupil, as a dependant, as a kind of nurse. However it may be, the appearance of domestic life is no greater with this daughter or quasi-daughter than it was in the case of his quasi-yviie the Countess Althann : Metastasio had made himself into a hopeless and typical old bachelor.

Timorous he remained, timorous about his health and about his position. Farinello, the only remaining old friend, had, after long, wretched depression, finally consoled himself for his loss of power and for his loss of youth. The rest of his life should not be dismal: he took to him his nephews and nieces and got to think only of them. One day, in high pleasure, in intense friendliness, he asked Metastasio to become the godfather to his nephew's child. There were other people enough whom he might ask; Bolognese senators, and Cardinals, and Neapolitan princes; but Farinello disdained them for the sake of his old friend. His old friend answered in most affectionate terms that he regretted, it was an immense mortification to him to disappoint his twin-brother, but he had recently refused to be godfather to the son of a very great personage, and great personages must not be trifled with. Farinello was vexed, but called the child after Metastasio all the same; and soon after, having forgiven, astounded the poet by the proposal that he should leave Vienna and live the rest of his days in his house at Bologna. It seemed quite simple to the singer that Metastasio, having ceased to be of any use in Vienna, should be but too glad to abandon a sinecure, to realise a dream

of which he was always talking, the dream of ending his days in Italy, out of that cold, proud, beggarly Austria where no one cared for him. Metastasio had indeed talked about his dear Italy, about tlie pleasure^ of seeing all his old friends again, of meeting his innumerable admirers ; perhaps he even thought once over the plan. But to move, to travel (he was in the best health), to leave his tiresome old Viennese acquaintance, to give up drawling througli Horace, to cease to be what he had been, and then to take up his abode in Farinello's house, a house too in the country (Metastasio considered the country most unhealthy), full of noisy brats, of visitors, with a constant bustle and hubbub; to be dragged out of his dear, dull routine into the life of other people—he shrank from the idea; his nerves, his sensitive nerves, could never endure it. He thanked his old friend and chose the philosophical course of staying where he was, of continuing the philosophical life he had hitherto led.

So he did. The century drew towards a close, and Metastasio, who had been born with it, shrank and withered. Things had gradually changed: mysterious forces were converging to form the revolution; all was palpitating with strange life, even at Vienna. The Viennese were beginning to remember that they were Germans, and instead of translations of Metastasio's plays they crowded to see Emilia Galotti and Goetz von Berlichingen. The last years of Maria Theresa were being watched with impatience. In 1780 she died, and with her seemed to die the old state of things. The bilious, impetuous Joseph cleared out a new road ; down with the old ceremony, the old prudery, the old bigotry. He was a Frenchman at heart, a passionate admirer of Frederick the Great, a passionate disciple of Voltaire, of Beccaria, and of Filangieri; he would reform everything, and he began by thrusting out the clergy ; seized by that vertigo which made even the kings and emperors of the late eighteenth century hasten on the revolution which was to sweep them away. Metastasio disliked all this movement, this pulling u\'7d) of the bad old pavement over which he had jolted for sixty years. Moreover, new poets were arising in Italy, and a new mode of thinking. A wild young man, whose tragedies were fast supplanting Metastasio's plays, came to Vienna with the intention of paying his respects to the old poet. But one day, as Alfieri was walking about the promenade, he saw a modest carriage stop before a splendid gilt coach, the door open, and a little bent old man of eighty get out, go up to the coach, and stand obsequiously at its window, hat in hand. Alfieri saw it, and left Vienna without visiting Metastasi*); a foolish, conceited, unthinking, unsympathising piece of swagger, but which showed that the attitude even of the Italians was undertroinc a change.

Meanwhile, all Metastasio's friends were dead, those friends with whom he had kept up a dull vacant correspondence for years; even those whom.

like Jommelli, he had encouraged as youths, were fast going; the century was dying: he who had belonged to it so comiDletely, so slavishly, must die also. He shivered and moped in his third floor in the Kohl-markt, surrounded by the obsequious, cool Martinezes, to whom that third floor, with all its contents, must so soon belong. Farinello, the only surviving old friend, and who was still as active and friendly as at forty, not being able since his departure from Spain to send the poet snuff or chocolate, sent him Bolognese grapes, gingerbread, preserved peaches, and other indigestible good things. Metastasio smiled faint thanks, let Marianna Martinez eat the grapes, gingerbread, and preserves, and looked on vacantly. He was beginning to feel a great yearning after affection; to his singer friend he wrote oftener and oftener, short, tremulous notes ; he thought of his twin-brother as he had been fifty years ago, the slender, light-stepped youth with the broad shoulders and triumphant voice; he let himself, perhaps, be led back by this phantom of a man still living but long altered to his own young days, to the summer walks across the park in Moravia, to the chats and games at cards in the Countess Althann's rooms, perhaps even to the musical parties at Naples, when sixty years ago he, a brilliant young man of twenty-four, had seen the Komanina lead the boy Farinello to the harpsichord, while Scarlatti, Por-pora, Leo, Vinci, Hasse, all the great composers whose settings of his plays had been forgotten for forty years, looked on and listened. " Ah ! adorable twin-brother, dearest Carlucciello," he wrote, " how much I have to say to you and how little I can say ! What can we do when we can do nothing?" What would he have said had he been able? Perhaps nothing ; memories of old affections, vague desires for love, were sadly and confusedly inarticulately speaking within him. All that he would have said remained unspoken. He wrote no more to Farinello, nor to anyone. In the spring of 1782 he caught cold, fell ill, and in a few days was beyond recovery. Pius VI., who had come to Vienna to humiliate himself and Catholicism before Joseph II. (who, having sore eyes, did not even go to meet him), sent his benediction to the dying poet; the Nuncio brought him the sacrament, and as he took it he sang, with sti-ange self-assertion, a verse of his own paraphrase of the psalm Miserere; then he subsided into lethargy and silence. In those hot^rs of isolation did he go over the past, remember Gravina, the Romanina, and the Countess Althann, ask himself how much sweetness he had got out of that long life of philosophic prudence, of sacrifice to peace and safety?

A little later Marianna Martinez, most cultivated and best mannered of spinsters, sent off a long letter to the Cavalier Don Carlo Broschi, commonly called Farinello, at his villa outside the Porta San Felice at Bologna, beginning, " The loss of a mortal who did honour to humanity

must be felt by all," &c. and winding up with thanks for a box of preserved fruit; the whole to inform him, with all due ceremony, indifference, and frigidness, that the Abate Pietro Metastasio had died on April 14, 1782. Very cold was this letter of the woman to whom, with her brothers, Metastasio had been as a father, and had left his whole fortune; cold as had been the letter, written sixty-four years earlier, by which Metastasio had informed those concerned of the death of Gravina. Farinello did not take it so coolly; to him Metastasio had never ceased to be the greatest of poets, the noblest of men, the dearest of friends. A few months later the great singer died, giving his last thoughts to a certain harpsichord and music-books ; all the rest his nephews might dispose of as they chose, but that they must keep, for it had been the gift of a saint, of the wife of Ferdinand VI. What became of harpsichord and music-books heaven only knows; the heirs of Metastasio's " adorable twin-brother " left Bologna, and abandoned his villa to utter decay. For ninety years did it stand empty and tenantless, dismantled and crumbling ; a strange weird sipot of desolation in the beautiful fields of corn and vines, forgotten like the fame of its owner. The next year, 1783, in a little house of the Campo S. Mnrcuola, at Venice, died an old couple, a German and his Italian wife, and no one noticed their end ; the husband was Johann Adolph Hasse, the most famous Italian composer of the second quarter of the eighteenth century; the wife, Faustina Bordoni, the greatest singer and most beautiful actress of the day. Of the great melodrama of the year 1730, the joint work of poet and musician, these four,—Metastasio, Farinello, and the two Hasses,— were the last, late survivors. A new school of music had arisen, a new school of poetry was arising: Cimarosa and Paisiello reigned without rivals; Altieri and Monti were about to accede; the old heroic opera, the school which had produced the Olimplade, Demofoonte, and Regolo, was extinct.

VIII.

The news of Metastasio's death gave a shock to the Italians: to that generation he seemed ever to have lived, his works seemed always to have existed; many people had probably not realised the fact of his being alive until they heard that he was dead. He had been a name, familiar beyond all others, a name associated with a hundred plots of operas which everyone seemed to have known ever since he existed, and with innumerable rhymes, strophs, and quotations which everybody seemed to have known almost before he was born. But, living at Vienna for fifty years,

J

he was not a personality to his countrymen, and even the few who had known him, in person or by letter, knew nothing whatever of his history. His death was felt as a surprise. A number of new editions of his works were published, and the printers hunted greedily for every letter of his that could be discovered; all the hungry literary priestlets set about compiling biographies of him, bare, barren, and most often apocryphal. All the would-be men of letters penned his eulogiums, gushing, pedantic, full of quotations from Horace and Rousseau, enriched with foot-notes, in which they displayed their learning and lampooned their adversaries with equal Avant of connection. All the academies convoked all their members to a great Church ceremony round a richly-scrolled catafalque, or to a meeting in the black-draped academic rooms, and speeches were made, and sonnets read and distributed. At Turin the literati gave Metastasio a grand funeral, with the famous Marchesi to sing ; at Alexandria the clever ex-Jesuit Cordara extemporised an immensely long and complicated oration; but the most was of course done at Metastasio's own birthplace, Rome. The Arcadians all met at the Bosco Parrasio, heterogeneous, cosmopolitan, and rather frivolous Arcadians, very unlike those Metastasio had seen there sixty years before: English milordi led about by tutors; German princes led about by equerries; artists, antiquaries of all nations, Angelica Kauffman, Piranesi, Gavin Hamilton, Tischbein, and Zeoga; a motley crowd, not knowing very well nor caring very much what this Arcadian business might be. To them, the Abate Taruffi, former secretary to the Nuncio at Vienna, most Voltairian, Ossianesque, altogether fashionable of ecclesiastics, friend of Goldoni, of Gluck, of Beccaria, of all that in those days meant rebellion, held forth in praise of his dear friend Metastasio, showing how great a man and how very great a poet he had been. And winding up his discourse the Abate Taruffi declared, that, though the Italian stage had lost much in Metastasio, there was present one who could repair the loss ; and he waved his hand gracefully in the direction of that singular, violent, red-haired young man who drove the many horses and wrote the tyrannicide tragedies, and made love to the wife of the last of the Stuarts; singing, in the same breath, the requiem for Metastasio and the Te Deum for Altieri.

This incident represents a vast fact. Metastasio's fame was indeed still alive, but it was a fame born of the past and not destined to live in the future. People continued to write, speak, and even think of him as great, but the reality of his greatness came less home to them year by year. The civilisation of which Metastasio had been the spokesman was breaking up ; the work of art of which he had been the chief craftsman was falling to ruins. Metastasio had represented the awakening of the purely Italian mind out of the long slumber of the seventeenth century, its spontaneous shaking-off of Spanish and erudite influences; but this movement

was now over ; Italy had become cosmopolitan and eclectic, borrowing French, English, Gorman, and antique modes of feeling; and tliinking already of borrowing topboots, guillotine cravats, and Grecian sandals, Metastasio's strong, delicate, natural, simply speaking and rapidly moving characters were even more insipid to the enthusiastic admirers of Lovelace, of Julie, of Fingal, of Werther, and of Brutus, than were his old-world wisdom, his old-world morality, to the readers of Diderot, Eousseau, and Chamfort.

To the Italians of the latter eighteenth century, saturated with every sort of exotic fashion, medleys of every sort of cosmopolitan exaggeration, Metastasio was necessarily insufficient: he did not satisfy their craving for morbid sentimentation, for strong action, for bold theory; he did not help to drag them along towards that mysterious, magnetic future which hid the revolution.

Moreover, Metastasio, who could no longer command sympathy in the closet, was rapidly ceasing to awaken admiration on the stage. The opera, such as he had known and treated it, had put all the action and dialogue into recitative, and had retained only the solo air or at most the duet for expressions of lyrism or passion. Very early, as soon as the public had grown fairly acquainted with his plays, the recitatives had begun to be curtailed; later, the words of airs were changed to suit composer or singer; little by little his plays became mutilated patchworks. Moreover, a gradual change took place in music; rhythm, accompaniment, and concerted pieces developed, while at the same time musical forms became softer, slighter, less massive and heroic; boldness of modulation diminished; and the recitatives, become threadbare and monotonous, were gabbled over unnoticed, except when relieved by instrumental passages. As the recitatives became worse and less noticed, concerted pieces became more complicated, better and more popular: trios, quartets, and quintets were made out of Metastasio's pages of recitative. The effect was obvious Not only did the verses thus inserted by theatre rhymesters disgrace the original play, but the very play was deformed by the action, whose rapidity was its great merit, being arrested or rather forced to move in the treadmill of concerted pieces. Anyone curious to see what a play by]\Ietastasio had become by the year 1790 may compare the Clemenza di Tito as printed in his works with the Clemenza di Tito as set by Mozart: the powerful opening scene between Sextus and Vitellia is fiddle-faddled into a duet; the rapid scene of the discovered conspiracy is drawn out into a quintet; the pathetic meeting of 8extus and Titus is fugued and twisted into a trio, and the exquisite outburst of Sextus's remorse is frittered away into a long rondo, in which he repeats a dozen times and to all sorts of tunes—" Tanto afifanno soflfre un core—ne si niuore—di dolore."

Meanwhile the universal taste for whimpering, semi-serious comedy,

Q

which had already done so much harm to Goldoni in Italy and to Lessing in Germany, affected even the opera. A famous singer, Marchesi, thought he could show off his fine figure to better advantage in modern dress than in the pseudo-antique works of Metastasian tailors, and could move more ladies to tears as a deserter, a reformed prodigal, or a gamester, than as a Roman consul ; so he imported from France a number of plays of the lachrymose, middle-class sort, which were duly transformed into Italian opera texts. The heroic subjects, with Greeks and Romans, kings and dictators, were still kept for the stately gala performances, to which people went in full dress, in the powder, hoops, stockings, and embroidered coats which were replaced in ordinary life by dresses a la Brutus and a la Pamela, limp, lank, and draggled; but the semi-serious plays, like the Nina pazza per ainore, the Disertore, the LodoisJca, the Agnese, were what people really enjoyed, what the great composers, like the delicately sentimental Paisiello, worked at with the best will.

The revolution had burst out; the old Italian states had been broken up, the Venetian republic had been dissolved for ever, the Papacy had been extinguished for the moment: a new state of things had suddenly arisen: it was the dawning of the nineteenth century; the last hours of the eighteenth were striking. Alfieri and Monti were at their zenith. Ugo Foscolo was arising, the children were already born who were to be/ known as Alessandro Manzoni and Giacomo Leopardi; Metastasio was a thing of the past. Yet even then his name carried with it authority; he was no longer liked, no longer read, but he was still respected. About 1798 there came to Rome with the victorious French a strange republican sibyl, once a nun, a mystic, a saint; now a democrat, a philanthropist, a prophetess of progress, the Citizeness Clothilde Suzanne Courcelle La-brousse, who held forth before the Roman patriots in the mixed language of an encyclopaedist and a fishwife, and whose long, rambling discourses, droll, sickening, pathetic, mixtures of politics, midwifery, and scriptui-al quotations, wei'e printed by the republican printer Puccinelli; the original in wondrous French on one page, the Italian translation on the other. In this exceedingly rare little pamphlet, which gives a greater insight into the French revolutionary invasion than all Botta's volumes put together, there is the following curious passage, which we transcribe with the Citoyenne Clothilde Suzanne Courcelle Labrousse's own spelling and punctuation:

" Vous Romaines, qui vous pleignez de toutes ces choses, je va vous faire voir encore comme quoi tout vient en haut et que c'est d'un Remain dont est venue I'origine de tout ceci au reste je va vous dire ce qui ma ete raporte, car je n'en sai point positivement I'histoire ; mais cela me paroit si vraisemblable que cela m'engage a le raporter, le principe de tout ceci vient dont d'un sertin Metastazc qu'on dit etre de son origine un petit

pauvre enfant de Rome, et qui se trouvant avoir la voie agrable chantoit souvant et vercifioit avec une grande facilite, gens d'etude, I'entendant lui dirent s'il vouloit venir avec eux qu'il lui aprendroit quelque chose qui lui facilitoroit a ce tiror d'affaire, lui soudain accepta, et fit tant de pro-gres quo dans pcu temps il Ics surpassa a tons, cela etant il denianda au Pape dece temps I'ii une pension pour vivro afin de nepenserqu'a I'etude, le Pape I'ayant constamment refuse il s'en fut a Viene, soudain ses talens fircnt du bruit, et parvinrent a Marie Therese Imperatrice, qui le voulut voir, et elle en fut si satisfaite qu'elle le fit Regent de ces enfants qnr comme tout le monde salt etoient en grand nombre, comme ce Metastase etoit vraiment eclaii'e, il faisoit presenter a cette cour que I'liomme quoi qu'il soit d'une grand naissance, il n'est pas pour cela dans le vrai plus grand que le reste des hommes, et qu'il n'est pas pour cela plus a I'abri des evenements de la vie que tout autre; enfin en consequence des prin-cipes qu'il insinuoit a cette cour I'lmperatrice fit aprendre a tons ses enfants un art comme I'agriculture etc. tout comme s'ils eussent ete oblige d'avoir besoin de cela pour vivre, a ses filles, elles leur faisoient balier leur chambre etc. et lors que les grands de sa court le voyoient, et qu'il lui observoient qu'elles n'auroient jamais besoin de ce savoir etc.; elle leur I'opondoient liela! qui le salt, de sorte done que se soit par principe ou par pressentiment que ce fesoit cette cour; mais reste qu'ctant imbue de ces sentiments; ils se disposoient deja, et disposoient tout chose aux evenements du temps .... de maniere que toute ses lumieres s'ctant re-pendues dans toutes los cours et des cours dans le peuple il en resulte joint a tant autres circonstances favorables; a 5a que les choses en sont venues ou elles sont, ainsi Romaines prenez vous en a vous memes, et non a d'autres."*

Whether the Roman citizens, citizens ox-abati, ex-princes, ex-spies, and ex-flunkeys, assembled at the republican club in the month of Floreal of the year six, were deeply impressed by the truth of Citizeness La-brousse's remarks, whetlier they ever took Metastasio into consideration as a philosopher, a philanthropist, and the original cause of the revolution, we shall never know. All that we do know is, that as a poet Metastasio was daily losing ground. By the end of the last century his plays had been transformed into monsters which could scarce be recognised as his; in the first years of this century they had disappeared altogether from the stage, routed by the invasion of pseudo-knights, pseudo-c/io^^/rtm^s, pseudo-pages, pseudo-ghosts, and all the other supposed representatives of chivalry which came with romanticism from Germany to France, and from France to Italy.

* Diseonrs prononees jJdT la Citoyenne CourccUe Lahroussc aw Cluh dc Home danx le mois Floreal de Van VI. faitsii: revus par ellc-meme. A Rome chez Puc-einelli Joachim Imprimenr National, p. 224.

q2

Driven from the opera stage, Metastasio could find no asylum on the tragic stage; his plays were now useless as operas, and liad always been unavailable as tragedies: they could never be declaimed, and they now ceased to be sung. Off the stage everything was against Metastasio ; he was not descriptive, not oratorical, not elegiac; he was dramatic, and his swift, impetuous action, his light, firmly-marked points of pathos, appeared to the reader dry and bare, thin action and thinner pathos, imbedded in insipid gallantry and entangled in complicated plots. The eye, running rapidly over his blocks of blank verse, was for ever arrested by those continual little lyrical strophs, insignificant little appendages which stood out like flourishes from the white paper. If anything was remembered it was these strophs, these pretty, insignificant little similes and conceits, formerly given over by the poet, who had done his work, to the composer who was to begin his ; trifles of little value save as a theme for melody and vocal execution, trifles in which the opera of the eighteenth century paid for having been almost an acted tragedy by becoming almost a motionless concert. These remained, and on these Metastasio's fame began to rest; on these rhymes, which had been intended to be enlarged, changed, given new metre, new movement, new life, breadth, and dignity by music, but which, when read off, were a mere pretty, ridiculous little fiddle-faddle.

Thus Metastasio was gradually placed in a position in which he could never be fairly judged, the position of an unacted dramatist, of an unsung song-writer; while, at tlie same time, the general way of thinking and judging became necessarily hostile to him. The Italians, checked by the French invasion in their self-elaborated civilisation of the eighteenth century, had become pedantic and utilitarian ; the literature of the days of former freedom, and the literature of aspiration after future liberty, were alone valued ; in their reviving national spirit, in their state of struggle against oppression, the Italians disdained that artistic life which had made them, as it seemed, the festhetical slaves, the jesters of the rest of Europe. Metastasio had belonged to the slavish eighteenth century, had been a court pensioner, a flatterer of the house of Austria ; he was utterly scorned; his works, which had been opera texts, Avere reviled as effeminate pieces of trumpery, which, with their falsified history, their royal pieces of perfection, their love-sick heroes, their roulades and their ritornellos, had been good only to amuse tyrants and to enervate slaves ; artistic Delilahs, sending the nation to sleep with meretricious delights, that it might aAvake to find itself shorn of its strength and blind to its shame. Even now, when criticism is getting the better of enthusiastic injustice, Metastasio is scorned and, at the best, condoned; his jesting and unconscious prophecy has been fnlfilled, and people write of him almost in his own mock humble words: " In the eighteeuth century there

lived a certain Abate Metastasio, a tolerable poet among bad ones." This is all the recognition ho receives from the intellectual classes: if his Avorks are still re-iirinted, it is for the benefit of old-fashioned prigs, who think him a safe moralist; of uncultured gushing women, who think him a consolation in unhappy love; of illiterate peasants, who use his plays on their own stages of planks and sheets. His true worth, which is his artistic worth, will be recognised only when the eighteenth century shall cease to be studied merely as a precursor of the nineteenth; when the musical efflorescence of the last century shall be recognised as a national and artistic phenomenon analogous to the plastic efflorescence of the Renaissance; and when with this musical efflorescence shall be associated the efflorescence of the Italian tragic drama; when, in short, the Italians shall recognise that their last great artistic gift to the world was the opera.

THE COMEDY OE MASKS.

THE COMEDY OF MASKS.

The Comedy of Masks, the farce partially improvised by typical buffoons, is as old as the Italian race. It has existed in rudiment ever since the earliest days of Latin, Oscan, and Italo-Greek civilisation: it is the elder comedy, for ever thrust aside by the younger comedy, the unwritten for ever banished by the written, driven out of sight by Aristo-[)hanes, by Plautus, by Terence, by the erudite comic writers of the Renaissance ; despised, reviled, ignored ; forced to hide in fair-booths and village taverns, till at last, after two thousand years of ignominious lurking, it issues forth strong, brilliant, and victorious with the great invasion of the dialect literature of the lower classes, of the peasants and lazzarcni and vagabonds who saved the Italian nationality in the sixteenth and seventeenth centuries.

One or two allusions of contemptuous ancient satirists and furious fathers of the Church, one or two terra-cotta statuettes and comic wall-paintings, have sufficed to prove not only that the Comedy of Masks was a mere continuation of the Atellan farces of old Italic days, but that the principal buffoons have undergone little change since the days when Pulcinella, under the name of Maccus, displayed his double-hump and prodigious nose to the ancient Neapolitans; when the Oscan Pappus and Casnar let themselves be duped by valets, daughters, and wards, just like the Venetian Pantalone and the Koman Cassandrino; when Harle-c|uin, once the satyr-like buffoon of the dionysiac revels of Sieyon, played his pranks and danced on his head, flatshod (planipes), begrimed with soot (fuligine faciam obductamj, and dressed in motley patches (mimns centunculus). before Cicero and Apuleius. ~ In the days of Poman civilisation and eclecticism the old Italic farce, the Comedy of Masks of antiquity, was rejected as coarse and rustic by a society requiring the more refined and artistic filthiness of Greece; but when the austerity, , which is always the companion of the highest depravity, began to grumble with the Stoics and thunder with the Saints against the wi'itten and polished comedy, when the Christian

Emperors and Popes began to proscribe the elegant abominations of the stage, the old Italian farce, safe from imperial and ecclesiastic censure in its unwritten licence, began once more to raise its head.-V xVnd, in proportion as the intellectual culture of antiquity diminished, and the austerity of Christianity increased, the

Italian mimes returned to power. We can dimly watch the buffoon masquers, with tlieir gibbosities and sootiness and patches, playing their antics and cracking their jokes amidst the crumbling remains of antiquity, in the fast increasing darkness involving the world; until at length, when Rome has been reduced to a heap of ruins and Italy to a Babel of nationalities, when memory of the past, consciousness of the present, and care for the future, seem simultaneously extinguished, we lose sight of the old Mask Comedy in the general obscurity, and strain vainly through the gloom to see the silhouette of the buffoons of antiquity. What became of them during that long period of darkness ? Did they lurk, with the last remnants of paganism, in the rural festivals, playing their pranks in honour of antique gods disguised as mediaeval saints ? Did the Church absorb them, as it absorbed all the life that remained, and let them loose to dance, gesticulate, and jest among the donkeys and drunken clerks of the feast of fools or the mummers of shrovetide, humouring the love of the ridiculous and the gi'oss in the same way as it did in the dirty and grotesque apishnesses of the cathedral fronts ? Be it as it may, the old buffoons continued to live, perhaps to hibernate, throughout the Middle Ages ; they doubtless showed themselves in the carnival processions of Italy, by the side of the mummers of shoemakers, of pastrycooks, of grasshoppers, and of antique divinities for whom Lorenzo de' Medici wrote his clever indecencies. But, as the culture of Greece had thrust them aside in Rome, so also did the revival of antique literature thrust them aside in the Renaissance ; the humanists of the fifteenth century would hear only of Plautus and Terence, and drove back the barbarous mimes, little dreaming of their antiquity, into the arms of the uneducated classes. Macjiiavelli, Ariosto, Bibbiena, Speroni^ T^is-sino, devoted their talents to imitating the ancient comic writers; Baldas-sare Peruzzi constructed ingenious stage scenery ; prelates, like Fedra Inghirami, learned the parts of antique prostitutes and panders, and Leo X. and Clement VII. laughed like schoolboys at humanistic adaptations such as the Calandra and the Suppositi, which would have made even an^ ancient blush.

But when the brilliant civilisation of the Renaissance broke up, when humanities were forgotten in the strife for existence, when Popes and prelates began to think of Luther rather than of Aristophanes, when the Italian merchants, turned into thriftless nobles, began to be Aveighed upon by Spanish solemnity, when the Inquisition began to prick up its ears at every profane joke, when the misfortunes of Italy had set in, then the old buffoons reappeared, Maccus become Pulcinella, Casnar grown into Pan-talone, the sanwiojjes turned into the two zanni, Arlccchino and Brighella; tlicn the unwritten comedy came as a consoler. It is a strange and suggestive fact that the man who first gave to the Commedia delP Arte a

separate and honourable position, who counterbalanced with his frank, tender, genuine comic genius the clever imitations and adroit obscenities of the humanists, the Paduan actor and dialect poet, Angelo Beolco, sur-named Ruzzante, was also the man who first mourned in the simple and touching dialect of Venetia the misery of Italy in the second quarter of the sixteenth century, the wretchedness of the peasantry and townsfolk ruined by the long wars and continuous massacres of the French, the (jermans, and the Spaniards. " The world is no longer what it was," said Ruzzante; "there is nothing but slaughter and famine; in the fields there is no longer any sound of laughter and singing ; the young people no longer make love and marry; we seem choked by the plague in our throats; the very nightingales no longer sing as in former days ;

happy are the dead quiet under ground. Let us therefore, since we cannot cry freely, laugh in our misery." .

H Laughter in misery, such was the origin of the revived Comedy of Masks : buffooneries to drown the recollection of ignominy, merriment to hide seditious sorrow, local satire to hide national satire, dialect to save Italian; the typical mask as a mantle wherewith to cover the object of derision, and the improvised jest, obscene and fleeting, wherewith to strike without leaving a trace. The police of the Viceroy, or the censors of the Holy Office, may indeed get scent of some stir in men's thoughts: let them come and pry; what can they find ? merely Harlequin kicking Pantaloon with some rabclaisien drollery; there is no proof, no paper, no definite action to lay hold of, the sedition has evaporated. Thus the Comedy of Masks kept alive the interest of Italy in itself at a time when Italy had been superseded by so many Spanish fiefs and Spanish king-dnius ; crushed and mangled as a whole, the country maintained its vitality in its fragments: fragments too insignificant, too heterogeneous to create suspicion, living on separate and unnoticed until at length permitted to reunite ; and the Comedy of Masks, the jumble of Bergamascs and Sicilians, of Neapolitans and Bolognese, the Babel of dialects the most dissimilar, is the product and the expression of this provincial life ever tending towards forbidden national unity.

V The wonderfully rapid development of the Comedy of Masks proves its intense vitality : by the middle of the sixteenth century the priuci\'7d)al masks had already become traditional: old men were typified in Pantalone dei Bisognosi the Venetian merchant, wearing the obsolete costume,—the scarlet stockings, black robe, and long-tailed hood, of the burgher of a mediaeval commonwealth; the two ideal classes of servants, the hypocritical rogue and the gliTttonous sly simpleton, were represented respectively by Brighella, dressed in the loose-striped shirt and linen cap of the artisans of the sixteenth century; and by x\rlecchino, wearing tight-fitting hose and jerkin of motley stripes and patches, suggestive of the grotesque dress of the youths

in Signorelli and Carpaccio's paintings. Both Brighella and Arleccliino came to be associated with the town of Bergamo, the Lombard dialect of which, wholly distinct from the Venetian of Pantalone, they continued to the last to employ. These two servants, the arch buffoons of the play, were called the two Zanni, perhaps in reminiscence of the Sanniones of antiquity; and Harlequin in especial never lost his antique character of mime,— dancing, playing tricks, and performing gymnastic feats in the midst of his parts. To these three was added the Doctor, sometimes called Doctor Graziano or Doctor Balanzon, the typical man of learning: dressed as a jurist, with an immense wine-stain on one cheek : always a Bolognese, always blustering and pedantic, oscillating between a knave and a fool, holding forth in maccaronian Latin. These four, Pantalone, Brighella, Harlequin, and the Doctor, were called the four masks; they were the most popular, the most typical, the most universally known and the longest of life. But opposite this quartet of North Italians arose another quartet of Neapolitan buffoons: Pulcinella, the ancient Maccus, the modern Punch '^r Polichinelle, with immense nose and double hump, dressed in white, a terrible violent sort of comic Bluebeard or Nero ; the J bully and intriguer Scaramuccia, dressed in black, the archetype of the military adventurer; the simpleton and stammerer Tartaglia; the long, dancing, fiddling, singing vagabond Coviello;— these Southern masks being more violent, more savage, more indecently antique, than the Northern, and perhaps more restricted to their own provinces. Round these two quartets of masks swarmed an infinity of other buffoons, varieties, individual or provincial; rising up and dying away, altering, multiplying to all infinity: the Milanese Beltrame and Meneghino, the immense class of Scappinos and Trivelinos of various shades, born of the Brighella tribe; the Truffaldinos,

Mezzettinos, Pedrolinos, and Cavicchios, children or brothers of Harlequin; and a legion of others, Burattinos, Francatrippas, Giangurgolos, Pasquariellos, Travaglinos, whom, in their rapid appearance, disappearance, and metamorphose, we cannot even plainly identify. To these masks—half actors, half acrobats, half jesters, —were added regular actors and actresses, speaking Tuscan and probably improvising but little, the pair of lovers Ijorrowed with but slight alteration from the written comedy and retaining its pseudo-antique names : Lelio, Leandro, Orazio, and Florindo; Lavinia, Flamminia, Ortensia, Giacinta, and Rosaura, dapper figures with no comic work to do, but necessary for the action of the play. And finally, superposed as it were on to the Italian comedy, was the type of the military adventurer, of the Spanish hidalgo, violent, tyrannical, overbearing and rapacious : a mixture of Don Juan, Pizarro, and Don Quixote; at first rather terrible than ridiculous, and growing into a bona tide comic figure, into a threadbare and hungry adventurer, a cowardly sonorous fire-eater, a Captain Fracassa or Mata-

moros, only in proportion as the redoubtable kingdom of Philip II., odious but dignified, turned into the tattered Spain of the seventeenth century, execrable but ludicrous.

j\Ioreover^thc_stabilijtj of the cbaractors was only one peculiarity of , / the improvised comedy ; the types were not only fixed, they were absolutely personal; a man who had once chosen to play Pantaloon, Harlequin, Pulcinella, or the Captain, never played anything else; the part was a costume which, once worn, could never be changed ; the viirious characters wore not abstractions like the characters of other comedies, they were concrete individuals. Instead of the playwright inventing a figure, a Falstaff or a Tartuffe, and then instructing an actor how to embody his conception, the playwright of the Comedy of Masks was given so many living creatures, so many embodied types, not Jacopo, Andrea, or Giovanni, whom he must bid strip off his every-day dress in order to assume some characteristic costume, and paint his face with any new device of wrinkles, but Arlecchino, with his patches and stripes, his black mask, his kicks, capers, and jokes; or Pantalone in his red hose and long black hood; or Lelio in his dainty slashed silk doublet and curled mustachios ; each as complete, as ready-made in character, gesture, intonation, and moral being, as in exterior appearance. The Mask actors were in short scarcely actors at all: they were fantastic realities, they no more needed a part to be written for them than does any other reality; they neces- "^ sarily and from their essential nature felt, acted, and spoke in a consistent and characteristic way. The consequence was evident: no parts were wnitton for them, they were placed opposite each other, and the meeting of Pantaloon and Brighella, of Harlequin and the Doctor, of Pulcinella and Scaramuccia, produced, by the automatic movement of the characters, an action and a dialogue ever new and ever natural. Ideal types of buffoons, made up of local caricature, of obsolete fashions, of antique traditions, moulded together by the reckless fancy of the people ; and real friction of character, real dialogue, real action, real repartee; such was the strange dual nature of the Mask Comedy, such the secret of its long fascination for the fancy and its ever renewed dramatic interest.

The Comedy of Masks had started with being but a sort of extravagant offshoot of the written comedy imitated from the antique, an adaptation thereof to the wants of less refined classes, and to the peculiarities of popular actors; the buff"oons had at first tried to perform for the lower classes what the academic actors performed for the upper ; Pantaloon and Harlequin had wished to act Terence and Ariosto. But, as the Comedy of Masks developed, it separated from the classic comedy and diverged further and further, till it stood perfectly alone, a unique])henon)enon in the history of the drama. About 1540 Beolco and his imitator Calmo had still written their comedies, leaving but little to the improvisation of

the actors, and their plays can still be read and thoroughly enjoyed in the reading; but their successors were obliged to leave half of the dialogue to be extemporised, and in a very few years the written part of the plays was reduced to a mere skeleton plan of the action divided into scenes, which was hung up in the green-rooms for the instruction of the actors, who filled up all the outlines according to the whim of the moment. Thence it is that nothing has come down to us of the Comedy of Masks of the late sixteenth and seventeenth centuries save a volume published about 1610 by the actor Flamminio Scala, containing fifty outlines of comedies in narrative form, which read like some duller Bandello or Cintio, threadbare tales of scurrilous intrigue, which are to the Comedy of Masks like the shapeless scaffoldings which remain after some wonderful exhibition of fireworks: of those enchanted palaces of light springing suddenly from the ground, of those fountains of flames, of those showers of sparks and sheaves of rays, of all that wondrous world of fire, there remains nothing but dreary rows of posts and bleak archways of wire.

The Comedy of Masks was not an invention, not a revelation, it was a natural product; it did not sieze hold of national taste, it sprang up and developed everywhere because its seeds had long existed in the Italian mind, and because the intellectual temperature of the latter sixteenth century necessitated its germination and development. From the humbler quarters of the towns it spread to the nobler, until the high-born and learned Academicians, reciting antique and pseudo-antique plays in their palaces, were interrupted by the yells of laughter of the spectators of Pantaloon and Harlequin over the way. The noble amateurs, trying to reconstruct Attic drama, strutting about in antiquarian splendour of toga and cothurnus, yelling choruses according to Pythagorean recipes and stumping pyrrhic sarabands after the fashion of Batthylus, looked down with infinite scorn upon these ignoble modern buffoons who dared to be more amusing than themselves. They refused to prostitute the noble name of comedy to the farces which, as the learned Niccolo Secchi contemptuously writes, " are performed here, there, and everywhere by dirty mercenary raggamuffins, who introduce the Bergamasc Zanni, Francatrippa, Pantaloon, and such like buffoons, who can be compared only with the Atellan mimes and planipedes of the ancients." The dirty mercenary raggamuffins of Messer Niccolo were by that time, about 1580, neither dirty nor raggamuffins, and could afford to snap their fingers at the written comedies and the would-be Rosciuses of the Academies. Mercenary they were, they lived off the laughter they could command, and lived honourably \ and even magnificently; and they accepted for their unwritten comedy the contemptuous epithet given it by the academic actors: professional comedy, artisan comedy, trade comedy, in the Italian of the sixteenth

ccntuiy, whicli associated no a'sthetical ideas with tlie word art, Qqm I media deW~Arte.. In the last quarter of the sixteenth century Italy was fidl of comic companies,—Venetian, Lombard, Tuscan, and Neapolitan, but more commonly mixed, who wandered from place to place performing with incredible success. The upper classes and the prelates and princes patronised superior companies of highly-trained actors and beautiful actresses, richly remunerated and highly honoured. The very Academicians became proud to recite verses in honour of some famous Harlequin or some lovely Flamminia. The Church, so far from excommunicating and refusing Christian sepulture to actors, did all to attach them to religion, and was rewarded by occasionally discovering that some celebrated buffoon had been in the habit of wearing a hair shirt beneath his motley garb, and had died almost in odour of sanctity; nay, a real saint. Carlo Borromeo, Archbishop of Milan, was in the habit of examining, correcting, I and annotating the skeleton manuscripts submitted to his censure by pious managers, and some of these curious, half holy, half profane relics, \ were still extant in the eighteenth century. At the end of the sixteenth century Italy was still the teacher of fashions, and the young foreigners travelling about with their tutors and their fencing-masters brought back to

England, to France, and to Germany, the taste for Mask Comedies, until at last they encour-aged Italian actors, as their great-grandsons of the days of Queen Anne were to encourage Italian singers, to try their fortunes abroad. About 1570 the Austrian and Bavarian courts already kept Italian companies with Arleccliino, Brighclla, and the Doctor; in 1577 a company of Mask actors headed by a certain Drusiano migrated to England, (introducing the clowns and fools employed by Shakspeare ; about the same time Juan Ganassa attempted, with but small success, to graft the Italian masks on to the Spanish drama of Lope and Moreto; and in 1577 Henri III., himself the strangest buffoon that ever played a part in tragedy, called to Blois, to amuse the Hugnenots and Ligueurs there assembled, the comic company of the Gelosi, whom he had perhaps seen during his Italian journey, and which numbered, besides the director Flamminio Scala, the two excellent Zanni, Simone Bolognese and Pedro-lino, Francesco Andreini, famous by his stage name of Captain Spavento della Valle Inferna, and his wife the beautiful Isabella, queen of Italian actresses, celebrated throughout Italy for her beauty, her learning, and her excellent conduct. The taste for things Italian increased with (he marriage of Henri IV.; the Gelosi were again invited to Paris, subse-(|uently succeeded by a new company called the Fedeli, headed by a younger Andreini; and finally, in 1G45, the Italian Mask actors were established in the Hotel du Petit Bourbon, where they performed alternately with French actors, and where the young upholsterer Jean Baptiste Poquelin, known on the stage as Moliere, studied acting from

the admirable Hcaramuccia Tiberio Fiorilli. Moliere not only learned from the Italians how to construct his plays and how to perform them, but he also borrowed from them largely, takinsf several of their Mask typos, like Truffaldin, Sganarelle, Pantaloon (Geronte), and Brighclla (Scapin), and deliberately using Mask frameworks for several of his plays, such as L'Etourdi und Le Festin de Pierre; nay, some critics go so far as to assert with M. Moland that wherever in Moliere there is complicated action and comic movement we may trace the influence of the Italian comedy. Thus the Commedia deW Arte, which had perhaps^ afforded suggestions to Shakspeare and to Lope de Vega, proximately y produced the comedy of Moliere by offering a definite artistic mould in which to cast all the heterogeneous comic elements which had existed chaotically in the old French fabliaux, nouvelles, and farces.

The historians of the Comedy of Masks, from the archaeologist-actor Eiccoboni, " dit Lelio, comedien ordinaire du Roy," down to M. Maurice Sand and M. Moland, have universally declared that the establishment of these colonies in England, Spain, Germany, and Franco, marks the highest point, the golden age, of the Commedia delV Arte, and that its decline dates from the year 1600. In this decision we cannot possibly concur. That the Comedy of Masks obtained its most artistic shape and its highest polish in the days of the Gelosi and the Fedeli; that in the hands of these admirable actors it was a happy mixture of written and improvised dialogue, of Tuscan and of dialect, of classic tradition and popular inspiration, is undeniable ; but the very nature of the Commedia deir Arte was to be deficient in artistic shape and literary polish, to be wholly improvised and totally unliterary, to be unhampered by traditions and fluctuating according to the caprice of the people. The comedy of the Gelosi and of the Fedeli stiW partook too much of the written comedy of Machiavelli and Bibbiena, the actors were still too much influenced by academic models, and spectators were still too accustomed to humanistic unities. Italy in the sixteenth century, broken as was its nationality and crumbling^as were its institutions, was still too much of the well-organised, polished Italy of the Renaissance to permit of the full development of the Mask Comedy: for that was required the final stage of national stagnation and ferment. The golden age of the Commedia delU Arte is precisely the period which has been assigned to its decline, the time when the restraints of culture and civilization had rotted away, and when comedy fell into the hands of the rabble; the Commedia delV Arte flourished most luxuriantly in the depth of that strange swamp, bog, and quagmire of the Italy of the seventeenth centmy.

~~A swamp, a bog, a quagmire indeed ; a confused expanse of stagnating ideas, of rotting forms, of rank and inextricable abuses, of melancholy dried vegetation of better times ; a slippery, muddy, puddly

piece of noisoniene?s, from whose ajiiiroacli we are scared liy the monotonous croak of a loq-ion of literary reptiles; such is the Italy of the seventeenth century. Yet let us be fair even to this evil piece of historical land ; to this putrescence of tlie vigorous things, good and evil, left liy the Renaissance. Hitlden in the corruption of death are tin* genus of life; among the putrid waters trickle little invisible streamlets, pure and limpid, acquiring daily more volume and more current ; hidden by the rotting vegetation of the insolent rank marsh-grass are little plants, gradually pushing their shoots upwards till they will have overtopped the evil weeds ; in this atmosphere of death there is a microscopic, infinitesimal but infinite life, a life as of maggots, or of millions of ugly little vermin, born of the very putrefaction : the swam.p, which seems dead, is alive, and the day will come when it will be redeemed and fruitful for the world.

Let us not, therefore, turn away in contempt and disgust at this ugly Italian seventeenth century ; let us remember that in this miserable, loathsome period took place that process of disintegration and revivification of national elements which gave us, instead of Machiavelli and Guicciardini,!'! Vice and Beccaria ; instead of Politian and Ariosto, Metastasio and Goldoni; instead of Leonardo, Michel Angelo, and Titian, Marcello, Pergolesi, and Cimarosa. In those dismal days when the solemn ostentatious houses of the rich were full of domestic degradation, when the husband would fall by his wife's side stabbed by the wife's lover; when the wife would pine away for months with the sickness of mysterious poison ; when the father, stained with every vice, would be strangled by night and cast by his sons into some foul hiding-place; and people would shrug their shoulders and the police raise their eyebrows as sole comment; when the dapper young men kept retinues of murderers dangling at their heels, and the sainted nuns filled the convent wells with little children's bones ; when the learned academies disputed in Greek, Latin, and Italian, whether the stone hurled against the Virgin's picture was to be considered a holy relic or a sacrilegious abomination ; when old | women and young were burned for going to the witches' meetings in the , shape of cats ; when poets were crowned for calling the heavens a shining ' sieve; when the upper classes had become poisoned and bewitched maniacs, and the literati exuberant superstitious pedants; when the society, literature, and language of Italy, sick with the excesses of the Renaissance, were weighed upon and oppressed by the huge rotting mass of dead Spain ; then in that dismal seventeenth century the lower classes, the beggars, the vagabonds, the illiterate, the whipped serfs of Naples, the malaria-poisoned peasants of the Maremma, the starved artisans of the towns, all the tattered, bruised, ulcerated, homeless, workless, nameless •' oppressed, upon whom national degradation and foreign tyranny fell

R

hardest, arose in their rags and their filth, and jDroclaimed in their multifold jargon of dialects that Italy was not dead. While the upper classes became day by day more grave, more sad, more imbecile with their Spanish solemnity and vacuity ; while the Italian poets, with Marini at their head, became day by day more nauseously insipid with their Spanish unmeaningness and inflation ; the lower classes became daily more waj^-ward, more powerful, more passionate, and their dialect poet more fantastic and original. While the upper classes sat yawning in their plaster-bedizened palaces, listening to some vapid, turgid pastoral rubbish, some bastard Amyntas or mongrel Pastor Fido; the lower classes in the open squares, in the fairs, among the nostrum vendors, the gibbets, the wineshops, the pillories, the strings of onions and tin ware, among the maimed, armless, legless beggars, the giants and giantesses, the preaching friars and the fortune-telling gipsies, the whole squalid, fantastic, grotesque world which Callot has etched in his " Fair at Impruneta," listened to the wandering dialect poets, singing of Bertoldo and Bertoldino like the Bolognese Croce, and to the vagabond actors of the Mask Comedy. Then it was that, without poets and without actors of any fame, the y Commedia delV Arte attained to its full size; gigantic, gigantically vigor-^ ous and monstrous : born of laughter among misery in the days of Ravenna and Marignano, it attained to maturity amid oppression, starva->/ tion, and squalor in that dreary half-century of lethargy during which Italy paid for the Thirty Years' War in Germany, and was bled of money and men for the great strife between Catholic Austria and Protestant • Sweden. Plays and playwrights there were none ; subjects were taken helter-skelter from Spain, from the older comedy, from the written comedy; the dialects were in their most wondrous vigour ; the burlesque style, under Tassoni,Maggi, and the great Redi, was triumphant. Everywhere swarmed new varieties of masks, acrobats, jesters ; grotesque, terrible ; obscene and ludicrous shapes, only half-human, suggesting the .^<r^^. broken egg-shells, melon-rinds, and bundles of rags of their native dust-holes and drain-vaults. Spanish Rodomonts, wondrous in deed, w with slashed jackets and cobwebbed swords, of names without end, Cocco-drillo, Spezzamonti, Bellorofonte, Martellione, Basilisco, Rinoceronte, Escarabombardon della Papiroutonda, swaggered about with bristling whiskers and mangy plume before the Spanish garrisons, boasting that they were sons of Earthquake and Thunder, cousins of Death, and bosom friends of Beelzebub; Trivelinos, Fritellinos, Formicas, Coviellos, dancing, fiddling, kicking creatures, Avith long noses and slit mouths, tumbled about in the face of the monks and Jesuits, singing heathen songs with jargon burdens; Giangurgolos and Scaramuccias, ceremonious and stately, with tattered clothes and spectacles, fandangoed about before the terrible coaches of Neapolitan Viceroys ; Pulcinella, ogre-like, terrific, a volcano

of jest and pfibe, lashod up the lazzaroni like a precursor of Masaniello. The Inquisition, tlie Jesuits, the Viceroys were powerless against this ever-increasing and ever-varying swarm of buffoons; the va.q'abonds, the raggamuflfins and their dialects, were saving the Italian nationality : the masks of the comedy,—bold, insolent, serious, jesting, unseizable Pro-teuses,— were saving the Italian lower classes from the fate of their Spanish fellow-sufferers. Yes, this middle of the seventeenth century was the golden time of the Comedy of Masks ; and the representative man, the supreme and universal genius of the day, the Michel Angelo of vagabonds, as Bernini was the Michel Angelo of nobles and pedants,— Saly ator Rosa —was one of the shining lights of the Commedia delV Arte. This strange jumbled genius,—wild, pedantic, ferocious, gentle, and playful, whose cynically imaginative paintings, with their smoking battle-fields, their brawls of ragged soldiers, their grimacing beggars and bandit-haunted ravines, contrast so singularly with his coarse verbose satires, sweepings up of erudite dirt-heaps, and with his charming, quaint, half-undeveloped music,—this arch-adventurer and arch-rebel wandered about in his youth with other tattered artist vagabonds, acting the part of the Neapolitan buffoon, dancer, singer, and jester, Coviello, in a masterly manner, as another confused and ragged genius, caricature of poet and composer like Salvator Eosa himself, Hoffmann, has shown him us in his admirable story " II Signer Formica," in which Salvator Rosa, with his opponents the Pyramid Doctor and thelittle deformed soprano Pitichinaccio, form a group perfectly in the spirit of the Comedy of Masks. Later in life, when Rosa had settled down in Florence, he continued to play his parts of Coviello and Pascariello in the comedies improvised at his own house, in which Torricelli the mathematician, Viviani the brother of the astronomer, and Carlo Dati, the Hellenist, performed the other mask characters ; while Carlo Dolci, Alessandro Stradella, and Redi, the author of the magnificent rollicking dithyramb in Tuscan dialect, may have been present as worthy spectators.

With Salvator Rosa the improvised Comedy of Masks, the proteus-like representative of the vagabond life and dialect buffooneiy of the seventeenth century, culminates and begins to decline. As the seventeenth century drew towards its close, as foreign oppression and national exhaustion diminished, as brigands and bravos vanished, a s_so.cic tj became reorganised in its upper strata ; as, in short, the marsh, with its stagnation, its garish weeds and vermin inhabitants, gradually turned into arable land, so also the .Comedy of Masks began to lose vitality. The opera, attaining to maturity, gradually usurped its national powers; in the southern provinces comic musical interludes began to supersede the mask buffooneries; in the northern, French imitation began to substitute bad tragic declamation for comic improvisation. The Commedia deW Arte

R 2

maintained, it is true, its possession of the smaller theatres for another half century; all actors were mask actors, all comedies were mask comedies; but the life of the style was fast ebbing ; no new types appeared ; the old became stereotyped ; the jokes and gestures and aero- . batic feats became traditional; the Comedy of Masks began to be considered as legitimately enthroned as perpetual sovereign of the Italian comic stage; its days of battle and adventure were over. The day of its dethronement was fast approaching; and the man Avho was to disintegrate the old national comedy, and to cast its elements into a new Tnould, was already born.

GOLDONI AND THE EEALISTIC COMEDY.
GOLDONI AND THE EEALISTIC COMEDY.

I.

Carlo Goldoni was born at Venice, in a liouse at the corner of the via Ca Cent' anni, in the parish of St. Thomas, somewhere in the year 1707. Sent into the world with the sole object of moulding into an artistic whole the heterogeneous elements of the mask comedy, and of substituting a national for a local stage, his birth, parentage, education, his whole life and whole character, were ingeniously arranged by fate for this purpose. He was an admirable luechanism, such as can be evolved but not constructed, for producing the greatest possible number of excellent comedies ; and he was interesting only as such, as his life is interesting only inasmuch as it served as a long apprenticeship to his art. A man of insignificant temperament, of limited intelligence, Itut with an enormous endowment for comic observation and construction, and a series of influences calculated to develope this genius,—such is Goldoni, and such Goldoni's life. Nature would waste no other material upon him, and fate would give him only comic adventures: his character and his life resemble nothing so much as his works.

Born a mongrel Italian, half Modenese and half Venetian, in the house of a grandfather who squandered his fortune upon actors and actresses, Goldoni was made a present of a puppet-show when he was four; he was encouraged to compose a play when he was eight, and was, in his earliest childhood, bundled off on a series of journeys throughout Italy. His father, a sort of irregular genteel physician, and his_amiable intelligent mother, made several attempts to turn him into an ordinary child and an ordinary youth by means of teachers, colleges, logical barbaras and bara-liptons and theological transcendental metaphysics ; but even they were forced to help the irresistible fate which destined Carlo Goldoni to be a comic writer and nothing else. At Perugia the urchin was made to play a woman's part in a comedy performed by the seminarists in the Antinori

A

palace ; a few years later, being left at school at Eimini, he was so fascinated by a company of actors as to leave all his books and shirts behind, and embark with them for Chiozza, where his mother was living, enjoying beyond all things the life on board, among the harlequins and pantaloons, the parrots, cats, dogs, monkeys, and pseudo-mothers of the actresses. At Chiozza the boy, intensely anxious to see his family, cannot summon up courage to present himself at home ; the good-natured Leander of the Company offers to help him, takes him home, and hides him in the passage while breaking the news of his arrival to his mother. " Signora," says the Leander, " I have brought you news of your son from Rimini." " My son ! how is the boy ?" " Very well, but he does not like his position ; he suffers very much from being parted from his mother." Signora Goldoni is intensely moved by the pathetic words of the buffoon. " Poor child ! How I wish I had him with me !" Leander siezes his opportunity. " I offered to bring him here." " You did ! and why has he not come?" "Would you have approved of such a step?" gravely asks Leander. "Of course," cries Signora Goldoni, in an agony of motherly affection. " But his studies—what of his studies ?" " His studies ! Oh—why—he might have gone back to them later." " Then you would really have been glad to see him, Signora ?" " Glad! I think so, indeed!" " Signora, here he is," and Leander throws open the door, and the boy rushes into the good woman's arms. The same scene, with the addition of hiding under the valance of a dressing-table, is repeated on the return home of the father; comic scenes, absolutely of the kind which Goldoni used in his plays. At fifteen Carlo is sent to finish his studies at the ecclesiastical college of Pavia—studies which had mainly consisted in reading the Latin, French, and Spanish dramatists, and, on these being confiscated as unfit for youth, of the horrible comedies [M -^^ of MachiavelJi, innocently furnished as a consolation by an unsuspecting old canon. At Pavia more surreptitious reading of comedies, varied with flirtations with sundry professorial young ladies ; the whole wound up by the writing of a dramatic satire, on the model of the ancient Atellanae, , an immense scandal and hubbub in consequence, and ignominious expulsion from college.

Goldoni's Memoirs—a huge work undertaken in his extreme old age— are unlike anything else of the kind. They are neither romantic, nor scandalous, nor philosophic : they are intensely professional; they are neither the outpourings of a man of feeling, nor the gossip of an old man of the world, nor the psychological study of a novelist or metaphysician ; they are a series of analyses on all of his innumerable plays, embedded in a biography which reads like a running commentary upon them ; the man's feelings, actions, and adventures appearing like the rough material for his works. As in his plays, so in Goldoni and in Goldoni's life there

is nothing sentimental, tragic, libertine, and adventurous ; all liis emotions and impressions have the levity, the good-natured simplicity, of bis works; all his actions and adventures have the light movement, the comic complication of his comedies. "We no more expect a deep mental conflict, or a real catastrophe in this book, than we do in the Smanieper la ViUeggiatura or the Putta Onorata; neither Goldoni nor any of the other actors in the Memoirs will ever commit any desperate action, experience any violent passions, or suffer any great misfortune; all the mistakes will be cleared np, all the peccadilloes condoned, all the scrapes got out of; all will come right at the end of the comedy. Gol-_ doni is the hero or the victim of a dozen love adventures and matrimonial schemes with citizens' daughters, lemonade sellers, waiting-maids, and smart young ladies ; from the first love for the charming girl whose abigail, in true Goldonian-Colombina style, fomented his passions with forged letters and interviews at windows, in which she acted her lady's part, until she finally deluded the youth into expressing his love by means of a set of glass beads, worth six sequins, which she sold for double the price to her unsuspecting mistress ; from this little early comedy down to his final breaking off his match with the lovely young lady of the Friulian journey, on the sagacious reflection that if she were to fall into ill health and fade as her elder sister had done he would find it difficult to remain faithful in his affection ; these loves are a series of strange little imbroglios, out of which Goldoni invariably emerges, crestfallen indeed, but never broken-hearted or remorseful. As it is with love so it is with all else: Goldoni slips in and out of social positions and professional arrangements with the same light-hearted, well-behaved, imperturbable slipperiness. Educated for the law, and successful at the Venetian bar, he throws up everything at Venice because he doubts of the wisdom of an<Hher matrimonial scheme, and because he is seized with the desire to present a tragic poem to the opera directors of Milan. The reading of the opera libretto being interrupted by the criticisms, harpsichord strummings, and general impertinence of the singers, and the manuscript committed to the flames, Goldoni, with nothing, or next to nothing, in the world, takes service as secretary with the Venetian minister at Milan. A little later, being accused of treachery by the minister, he goes off with a company of actors; arrives at Genoa, and seeing a beautiful young lady at a window, makes a deep bow, and gives her a tender glance. The young lady curtsies ; Goldoni returns again next day and the following days ; more bows, more curtsies, more tender glances : a perfect little comedy courtship, with a stage-like quiet street and balcony, and two stage-like little graceful silhouettes, Florindo and Rosaura. After a few days Goldoni is introduced to the lady's father; invites him, like some Signor Pantalone de' Bisognosi, to the play ; asks for the hand of his daughter,

ami is immediately accepted, and almost immediately married. And, like the marriages in his plays, this off-hand marriage, a marriage neither of passion nor of interest, but of whim, proves extremely happy ; Goldoni and his wife live childless, without quarrels or jealousies, for more than fifty years, as we imagine that Sior Menegheto does with 8iora Lucietta, or the Signor Evaristo with the Signora Chiara. For ever falling on his feet, or, if falling elsewhere, up in a trice and with no bruises upon him, Goldoni, amiable, honest, superficial though perfectly sincere in all his attachments, never once, as he himself tells us, lets any misfortune interfere with his supper. He is no cynic; on the contrary, all his feelings are on the right side : he never succumbs to temptation, he is never drawn down to vice ; he is for ever flitting about, skimming over the surface of life with a little reproachful shake of the head for the unfortunates who stick in its mire, and a little nod of approbation for heroes Avho trudge manfully up its rough and dangerous paths. For ever shifting his quarters, Goldoni saw a great deal of the world, and a great deal of life : he never failed to visit Roman ruins, alum-mines, or celebrated writers ; he never failed to hear^11 good music and to attend all good sermons; but though he forgot nothing, and could tell the number of arches of the amphitheatre, of cartloads of alum in the mines, of subjects of conversation of the writers ; although he remembered the tunes of the operas and the arguments of the preachers, nothing of all this ■was assimilated by his own nature, neither history, nor art, nor literature. The man's nature was capable of really absorbing only those commonplace comic scenes and incidents which came before him. He was for ever getting into the way of that lightly treated but serious and most eventful war of Bourbon Spain against the house of Hapsburg, continually renewed from about 1732 to 1745. He almost witnessed the battle of Parma; he was jammed up between the Austrian and French armies in the Milanese, seeing sieges and capitulations ; he was robbed of his clothes and money by marauders, and fled before the enemy reading a comedy of his—the only thing remaining to him—to a fellow traveller ; he was retained,—after being abandoned by his coachman, losing his trunks, and can*ying his wife on his back through swollen torrents and along broken roads,—as a sort of comic prisoner by the Austrian troojis at Rimini; but all these personal experiences of warfare left only comic impressions in the cheery, flighty, little man, and served to produce no other pictures than those of officers gambling and making love to quartermasters' daughters, of soldiers stealing fowls and eggs, of wandering hucksters selling their wares at monstrous prices; of the misery, the ruin, the wounded, and the widowed. Carlo Goldoni, true son of the light, cheerily benevolent eighteenth century, appears to have remembered nothing. Goldoni was eminently respectable : to swindle, to live oflt"

others, to live the Gil Bias life of many another Venetian of his clay, was impossible for him ; it savoured too much of romance, and romance was quite out of his line, as the rojjc ladders, daggers, disguises, and other cloak and sword paraphernalia of Moreto and Calderon were foreign to his comedy. A good husband though not a passionate lover, an agreeable acquaintance though not a devoted friend, an honest and kind-hearted man though not a hero, he was fully persuaded of the necessity of a decent mode of life. He was first a lawyer at Venice, then attached to the Venetian resident at Milan, then Genoese consul at Venice, then lawyer again in Tuscany, working just as much or as little as was required by honour and poverty ; doing what had to be done jiroperly, with indifference, and then throwing up the profession without reluctance: neither love of work, nor avarice nor ambition, could anchor him to any occupation.

Jjut light as was Goldoni's character, and fickle as were his habits, he had one mental ballast, he had one loadstone ; the ballast was his co mjc genius, the luailstdue was j.he conaic stage,. Comedy, either in the shape of plays which lie had wi-itten and acted, of actors and actresses whom he had followed, or of comic accidents which had befallen him, had been wound up with his whole life : comedy absolute was for ever haunting bim. He had from the earliest a vague feeling of dissatisfaction at the absence -dfe of really Italian written comedies; EeTiada hazy notion that he might dfe something himself, a notion which gradually developed into a quiet, self-satisfied belief in his own mission to give Italy what it lacked. As a youth he had written one or two comic interludes for his Friulian lady-love ; at]\Iilan, while attached to the Venetian minister, he wrote some scenes for the excellent mask actors in the service of a quack doctor. Buonaf ede Vitali, ' who, after wandering through Asia, had made his fortune in Italy by the alexipharmacon which lie sold in the streets with interludes of mask comedy to attract the crowd. The (^uack introduced Goldoni to Qisali, generally called the Tooth Extractor, a famous cq^fiQcomico, for whose company some more trifles were written. Expelled from the house of the Venetian resident, and buffeted to and fro by the war of 1734, Goldoni made acquaintance in the amphitheatre of Verona with another Qopo comico named Imer, and was engaged by him to write for the tlmitre of 8t. JohrrG^trysostom at Venice. For St. John Chrysostom he continued to write after his marriage and during his tenure of the Genoese consulate at Venice, but on losing this post he gave up the stage for good and sought his fortune elsewhere. But_comedy would not let him slip : taken prisoner with his wife by the Austrian army at v Cesena, he was immediately set to work writing plays by military command. At length, delivered from this courteous servitude, he settled at

Pisa as a lawyer, and in a year or so obtained a promising practice : jao ^ore comedies for the rest of his life. _So, at least, it seemed. But one day an enormously tall and fat man, dressed in Quakerish fashion, stalks into the Advocate Goldoni's study ; he has come on business. Doubtless some steward or shopkeeper wishing to consult on legal matters. The fat stranger seats himself, and rolling to and fro on his chair, and making the most wondrous grimaces, explains his errand. He has come to offer employment to tlie Advocate Goldoni, come with sequins in his pocket, and full liberty to treat: the employment is that of comic writer to the company directed by the ca po co rudcA Medebat'^; he himself is Cesare Darbes, pantaloon of the above company. Will the Advocate Goldoni name his terms? The Advocate Goldoni declines : he has made law his profession, he is very sorry to be unable to give his time, &c. &c. Pantalone Darbes j)resses; Goldoni becomes obdurate ; Darbes supplicates, making the most deliciously comic grimaces the _ I while; the man of law protests ; but the grimaces of the pantaloon are too much for him; while refusing louder and louder he is in reality giving way ; he smiles, he laughs. Darbes siezes his opportunity ; Goldoni is lost for evermore to the legal]irofession. Medebac drags him to Venice, where he has hired the theatre of S. Angelo, places at Goldoni's disposal his magnificent comic company, and bids him write any-\ thing, everything, bids him summon up all his powers to please the most lingenious, the most fanciful, the most artistic, the most fastidious and jfickle comic audience in Italy.

In 1740 Venice was still something of what she had been in 1540. The development of northern nations and of northern commerce which had, in a moment as it were, broken to pieces and bled to death Florence, Milan, and Genoa, had not dispatched Venice, but had imprisoned and ■'starved her: she had been let off with her life, permitted to linger on and die slowly of paralysing inaction and bloating anemia. In the eighteenth century she had become very incapable of exertion, very subject to ailments, so wretchedly sick that she died of the first storm-blast of the revolution; but she retained her general aspect of manner of other days. The mode of life and way of thinking of the Renaissance were maintained in Venice, as were the institutions and dresses of the sixteenth century. It is this something of former days, mixed with the modern, which gives Venice in the eighteenth century so peculiar an aspect, something analogous to the portraits of doges in the robes of the Middle Ages over knee-breeches, and the cap of Byzantine days stuck upon a powdered bagwig. The Spaniards and the Jesuits had not been at Venice and covered all things with the dirty white monotony of their social and moral whitewash: the old colours, the old patches of half-mediieval, half-

oriental gold and colour, the old dabs of sea-stain and filth, still remained in tho spirit of Venice as on its walls. It had kept the licence, the . practical spirit, the incredulity, the magnificence, fancifiilness, and splendid cynical corrujition of the Renaissance: it was the town of brocaded courtezans and dare-devil adventurers; of learned dissipated nobles, who spent their mornings in the council-room, their evenings in their libraries, their nights, masked and dominoed, over the great \'7d)ublic gaming-table : half Cato, half Petronius; it was the town of enterprising booksellers, who,^\mder the eye of a censor who cut out .all which " offended princes and good morals," openly sold the boldest diatribes, the foulest romances of the encyclopanlists; it was the town whence medals were sent to Voltaire, and in which Montesquieu, crossing the lagoon, threw his note-book into the water for fear of the terrible Messer Grande and his spies; the town of all the strange picturesque anomalies of the Renaissance, with a semblance of Renaissance life about it; with

f _an art and a literature, and a corruption and a beauty of its own ; with Marcello, Lotti, and Galuppi composing, instead of Giorgione, Titian, and Tintoret painting; with an infamous Baffo instead of an infamous Aretino ; ^nth a clever local poet Gritti instead of Beolco; with a judicious, elegant purist Gasparo Gozzi instead of Bembo; with all it had once possessed

• except vitality to endure. Venice, in the year 1740, was the headquarters of Italian gaiety, and as such the head-quarters of Italian comedy. The Coniedy of IVIasks, gradually degraded into puppet and acrobat performances liy the music of Naples and the della Cruscan purism of Tuscany, was in full force at Venice; indeed its characters had become gradually reduced to the four Venetian masks, Panta-

H.lone, Arlecchino, Brighella and the Doctor. Venice, where the mask and domino were habitually worn for several months in the year; where high-born nuns frizzled their l;air, and invited their friends to see harlequinades and to dance/«?■/one in convent refectories; where the people crowded round story-tellers and extempory poets under the Palace arches; Venice, whose whole superficial life was a profane farce, was the natural home of the Commedia delV Arte. The whole population crowded the comic theatres : the senators in their robes and perriwigs, the priests and monks disguised in domino, the flaunting jjainted Jezebels, the severe ascetic merchants Avith their quaker-like wives and daughters, the ribald scum of the square of St. Mark's, the simple, patriarchal fisherfolk of Torceles, the blustering gondoliers in red sasli and loose jacket, th(^ quiet black-dressed familiars of the State Inquisition; all this motley mixture filled the theatres, forming aja audience fastidious like the effeminate nobles, judicious like the solid men of law, austere like the merchants' wives of the Mercei'ia, free and easy like the libertines of the Piazza,

wonder-loving like the townsfollc, rough and violent like the fisherpeople, intriguing like the spies and adventurers; and altogether laughter-loving and fickle, like all good Venetians. How please, how satisfy, how fascinate such a chaotic audience ?

Goldoni, violently pushed forward by the manager Medebac, looked round him, doubted, advanced a few steps, receded a little ; felt his way, looked from one side of the audience to the other, fumbled, and only gradually began to understand what to do. He was to amuse this many-headed monster: he began by examining the instrument upon which he

[had to play for its amusement. This instrument was the Comedy of Masks; in 1748 it was ali'eady going to pieces. The old masks were daily dropping off, and no new ones arose to take their place; the significance, local and historical, of many of the types had been lost. The people of the eighteenth century, accustomed to pacific soldiery and rapid, orderly, almost courteous warfare, forgetful that any Spanish had ever been spoken in Italy, took no interest in the rodomontades of Captain Matamoros or the ceremonious swagger of Giangm-golo ; they had ceased to delight in the mouthings and caperings of such children of the dust-^ftt^^ heap as Francatrippa, Fritellino, and Coviello ; all this had too much of the fair-booth and tavern smell to be endurable in a civilized theatre; the upper and middle classes, once more the life of the country, took no pleasure in the ruffianly bufSoons who had arisen triumphant out of the slums of Naples and Rome. A j the C omedy of Masks had left the streets andthe fair-sheds for tidy urban theatres, and found itself before a cultivated and resjiectaUle audience, it had been obliged to trim and clean itself, to~conform to the decencies!)? civilized life ; to exchange its rags for smart fancy dresses or for gala suits. The actors were once more a class of educated artists, instead of being mountebanks and ballad-singers as in the days of Salvator Rosa ; they had more artistic sense, but less spontaneity than their predecessors ; in proportion as they were well-trained they ceased to be inventors; the jokes and acrobatic feats

I began to be learnt by rote. To interest the public something new was

I required, and that something new could be found only in the written ^ lelement ; th e impr ovisations were all stale, the only hop_e_ofjiovelty was

\v5n_jthe j)lots of the written dialogue. Goldoni set about weaving his works on the old frame. He began by merely new setting old stories like that of Don Giovanni Tenorio and of Griseldis, adding a character or an incident here and there to some old play of Spanish or French origin; manufacturing new frameworks for the improvisation of the masks, as in the Thirty-three

Misfortnnes of Harlequin, adding more and more of his own as he was emboldened by applause. '\He, left the fciur old masks. Pantaloon, Harlequin, Brighella, and the Doctor, to their own

devices, merely giving them a rough outline of action,* and turning all his attention to the other characters, those not belonging to the Mask Comedy, and wliich had been in it mere insignificant lay figures. Those parts, which he was free to dress, employ, and write for as he pleased, he made into clever sketches of living types, slight at first—card-sharpers, waiting-maids, cavalieri serventi of the eighteenth century—gradually assuming new importance by the side of the masked and fantastic buffoons who were wont to lord it over them. Heunconsciously to ok u p a nd dc-vejopetl tlii> t\v(i most insignificant parts of the comedy,i ke two Ig vcrs, who had been there merely to give opportunity for the action of the other cliaracters ; these dramatic shadows, with but a dim outline, vague features, lifeless voice, and limp action, gradually took body and shape, became alive, rea l m en an d women, strongly marked, vigorously acting realities ; and at length,—^!! wonder of wonders !—the audience began to be perfectly engrossed in the loves and adventures of Lelio and Beatrice, of Rosaura and Florindo, of Leandro and Giacinta. One day the mask actors awoke and found themselves subordinate : H arlequin niiglit tumble and giggle, Brighella might plot and caper as he pleased, the audience

\i * As a sample of Goldoni's treatment of the masks, we give the following:— II Biion Compatrloiio, alto 1".

Leandro. Quest'uomo, signora contessa, mi figuro che sara il vostro servo. Roslna. Si certo, e il mio servitore.

Traccagnlno (Tarocca, c dice jnano a JRosina che note vuole passare per servitore).

Ro.una. Tase, abie pazienza ; za nol ve cognosse ; no perde gnente del vostro. Traccagnlno (Insiste che non vuole, e scoprira tutto,') Rusina. Tase, no me rnvino, no nie prccipito : Soffri per mi e per la patria. Traccagnlno (che nun vuul far qneato dlsonorc at skoI parentl, chesono cenfannl che fanno a Bergamo i clahattini, e non vuole passare per nn servitore), Sec. &c.

ScENA V.
Rosina, e detti.
Segue come in soggetto.
SCENA VI. Rosina e Traccagnino.
SCENA VII. Costanza e detti.
SCENA VIII. Ridolfo e detti.
SCENA IX. Pantalone e Brighella.

gave them but partial attention. Goldoni developed the. nnma.^Jved-aml ") w ritten part s, and in so doing naturally restricted the masked and improvised parts; as the lovers, the housekeepers, the mothers, and tutors became all important, so gradually the buffoons were reduced to littl e o r nothin g; H arlequin, as a servant br inging a message, or Brighella i as an innkeeper, had little time to amuse the public; Pantaloon him-iselt, the immortaFVenetian father, was hurried through his parts by ,the all-engrossing interest in his offspring. Moreover, in proportion as Goldoni imitated the leal types and habits of his time, the old ideal buffoons were forced down to reality ; Harlequin could not jabber and stand on his head in the midst of a real scene of Venetian life with the freedom he had enjoyed when surrounded by the fantastic world borrowed from Tirso de Molina or Lope de Vega. It was one thing to be the servant of Don Juan, introducing the marble visitor; and another to be the hus-I band of Catte, the washerwoman of Castello. For a long while indeed the four masks continued to form strange spots of outlandish colour in the midst of the sober reality of Goldoni's comedy ; for a long time, and even in some of Goldoni's masterpieces, Pantalone dei Bisognosi, in his grey beard, mediaeval hood, and scarlet stockings, is the father of some modern Venetian girl, with powdered hair beneath her black net zendado, and buckle-shoes peering from beneath her hoop. I^podeciJiin, in his patches, with his rabbit's tail and lath, is the brother of some gondolier in scarlet scarf and velveteen knee-breeches; Biig^Ha, in his Avhite-striped dress of the sixteenth century, is the valet of a well-shaven, pig-tailed Sior Momolo, with his three-cornered hat beneath his arm, and his snuff-box in his hand ; once or twice the old Bolognese man of law, D octor Graziano, habited like Portia's uncle, comes forward to draw out his marriage contract between Venetian contemporaries of Clarissa and Sir Charles Grandison. The_tradiiionj)f_c.mitmi iji_a^a y, no rj^mild-ffienTTgrrdream of destroying it. Gradually Goldoni I* began to feel that these buffoons were anachronisms, that these Tnasks_ on the faces of some of the actors were wholly out of harmony with ithe subtly moving features of the others ; the pantaloons and harlequins also began to feel that their talents were beginning to be hidden, to be wasted on parts which had become unimportant, that, if they would regain their former popularity, they must strip off their fanciful costumes and appear as realities. But they shrank from throwing aside those beloved absurd old garments, from showing their real face, hitherto hidden by the black mask, to the audience ; the audience, on the other hand, though tired of the masks would not summon up the courage to bury the old friends of its childhood, the friends of its grandfathers and great-grandfathers. But the step must be taken. Goldoni, without any sentimental attachment for the past, bold from levity of nature as well as from con-

viction,. to ok tlie fatal step : Collalto, a Iiandsomc and intelligent young man, recently cni>-aged as pantaloon to replace Darbes, was sent on to the stage in plain clothes and unmasked, t rembling at his own transf ormation into a real human being. The audience applauded ; it had given its consent to the final demolition of t he old Comedy of Masks, and to the building up of a modern national comedy in its stead.

But the new comedy owed its existence to the old ; it was built with the old nuiterials, not only with the old bricks and stone but Avith the old pillars and lintels; it was also built upon the same basements. The ground-plan could not be altered, the fragments of old masonry could not be displaced ; the site, the substnictions, and the materials of the old building necessarily implied also its general shape. The comedy of Goldoni was constructed out of the old Comedy of Masks ; its audience, its aptors, its habits, its whole being was dependent upon the national improvised comedy : it was therefore a national Avritten comedy. The old elements left by Beolco and Calmo could not be moulded into imitations of Moliere and Regnard ; the old popular types born of the market-place and the tavern could not be metamorphosed into types borrowed from La Bruyere and La Rochefoucauld ; the old multifarious, largely plebeian audience, from the shops and canals quite as much as from the palaces, could not be turned into a polished and subtle audience like that which filled the French theatres; the actors who had been trained to talk dialect in grotesque costumes, and to cut capers while nudcing extemporary jokes, could not be taught to declaim verse with nobility, and to rei)resent a subtle, delicately-marked character: add to all this, that Italy in the eighteenth century was far less feudal, less aristocratic, less polished, less intelligent, less cynical and depraved than Fjance even in the seventeenth; and that Goldoni, its comic representative, was as frivolous, as plebeian, as frankly cheerful, as unpsychological as Moliere had been the contrary. Add up all this, and it will be clear that the theatre of St. Angelo at Venice could never produce the Misanthrope or Tartuffe, as the theatre of the Petit Bourbon could never have produced the Baniffe Chiozzotte, or Zelinda e Lindoro.

The basement of the new comedy was the basement of the old: the whole general cut and tendency of the jtlay was therefore the same. The Comedy of Masks, popular, unliterary, improvised above all things, was essentially a comedy of action. There could be no psychological interest in a play intended mainly for the lower classes and performed by typical buffoons; the analysis of character and of feeling would have been unintelligible to the audience and unfeasible to the actors ; the illiterate artisans, boatmen, labourers, and bravos, the violent or business-like nobles, wanted to be interested by action and amused by buffooneries; the pantaloons and harlequins, in their traditional fantastic costume,

with their grinning pieces of black leather instead of faces, with their local dialects and acrobatic tricks, could wrangle, tussle, scream, kick, fly at each other; they could pour forth volleys of street jests and street abuse ; they could dance and tumble, and play tricks ; they could move and amuse, and that was all. Moreover, the traditional, conventional tyj)es, and the extemporarising of the parts, precluded any original study of character, any class satire, any defined impersonation : the words and the gestures were left to the individual actor's whim,— how then could the writer instruct him to produce a given effect ? The actor's movements and sallies depended on the other hand on the movements and sallies of his companion ; where all was extemporaiy nothing could be concerted, and, where nothing could be concerted, only the roughest outlines of character and situation were possible, only effects of movement and plot could be directly counted upon. /Thus, then, the comedy I of Goldoni, inasmuch as it was founded upon the Comedy of Masks, was! aiecessarily a comedy not of character, type, and satire, hut a comedy of] movement; derived from an unwritten performance, it could not pos^ sibly"be a thing for the closet. The Comedy of Masks gave Goldoni not only action, but natural action; the business of the play, being extempory, was almost a reality; the actors had so great a habit of realising their parts, of moving and speaking really on the spur of the moment, that, even when their words and their actions were prescribed to them, they retained their old naturalism : the word had so long been spontaneous that the intonation long continued to be so. Moreover, these actors couLl nut deliver artificial speeches ;.their sole art had consisted in having none, in being real ; they had no habit of artistic, ideal performance; they woidd have repeated, like a page of catechism, without inflexion or gesture, the speeches of Moliere's Alceste or Chrysale ; unaccustomed to rhetoric, nay, to anything written, they could be trusted only with such words as might have been improvised by themselves. Thus, while the general framework of the old comedy, the, absolute 2)reponderance of movement over character, remained unchanged, the written dialogue with which Goldoni filled it up remained also equivalent to the improvised dialogue of former days. M oreover, the m ask_acto.rs, i a ccustomed to perform the typ ical buffoons^ of the populace , could scarcely Y^ I be _used except in the parts of midd le and lower class^people ; the Har-\ lequins and Columbines, Pantaloons and Brighellas of the Comedy of M asks, could turn into g ondoliers and maid-servants, into shopkeepers and card-sharpers, but never into dapper Dorantes and stately Dori-meiies ; they could never learn to talk and sit and walk with courtly elegance ; they could never forget to cry, shout, jabber, jump, scuffle, and • tussle together. The written offspring of the plebeian Comedy of Masks . was necessarily democratic. At the same time the old comedy, which had

Goidoni and the Realistic Comedij. 259
indulcfed largely in pccnos of magic and other raree shows, gave to the comedy of Goidoni great scenic and mechanical means which despised ' the monotony of the no-place no-where of Molicrc, and encouraged a reckless changing of scene, from house to street and from street to canal, and whicTTproduced those wonderful complete pictures of everyday life_ like the village street in the Ventaglio, the outside of the theatre in the Ftttta Onorata, the whole camp in La Guerra, and the street, the strand, and the shipping in the Bariqfe Chiozzotte. Above all, the Comedy of Masks had bequeathed to Goidoni its m ixed audience^ The nobles and the men of letters in the theatre might, perhaps, have enjoyed a comedy like that of Moliere, a comedy of psychology, of satire, and of wit; but on the innumerable shopkeepers, artisans, and fishing-

people, everything of the sort would have been lost; they would have clamoured for intelligible dialect, for feats, for scenes of common life, for intrigues and squabbles. And this audience, inasmuch as it was mixed, required a comedy purified of theevinvEtch each class, taken in itself, might have required: the healthy feeling of the lower classes precluded any Congrevian im])urity of subject and inuendo which might perhaps have pleased the nobles; the refinement and elegance of the upper classes precluded that clownish grossncss of word and gesture which might have been relished by the artisans and boatmen ; the austere and patriarchal shopkeepers kept in check the giddy buffoonery of the idlers; and the wit and love of fun of the idlers leavened the over domestic gravity of the shopkeepers.

Thus the comedy born of the Comedy of Masks was by virtue of its parent age a comedy uiit of character but of movement, not of wit but of fun; not of eloquent speeches but of easy dialogue; not courtly but popular; not confined to an ideal nullity of place but indulging in scenic realisation; not a satire but an amusement; neither elegantly dissolute, nor coarsely simple, nor giddily farcical, nor whimperingly serious; the offspring of the Comedy of Masks could be neither the comedy of Con-greve and Wycherley, nor the comedy of Tabarin and Hanswurst, nor the comedy of Goldsmith, nor the comedy of Diderot: it could be nothing except the comedy "f Goidoni.

32

II.

The genius of Goldoni, like his character and his life, was in perfect harmony with his allotted work. The artistic perfector of the democratic, unliterary, essentially natural and dramatic Comedy of Masks, was by nature and education a man qf the middle classes— ungenteel and un-aristocratic, a man of no literary faculty, incapable of regarding writing a§^jm art; without the moral fibre or intense sense of disproportion of the satirist ; cheerfulj good-natured, regarding mankind with indulgence ^ and optimism, disbelieving in great evil, refusing to examine beneath an agreeable surface; a man of immense powers of light dialogue and light acti^on. Given the style, no individual could be imagined more supremely its master : he had the perfect facility of conception, the perfect ease of execution, the absolute felicity of finish and detail, the immense fecundity of the providentially sent artist. He was never at a loss for a subject, and never at a standstill for its treatment;—a moment at a window, a glance round a drawing-room, a word caught in the street, was sufficient material for a comedy. The sight of the dirty grey-beard Armenian goody-seller, snarling out " Baggigi, Abaggigi" over his basket of lollipops, near the clock-tower of St. Mark's, produced the delightful little play, " I pcttegolezzi delle donne ; " Goldoni's mind immediately caught at the ludicrous notion of making this nasal old Oriental the supposed father of a Venetian girl ; and in a second he heard all the sneers, the whispers, the mocking words, he saw all the "^ movements and gestures, which such a situation would produce. When no external incident suggested a plot, Goldoni would quietly take a piece of paper and boldly write, " Act I. scene I. Rosaura and Florindo," and by the time the two names were down a fragment of dialogue was ready, and after that another, until at length, without any apparent Avhy or wherefore, the play had taken shape. When Goldoni, liaving achieved the almost supernatural feat of writing sixteen comedies in a twelvemonth, fell ill and exhausted, the exhaustion was more bodily than intellectual, for as soon as he had recovered from his prostration one

comedy flow from under his \'7d)en after another, comedies showing a greater richness and elasticity of invention than their predecessors. , (Jol- ,^ d oni's genius lay particularly in this power of making something out of nothing, of creating a]ilivy-uiit of an incident the most insignificant, out "Of a "situaTion the most ordinaVy'f~ne~'did not construct his plays, he creaied them—blewjhom out like soap-bubbles ; a drop of prose dilated into a delicate, delicately-tinted, winged bubble by the breath of genius. He never manufactured a plot like Calderon and Goldsmith, he never borrowed one like Moliere ; a plot, a stiff, angular, awkward piece of mechanism, whereon to stick bits of character and satire, whereon to hang out elaborate humour—Avhat could he want with such a thing ? Had he not what perhaps only Sterne possessed in equal degree, that subtle, fluid, floating essence of action; that ever-shifting, moving, oscillating reality of incident and feeling, which disdained fixed and ready-made shapes ? Goldoni was a Sterne in dramatic form; the same power of realising with a single touch, of filling trifles with the importance of life and feeling, of riveting and charming us with a couple of figures employed in unimportant action, with a simple every-day incident, with a simple every-day character; Sterne on the stage in short, but of a simpler, purer essence than Sterne, with the indefinable, just perceptible relish of good bread or pure water, not made up and flavoured like Sterne with the mysterious and subtle mixture of poetry and nastiness, and having no insipid or nauseous aftertaste. Goldoni was entirely destitute of either wit or poetic feeling, and wholly without any hankering after i either: in him this was less a deficiency than the absence of faculties | which would have marred his particular style. Goldoui's excellence lay in his realism and life; his artistic merit consisted in the perfect spon-ttaneity and simplicity; in the absence of the artist in his own work ; the lifelike scenes, carefully sifted and arranged by a delicate intention, have the additional charm of apparent absence of arrangement; a conscious ornament of poetry or wit, an underlining of any thought or feeling would mar the whole. In these bright, light, fresh, and spontaneous pieces of realism there is not a metaphor, not a thought, not a jest; Gol-doiTfs figw res, mth their wonderful ease and grace of movement, neither altitudinize n(jr grimace. They are never caricatures, as they are never made-up ideals. Goldoni never blunted his pencil-tip from the anxiety to bring out a salient characteristic, he never dabbed colour on to a given feature; such an emphasized figure as Tartuffe, as Trissotin, or as Oronte, he could not conceive; his instrument was the etching-pen, sharp, light, delicate, leaving the lights white and clean, distinctly marking the shadows, avoiding every unnecessary line, giving the living, moving, individual outline, graceful and natural in gesture. The Hogarthian

satire, coarse and insipid, alternations of ugly vacuity and ugly grimace, as of some dull old almanack caricatures or would-be humorous Longlii, of his imitators Albergati and Pepoli, was entirely hostile both to Gol-doni's genius and to the nature of his comedy, Goldoni, averse to caricature, preferred subjects where it could be avoided; and, where satire there must be, it was attenuated away into mere comic drollery. The_ gentry, the small titled nobility, as distinguished from the patrician class, which no Venetian dramatist could handle, he did not like : it was too tight-laced, too tight-shoed, too painted and dancing-master'd, to afford the light comic elements he required; it might suggest strongly-marked and heavily-coloured caricature, but that he did not want; it was too artificial, too vicious, and too ridiculous for him. His aristocratic figures, when not mere dummies, are usually insignificant outline satires : ruined gamblers, cardsharpers, rakes and prigs, kept in the ,-1)ackground of the play. When he dealt with the upper classes he approached as far as possible to the burghers: counts and marquises of 1 little fame and modest habits, different from shopkeepers only by the ^ prefix Don to their names, as in the VoHaglio, Zelinda e Lindoro, La ViUegglatura, and other comedies not in dialect. In all cases he simplified aristocratic society, attenuating its vices and absurdities, turning the ridiculous and the disgusting into the merely amusing. The cava-Here servente, that miserable and loathsome piece of rococo drawing-room furniture, is never in Goldoni what he is in Parini, in Gasparo Gozzi's satires, or in the Marchese Albergati's plays: a social disgrace, a bedizened conceited puppy, a sort of fashionable fungus. Even in the Cavaliere e la Dama, a play directly turning upon this stale and prescribed sort of gallantry, the cavalieri serventi are mere light idiots, dangling, without any harm, after their ladies; Goldoni shrank from any thought of domestic corruption. In the delightful Dama Prudente Goldoni has turned the cavaliere servente theme into a most charming comic stuff totally without satire or inuendo. Don Eoberto, madly jealous of his wife, and nervously desirous of hiding his jealousy, mortally afraid of a cavaliere servente, and mortally afraid of appearing to be afraid, insists upon giving Donna Eularia not only one, but two of these appendages, the one to check the other. Donna Eularia, devoted to her husband, is continually pulled from side to side by his jealousy and his desire to appear indifferent, by his wish that slie should appear perfectly unwatched and his desire to watch over her ups and downs of temper; which cause continual absurd blunders and scrapes, heightened by the rivalry of the two cavalieri serventi, both indifferent to the lady but jealous of each other; a concatenation of bungles and contradictions from which the prudent lady gets loose only by carrying off her husband.

unknown to everyono, to a remote country town, wbei*e a husband may walk out and pay visits witli liis own wife and where the fashion of cavalieri serventi has yet to be introduced.
,

To these attenuated, simj)lifi('d gentry, Gohloni vastly preferred tiio "Tv middle classes, shopkeepers, doctors, and lawyers, people of more domestic life and easier manners, into whose houses it was less difficult to introduce the audience. He enjoyed giving, as it were, a vertical section of a middle-class honse, showing at the same time the inhabitants of the various floors, letting Uf' see the richer and poorer inmates at their amusements and occupations, at their meetings; dis])laying two or three households at once, with their efforts to make a fine show to each other, with their whole life not only of the parlour and the office but of the staircase and house-door. He would let us see the supposed head of the family walking about in dressing-gown and slippers, eating dates out of a paper, assenting feebly to every order of a younger brother, always referred to but never displayed in i)ublic ; or tli(> old bullying dotard, continually blustering with his children and led by the uose by some sly housekeeper or deferential agent,^endless types of Pantaloon, lightly and rapidly sketched; ho would display the son and heir running into debt, attempting to reform, determining to marry and live an orderly life, and then borrowing more money in order to entice a wife. Above all, Goldoni delighted in pulling the wires of his female puppets, of his charmingly simple, vain, lecturing, half stupid, half sensible girls, from the little weak-headed daughter of Pantalone, who plays with her dolls at fifteen and asks the first man she ever meets to marry her, up to the independent and serious Giacinta of the Villeggiatura trilogy—gentle, self-sacrificing, resisting her own passion, but with just a little vanity and desire to be better dressed than her sister-in-law; Beatrices, Rosauras, Vittorias, Giacintas innume-ra])le, little figures, lively or sedate, malicious or forgiving, invariably graceful and sym\'7d)athetic, alive and individual, nifinitely different from the insipid, ever bashful and resigned, over properly behaved young ladies

I of Moliei'e; for Moliere's girls were mere pieces of stage mechanism, required for the plot, and replacing for the moral public of the seventeenth century the slaves and light damsels of Terence and Ariosto; whereas (Joldoni's girls were realities, really moving and chattering in every burgher's house in Italy, reproduced by the dramatist for their own sake. Goldoni shows us these young women in their visits, affectionate and sarcastic to each other, kissing on both cheeks while counting up the yards of ribbon on each other's dresses; in their agonized consultations with dressmakers and ladies' maids; in their tragic rage at not going to the country, in their malicious jubilation at their neighbours staying in town. The country ! that was Goldoni's richest theme : not the trees, and skies

C'.- and flowers, for which he cared as little as did his dramatis perso7icE, but

^

__the villeggiatura, with its financial and tailoring preparations, its prologue of entreaties and sulks and rages, and usurers and dressmaking and family agonies; its joys of card-playing, flirting, chocolate-drinking and scandal-mongering, and its tragic sequel of unpaid bills, recriminations, and domestic shipwreck. Goldoni wrote at least a dozen plays about rilleggiatura, its preparations and consequences: villeggiatura on the Brenta, in the Euganean hills, on the Montagnola of Bologna, and at Montenero near Leghorn, summing up everything in that almost epic trilogy, the " Smanie per la Villeggiatura," the "Avventure della Villeggiatura," and the " Ritorno dalla Villeggiatura"—Villeggiatura! talismanic word, which now means solitude in a country-house or town-life at a watering-place, but never fails to evoke in our mind, thanks to the genius of Goldoni, the thought of those immense parties of five or six families, huddled together on the top of some hill or on the banks of some stream, for ever going in and out of each other's houses, for ever gambling, eating, drinking, singing, dancing, love-making, gossipping, squandering during a month the revenue of a year—villeggiatura! delightful pastoral life among ^ autumn rains, floods, mud, mosquitoes, and damp yellow foliage, bought cheaply by a winter without carpets or fires, and a summer Avithin red-hot city walls. Yes, the word has retained a quaintness and a charm, and we cannot now pass before the rusty gates of the melancholy suburban gardens, with their drenched sere groves and broken earthenware statues and vases; nor go up and down the long flights of steps between the congregated stained houses, with battered shutters, blackened escutcheons, faded sun-dial, and tawdry soaking autumnal flowers, without thinking of the Pantaloons and Rosauras and Leandros whose delight they wore in the days gone by. And when we enter that vast half-furnished entrance, with gilded high-backed chairs marshalled stiffly round the walls, and card-tables pushed into every corner, we cannot help fancying that Giacinta and Lelio may be whispering behind yonder screen; that the parasite Ferdinando may just have shuffled the cards on yonder green baize; and we catch ourselves half expecting that the folding gilded doors may open, and the foolish, jolly old Signor Filippo, in his knee-breeches, embroidered waistcoat, and little Avig, enter, beaming with vanity and pleasure, and cry out, rapping his snuff-box: " What, children ! no one playing, no one eating, no one drinking? The country is made for amusement, and in my house it shall never be wanting. Quick! cards and lights! and chocolate and lemonade; and afterwards call the fiddlers, and we'll dance a couple of minuets—and those who won't, need not; let all do as they choose ! Long live liberty and long live the villeggiatura!" jCr Goldoni was best pleased with the humblest, forming in this a strange contrast with the French comic writers; the shopkeepers, ridiculous gullible M. Jourdains and Sganarelles in the eyes of Moliere, never

ceased to be respectable for Goldoni; in the Putta Onorata he made the Venetian shopkeeper Pantalone address the half-feudal card-sharping Marquis of llipavcrde, bidding him onler people about elsewhere: " La vaga a cnnimandar en tel so marchcsato," in a nninner which would haveshocked the public of Hrc'^sct and of Diderot. In the delightful Lo^andiem he showed a noble who had just sold his title, and another "wEo^Tuid just bought his, treated like monkeys by a pretty and inde-licndent hostess, who, after bringing them and another woman-hating and gruffer specimen of nobility on to their knees, laughs in all their faces and marries her faithful head-waiter; while in the three comedies, bearing the names of Zelinda .and Lindoro, he showed the loves and jealousies of a poor secretary and a waiting-maid with a sympathy, a tender homely admiration, which makes this trilogy tlu^ most suggestive companion-piece to Beaumarchais' picture of the courtship of Figaro and Suzanne. This democratic, domestic Goldoni naturally refused to show us the effeminate, corrupt Venice of nobles, and spies, and courtesans, which shameful Q,dventurers like Casanova, heaping up all the ordure of their town and times, have made some of us believe to have been the sole, the real Venice of the eighteenth century. But Goldoni has another Venice to show, a Venice undiscovered by gallant idlers like the President de Brosses, or pedantic guide-book makers like La Lande. Let us follow Goldoni across the square of St. Mark's, heedless of the crowd in mask and cloak, of the nobles in their silk robes, of the loungers at the gilded coffee-houses, of the gamblers and painted women lulling out of windows; let us pass beneath the belfry where the bronze twins strike the hours in vain for the idlers and vagabonds who turn day into night and night into day; and let us thread the network of narrow little streets of the Merceria. There, in those tall dark houses, with their dingy look-out on to narrow canals floating wisps of straw, or on to dreary little treeless, grassless squares, in those houses is the real Avealth, the real honour, the real good of Venice; there, and not in the palaces of the Grand Canal, still lingers something of the spirit and the habits of the early merchant princes. Merchant princes no longer, alas ! only shopkeepers and brokers, but thrifty, frugal, patriarchal as in olden days, the descendants of the great Pantalone de' Bisognosi, once clothed in scarlet-lined robe and pointed cap, now dressed austerely in black, without hair-powder, gold lace, swords, or scarlet cloaks; active,honest.gruff, and puritanical; with wives and daughters forbidden to wear silk, permitted to go alone no further than to church, early and with rapid step, their face half concealed beneath the black net zenda; with sons in the counting-house and the storerooms, working from dawn till dusk, strictly forbidden to go near the square of St. Mark's, and too afraid to even wish for the forbidden joy. Over all this family the father, the merchant, the patriarch, lords it undis-

puted, the married sons and daugliters submitting as if they were ten years old. The father is sometimes an intolerable puritan tyrant, like Sor Todero Brontokm-and the four Rusteghi, making his unfortunate family live like anchorites, and driving his servants like negroes; but more often, beneath all the puritanism and gruffness, there is deep kindliness and charity; and in the austere dark house there is excellent eating and drinking, and hearty laughter and bluff merriment when the master invites his friends and their wives and dausfhters.

This is all that remains in the eighteenth century of the frugal, industrious, austere Venice of the Middle Ages. Let us follow Goldoni yet further from St. Mark's to the distant wharves, to the remoter canals and campieli, to the further islands of the archipelago of Venice, and he will show us all that remains of the force of the city, of the savage simplicity and austerity of the boatmen, and fishers, and working classes. There are the gondoliers, forming a link between the artisans and the seamen— a strange, Janus-like class which Goldoni loved to depict: servants of the upper classes, devoted, faithful and pliant; steering along with equal indifference political conspiracy, household corruption, or venal gallantry beneath the black, tasselled roof of their boats; witnesses of all the most secret life of the nobles and merchants, and, while on their prow, mute and cynical; but, once on shore, independent, arrogant, despising the in-door servants, contemptuous towards their masters, whose secrets they possess, frugal and austere at home, jealous and revengeful among each other. Goldoni has shown us the gondoliers seated on the slimy steps by their moored boats, exchanging witticism on witticism, criticising the performances at the theatres, discussing city life with ineffable arrogance: he has shown them coming along the Grand Canal, chanting the flight of Erminia through the ancient forest; he has shown them again, quarreling in the narrow twisting channels, each refusing to make way for another, yelling and cursing, forcing their passengers to alight in terror, and then pursuing each other with their oars and their short, sharp tatare daggers. The gondoliers, besides being good comic stuff for Goldoni, were an influential part of his audience, and had to be propitiated by being shown on the stage in all their originality and waywardness. The gondoliers lived, when off their boats, among a savage population of ferrymen, bargees, and fishers; poor, violent and austere, whose daughters had at once the freedom of speech and strength of action of amazons, and the purity, nay prudery, of nuns: large-limbed, sun-burnt, barefoot creatures, Avith the golden tints of hair and cheek of Titian and Palma, with the dark, savage eyes of an animal, with the arms of an athlete and the language of a trooper, of whom Goldoni has painted a magnificent portrait, idealised but intensely real, in his Bettina, who, in her perfect self-reliance, her complete knowledge of evil and detei-mination to avoid it,

her ferocious chastity, refusing to let her own betrothed enter the house, and her passionate tenderness and dog-hke attachment, is one of the grandest female figures which any stage can boast. Such deep appreciation of the lower classes, such a really idyllic conception of the life of the pco^jTe, equalled in Italian literature, tliough in more poetic realism perhaps, only by the Nencia of Lorenzo doi Medici, can be explained in the middle of the eighteenth century, in the midst of the Dresden china shepherdesses and cotton wool, beril)bone(l lambs of Boucher and Dorat, of the fashionable milkmaids and cow-boys of Rousseau and of Greuze, only by the fact that the comedy of Goldoni, as the offspring of the Comedy of Masks, had its origin in the very heart of the people.

Betlina is a single individual a splendid savage creature, half lost in the artificial woi-ld of gentlemen who cheat at cards and ladies who borrow money from gondoliers; but Goldoni can show us the world to which she belongs, which is made up of nothing but her brothers and sisters. Let us call Goldoni's favourite gondolier, the rough and caustic Menego Cainello, and bid him steer us through the last canals, among the remotest Venetian islands, leaving the towers of Venice behind us; bid him row us across the shallow open lagoon, with its vast snake-like rows of sea-corroded posts, its stunted marine reeds, and its tangled sea-grass waving lazily on the rippled water; row on till we get to that tiny other A^enice, still perhaps like the greater Venice in the days of her earliest doges, to the little fishing-town of Chiozza. There, in the port, Goldoni will show us the heavy fishing-boat, grimy and oozy, just returned from a weelv's cruise in the Adriatic, with her yellow sail, emblazoned with the winged lion, leisurely flapping, and her briny nets cast over her sides; the master of the boat, Paron Fortunato, is shouting in unintelligible dialect, Venetian further insularised into Chiozzot, and Chiozzot rarefied on sea into some strange nautical lisping jargon; the rest of the fishermen, Tita-Nane, and Menegheto, and Toni, are collecting the fish they have brought into baskets, reserving the finest for his Excellency the Governor of Chiozza. And, when the fish are disposed of, follow we the fishermen to the main street of the little town, where, facing the beach, their wives, daugliters, and sisters sit making lace on their cushions, chattering like magpies; some eating, others holding disdainfully aloof from the baked pumi)kin with which the gallant peasant Tofiblo Marmottina regales them. Suddenly a tremendous gabble begins, gabble turning into shrieking and roaring, and upsetting of chairs and cushions; and a torrent of abuse streams forth in dialect, and all is lost in scuffling confusion; the men come up, seize sticks, daggers, and stones, and rush to the rescue of their female relatives, till the police hasten up and separate the combatants. Then let us watch the recriminations of the lovers, hear them accusing each other of perfidy, calling each other dog, assassin, beggar, gingerbread, jewel, pig, all in turns; clinging and nudging, weeping and roaring, till at length the good-natured little Venetian magistrate of Chiozza, contemptuously called "Mr. Wig-of-Tow" \'7bSiorpai'uca de stopa), makes i;p all the quarrels, bids the innkeeper send wine and pumpkins and delicious fried things, and, after regaling the pacified Chiozzoti and Chiozzote, calls for fiddles and invites them all to dance some furlane. Is it a reality ? Has Menego rowed us over the lagoon? Have we seen the ship come in and the fish put in baskets? Have we seen the women at their lace cushions ? Have we heard that storm of cries, and shrieks, and clatter, and scuffling feet? Have we really witnessed this incident of fishing life on the Adriatic ? No ; we have only laid down a little musty volume, at the place marked '• Le Baruffe Chiozzotte."

The public of the theatre of S. Angelo were delighted and dazzled by this series of ever new, ever varying pictures, which Goldoni projected for them through the wonderful magic lantern of his genius. The plays were printed at Venice, at Florence, at Pesaro, at Bologna; Venetian nobles formed an association to smuggle in pirated editions; Goldoni, travelling about Italy during the dead season of the Venetian theatres, was everywhere beset by entreaties for new comedies; a custom-house officer, overwhelmed with enthusiasm, risked his position rather than let the illustrious dramatist pay duty on his parcels of snuff and of chocolate. About 1755 M. de Voltaire himself addressed to Goldoni a strange polyglot epistle, half prose, half verse, saying : " Je voudrois appeller vos comedies ritalia Liberata dai Got!," exclaiming " Che felicita ! mio signore, che purita!" and winding up by making Nature declaim some verses to the

effect that—

Tout auteur a ses defauts

Mais ce Goldoni m'a peinte ;

and about the same time Lessing, then Avorking at his " Hamburgsche Drammaturgie," and Emilia Galotti, wrote that he was Misy reading and adapting some of the plays of Doctor Goldoni, a Venetian lawyer, whose name at least must be familiar to his correspondent Moses Mendelssohn. Goldoni, beset by managers and actors, petted by cardinals and senators, praised by a liost of critics and imitators, and receiving a sort of preliminary immortality from the 8age of Ferney, seemed at the very summit of all possible good fortune. But while the fabric of his fame spread wider and rose liigher and more splendid, it was being sapped at the base, and, strange to say, Goldoni himself was blindly helping to undermine it. As soon as the written comedies of Goldoni had begun to be popular, he had been attacked by the managers of rival theatres, whose audience streamed to the Teatro S. Angelo; and by mask actors, whose buffooneries and repartees were being thrown into the shade by the written parts of the unmasked actors, mere obscure and

stupid libels, \'7bu-icks of invisible critics. But they caused Gnkloui to look up. He thought fit to auswor his accusers by his seventeenth comedy, // Teatro Vomico, in which he brouglit on to the stage the masked actors and the unmasked actors in succession, and held forth to prove/ that leathern faces and clie(|U(n-ed bodies were detrimental to real dramatic; interest. This answer jirovoked a reply, and the reply produced a retort. Goldoni, attacked in his practice, took refuge in theory, and the theory in its turn had to be supported by practice; thus, little by little, Goldoni let himself be goaded into entirely suppressing all improvisation, into entirely rejecting the masks; into abusing the old Commedia delV Arte, from which his own style had originated, and into appealing to French models with which his own style had nothing in common; injustice made him unjust; folly was to make him foolish. His detractors, ever multiplying, acci;sed him of being incapable of anything above prose dialect plays. Goldoni immediately set to work on rhymed comedies, ill versified, in bad Italian, and extremely dull;

they accused him of being unable to rise above the squabbles of boatmen and the intrigues of servants. Goldoni instantly scribbled off half-a-dozen romantic plays, with bravos, daggers, sultanas, noble savages, and every species of dramatic vermine. They accused him of being deficient in pathos and moral tone; Goldoni forthwith patched up a number of whimpering, paternal, maternal comedies, with patterns of virtue, attempted seductions, refoi'med prodigals,]\filor Bonfils, Miledy Duvres, Mosii Wamberts, and scraps of morality and sentiment cut out of Richardson, Diderot, and Mmc. Riccoboni. He was accused of being new-fangled and incorrect; Goldoni rushed off and dramatised the persecutions of three other literary innovatwn^Terence, lj:r^Q Tasso, and Moliere, who turned out respectively a sentimental professor of ancient literature, a crackbrained academic sonnetteer, and a melancholy jocose comedian. He was accused of being limited; he immediately jumped over the limits of his genius in order to show himself limitless. Goldoni, the author of master\'7d)ieces in his own style, weakly and foolishly let himself be deluded into writing inanities in the style of other people; he was accused of ruining the national Italian stage; he declared that he had come to reform it. He was told that he was nobody; he answered that he was omnipotent and providential. The faults of Goldoni's bad j^ieces were exaggerated by numberless imitators, by the scribes who worked for -,Jl the other comic theatres, which, without having a Goldoni to Avrite, followed the fashion of written plays ; the pretensions of Goldoni as a reformer and destroyer were exaggerated by numberless foolish fashionable critics, who, without really understanding Goldoni's genius and position, made his theories a theme for invective against things Italian and laudation of things French. Little by little the trumpery libels of theatre proprietors and rival authors turned into criticisms of greater importance;

Goldoni, serenely conceited, answered in prose and in verse, answered stupidly and offensively; the number of critics increased. In a few yea;'s the most original dramatist of the eighteenth century, the most intensely Italian of writers, the most moral of humorists, had raised against himself nearly all the original thinkers, the patriots and the moralists of Italy, and found himself supported only by those very frenchified, vicious, vapid people of fashion whom he most despised. In the rapid succession of his plays, the critics of the eighteenth century, uncritical and hasty, did not distinguish the genuine style of the man from his imitations ; they confounded masterpieces with imbecilities; they condemned the grace, the life, the truth of such plays as La Locandiera and Le Baruffe Chiozotte on account of the dullness, the vulgarity, the falseness, the lachrymosity of the Sposa Persiana, the Bella Peruviana, and the Pamela. Moreover they credited Goldoni with all the imbecility and immorality and gallicisms of the numberless scribblers whom the destruction of the improvised, comedy had brought into existence; they tied like a stone to Goldoni's neck the immense weight of nauseous idiotcy of the plays of a certain Abate Pietro Chiari, the dullest, coarsest, most sentimental scribbler of melodramatic rubbish about Polish castles, Kussian shepherdesses, artificial cows, harems, negroes, and slave-dealers, that ever lived. Goldoni had no connection with Chiari, either personal or literary; he hated and despised the reptile, yet in the furious polemics which his own thoughtlessness had produced it was Goldoni's fate always to have this odious idiot as a companion, never to be mentioned except in the same breath as Chiari. The confusion between Goldoni's good and bad plays, the confusion between Goldoni and Chiari, the connection between Goldoni anil the odious French imitation, raised a hurricane against the unfortunate refoi'mer. Every immoral novel translated, every lachrymose play imitated from the French, every encyclopedic disbelief, every un-crnscan expression, was more or less put down to Goldoni's baleful influence; he was confounded with Helvetius and Rousseau; he was associated with the too open boddices of ladies, with gambling-tables, with the use of newfangled words like Toelette and Fricando, with pastoral inanities, with masonic mysteries; and this miserable depraved idiot, who was perverting Italian morals and corrupting the Italian language, was in reality the mere tool, the toy, the laughing-stock of that horrible M. de Voltaire, whose mixture of royalism and irreligion, of morality and indecency, of jest and earnest, whose strange laugh of scorn, indignation, and cynicism entirely baffled the good Italians of the eighteenth century. . This Goldoni was destroying the Italian comedy, the national comedy which Italy had possessed for two centuries, in order to introduce French lachrymosities and inmioralitics, and was being told that he had liberated Italy from the Goths— by whom ? By the evil being who had twitted Tasso, patted

Maffei contemptuously on the shoulder, and had declared (oh sacrilege of sacrileges !) that Father Dante was crazy and the Divina Cominedia a monster, and had carried his audaciuus and insolent ignorance so far as to call Can Grande della Scala " Le Grand Khan." No, Goldoni could never be forgiven his unpatriotic imbecility and insolence, his frivolous frenchified wickedness, his criminal attempts upon the old Italian comedy; all the pedants who two centuries before would have spat upon the Com-mcdia deW Arte with Mosser Niccolo Secchi and Messer Giorgio Trissino, now rushed forward to defend the honour and existence of the ever venerated Harlequins and Pantaloons. Pamphlet upon pamphlet, and volume upon volume, was hurled against Goldoni; Baretti, the patriotic and rabid, lashed Goldoni's plays to rags with his " Literary Whip," and '^'^ the two Gozzis poured forth epigram and sonnets by the bushel to annihilate him; the storm was raging.

In the middle of it, one fine day about the year 17G0, rumour was spread through Venice that the advocate Carlo Goldoni had accepted an offer to go to Paris and provide plays for the Italian stage, which had been established there ever since the days of the Gelosi and the Fedeli; a few months later, while the enemies of Goldoni were still wondering whether they were to believe their ears, a new play called " One of the last Evenings of Carnival " was performed at the Teatro S. Angelo. It was one of those charming, simple pictures of Venetian merchant life which were Goldoni's masterpieces ; in it was represented the departure from Venice of a certain Sior Anzoleto, a designer of patterns for silk stuffs, who had been called away to Russia, and was leaving with a heavy heart the weavers whose looms he had so long provided with patterns ; the allegory was evident: the weavers were the comedians of S. Angelo, the designer of patterns was the comic writer. Russia meant Paris, and when Sior Anzoleto came forward for the last time, and said, in the quaint, graceful Venetian lisping dialect, "This is not the first time that I go away, and Avherever I have been I have carried the name of Venice engraven in my heart; I have always remembered the good offices and kindness I have received; I have always wished to retmui; when I have returned, it has always been with joy .... and so it will be this time also, if Heaven permit me to return. I attest on my honour that I go away with a sore heart; that no pleasure, no fortune, if I have any, will be able to compensate the pain of absence from people who are fond of me. Preserve your love for me, dear friends; and God bless you. I say so from my heart—" when Anzoleto, moved by the part he was playing, bowed before the spectators, the audience, half crying, half laughing, forgetful of whatever pasquinades they might have written, and awake once more to the greatness of Goldoni, burst out like one man, shouting, " Good-bye, Goldoni! A good journey to thee ! Remember thy pro-

niise ! Return soon ! Return soon!" Goldoni did not show liimself; he Avas perhaps crying behind the scones; in the midst of his hopes of future success and of speedy return, tliis farewell of iiis old public saddened even his light and cheerful nature. " A good journey, and return soon !" cried the last spectators in their dominoes, as they left the already • darkened theatre. Goldoni never returned, never saw again the theatre of S. Angelo, never again heard his beloved Venetian, never again wrote a masterpiece.* A frivolous, cheerful old man, called Carlo Goldoni, was indeed destined to live some thirty years more, obscm-ely and happily, and to leave the world unnoticed in the midst of the chaos and darkness of the year '93 ; but Carlo Goldoni, the great Venetian comic writer, the incomparable author of the Ventaglio, the Locandiera, and the Bamffe Chiozzotte, ceased to exist as the curtain of the Teatro Sant' Angelo fell upon that " last of the Evenings of Carnival."

      * The charming plays Zdlnda c L'nuhn-o were merely corrected and copied out in Paris, as ihey had long existed in rough form under the name of " Gluimori di Arlecchino e Cammilla," in Goldoni's portfolio ; the Burhero Scnefico (Le Bourru Bicnfaisant) is a weak and insipid French adaptation of the " Casa Nova," with all the best parts left out. "^^

CAKLO GOZZI

AND

THE VENETIAN FAIEY COMEDY.

CARLO GOZZI AND THE VENETIAN FAIEY COMEDY.

      Goldoni's plays had been the artistic development of the purely comic and realistic elements of the Commedia deW Arte; its other elements, fantastic and humorous, its masks, its transformations, and its extemporised quips and cranks, Goldoni had roughly eliminated and contemptuously cast aside. There they had lain during the days of Goldoni's l)opularity, neglected and despised; but the eyes of one man had been fixed upon them with sorrow and admiration in their ignominy, and when Goldoni's style was on the wane, he had silently approached the heap of degraded tinsel and gimcrack, and tenderly, reverently, picked out of the dustbin the ragged checks of Harlequin, the battered mask of Pantaloon, the tarnished tinsels of the fairy Morgana; had carried them away like relics under his cloak, close to his heart. What would he do with them ? The tall, gaunt man, stalking about in his old-fashioned clothes, splashing into every pool of water, letting his scarlet cloak trail along the muddy steps of every Venetian bridge; always silent, self-absorbed, his eyes fixed on an unseen world, his lips smiling at unspoken jests; the kindly, idle, half-crazy Count Carlo Gozzi could himself not have explained why he had treasured up all that discarded trumpery of the Commedia delV Arte. Had you asked him, \w. would have answered with some half-serious, unintelligible jest, he would have told you that it was his veneration for the antiquity of Harlequin's lath, his gratitude for the laughter the poor dethroned buffoons had given him as a child, his hatred of ucw-fangled French things ... a hundred ill-defined reasons, pedantic and grotesque and pathetic, jumbled up into an argument which you could not understand, at which you laughed and felt the Avhile as if you would have cried . . . Enough, Carlo Go zzi was whimsical , sentimental, metaphysical; in short, a humourist of the temper of Sterne and of Jeai Paul: he believed in tlie superior wisdom of childishness, in the philosophy of old nurses' tales, in the venerableness of clowns; why, he knew not. So he scolded against the prosaic Goldoni, who was driving-romance and buffoonery off the stage; sighed at the world growing daily more dull, more obtuse, more philosophical; and cherished the cast-off mummeries of the Commedia delC Arte as if sunshine and youth were

    t2

    1

lurking in their tatters; objectless and heedless, until one day it flashed across him to build a temple in which the dear and venerable relics would be enshrined and worshipped.

      Baretti tells the story how one day Goldoni, with the swagger of success, sauntered into the shop of the bookseller Bottinelli, in the narrow streets behind the clock-tower of St. Mark's, and began holding forth to the literati there assembled on the grandeur and success of his reformation of the Italian comedy; until at length Carlo Gozzi, outraged by the upstart's insolence towards the Commedia delV Arte, jumped up from the pile of books on which he was seated, and cried out: " I wager that with the masks of the old comedy I will draw a greater audience to hear the story of the Love of the Three Oranges than you can with all your Ircanas and Bettinas and Pamelas ! " Goldoni burst out laughing at this threat: the Love of the Three Oranges was a fairy tale told by every nursemaid from Venice to Naples, a ridiciilous childish piece of nonsense, whose mere name was enough to make people laugh: it was like telling Sheridan that Jack and the Bean Stalk would draw a larger audience than the School for Scandal.

But Carlo Gozzi was sincerely persuaded that nursery tales were worth all Goldoni's volumes of comedies : the Love of the Three Oranges had a charm for his mind, the charm of fancy and of association; the Pamelas and L-canas had his hatred as a hater of French things, as a hater of false sentiment, as a hater of modern philosophy, as a noble, a Venetian, a poet, and a humourist; so Carlo Gozzi set to work to make_go od his tlireat. Some weeks later the comic comjja-ny, dii'ccted by the famous TrufFald iuo-Harleciuin Sacchi, which had recently rctunuMl i'rom Portu-gal in coiisccpicnce of the earthquake at Lisbon, announced at its theatre of S. Samuele a new comedy entitled The Love of the Three Oranges. All Venice stared at this announcement. Was Sacchi gone mad ? Had they read correctly? Were they really invited to hear a nursery tale? Everyone rushed to S, Sa muele for the explanation of this mystery. The curtain rose, and displayed the strangest medley ever conceived. The King of Clubs, dressed as on the playing cards, consulting with Pantaloon, in his mediaeval robe and scarlet hose, about the mysterious melancholy malady of his son, the Prince Tartaglia; Pantaloon, the inimitable fat Cesare Darbes, who, with all the best mask actors, had left the Medebac company in consequence of Goldoni's reforms, ansAvering the King of Clubs that the malady of the prince must be attributed to his having been poisoned by the opiate verse of Goldoni and Chiari; the Prince Tartaglia, stammering heroic verse, with his thick Neapolitan utterance, smitten with the Love of the Tliree Oranges, and going out to seek them in company with the harlequin Sacchi; the first orange being opened, giving birth to a beautiful maiden, who withered into thin air for

want of a dvaiiglit of water. Harlequin, in his anxiety to slake her thirst, breaking open the second orange, and thus liberating a second princess, who vanisliod like her sister; the agony of Prince Tartaglia at the thought of losing his only remaining ^bride, enclosed in tlie rind of the third orange; the jealousies of the nogress, Smcraldina, who, cast into the flames, issued forth white like a clay pipe; the battles between a hideous witch, Margana, talking the tumid gibberish of Chiari's plays, and a ridiculous wizard spouting the semi-legal verses of Goldoni's bad plays; . . , enchantments, harlequinades, satire, nursery tales, all mixed np together. The Venetians were puzzled, then amused, then delighted : ^they shouted that the old masks and their improvisations were after all lore amusing than the Pamelas and Monsili Wamberts, that the en-cTiantments of nursery tales were more delightful than the whimperings of French translations, that the Love of the Three Oranges was a masterpiece. Like the Prince Tartaglia of the play, the Venetian public, sick with the stupefying drugs of the pseudo-wizard Goldoni, and the dotard-witch Chiari, had laughed and found itself cured, /-^he popularity of Goldoni began rapidly to sink; the popularity of the \ Sacchi company began to rise; the fickle Venetians abandoned S. Angelo \for S. Samuele: the old centenarian masks, banished out of sight for a few years by the real men and women of Goldoni, re-appeared with all the 'charms of youth and novelty. No more realisms, no more lachrymositios, away with the unpatriotic prosaic Goldoni: fairy tales, harlequinades, wizards, witches, kings of clubs, pantaloons, and brighellas, aristophanesc absurdities improvised in dialect,—that was what really and truly suited the poor deluded Venetian public. Truff'aldino-Sacchi, overjoyed at the miracle, beset and clung to Carlo Gozzi, entreating him for more fairy plays, more Jiabe, Jiabe da putei, more Loves of the Three Oranges. Carlo Gozzi, dreading to become a regular hack playwright, who might be called ujjou , to produce sixteen plays in a year, like Goldoni,—lazy, whimsical, and ■with the instinct of a dilettante,—refused all Sacchi's offers of money, refused to enter into any engagements, refused to promise to wi-ite. But Carlo Gozzi had created a new style, and he who creates a style becomes its slave; he had, unconsciously, evoked the weird grotesque world of the supernatural, and the supernatural would not let its wizard

go-

Carlo Gozzi himself was of opinion that the invisible world obtained some mysterious power over him from the moment of his writing the Love of the Three Oranges, and that the series of persecutions which he relates in liis very quaint autobiography were due to the vengeance of the fairy world, which he had dared to bring on to the stage. But in this Carlo Gozzi was certainly mistaken; his connection with the supernatural world was much older. Carlo Gozzi had been destined from his birth to

be the familiar, the crony, and the butt of all the fairies and goblins ■who still haunted Venice in the first half of the eighteenth century; some crabbed and contradictoiy fairy godmother must have been present at his birth, have endowed him with the humour and fancy of Beckford and Jean Paul and Hoffmann, and then, irritated at the sceptical levity of Count Giacomo Gozzi and the patrician haughtiness of the Lady Tiepolo, his wife, have cursed her godchild with the terrible curse of being misunderstood by his contemporaries and forgotten by posterity. The ancestral Gozzi palace at S. Canziano, at Venice, was the chosen abode of all the hobgoblins of the lagoons: the doors were off their hinges, the window-panes broken, immense spiders dangled from the rafters. Of the magnificent furniture of former days, long since gone to the pawnbrokers, there remained only a couple of senatorial portraits by Titian and Tintorot, looking down grimly in their \'7d)urple and ermine and cobweb upon the miserable disorderly household of the noble Counts Gozzi. All in this Gozzi palace was melancholy, ludicrous, and grotesque: an old, paralysed father, dying by inches, with every piece of ancestral property which had to be sold; an elder brother. Count Gasparo, absent-minded, slovenly, contented, poring over his books and writing his satires and commentaries, while his innumerable brothers and sisters were growing up without profession or chance of marriage; devoted to a blue-stocking wife considerably older than himself, who translated plays and set up journals, while her babies, hungry, dirty, and tattered, played with the ragamuffins of the quarter; money continually wanting, squabbles for ever arising; state halls turned into dirty kitchens, gala clothes cut up into children's pinafores ; musty books encumbering the floors : dust, cobwebs, rats, ink-stains, howling brats—such were the surroundings of Carlo Gozzi on his return from military service in Dalmatia at the age of twenty. About 1740 his combat had begun with those invisible enemies who were to persecute him throughout his life. Carlo Gozzi manfully determined to break the spell which hung over his family: he went about examining the Gozzi property on terra-firma; he tried to let part of the premises; he sought for the title-deetls of bonds left by his father; but the goblins met him on all his journeys with flooded roads and broken bridges, with bugs and thievish stewards. They sent to him polyplike tenants who never paid, scandalised the quarter by their doings, and, when legally ejected, clambered back into their former premises during the night; they inspired the Countess Gasparo Gozzi with the happy thought of selling all the family papers and parchments to a neighbouring porkshop. However, Carlo was victorious: he reclaimed the terra-firma property; he finally ejected the non-paying, disreputable tenants; he recovered, among the heaps of cheeses, the rolls of sausages, and the compact rows of hams, the venerable documents of his family; he put his younger brothers into

government offices, his sisters into convents; had the little Gasparo Gozzi swashed and shoed and stockinged; quietly shipped off the resigned philologist Gasparo and his furious poetess wife to Pordcnone; and then, with a few books and just sequins enough to eat meagrely and dress tidily for the rest of his days, he established himself alone in the haunted palace at S. Canziano, with his Spanish plays and his collections of Arabian and Xeapolitan fairy tales. But the goblins did not let him off so easily: they delighted in pulling, pinching, twitching, and tripping him up; they led his silk-stockinged feet into every pool of water; they jolted his coffee-cup out of his hand on to every new pair of satin breeches; they enveloped him in some mysterious cloud which made people mistake him for opera directors, Greek merchants, and astronomers, and give him playful blows intended for other persons; thoy lost tlie letters addressed to him, and wrote answers of which he knew nothing, so that one evening, returning travel-worn, weary, and ravenous, from Friuli, he found his own house brilliantly lit up and garlanded, filled with cooks and lacqueys, and with a crowd of masked rioters eating, drinking, and dancing to celebrate the accession to the patriarchal chair of Monsignor Bragadin, whose fhmkeys politely told the astonished owner of the house that he had written to give permission for the momentary annexation of his palace, and that for the three days and nights of Monsignor Bragadin's festivities he had better retire to the nearest inn. The hobgoblins, the fairies, the enchanters, and their earthly representatives, the fantastic Pantaloons and Harlequins of the Commedia rZe/Z'Ar^e —unearthly, swarthy, gibbose, imp-like creatures, two thousand years old—this world of the supernatural and the grotesque, in which Carlo Gozzi had been born and bred, completely enslaved him immediately on the appearance of the Love of the Three Oranges. He had written one fairy comedy, one fiaba teatrale, as he styled it; the fairy comic style, the fiahesque, was created; he must continue.

And we must not be astonished that this grotesque and fanciful mixture of the comic and the supernatural, which at first sight seems the exclusive creation of northern imagination, should have originated in this humdrum Italy of the humdrum eighteenth century; for in the midst of this Italy of the eighteenth century, with its prim little ways, its dapper little costume, its minuet-tripping cavalieri serventi and sonnetteering abatini, its stuccoed house-fronts and shell grottoes and volumes of academic verses ; its novels, caps, boddices, and philosophy supplied by third-rate Parisian milliners and philosophers—in the very midst and heart of all this was one strange, weird, beautiful, half oriental, half mediaeval thing, one city of gorgeous colour and mysterious shadow, in which the creole wizard of Fonthill felt as if he were moving in his own magic world of Yathek; and that city was Venice. Even now-a-days, when we return to

Venice after an interval of years, melancholy with the first impression of the livid green canals, the dilapidated discoloured palaces, the black and brown stains and shadows on stone and water, lugubrious beneath the grey twiUght, our first sight of the squares of St. Mark's in the summer evening is like the transition from the world of Childe Harold to the world of the Love of the Three Oranges. The two squares, smooth like huge ball-rooms, enclosed by the lace-like stonework of the Proccuratie and the Ducal Palace, the arcades brilliant with yellow light of the jewellers and bronze and glass shops, and of the gilded and painted coffee-houses crowded with loungers; the middle of the square, where the yellow light from the porticos dies away into the white twiliglit, with its scantier pro-menaders; the indistinct shapes and colours of St. Mark's, with its confused stories of pillarets and piles of cupolas and gleaming mosaics and gold, facing the hazy sea; the great belfry rising, shooting up into the dim, distant sky;—all this is iQxvy-\\\<.Q, fiahesqne in Carlo Gozzi's sense of the word. And if we re-people it with the crowd in domino and mask, the nobles in their scarlet tabarro mantle, the Greeks and Dalmatians in their plaited skirts and red caps, the fiddlers and singers at the coffeehouses, the mask buffoons surrounding the nostrum-seller shouting the virtues of his alexijihai'macon, the story-tellers and improvvisatori beneath the half-lit arches of the palace: if we do this, we get the background of one of Carlo Gozzi's comedies, and we can imagine how in the last gay days of Venice, when Marcello was teaching his psalms in the palace near the Eialto, when Porpora was directing the choruses of girls at the Mendicanti, when Longhi was painting his carnival caricatures and Gritti writing his dialect drolleries, when the dying republic gathered its tarnished grandeur about it and awaited its death in merriment, the Jlahesqne comedy, the precursor of Beckford and Hoffmann's fantastic buffooneries, originated in the brain of the amiable, crochety, humorous, haunted Carlo Gozzi. We can fancy him sauntering lazily through the crowd of masks and idlers, unconscious of greetings and nudges, dreaming over his boyish loves with the fierce little sultanas of Zara, of his serenades beneath Ragusan windows, of his wanderings in the Epirot hills among the fierce Morlac brigand-peasants and the half-oriental Greek women, listening to their tales of revenge and murder, to their nasal, dirge-like songs: we can fancy him meditating over the hobgoblins in the Palazzo a S. Canziano, over the squabbles with Goldoni, over the ignominy of the dear, venerable,Comedy of Masks; thinking perhaps how best to make a play, with Pantaloon, Harlequin, and Smeraldina, of some Arabian tale of Turandot or Zobeide, of some nursery tale of the Stag King or the Little Green Bird, just heard for the hundredth time from the red-sashed storyteller Cigolotti, vociferating " c cussi, sior mio benedetto , . , le piii bele

cose,le pill maraviose," to his audience of gondoliers, even as Carlo Gozzi was to make him appear on the stage, carrying the magic parrot of the sorcerer Duraudarte.

Carlo Gozzi, as we have remarked, took up and artistically manipulated just those elements of the old Commedia delC Arte which Goldoni had rfj(vto(l—the masks, the buffoonery, the supernatural, and the tragic. The stuff upon which he worked was essentially different from that of Goldoni; the artist's own nature and endowment was also essentially different. Goldoni was much less a Venetian than an Italian, and less an Italian than a man of the eighteenth century. Of the middle class hijii-self, and wholly without imagination, he saw of the upper classes only the despicable artificiality: he detested illusions, having none himself; he enjoyed the manners of the shopkeepers and gondoliers, and painted them as he saw them, with a keen interest in natural character, action, and speech ; the past for him was neither a reality as to the student nor a poem as to the dreamer ; it Avas an uninteresting blank for which he felt no sympathy ; to him Venice was merely a state rather older and more eccentric than any other; the canals of Venice were the same canals as the canals of Leghorn or the canals of Holland, had he seen them; the ducal palace was a large building with arcades very convenient in rainy weather; the motley dress of the old comedy, the magic and transformations of tlie Spaniards, were to him imbecilities good for children, and children, in the eyes of Goldoni, were silly ignorant little donkeys. With an immense power of sympathising with everyday feeling and arranging prosaic plots, Goldoni was wholly destitute of the power of weaving subtle and fanciful shapes, of colouring and gilding with the imagination, of realising, in dream or nightmare, the distant and the impossible ; he had all the faculties required to do what he wished to do, he was complete because he was limited, and his work was executed with the same felicity with which it was conceived; there was no horizon for Goldoni, he could grasp all that he could see. Carlo (jozzi was totally different ; he was as fragmentary, as inconijilete, as those very elements of humour and fancy which he had saved out of the wreck of the Covimsdia dell' Arte ; he was full of poetic aspirations, and humorous fancy, thrust back by reality,~aud without the force to create a world of their own. A Venetian citizen on his father's side, a patrician on his mother's, he clung with tenderness and veneration to the Republic: he loved its traditions, its glamour, its unrealities; its realities, its corruption and meanness, pained him intensely; he was neither a bigot nor a retrograde, but, though seeing the good which might come of the revolutionary and pre-revolutionary movements, he shrank back from their hardness, their prosaic materialism: a poet and a humourist, he loved the ivy and the delicate fanciful cobweb; the ivy might mean ruin and the cobweb might mean

dirt, but he had not the heart to tear off the one and sweep down the other. He did not like reah'ties like Goldoni; an aristocrat and a dreamer, he did not sympathize with the people; he would accept their poetry, their fairy tales and quaint sayings, but he would not endure their prose. His matter-of-fact century, philosophic and pedantic, drove him back upon himself, and made him brood over his fancies and whimsies more than is healthy for an artist. He found little sympathy without, and he had not enough in himself to suffice for himself. The world surrounding him was prosaic and dull and could not satisfy him, and he had not the power to create a world for himself which should be satisfactory. Every great poet and great humourist creates a sphere into which he can rise and in which dwell in happiness, be it among clouds and rainbows like Shelley, among moss and leafage like Keats, or among Uncle Tobys like Sterne, or advocates of the poor like Jean Paul; Carlo Gozzi could not do this ; both as a poet and as a humourist he could rise out of reality only for a few minutes, and then drop back into it wearied and bruised ; he was full of aspiration and suggestion: wondrous dreams, beautiful and grotesque, flitted before him without his being able to seize them, like that fiddler trying for a lifetime to reproduce the exquisite sonata heard in sleep from the fiend ; here ! here it comes, the wierd melody—quick ! the bow across the strings —alas !—that was not the piece. Carlo Gozzi, like every imaginative mind, saw in everything much more than it contains ; but, unlike the great artist, he could not extract that something and make it his own. In his plays he seems for ever pointing to some suggestion of poetry, of pathos, and of humour, calling upon us to lander-stand what he would do but cannot ; saying almost piteously, " Do you not see, do you not feel ? Does not that situation, that word, appeal to your fancy ? Do you not see dimly those fairy princesses, too beautiful

to be seized, t^here, do you not hear the music ? Do you not feel

that a world of wonder is half visible to you ? Always suggestive, and sometimes successful in working out the suggestion; such must be the final verdict on Carlo Gozzi's plays ; and it explains why they have been so warmly admired by individuals and so completely forgotten by the public. Give the world of suggestion contained in The Stag King, in Turandot, in The Raven, to such readers as Goethe and Madame de Stael, as Schiller and Hoffmann, and it will suffice; they will see what poor Carlo Gozzi can only point to. They can sympathize, imagine, and complete. But humanity at large cannot: it can see only what is absolutely shown it; mediocre Mr. A, B, or C, must have complete realization, absolute perfection; he must have Homer, Shakespeare, Raphael, the finished statue with every inch properly chiselled, the finished picture with every line in its place and every colour well laid on; the block of stone with the mysterious figure still veiled in its rough mass, the sketch with its vague

faces and forms visini,' sliadowlike out of the confusion of blurs ; the indistinct voice in the wind, tlie li.azy shapes in the moonlight, all this is incomprehensible to him; he wants art, and he is right; but below art, below the clear, the realized, the complete, is a limbo of fair unborn ghosts, shadowy and vague, of distantly h(>ard melodies, of vaguely felt emotions of patlios and joy. Let us not despise that limbo, that chaos; out of it emerges every masterpiece, and in it lies hidden many a charming or sublime sliape which those who know the secret spell can evoke out of the mist of ever-clianging forms which surround it.

To this limbo belong the fairy plays of Carlo Gozzi; they are things which in order to be thoroughly enjoyable must he completed; in our days they can be thus completed only by the fancy of the reader; in his own time they were completed by the scenic realization of the excellent comic company directed by Sacchi. The machinery, improvisations, acting, and dresses of the Teatro San Samuele filled up the gaps left by the insufficient talents of the writer; the grotesque shape of Pantalone Darbes, with his immense paunch protruding beneath his mediaeval robe, the mouthings and gestures of Fiorilli-Tartaglia, stammering Neapolitan brogue and blinking through his goggle spectacles, the capers and jests of the admirable Truffaldino-Sacchi, witty, quaint, and graceful ; the coquettish audacity of the servant Smeraldina, the dignity and passion of the beautiful Teodora Eicci, Grozzi's capricious platonic flame; the outlandish and shrovctide dresses, the admirable effects of scenery, and lighting, and mechanism—all this realised and rendered visible upon the stage of San Samuele that grotesque and fantastic world of the Three Oranges, the Blue Monster, the Serpent Woman, and the Stag King, which Gozzi had conceived and suggested, but unlike the greater masters of the art, Shakespeare, Beckford, and Hoffmann, had been unable to display. With the Sacchi company at his command. Carlo Gozzi appeared a genius; as soon as the Sacchi company broke up he was forgotten; and ifj^nother such company could be formed, if jye could have another Truffaldino-Sacchi, another Brighella-Zannoni, another Panta-lone-Darbes, another Fiorilli-Tartaglia, another Teodora Ricci, if we could resuscitate those admirable last buftbons of the Commedia dell' Arte the fiahescfie comedies of Carlo Gozzi would once more be as popular as a hundred years ago; and Carlo Gozzi would seem as great an author to those compilers of histories of Italian literature in which his very name is omitted, as he seemed to Hoffmann, to Schiller, and to Schlegel.

There is, however, one of Carlo Gozzi's plays which, by some fortunate accident, is almost perfect, which might be read and enjoyed even after Vatheh or Chapelmaster Kreisler, or Alfred de Musset's Fantasia; and that is the philosophic fairy play V AugelUno Bel Verde, or, if we may translate the uutrauslateable— The Little Bird Fair Green; for in it

Gozzi lias almost shown us the masks, almost let us hear the improvisations, and has given all the quaint charm of the old nursery tale, originally told by some ancient Hindoo poet to the Persians, moulded into shape by some beautiful Sheherazade, written out in grotesque Neapolitan dialect by Basile in the sixteenth century, re-written in dainty and stately French by Perrault, the architect of Versailles, wandering from country to country, changing now into Princesse Belle Etoile, now into Peau d"Ane, and still repeated, as the Uccello Biverde, in thick-mouthed Roman or lisping Venetian, by many an illiterate granny beside the blazing ruddy mouth of the bread-baking oven, or in the cool gloom of the farmyard beneath the spreading fig-tree, to the sound of the sawing cicala and the splashing fountain. In this comedy Carlo Gozzi has woven together with wonderful art the pi'ose buffoonery of the Comedy of Masks with the stateliest tragic verse and the sharpest moralising of a satire; his love of the droll Venetian dialect, of the supernatural, of the grotesque, and his moral indignation against the philosophic sophisms of his day, have balanced each other, and united to form a little masterpiece, in which for the only time perhaps in his life Carlo Gozzi has succeeded in making us see and feel completely and satisfactorily all that he wants us to see and to feel. The wicked old queen-mother Tartagliona has buried alive her daughter-in-law Ninetta, on the pretence that she has given birth to two spaniel puppies, and has bid Pantalone, the prime minister, drown the real twin children of the King and Queen. Good old Pantalone has not had the heart to execute the order, but has made a parcel of the twins with twenty-four ells of oilcloth and let them float down the river, whence they are rescued by Smeraldina, the -wife of the pork-seller Truffaldino, who adopts and educates them as her own children. But Truffaldino, who is a lying, bullying, and cynical sort of harlequin, hates the twins, and when they are grown up turns Renzo and Barbarina out of doors. The brother and sister, who have read odd pages of Helvetius and Holbach, in which Truffaldino was wont to wrap up his cheese and sausages, wander about destitute but philosophical, having come to the conclusion that morality is a social fiction, that all human action springs from self-love, and that the only wisdom is to suppress every feeling and to hold aloof from mankind. While thus philosophising they are met by a broken, noseless, ancient statue, who tells them that four hundred years before, he also, Calmon the philosopher, reasoned as they reason, disbelieved in good, and hardened himself against his fellow men, until by degrees his heart became a stone, his limbs turned to marble, and he fell upon the ground there to lie, the butt of ignominy, among weeds and filth, for four centuries. Renzo and Barbarina argue with him, try and persuade the statue that according to all natural laws statues cannot speak, and go off as philosophical and famishing as ever. But at last

this hunger humbles their reason, and they throw into the air a magic stone given them by Cahnon and invoke the philosopher statue. Immediately a fairy palace, full of magnificent furniture and splendidly-arrayed servants, rises out of the ground and receives them as its owners. This sudden change of worldly position entirely changes the philosophy of the twins ; and when Truflfaldino, who is also a philosopher of the modern school, comes to them, and, thinking to please them, cynically avows that lie drove them away when they were poor, but that ho comes to them when they are rich because self-love is the sole motive of human action, Renzo has him kicked out of the palace as an ill-conditioned cur, and consents to re-admit him only when Truffaldino goes in for the most abject hypocrisy and knee-kissings: a humorous scene admirably indicated by Gozzi, and which must have been magnificent in Sacchi's hands. Barbarina, on her side, becomes so vain and conceited as completely to despise the attentions of a certain little green bird, the " Augellino Bel Verde," whose courtship had been her solace while living in poverty. Meanwhile the unwitting father of the twins, the blinking, stammering Tartaglia, King of Shadowland, little guessing that his wife is still alive (owing to the provisions brought her in her tomb by the benevolent Little Green Bird), is for ever whimpering over his lost spouse, shedding tears at the sight of the floor upon which his Ninetta (one of the magic damsels of the Love of the Three Oranges) was wont to tread, of the kitchen in which, appearing in the shape of a bird to the cook Truffaldino, she had caused the royal dinner to be burnt; lamenting and cursing his mother Tartagliona, who vainly tries to cheer him by suggesting that he should play at blind man's buff and similar games; nothing can amuse him. At last Pantalonc the minister rushes in to tell the King that a palace has risen up in one night opposite his; the King languidly consents to go on to his balcony, and there, with Pantalonc, he examines the magic palace and its inhabitants through an opera-glass. He has scarcely seen Barbarina on his terrace before he falls madly in love with her—" Pantalonc," he cries, " she has on a dress made by the dressmaker Canziani ! Her hair has been dressed by Carletto ! I am in love as a donkey; look at my eyes, do thoy not shed sparks? " Pantalonc entreats his Majesty not to lose his gravity, es\'7d)ecially as the young woman on the balcony is turning her back upon him. King Tartaglia kisses his hand at Barbarina, who laughs contemptuously; he entreats Pantalonc to teach him some pretty speech to make to her. Pantalonc, disapproving of such undignified conduct, demurs, so Tartaglia begins, "Wait a bit; I want to begin the conversation in a brilliant way. Beautiful lady, do you feel tliis scirocco blowing? Do you not think the sun has risen very bright this morning?" Barbarina, determined to conquer the King, answers rudely and leaves the terrace; and Tartaglia immediately despatches

Pantalone to ask her to marry him, little dreaming that she is liis daughter. But the old wicked Queen Mother has a cavalierc servente who is a poet and a prophet, Brighella, whose mixture of Bergamasc prose and tumid prophetic verse is intensely funny, and he warns her that danger bodes her from Barbarina, bidding her refuse her consent to the King's marriage unless the bride can bring as dower the Singing Apple, the Dancing Water, and the Little Green Bird, all of which are in the possession of a fairy, who guards them with numberless monsters. Of all the princes who have gone in search of the Singing Apple, the Dancing Water, and the Little Green Bird, not one has ever returned; but Barbarina, blinded by ambition, entreats her brother to go in quest of them. Renzo refuses to risk his life ; but, when he hears that a feather of the Little Green Bird (who has ceased visiting his sister) is necessary to give life to a beautiful female statue of which he is enamoured, he sets off with Truffaldino, leaving with Barbarina a magic knife, whose blade, clean as long as he lives, will be blood-stained as soon as he dies. After some time Barbarina looks at the knife and sees it is bloody; forgetting all her vanity and ambition, and in despair at having caused her brother's death, she sets off with Smeraldina to share his fate. This generous impulse breaks the spell hanging over the twins ; Barbarina meets Calmon, who, calling to his assistance the statues of Moors of the Campo dei Mori at Venice, who hold open the magic door with their shoulders, and the fountain nymph of Treviso, who spirts water out of her breasts and extinguishes the magic flames, he enables her to get the Green Bird in his cage. The Little Green Bird bids Barbarina tear a feather out of his mng and touch with it his brother and TruflFaldino, who stand turned into statues in niches among many other seekers of the Singing Apple and the Dancing Water; Barbarina does so, and Eenzo and Truffaldino resume life. Then Barbarina touches with the feather all the other statues, kings and princes and sultans, among whom is also Cigolotti, the story-teller of St. Mark's, who, taking a pinch of snuff, remarks in Venetian that he ought never to have let himself be tempted by the hope of getting the Apple, the Water, and the Green Bird, and making a fortune by showing them off at Venice, and that henceforward he will be faithful to his tales of Bovo d'Antona and King Pepin. Tlie Green Bird reveals that Renzo and Barbarina are the children of Tartaglia ; Eenzo marries his statue vivified; Barbarina the Little Green Bird, who turns into a handsome prince ; Truffaldino returns to his pork-shop; the Queen Mother and her poet Brighella are metamorphosed into a toad and an ass, and the good stone philosopher, Calmon, is promised a restored nose as soon as the audience of San Samuele shall have paid their money. Tlius ends the comedy of the Little Bird Fair Green, which, with its buffooneries, its transformations, its tragic passion, its philosoiihising, its

uioralising antique statue, its apple singing opera songs, accompanied by the dancing water as orchestra, its whimpering comic king, its mophis-tophelian pork-selling harlequin, its clown poet-seer Brighella (who restores hi^ iiroi)hetic vein at the tavern), its hero Renzo madly enamoured of a woman of stone, its bird in love with a mortal, its fantastic, semi-philosophic suggestiveness, has altogether a strange analogy Avith the second part of Faust; an enigmatic work, we know not whetlier too loftily meaningful or too childishly meaningless for full comprehension; amusing, tickling, \'7d)leasing; above all filling the mind with a queer and delightful medley of thoughts. The Jiahesque comedy of Carlo Gozzi was, in its mixture of humour and pathos, of the grotesque, the fanciful, and the supernatural, the apotheosis of the Comedy of Masks, its highest triumph given it by its most fervent votary; but the apotheosis is a funeral rite, and shows that the old Commedia deiV Arte had expired. Little by little discord began to arise in the once united company directed by Sacchi. Teodora Ricci, Gozzi's pupil and goddess, behaved scandalously and went off to France. Sacclii, old and worn out, became cantankerous and headstrong. Darbes died or retired; the other actors, one by one, took other engagements or entirely left the stage; the finances of San Samuele got into disorder, furniture and stage properties were seized ; lawsuits began among the various actors ; the owner of the theatre ejected the manager ; the magnificent Sacchi company, the last company of mask actors in all Italy, was dissolved.. One day, about 1782, poor old Truffaldino-Sacchi came to see Carlo Gozzi, and took leave of him all in tears. " You are the only person to whom I pay a farewell visit; for my departure from Venice must be secret," said Sacchi, " I shall never forget the favours you have bestowed upon me, Signor Conte ; vouchsafe to grant me your pardon for any offences, your pity, and the honour of embracing you." " Poor Truffaldino," writes. Carlo Gozzi, " pressed me in his Avithered old arms; he gave me a last sad glance out of his goggle-eyes full of tears, and then ran away, leaving me alone, wandering disconsolate through Venice, separated from my dear comedians, and twenty-seven years ohler than when they returned from Lisbon. Oh, my poor heart! Oh, national comedy! All around me I cannot find one single person who still shares my love for this comedy, so

original and so eminently Italian ! But I am waxing pathetic

Quick, let me wipe the cheek upon which Truffaldino has kissed me: the fellow must have been eating garlic.' At the same time I may brush away unnoticed the tears on my face ; and then I can go off and dine,])roud to have succeeded in appearing philosophical, that is to say, heartless."

The Commedia ddV Arte Avas dead. Carlo Gozzi relapsed into obscurity. Old, whimsical, and solitary, he Avandered about through Venice, with scarce a person to point him out as the author of the Little Green

/ 288 Carlo Gozzi and the Venetian Fairy ConieJy.

Bird. The tempestuous political and social horizon scared his fanciful mind; he watched with wonder and terror the bursting of the great revolutionary storm; he watched with vague heart-ache the fall of his beloved republic of Venice. His friends and relatives dropped away one by one; the eighteenth century drew to a close. We have one last glimpse of him, seated solitary and silent on a certain bench on the Quay of the Slavonians at Venice, watching vacantly the boatmen gambling at the coffee-houses, the water-sellers going up and down with their yoked pitchers, the women hurrying to and fro in their black skirt and veil; the fishing-smacks moored to the posts, the green water lapping lazily on the steps, the clouds sailing over the tower of St. George and the cupolas of the Giudecca; listless, wistful, seeing perhaps nothing of the life around him, going over the past, seeing again his loves at Zara, the haunted dismantled palace at S. Canziano, the theatre of San Samuele with its Harlequins and Pantaloons and Arabian princesses and transformations; thinking of his Jiahe, of the Stag King, of the Love of the Three Orariges, of the dear, venerable, dead Comedy of Masks. How often may poor old Carlo Gozzi have returned and sat upon that bench ? When did the boatmen and coffee-house loungers of the Quay of the Slavonians miss that familiar grey, bent old man, with the wistful, fanciful face? We know not; for, in the total oblivion into which Carlo Gozzi has fallen, n^ one has even recorded the exact year of his death; he and all that he did is forgotten.

Out of the old, venerable Comedy of Masks, born in Greek and Oscan days, given shape by Beolco and Calmo in the sixteenth century, developed to its utmost among the tattered buffoons of the days of Salvator Rosa, originated two forms of comedy, the realistic comedy of

Goldoni and the fantastic comedy of Carlo Gozzi, both essentially national and spontaneous artistic productions. But the fate of the two comedies has

(been as dissimilar as the talents of the two men: Carlo Gozzi, the fanciful, the suggestive, the romantic, the artist incapable of embodying his finest conceptions, has been forgotten ; Goldoni, the clear, the realistic, the positive, the intensely limited and concentrated genius, has been remembered. The bookstalls of Venice, crammed with quaint and useless literary rarities, may be ransacked in vain for a copy of one of the only two editions ever made of Carlo Gozzi's plays. If we ask for Carlo Gozzi, ten to one we shall be offered the works of his brother Gasparo: the clever mediocre, puristical satirist has survived; the quaint, fantastic, incorrect poet has been forgotten.

If we Avant Goldoni we need only enter the first best bookseller's, and we shall be offered our choice of twenty different editions of his plays ; or,

better, we need only bid our gondolier steer to the little theatre of San Benedetto, and, entering its pit, we shall behold a perfect resuscitation of Goldoni's men antl women, in their real striped coats and powdered hair and scarlet cloaks and Venetian skirts and veil, with their real evcry-day looks and intonations and movements: not so much an admirably-performed comedy as a magic evocation of the daily life of a hundred years back. And, returning home through the little silent squares, across the staircase bridges with their solitary gondola light in the distance, through the network of narrow streets behind St. Mark's, we have none of the feeling of having been to the play: Siora Menegheta, in her chintz and veil, may be wheedling some black-dressed, horse-hair wigged, snarly Sir Todero Brontolon behind yonder shutters .... Menego Cainello may be asleep on the prow of yonder moored gondola; the spendthrift Eugenio may be gambling in yonder lit-up coffee-house; and, hearing steps behind us in the narrow, twisting streets, we turn round and almost expect to see beneath the lamp at the corner the disconsolate, ruined Sior Anzoleto, flying from his creditors in his black cloak and three-cornered hat . . . ; for after more than a century after the fall of the republic of Venice, after the death of the Comedy of Masks, after every connecting link with the eighteenth century has long been broken, Goldoni remains ; and his men and women are realities to-day even as they were on that day a hundred and twenty years ago when, in the book-shop of Bettinelli, Carlo Gozzi challenged Goldoni with the Love of the Three Oranges, and the author of the Bai'uffe Chiozzotte laughed at the challenge of his rival.

CONCLUSION.

CONCLUSION.

In re-reading the foregoing pages there has come home to us an impression felt but vaguely while \vriting them ; the impression that in our search for art we have been wandering through rooms long closed and darkened; that we have been brushing away, perhaps over roughly, cobwebs and dust which lay reverently on things long untouched, that we have been intruding into a close weird atmosphere filled with invisible ghosts. The men and things of the Italian eighteenth century have not yet been exhumed and examined and criticised and classified; they have not yet been arranged, properly furbished and restored, like so many waxwork dolls decked in crumbling silks and lace, like so many pretty, quaint, or preposterous nicknacks in the glass cases of our historical museum, to be gaped or sniffed at by every vacant idler or heartless antiquary, like the men and things of our English, French, and German eighteenth century. They have been forgotten and neglected, but not insulted; the dust of their own day has lain thick upon them, and that dust has brought home to our hearts that the men and women once lived and felt, and the things once charmed or amused. An old book of cantatas of Porpora, an old volume of plays of Carlo Gozzi, does not affect us in the same manner as a darkened canvas of Titian or a yellowed folio of Shakespeare ; these latter have passed through too many hands, been looked at by too many eyes, they retain the personality of none of their owners. But the volume of Gozzi's plays was probably touched last by hands which had clapped applause to Truf-faldino-Sacchi or Pantalone-Darbes ; the notes in the book of cantatas may last have been glanced over by singers who had learned to sing them from Porpora himself ; with this dust, which we shake reluctantly out of the old volumes, vanishes we know not what subtle remains of personality. It is different with the Renaissance : its men and women are as indifferent to us as their calm effigies by Rossellino or Donatello; they are not dead because they have never, for our feelings, been alive. They are a superior sort of mummy. We buy their old garments to hang in our parlours, we knock against their old armour as we would knock against a brand new fender, we ransack their papers, their lives ; we feel no scruple in handling their dead personalities; they are totally dried, embalmed, turned into something wholly different from ourselves; we cannot, by the greatest stretch of imagination, conceive that they like or

dislike anything we do to them or say about them ; it is so long since they lived that the very ghosts of them are dead.

But no such stratifications of humanity and of events separate us from the people of the eighteenth century ; we indeed have never known them, but we have met occasionally men and women who have; like those two, now themselves become part of the past, to whom this book should have been dedicated, if dedications were not advertisments to the living rather than homage to the dead : that sweet and sunny lady, whose hand, which pressed ours, had pressed the hands of Fanny Burney, and that old musician who had sung with boyish voice to Cimarosa and Paisiello those airs which he hummed over for us in faint and husky tones. Thence it is that our study of the things of the last century ends with a sort of sadness which should not belong to historians or sestheticians.

Moreover, we must repeat it, the art of the Italian eighteenth century is extremely forgotten; indeed with the exception of a few plays by Goldoni, wholly forgotten. The music and the drama may, will, nay certainly must, sooner or later be exhumed ; but the revival will have taken place too late, they will be things of culture and eclecticism, the tradition will be gone. The old Italian Comedy of Masks, so quaint, so coloured, so fantastic in its humour, has long disappeared ; a few local masks revived and altered in our day, like the Florentine Stenterello or the Neapolitan Pulcinella, cannot in their isolation give a notion of the imaginative charm of the coming together of the various droll and uncouth figures of the mask comedy. Perhaps the performance we chanced to witness one autumn evening in a shed behind the cathedral of Perugia was the last real representative of the Commedia delV Arte. It was only a company of rough wooden puppets, a couple of feet high, jerking in rectangular fashion and bobbing with rotatory movement for the amusement of the artisans and apprentices of Perugia; and very humble, very shabby, and very much humiliated they all were, this Harlequin in his checkered doublet, this Pantaloon in his red hose and black Dantesque cap, this swarthy Brighella in loose-girdled garb; but they were the last of a long and mighty line. Their ancestors had amused men and women long before the brazen griffin had first spread his porcupine wings on the front of the grim battlemented townhouse, long before Augustus had built his gate, perhaps even before the first Etruscan wall had been planted upon the bleak steep of Perugia ; they were as venerable as anything in Italy, these poor little wooden mannikins, clacking their legs and bobbing their heads on their stage of planks, and we looked upon them with reverence.

"With respect to the Italian music of the last century, much has been torn up, much has been made into new paper, much has been used for the inner binding of books, much has been made into firework papers,

and has whizzed and flamed out of existence in the shape of rockets; much certainly still remains, carefully locked up and catalogued, and respectfully unopened, in public and private libraries, and much ought to remain, but perhaps does not (for no one takes the trouble to discover), in the archives of the chapels of St. Mark's, of St. Peter's, of St. John Lateran, and of other great musical establishments. But the men and women who could still remember how it ought to be performed are long dead, and while they were still alive no one cared to learn their art and their traditions. This music of Pergolesi, of Durante, of Lotti, of Jom-raelli, and of Cimarosa, will certainly soon be remembered and sought for, and printed and performed, well or ill. The Italian eighteenth century will, like Antiquity, like the Middle Ages, like the Renaissance, contribute its share to our eclectic culture; its men and women will be exhumed, restored, put into glass cases and exhibited mummy-fashion in om- historical museum ; we shall gape at them, pry into them, hit up against them, understand them and feel nothing for them, just as we do for all the other classified human fossils which we possess ; but that time has not yet come. The men and women of the Italian eighteenth century are still mere ghosts, whom we have scared in our search after art; for whom we yet feel we know not what vague friendship and pity. And now we turn away from them with reluctance, from these men and women whom we have met in our rambles through the forgotten world of the Italian eighteenth century, these poets, and composers, and playwrights, and singers, to whom we have listened so long and so often ; nay, even the poor crabbed little academic pedants and fops, at whom we have so often laughed, have become something to us, and even to them, with their absurdities as to the others with their greatness, we bid farewell with something akin to sorrow.

THE END

Made in United States
Orlando, FL
17 June 2025

62192854R00114